# Praise for Paul

'Riveting and all too realistic. Cleave

'Cleave leads us on a tantalizing, mouth-watering spectre of horror, never knowing what will be revealed around the next corner, or turning of a page.'

*Suspense Magazine*

'Dark, bloody, and gripping, *Blood Men* is classic noir fiction. In Paul Cleave, Jim Thompson has another worthy heir to his throne.'

John Connolly

'An intense and bloody noir thriller, one often descending into a violent abyss reminiscent of Thomas Harris, creator of Hannibal Lecter.'

*Kirkus Reviews*

'Anyone who likes their crime fiction on the black and bloody side should move Paul Cleave straight to the top of their must-read list.'

Mark Billingham

'A pulse-pounding serial killer thriller . . . The city of Christchurch becomes a modern equivalent of James Ellroy's Los Angeles of the 1950s.'

*Publishers Weekly* (starred)

'Paul Cleave writes the kind of dark, intense thrillers that I never want to end. Do yourself a favour and check him out.'

Simon Kernick

'Gripping and darkly funny.'

*Globe and Mail*

'An intense adrenalin rush from start to finish, I read *The Laughterhouse* in one sitting. It'll have you up all night. Fantastic!'

. Watson

# ALSO BY PAUL CLEAVE

*The Cleaner*
*The Killing Hour*
*Cemetery Lake*
*Blood Men*
*Collecting Cooper*
*The Laughterhouse*
*Joe Victim*
*Five Minutes Alone*
*Trust No One*
*A Killer Harvest*

# PAUL CLEAVE

# THE
# KILLING HOUR

MULHOLLAND
BOOKS
HODDER

First published in Great Britain in 2017 by Mulholland Books
An imprint of Hodder & Stoughton
An Hachette UK company

1

Originally published in New Zealand in 2007, revised edition published in 2013

A CIP catalogue record for this title is available from the British Library

Paperback ISBN 978 1 473 66463 0
eBook ISBN 978 1 473 66464 7

Typeset in Goudy Oldstyle Std

Printed and bound in Great Britain by Clays Ltd, St Ives plc

Hodder & Stoughton policy is to use papers that are natural,
renewable and recyclable products and made from wood grown in
sustainable forests. The logging and manufacturing processes are expected to
conform to the environmental regulations of the country of origin.

Hodder & Stoughton Ltd
Carmelite House
50 Victoria Embankment
London EC4Y 0DZ

www.hodder.co.uk

To my parents—who aren't as crazy as I make them out to be

# AUTHOR'S NOTE

Years ago, back in the early nineties, I had a friend ask me, *"What do you want to do in life? Really? If you could do anything?"* I was nineteen. I said I wanted to be a writer. A week later I sat down and started writing the first of maybe six or seven books nobody will ever, ever see. The first one was about a kid who couldn't die. He'd been taking some weird experimental drug to knit his broken arm together, but he kept taking it, and soon no matter what happened to him he'd just keep on repairing himself. Second one I wrote was about an alien. So back in the early nineties, instead of enjoying those years the way I should have, I spent them working and writing. More specifically, I was writing horror.

*The Killing Hour* came about at the end of the nineties. It's like watching a baby grow, I guess, how they can never walk then one day they suddenly can. That's what it was like for me. Five or six years of writing, and then suddenly I wrote

*The Killing Hour*, and it was a massive leap forward for me. Originally it was written as a horror novel. And it stayed that way for a few years. I am, at heart, more a horror fan than anything. My favorite movie is *The Thing*, my favorite show is *Fringe*, but it's crime that I write best. I didn't know that until a year or two after *The Killing Hour*, when I then wrote *The Cleaner*. *The Cleaner* is the first crime novel I ever wrote, back in 1999. I was making my way, figuring out what I wanted to write, and at the end of *The Cleaner* I knew. That book went through many rewrites over the next five years and eventually found a publisher in 2005. During that time, I would revisit *The Killing Hour* and rewrite it, and over time I removed the horror elements and replaced them with crime. There are still holdovers from the horror novel—you'll see them—only these are now all justified. My main character sees ghosts. Are they real? No. But he still sees them.

So *The Cleaner* was signed up, and before it ever came out anywhere, it was starting to sell to other countries. People in the publishing world were responding to it. What else did I have? Well, I had *The Killing Hour*. What's it about? Well it's about a guy who has a really, really bad week. It used to be a horror novel and now it's a crime novel and, truth be told, it's my favorite of all my books. So *The Killing Hour* got dusted off and signed up. What else did I have? I was working on another book called *Cemetery Lake*, but I'd only written twenty percent of it. That would get signed up too—it was the first time I had a contract for a book that didn't exist.

*The Cleaner* had five years' worth of rewrites, but I knew, like anybody did, it was going to be the book that made things happen. *The Killing Hour* didn't have the same amount of rewrites. Suddenly it was getting published. Suddenly there was a hurry. It would be released a year after *The Cleaner*. The

*Killing Hour* was my first book, but people saw it as my second. Of course they would. Because it came out second. *The Cleaner* was a better book—which means, to them, I had hit a sophomore slump.

Another five years have gone by, and now I've had the opportunity to rewrite *The Cleaner*, *The Killing Hour*, and *Cemetery Lake* for my US readers—along with a new editor, who is quite brilliant. It's been fun to do so, and it's been a real privilege for me because the American response to my recent novels—*Blood Men*, *Collecting Cooper*, and *The Laughterhouse*—has been amazing. *The Killing Hour* was always going to be the biggest challenge of those three books to revisit. But I was up to it. I've been given the chance to put the last five years' experience into it. It's always hard to look back at something you worked on long ago. I'd forgotten so many of the details because I'm constantly working on future material. So it was really interesting to see how far things have evolved since the nineties and my focus on horror.

This edition of *The Killing Hour* is over twenty thousand words longer than the original. It's sleeker. It's much better. There's more atmosphere, and the characters are more likeable. I was always proud of this book, but the book was written by a twenty-five-year-old, unpublished Paul Cleave who was finding his way, and I pat him on the back for it. But now thirty-eight-year-old, published Mr. Cleave has taken the work his predecessor did and has improved it. This will always be the book that was the turning point in my career, the book where I learned to walk and talk and, for that, I will always be thankful.

# CHAPTER ONE

They come for me as I sleep. Their pale faces stare at me, their soft voices tell me to wake, to wake. They come dressed in the clothes they were in before they died, though there is no blood on them. I know what they want, because when it comes to people who are ghosts because of you, there really is just the one thing. They cannot touch me because they have no real form. I cannot touch them either, cannot push them aside. I feel the guilt they want me to feel—I feel very little else. When I wake it is with a scream lodged so tight in my throat I start gagging until I can swallow it back down. It is five o'clock in the afternoon and I am bathed in sweat. The ghosts disappear, but their *It's all your fault* message doesn't disappear along with them.

It's Monday. I roll over and see my clothes lying on the floor and wonder if anything good in this world ever came about on a Monday. My shorts are covered in blood. My muscles ache as I sit up. When I touch the bump on my forehead my world sways and the headache grows. The stains on my shorts are made up of red droplets in various shapes and sizes and I wonder what my answer would be if a psychiatrist asked me what I saw in those patterns. I shiver in my hot bedroom. It feels as though a thousand spiders are weaving up and down my spine. Their furry legs and tiny fangs clutch and prod and bite me.

I walk to the bathroom. The house has been closed up since yesterday. The air is tainted. I open the bathroom window, strip off the clothes a dead woman gave me, and climb into the shower. A breeze enters the room. Occasionally it pushes the cold shower curtain against my body. I embrace the water, letting it wash over me but unable to be washed clean by it. I feel nauseated, foul, and a moment later I drop to my knees, vomit burning my throat and splashing on the floor. The water falls around my head and rinses my lips, but the taste of death remains.

I turn off the shower. Climb out. There are lots of little cuts over my body but nothing that needs stitching. In the mirror the dark blue skin on my forehead looks like a golf ball has been stitched beneath it. Seeing it invites the headache deeper into my brain. It builds a residence in there, hangs up a sign, and settles in for a long stay.

I wrap the towel around my waist and trudge through the house. Water rolls off my hair and down my body. I leave wet footprints on the carpet. The stuffy air feels like a damp overcoat. It feels like I'm walking through a tomb. Perhaps that's exactly what this is. I close my eyes and the two dead women waiting in my thoughts agree. In the kitchen I knock back two painkillers. How well the two words, *pain* and *killer*, go together. Is that what I am?

The answering machine has a light flashing. There are

three messages. I press play and I listen to one of the secretaries at school asking me where I am, telling me I have a classroom full of students waiting for me to show up. Then she calls back two hours later and says a similar thing, and an hour after that the headmaster, a guy by the name of Declan Burrows, asks where the hell I am. I don't return the calls.

I settle down in front of the TV in the lounge and use the remote. There's a show on that involves one women caked in makeup screaming at another woman caked in similar makeup, something important enough to involve the word *skank* getting used four times in the ten seconds I watch the show for. I change channels. The news has already started and the deaths are the lead story. The reporters and presenters are good-looking people full of smiles and bad news. I wonder if their salaries are on a sliding scale—the bigger the tragedy the more they make. They use phrases like *mega-murder* because they lack the real vocabulary to sensationalize human tragedy. They're talking about a community in shock. Not just one homicide, but two—the God-loving, taxpaying citizens of Christchurch are getting their money's worth. *Senseless crimes*, they say. A *brutal frenzy*, they say. Just how brutal they can't say, but they sure as hell like to guess. No motive, no clues, no leads. It's their favorite kind of story because it's equally as full of mystery as it is tragedy. They say *ritualistic killings* so often it's easy to imagine some soap company sponsoring them to do so, *because nothing cleans up a satanic massacre* like their product will.

I'm given the chance to learn what I couldn't last night as photographs from Kathy's and Luciana's lives flash across the screen. I didn't know the two women for long. Just hours, really, but sometimes that's all you need. Sometimes it's all you get. The photographs seem to be taken a few years ago.

In Kathy's photo there's an arm around her, probably her husband's. Her teeth are showing, she has an uncontrolled smile, a full genuine smile that comes about when somebody is trying to make you laugh and doing a great job of it. She has the blue eyes and blond hair of a surfer, and the tanned body to go along with it. Or it could just seem that way because the photo has been taken on a beach—you can see sand and water in the background and somebody wrestling a stick out of a dog's mouth.

Luciana's photo is a wedding photo, one snapped of her where she's staring into space. She looks beautiful but also a little lost. She is alone in the photo. Her dark hair is pinned up, her slender body hidden by the heavy white dress.

The reporter lists their personal achievements and ambitions as the photos are on display, the same way a salesman would list the best features of a car. Luciana was thirty-two, married, she was studying creative writing, and she taught piano. I had no idea. Last night was the realest night of my life, but thinking of that piano, thinking of the lesson she will have missed today makes it even more . . . what's the word? *Realer?* Kathy's the same age. She was a real estate agent. The two women had known each other since primary school. They grew up together. They hung out together. They died together. Family members and friends come on and share their anecdotes and pain. It's a smorgasbord of details I'd know had I kept them alive. But I didn't. Because I fucked up. Soon I'll be on the TV too. They'll thrust a microphone in my face looking for a sound bite. They'll ask the same questions the ghosts are asking—*Why?*

I switch off the TV. I get dressed. I drag a backpack from the bottom of my wardrobe and dump it on my bed and start packing. It takes me five minutes. I grab the bloody shorts from the floor and throw them in the laundry on the way out of the house.

It's nearly seven o'clock by the time I climb into my car. The evening is still light, but won't be for much longer. It's that time of the year where summer has disappeared, but its reach still remains. The air is warm and sticky and smells like freshly mowed lawn. A young boy with a baseball cap pulled on backward is biking along the footpath stuffing mailboxes with leaflets that might be advertisements for toasters or pleas for help to find his puppy. A few doors down an elderly woman is on her knees pulling weeds from her garden. She waves at me. I wave back. The boy puts a leaflet in my mailbox. I drive down my street and watch them both get smaller in my mirror.

A few minutes later I drive past the pasture where the early hours of Monday introduced me to this world, the Real World, where old women with green fingers are replaced by madmen with red ones, where no children play, where fresh pies don't sit on the windowsills of happy-go-lucky life. Jesus, I don't even know what life's about anymore. It certainly isn't about routine; it isn't about paying your mortgage and buying groceries; it isn't about singing "Happy Birthday," licking stamps, and changing flat tires. I used to think it was. I used to think there was justice in this world, balance. You want to think it's about living, about surviving, but no matter how hard you try it gets to be about dying.

As I look out at the long grass and trees, the soil and scrub, it seems obvious it takes only a couple of shovelfuls of dirt to form a shallow grave. There could be a dozen people out there in the ground—lost loves, lost lives, just lost. The trees at the far end look nowhere near as imposing as they did in the early hours of the morning. The killing hour is over, that's why. In the dying sunlight, during the day, these trees are a strip of nature in the city, they're a place that hasn't been bulldozed and developed, but at night those trees are dark and foreboding, the kind of trees that in a fairy tale would come alive and rip children limb from limb. There are no police cars, no tape cordoning off the scene, no clatter and squawking of radios. There are only ghosts. I can't see them, but I know they're there.

The Real World isn't about destiny and it certainly isn't about luck. If it is, Luciana and Kathy ran out of theirs around the same time I ran out of mine. I push my foot down, not caring about the speed limit. Before I can escape I have one more thing I need to take care of—one more woman I need to see.

# CHAPTER TWO

Detective Inspector Bill Landry is an angry man. He's been angry for the last five days, angry at the life-changing news. Though thinking about it, it was more life ending than it was life changing. Too many cigarettes. That's what it was. The doctor had warned him years ago. He told him it was like putting a gun to your head with a single bullet in it and pulling the trigger over and over. Eventually it was going to go off.

Five days ago he got the news that that gun would be going off within the next six months.

He's trying hard not to think about it, but it's always there, if not in the forefront of his thoughts, then at least lurking around the sidelines. Right now he's standing in the bedroom of a dead woman, having just come from a different house across town that had an equally gruesome scene. It's all he should be thinking about, but those cancer thoughts keep creeping in.

He looks at his watch, then at the red numerals on the alarm clock, then back at his watch. The two are disagreeing by two minutes. Either that, or there's a slight rift in the bedroom and he's two minutes into the future. He figures that would be a better superpower than the one seeming to dog the police everywhere they go—which is to be two minutes in the past. You can't save people in the past. He watches the last number change from an eight to a nine on his watch. The woman he's come to see has now been dead a minute longer than she should have been, and he's one minute closer to his grave. For that matter, everybody is.

He's struggling to stay focused. He's hungry and tired and it's been a long day in what is no doubt going to be a very long week. He badly wants a cigarette. Life isn't the same unless you're slowly ending it. He follows the shape of the dead woman's face and locks his gaze on her milky eyes. She would agree. She would agree he needed coffee too.

There is a jingle caught in his head. Music from somewhere and he can't figure out from where. It's been stuck with him for the last few hours and he can't shake it free. The kind of music you'd hear in an elevator or on a child's toy, only he hasn't been in any elevators today or hanging around any kids. Even if he could identify it, it wouldn't help the music disappear. Probably he'd just get more of it stuck in there. He looks down at the woman's hands, at her fingernails, wondering if any skin from her killer is trapped under them, wondering what she would have done differently the last time she had a manicure if she'd known how many people would be looking at them. He wonders just how much that manicure would have cost, whether she often had them, whether she was into small talk or whether she'd have held a magazine in the hand not being worked on. Life and death and the details in between all have price tags. The cost of death starts out small. Like a fifty-dollar visit to the doctor. You begin throwing good money after bad. You try to chase away the cancer or one of a hundred other diseases that riddle your body and ride it down. Sometimes it isn't even fifty dollars. Sometimes it's only five. Or ten. A ten-dollar investment. A knife, for example. Or a pair of garden shears. They slice through skin and flesh quicker than any disease. There are expenses no matter what savages you. New clothes to replace the bloody ones. Smaller clothes to replace the ones that no longer fit your wasting body. Booze to calm the nerves. The family of the victim shops through glossy catalogs for coffins, choosing color and craftsmanship and style, what's in at the moment, what was *so last year*. The graveyard plot, prime real estate these days, adds to the bill, along with a new suit or a dress for the corpse. New clothes for the mourners. When the bad news comes from a cop rather than a doctor the expenses add up faster. One murder and the cash is flying around. Man hours. Court cases. Lawyers. News stories. People charging and making money from evil. People . . . people . . .

He holds a hand up to his face and pinches the bridge of his nose and closes his eyes for a few seconds. He needs to get ahold of himself. He has to get ahold of these dark thoughts. Has to rein them in. But on the grief scale, he never made it through to acceptance. He's stuck on anger. He doesn't see that changing anytime soon.

The day is cooling off. It certainly needs to. The air inside the house is thick—it tastes and smells like aging fruit. He can't turn on the air-conditioning, can't open any windows— not allowed to do anything that will alter the temperature. The medical examiner and the forensic guys would all have fits. He moves over to the window, looks out at the slowly ebbing day and wonders if it will ever actually end. The neat backyard with its golden pebbles and expensive plants has been surrounded by yellow plastic evidence markers. With their black numbers they're larger versions of the order disks he's been given at pizza restaurants. He wonders if the same people make them or if they're made to order, then that thought leads him back to an earlier one about being hungry. A pizza would be good. And a beer. And since he's in the wishing mood, he'd like to sit on a beach somewhere and watch the sun dip into the horizon, have a few women in bikinis taking up his field of vision too.

Best he can settle for is to watch the sun as it bounces off the roof of the neighboring house. The roof is made from blue steel and the reflecting light makes the lemons on the nearby tree look purple. The people in the townhouse are standing by their windows. They're staring at him, their eyes wide and their mouths open as they watch in awe. They're probably thinking this is the next best thing since reality TV. Seeing them isn't helping with the anger. He wishes he could arrest them. Wishes he could fire the guy who hasn't got around to hanging large tarpaulins to block their view. He turns away in disgust.

The music is still stuck in his brain. He picks his way across the room, stepping carefully over and around the dried patches of blood, of which there are many, once again trying to identify where he heard that theme, and at the same time wishing he could forget it. The furniture and layout may be different, but aside from that it all looks very much the same as the crime scene he came from a little over an hour ago. Similar views, similar furniture, similar dead woman covered in blood. The room has a definite woman's touch—two vases of flowers, dreary paintings of romantic scenes, candles on the dressing table. It's the sort of mishmash of trinkets his own wife had lying around when she used to be his wife. His second wife was the same. The good thing about wives when they become ex-wives is they take all that crap with them. The sad thing about when they become ex-wives is when you find something under the bed or hidden in a drawer they missed packing, and it reminds you that being married was made up of good times too.

There's a collection of makeup and hair products scattered beneath a mirror on the wall with smudges of hairspray on the glass. A hair dryer lies on the floor next to several pairs of shoes. A garbage basket full of tissues and Q-tips. A pair of slippers made to look like cartoon lion heads. A calendar showing vintage movie posters on the wall by the wardrobe. March shows a pissed-off 1933 King Kong on top of the Empire State Building, fighting off planes while holding his damsel in distress. No dates have been circled, no messages jotted down. Nothing to indicate a bad day was coming.

The medical examiner is currently tying paper bags over the dead woman's hands and feet to protect any evidence beneath the nails. One of his kits sits nearby, containing a selection of scissors, blades, Q-tips, and needles. Small labeled vials containing specimens of hair and fibers and blood are lined up evenly inside a larger plastic tray. There's fingerprinting powder covering different surfaces, evidence markers, plastic bags—it wasn't this messy when he arrived. Now it's starting to look like a whirlwind came through here. Just inside the bedroom door waiting to take the cause of that whirlwind away is a neatly folded body bag. Aside from the bedroom the house has no other signs of violence—no broken furniture, no bloodstains.

The other crime scene is the same—similar kind of house,

similar neighborhood, similar amount of blood. Just two dead women and no reason why. That's always the way.

"Makes you wonder, doesn't it," the medical examiner says, standing up, his knees popping in the process as he moves over to stand next to Landry. His name is Sheldon. He's in his fifties and sounds like he's in his seventies. To Landry he seems like the kind of guy who'd yell at kids who stepped on his lawn. His dull and depressing personality could drive people to suicide—a neat trick for somebody who works with the dead.

"It does," Landry says, knowing what's coming.

"What the hell is wrong with people? I've been doing this a long time," Sheldon says, just like Landry has heard him say on other, similar occasions, "and I can tell you this with certainty—as bad as this is, there will still be worse. It's human nature," he says. Both men stare at the body. Landry looks into her eyes, and then he looks down at her chest where one of her breasts has been hacked off, wondering what kind of human nature Sheldon is referring to. "A million years ago we were crawling out of the sea," Sheldon says. "Now we have the ability to fly to the moon. Man is always trying to better himself, and killing is no different. Guys who can do this," he says, nodding toward the dead woman, "get better and more brutal. A guy like this, well, you can tell killing these woman wasn't enough. He wanted to put on a show. Probably wanted to put on a better show than the last guy who did something similar."

"It's a rat race out there," Landry says. "Everybody wants to be better than the last person. Everybody wants to put on a show."

"You think this was enough for him?" Sheldon asks. "Or you think he still has a point to make?"

Landry slowly nods, but doesn't answer. He's not nodding to say yes, it's the nodding of a man deep in through. "I don't know," he says, "and I don't want to guess."

A forensic examiner with a hairy neck and a nervous twitch starts photographing the body, images of death being saved to a memory card. Later they'll be put up on large screens and studied in detail. Sheldon signs off on the body and helps his assistant roll it into the body bag. Landry picks up the victim's address book, moves to the corner of the room, and starts going through it. The names are listed alphabetically by last name. He flicks through to the *F*'s and reads through the names three times, looking for a specific one that isn't there. Then he flicks through the rest of the book looking for it, getting the same result. Most of the people listed in here probably don't even know yet what has happened. Others are crying on shoulders or into drinks, wondering why in the hell the world is such a shitty place.

Two officers start to carry the body outside, Sheldon following them. Suddenly Landry has had enough. It's been months and months of killing. The Christchurch Carver stole all the headlines over the few years until his arrest, and he hasn't been the only serial killer to have walked the streets of what he now thinks of as a broken city. Landry has had enough of the death. He's sick of living two minutes in the past where he can't do a damn thing to save people. It's time to live in the future.

That's the perspective his cancer has given him. In six months' time, he won't be able to make a lick of difference.

He puts the address book into an evidence bag then makes his way out of the room. Detective Schroder is in the hallway talking to a few other detectives. Schroder is the man leading the case. That's what Schroder does. Last year it was Schroder who got the credit for arresting the Christchurch Carver, but it was also Schroder who got a lot of the blame for not having caught him earlier. Sometimes Landry thinks he'd like to lead a case, other times it's the last thing he wants.

He's going to lead this one. Only nobody else is going to know.

"You don't look so good," Schroder says to him.

"Something I ate."

"You going to be okay?"

"I just need some air, that's all," he says, handing the evidence bag over to Schroder.

"Got anything useful?"

"Nothing," Landry says, which isn't quite true. In fact he actually has a whole lot of something. He has a name. And he still has those bad ideas he's been trying to rein in.

Schroder starts to say something else, but Landry has to get outside, now. He moves quickly down the stairs and heads for the front door. He starts humming along with the music caught in his head, and it comes to him what it is when he steps outside. It's a radio jingle, an ad for security systems. Makes sense he'd be thinking about that kind of thing. Would this woman still be dead had she heard that ad? Maybe. No broken windows. No forced entry. A security system isn't any good if you're opening the door to your killer.

He makes it through the front door and onto the porch. He smears some sweat away from his face with the back of his arm. Dozens of tiny insects fill the air in front of him. He swipes a hand through the little bastards and a gap appears in the middle, then the cloud reforms itself. Where death goes the insects and bugs are quick to follow. That's the nature of nature. He tugs at his collar and rushes around to the side of the house where he squats down and gulps in the cool evening

air, then it hits him, the overwhelming sensation that he's
going to be sick and there's nothing that can hold it back. He
has no time to see if anybody is watching, barely has time to
even get the evidence bag out of his pocket and get it over his
mouth. Last thing he can do is contaminate a crime scene.
The vomiting is over within a few seconds. The bag expands
and is warm. He coughs the remaining dregs into it. He looks
up and sees that he's alone. He's thankful. He seals the bag
and carries it to his car.

He still feels sick. And a little light-headed too. It's been
that way since he started taking the pills. The pills are for the
coughing. The coughing is from the smoking. The pills helped
for a bit, then not so much when he learned the coughing
was cancer based. He still takes them—they help, but they
do have side effects. He bruises easily too. And his appetite is
pretty messed up.

There's no point going back inside, not feeling like this.
Best he can hope for is to not collapse and roll down the stairs.
So he climbs into his car. He pulls out his phone and sends a
text message to Schroder and tells him he's not feeling well,
which is true, and tells him that he's heading home, which
isn't true.

He doesn't mention the name he found, the name that
wasn't in the dead woman's address book, but on a bloody pad
of paper next to the body. Charlie Feldman. That pad had
plenty of blood on it. It's now inside an evidence bag inside
his jacket pocket. He tries to tell himself he doesn't know
why he's keeping that information to himself, only he actually
has a pretty good idea why that may be. It's a combination of
things. Part of it is the imbalance of the world. Good people
dying. Bad people getting away with things. Part of it is the
anger. The anger is leading to dark thoughts. Dark thoughts

that he can't rein in. Dark thoughts and nothing to lose by seeing where they lead. Mostly it's because he has six months to live. The cancer doesn't care about what he does, why should he? He's got six months to do what he can to make this city a better place. Better to make a difference in this world than spending his last six months at home, filling up his days with slow dying.

When that's all the time you have left, he can't see any reason not to bend the rules.

# CHAPTER THREE

I pull up the driveway. A dozen or so of the paving stones wobble beneath the weight of the car, stones I wanted to cement back into place but never got around to doing so. I come to a stop in front of a garage with freshly painted black doors and shiny new handles. The house is fawn with black trim and a black concrete tile roof. I painted it. The garden is full of small shrubs surrounded by dark brown bark. I helped plant them. There are a few weatherboards at the bottom of the house that have rotted more since I last saw them. I never got around to replacing them. I wonder who will do it.

I kill the engine and sit with my hands on the wheel and tell myself I've done the wrong thing by coming here, and I agree with myself too, but that doesn't make me start the car up and back out onto the street. I should. I should back out and never come back. Catch a plane somewhere. Things might look different from a pilot's point of view. None of my problems would fade as we climbed toward the sun, but they wouldn't get any worse. Most bad decisions you don't know are bad until you look back at them, but occasionally you know it when it's happening—and last night and today have been full of exactly those.

Staying is wrong. Leaving is right.

I stay.

I get out of the car. I walk toward the front door. I feel like I'm not really here, that this is all part of the same dream I've been having all day. I reach out and trail my hands along the weatherboards of Jo's house. The wood is hard and smooth. It's real. It's no dream. When I reach the door I suck in a few breaths and bite down on my lip and give myself a last chance to leave, but don't take it. I knock. My hand doesn't pass through the wood. I don't wake up.

Jo comes to the door. She has a smile that disappears when she sees me, and I feel an immediate sense of shame and rejection. She lets one arm fall to her side; the other she keeps up high on the side of the door frame blocking my entry. Her greeting toward me doesn't include the word *hello*. She has this look on her face that suggests she has just eaten a bad piece of chicken. I can smell freshly brewed coffee.

"Hey, Jo, can I come in?"

"Oh my God, Charlie, what happened to you?"

"I need to talk to you." She looks me over, studies the wounds on my face. The last time she saw me I also had wounds on my face. I guess I'm a wounds-on-face kind of guy. "Are you alone?"

"Have you been in a fight? You're still hitting people, huh?"

Hitting people is why we broke up. Maybe I'm a hitting-people kind of guy too. "Please, I just need to talk to you. Are you alone or not? Can I come in?"

"I don't know, Charlie. I don't . . . I don't really want you here, not looking like that."

"Come on, Jo, it's important."

She takes a few seconds to weigh up just how important it could be, then decides it's important enough. She steps aside. "Come in."

When I'm in she closes the door and leans against it as if to block my exit. Jo's a few centimeters shorter than me, a couple of years younger, but twice as mature. She has hazel eyes, soft until she frowns at me, which she's currently doing. The tanned skin of her face is sprinkled with light freckles. Her hair has been cut, stopping just above her shoulders. Her body is toned and athletic from her visits to the gym. She looks better than the last time I saw her, six months ago.

"So no *How are you doing, Jo?* or *You look nice, Jo,* or *I've been missing you?*"

"I didn't think you'd want to hear it."

"You're probably right."

"Look, I'm sorry about what happened."

"I know," she says. "You said that six months ago."

"And I'm still sorry. I didn't mean to . . . you know . . . it just happened. But you look good. I like the new haircut."

"I haven't had a new haircut, Charlie. So let me guess why you're here. You have a new girlfriend and got jealous and decided to try and beat up the next guy who looked at her wrong."

"Come on, Jo, it wasn't like that with us. You know that," I tell her.

"That's exactly what it was like."

"Bullshit. That guy at the bar was out of line," I tell her. "He got what he deserved. You should be thanking me."

"And I would have thanked you if you'd just gotten me out

of there. But you had to make a point," she says. "You could have been arrested. Or worse. You could have been seriously hurt."

"He touched you," I tell her. "Guys can't just go into bars and touch whoever the hell they want."

"I get that, Charlie, I told you that. But what you did—that scared me. You just kept hitting him over and over until I managed to pull you off. There's something inside you that scares me," she says.

"Ah, come on, Jo, don't say that."

"Well, it's true."

"At least it probably stopped him from doing it again."

"And that's your job now, is it? To go around teaching people a lesson?"

I knew this was going to be the kind of reception I was going to get from Jo. Six months ago everything had changed. It was a night out for dinner. Date night. When you're married or have been with the same person more than a few years, then date nights become few and far between as life and work get in the way. We had Thai. Then we went to a bar for a few drinks. I had a gin and tonic. Jo had the same. There was a rugby game on TV and a bunch of people were caught up in it, getting loud, and when you get loud bunches of people watching their team lose, you're always going to find the occasional asshole or two. In this case that asshole put his hand up Jo's dress as she was coming out of the bathroom and he was going in. She shoved him away and he called her a bitch. I didn't see it happen, but she told me. I'd never hit anybody in my life, but I hit him. I marched into that bathroom and Jo came with me, not to help me, but to stop me. I walked up behind him to bang his head into the wall, but he sensed me coming. He turned, pissing all over himself and over my feet, and took a swing at me. He got me in the cheek and split my lip open. His next punch got me in the chest. I stumbled back, and he came forward and slipped over in his own piss. Then I leaned down and hit him. The problem, as far as Jo sees it, is I kept on hitting him. One punch, I was defending her honor. Two punches was teaching him a lesson. But it turns out a dozen punches is ten too many. She had to pull me off him. We got out of there before anybody else came into the bathroom. We got out of the bar and nobody stopped us. We got back to our house and she didn't say a word on the way home. We sat and waited for the police to arrive, only they didn't. The assault didn't even make the news. The following day she asked me to move out. The person I'd shown her the night before wasn't somebody she wanted to spend her life with. It wasn't somebody she wanted to help bring up the children we used to talk about having. I'm pretty sure the person I was last night isn't somebody she'd want to spend her life with either.

"I'm in serious trouble," I tell her.

"If it's serious, go to the police."

"I can't."

"Why not?"

"It's complicated."

"I'm smart," she says.

"I know."

"You don't think I can understand?" she asks.

"That's why I'm here. I need somebody to understand."

"So you argue that you want my help, then argue against telling me?"

"I'm only arguing against going to the police. You'll understand soon enough."

"Understand what?"

"Can I have some of that coffee?" I ask, nodding toward the coffee maker.

"Will it get you out of my house any quicker?"

"Technically it's still *our* house," I tell her.

"If that's . . ."

"But yes," I say, interrupting her. "It'll speed things up."

While she pours me some of the coffee she's just made I stare at the magnetic poetry on the fridge door. I make a square and a triangle with random words, but I can't line them up to make sense of the last twenty-four hours. She pours a coffee for herself too, then we walk through to the lounge. It's warm from the afternoon sun. I sit on the sofa and lean forward. I'm frightened that if I sink back and relax the sofa will swallow me. I look around the room to see if anything has changed, but it's mostly the same. The only difference is what isn't here—no photographs of us. Nothing to show I ever existed. All those memories have been packed away. Thankfully there aren't any photographs of her with anybody else to have replaced them.

"Well?" she asks.

"This is difficult for me."

"Difficult for me too, Charlie. You think I want to spend my Monday night with you?"

"You have other plans?" I turn to face her and immediately I'm annoyed at the pang of jealousy we both heard.

"That isn't the point."

"Okay, okay, just give me a few seconds," I tell her. I stare down at the coffee table, at the small nicks and scratches that have built up over time. Some of them I remember happening, others had happened well before Jo inherited the table from her grandmother. "I was on my way home," I say, and I keep staring at the table, wishing that was the whole story just there—that I was on my way home and nothing bad happened. I was steering my Honda around the sweeping bends of the empty highway. The road was dark with half circles of light spilling across from the streetlights. I had my window down to enjoy the summer breeze. The air was warm and dry. The mercury was hovering around the shorts and T-shirt end of the thermometer. The highway was bordered by pastures. Thin wire fences stopped the large willow and oak trees, the poplars, the patches of knee-length grass and the thinning creeks from escaping. Cows and sheep and horses were standing vigil, all unaware that day by day technology was slowly making their homes smaller, that day by day their future as hamburgers and juicy steaks was getting closer. I was coming home from my parents' house. Mom had been convinced there was a mouse in the house, and equally convinced that my dad wouldn't be any use in finding it.

"It happened when I turned off the highway toward home. It was so . . ." I shrug. "I don't know. If it wasn't for the news and the blood. I don't know. I guess I would think it was all a dream. But I guess it's more that I'm just wishing it were one."

Jo leans forward. She looks concerned. I pick my coffee up, but can't bring myself to take a sip.

"What blood, Charlie?"

"I went around the corner and that was when she stepped out in front of me. I didn't even see her at first. In fact I almost ran her over."

"Who did you almost run over?"

"Luciana. Luciana Young."

Jo's mouth falls open and she leans back. All the air seems to rush out of the room. She says absolutely nothing. She doesn't ask if I'm joking, because there's no way in hell I'd come around here and make something like this up.

"Luciana Young from the news," she says, and she says it as if there was another possibility, as if I were talking about the Luciana Young who lives a few blocks away who wasn't murdered during the night.

"Yeah."

"So . . . so you were with her last night? And the other woman too?"

I look down at my coffee cup, unable to look at Jo, but I know she's staring at me.

"You killed them?" she asks.

Last night as I turned the corner, my headlights washed into the pasture opposite, lighting up the same bank of trees they always light up. The trees looked like large deformed fingers pushing through a farming landscape. Twisted and broken, they were the sort of thing Salvador Dalí would paint, along with some melting clocks and a naked woman.

"Charlie?"

"No," I answer, "of course not."

"You ran her over?"

"No."

"What happened?" she asks, and she sounds scared, scared because I'm crazy and making this up, or I'm crazy because I'm not. She sounded the same way when we finally started talking that night six months ago when we got back home, the night I still think of as Date Night.

The moment I saw Luciana I tugged on the wheel and jumped on the brake, swerving my car around her. In my rearview mirror I saw a woman drowning in the glow of my brake lights. All that red skin, red clothes . . . if I ever see that sight again I'll understand it for what it really is—a premonition.

"No, I didn't hit her, but I pulled over. It was obvious something was wrong. She climbed into the car. She was panicked. I wanted to go to the police. You would have too if you'd seen her. If you'd heard her."

"Then why didn't you? This isn't making any sense, Charlie."

"We didn't go to the police because her friend was in danger."

"Kathy," she says.

"Yeah."

Luciana's dress was shredded above her chest as if she'd been repeatedly clawed by a big cat. There were several cuts over her chest that looked like tiny canals, and a red sea was welling up over the edges. Her face was smeared with dirt and her eyes were full of desperation. She had to be desperate to jump into the first car that came along. Her blond hair was matted with twigs and leaves, stained with soil and blood that in the weak light of my car looked like oil. There was a line of blood on her leg. She wore a bandanna necklace that had been a gag. When she closed the door the interior light blinked off and we were plunged into darkness. Monday's darkness.

"You've . . ." was all she could say before breaking into loud sobs. She collapsed with her forehead pressed to my arm. Her skin felt like wet clay. She was shuddering, choking on her sobs and the beginnings of small words. I was half out of my seat belt when she pulled away and doubled her efforts to speak.

"You've . . . got . . ."

I put my hands on her shoulders and told her to take a deep breath. It worked. I kept staring at the blood on her that was becoming more real by the second. This was actual blood.

Like that B negative or O positive stuff that drips out of dead people. It gave her credibility, so when she pointed out my side window with hands that were bleeding and shaking and told me her friend Kathy was out there being held by a crazed lunatic I had no reason not to believe her.

I tell this to Jo.

Jo shakes her head. "Why didn't you call them on your cell phone?"

"Because I still don't have one."

"What? You never replaced it? You're kidding."

I shake my head. I'm not kidding. When that guy in the bathroom got his second punch in six months ago into my chest, it actually connected with my cell phone. It didn't survive the impact, and I didn't replace it. I was sick of being tied down to a phone. Sick of seeing people everywhere I go spending any free second they have to send a text or check an email.

"There was no time to get the police. I moved the car so I was out of sight of the trees," I tell Jo. I twisted my body and pocketed my keys then told Luciana to stay where she was. She asked if I had a weapon. All I had was whatever was in the trunk. That turned out to be a car jack, a spare wheel, a bike rack, a tire iron, and no shotgun. I settled for the tire iron. It was cold and heavy and boosted my confidence.

The night was twenty degrees, but each of them cold as I strode from the car. I wanted to be Action Man, but I felt more like the actor nobody recognized in an old *Star Trek* episode—Crewman Random who went away with Captain Kirk, but never came back. I actually thought about that guy in the bathroom as I strode into that field. I thought about it because that was the first and only time I'd ever hit anybody. I thought about it because it was his fault I didn't have a cell phone and, by association, anything bad to follow by me not being able to call for help would be his fault too.

Monday was twelve minutes old when I stepped into that field. It was about to become longer. Elastic hours. Even now, sitting opposite Jo, they're still stretching.

# CHAPTER FOUR

Landry doesn't even get half a block before he has to bring the car almost to a stop. The first barrier to get past is police cars and tape that's been put up to cordon off the scene. The next barrier is the hundred or so reporters beyond it. With all the killings over the last year, he's surprised journalists are still taking an interest. He has the windows down and can smell sausages and steak on a barbecue from a nearby yard. Music is booming from a neighbor's house, the sort of generic pop every teenager is recording these days for every other teenager. He remembers a time when he used to love suburbia, but now it's just another body count. The neighbors have gathered on their front lawns to watch the show. They're thinking the circus has just come to town. And it's free. They're inviting family and friends over. With neighbors like this, murder will always stay in fashion.

The police cars pull back and make room for him to pass

through. The station wagon with the body in it has pulled up behind him. The sun is falling from the sky and nighttime is nearly here. He closes his eyes for a few seconds, and he can see both women. The pictures are exposed perfectly and full of vibrant and violent colors. They're real Kodak moments.

He realizes he's just been asked a question from one of the reporters. Well, not quite asked, more yelled than anything. Then other questions are coming his way. He rolls the window up, but the yelling continues. He can see the street being canvassed. Tranquility Drive. That's the name of the street where this modern-day-Christchurch drama is unfolding. All the streets in this subdivision have similar names. Serenity Street. Harmony Drive. It's as if the council sent in a psychiatrist tanked up on Prozac to name them all. He's been in enough of these situations to know what questions are being asked, and to know it's a six-to-one ratio. For every question a cop asks, they themselves are asked half a dozen in return.

*Did you see anything suspicious?* would be returned with *What happened? Do you know who did it? Tell me all the gory details. Was there a lot of blood? Do you suspect her husband? Was she having an affair?* Everybody questioned wants a piece of the action. They want a story they can tell at work or on the golf course. *Hey, Jimmy, guess what? Those two chicks that were blood-let during the week? Hand me that nine iron. Well, you're never going to believe this, but I knew one of them. Crazy, huh? Now watch this shot. . . .* It makes them Mr. Popularity for half a week. It makes them the center of attention. Makes them wish their neighbors were getting killed more often.

Makes Landry angry just thinking about it. It makes him want a cigarette.

He reaches for his pocket, but of course there are none there. He threw them out five days ago.

A week ago he was miserable, alone, and without long-term goals, but he still had plenty of time to change that. He had two failed marriages and a mortgage he couldn't afford. Thirty minutes sitting with the doctor changed everything. Now he's racing to his grave. The smoking will help him get there quicker, but quitting isn't going to give him his life back, so why bother? It seems pointless not to enjoy every one he can fit in before his spring funeral. Jesus, forty-two is too young to be sitting in your doctor's office with your hands gripped tightly against the armrests and your skin itchy from your clothes and damp with sweat. It's too young to be told you've just drawn the short straw in the cancer lottery. Too young to feel your stomach turn upside down with the news that you're going to die. He listened quietly and he asked all the right questions and got all the wrong answers.

Chemo wasn't an option. Landry had had heart problems a few years back. His body wasn't strong enough to have one poison fighting another poison within him. He had six months tops. That's what the doctor gave him. And that's if he gave up the good life of smoking. Once that figure was out there, a calmness came over him, and suddenly the fear and anxiety he'd had disappeared. He was a man who knew his fate. He went through the seven stages of grief all in about sixty seconds, bypassing a bunch of them and coming straight to acceptance, then he stood up, thanked his doctor, and left. It was time to put his affairs in order. He got home and back-peddled somewhat on that grief list, settling on anger.

He's angry with himself for smoking for so damn long. Other people smoke forever and get away with it. He smokes for twenty years and now that gun he's been holding against his head has gone off. He's angry at life. Angry all the justice in his world was pissed away so long ago. Angry that the real cancer comes in the form of people like Charlie Feldman. Why the hell can't God start correcting His mistakes?

The police finally make a path through the ocean of journalists for him to drive through. Cancer and the media—he hates them both. Suddenly he has the desire to set fire to every camera and microphone within a half-mile radius. Everywhere he looks a reporter is talking to a camera or fixing their hair in front of a mirror. He wonders how attractive they'd look if he took them single file through the bedroom and showed them firsthand what rocked Charlie Feldman's world.

When he's past the journalists he winds the window back down. The air is cool, but his skin still feels hot. He isn't sure if it's from the black death running through his veins, or the anger. When he tries to turn his mind to calmer thoughts, he struggles. Everything in his world is darker now.

They've ruled out burglary—cash and jewelry have been found at each scene. Trace evidence has been vacuumed from each of the rooms as well as the road and the driveway—carpet and clothing fibers and hair. There's plenty of blood to process. It'll all take time. Every piece will strengthen the case against Feldman. Yet all of it's irrelevant. Only one piece of evidence really matters—the pad he found beside the victim's bed with Charlie Feldman's name on it. The top sheet of the pad was clean. That was impossible, unless it wasn't really the top sheet, but was in fact the second one down. The original top sheet had been removed after the woman was killed.

One reason for that would be if the killer didn't want what was written down to be read.

Landry had done one of the world's simplest tricks—he had run the side of a pencil over that sheet and read the impression left behind. That's where Feldman's name came from.

He has to pull over a few minutes later when he suddenly

feels nauseous again. He comes close to throwing up, but this time is able to resist it. This is now all part of the cancer merry-go-round. That and the weight loss. He can hear a dozen lawn mowers closing out the day in the distance. He's far enough away from the crime scene now to pull out his phone and spend a few minutes on the Internet.

He finds an online phone directory, looks up Charlie Feldman's name and matches it with the phone number he found on the pad, and a moment later he has Feldman's address. Best way to find out for sure why Feldman's name was removed from that pad is to go and ask the man himself. See what he has to say.

# CHAPTER FIVE

Monday is ending and I'm as scared as hell. The air is heavy with hay fever—I can feel it crawling into the back of my nose. I've suffered from hay fever ever since I was a kid. In my teens I had to start getting injections to keep it under control. Things have gotten better over the years, but not better enough to travel without pills. So I pop a couple out from my pocket and toss them onto my tongue and work up enough saliva to swallow them. A light breeze is coming through the open window, but nothing is normal on this normal night because I know what's really out there. I know about the Real World. I've seen some of its secrets, some of its pleasures, some of its evils. I glance at my watch and see I've been at Jo's for an hour. My unfinished coffee is cold and its surface has developed a skin. The ghosts are back, and though I cannot see them I know they're nearby. They always will be. I stand up and close the window.

Jo's backyard begins to shimmer. The trees become Dalí's trees. The grass grows and turns brown. The flowers disappear and become patches of stinging nettle. I'm back in that moment from last night, back to trying to find a woman I didn't know. I close my eyes and watch it all unfolding, narrating it to Jo along the way. I was halfway to the trees when the woman I was trying to save, Kathy, screamed. I ran forward, the keys in my pocket swinging back and forth. I put my hand down to mute them.

It's easy to see where I went wrong. My first mistake was thinking I could help. I was still living in the same world where the tiny forest of trees had been planted, but the world they had grown into was the Real World. There were no flashing bells, lights or whistles to signify my crossing over, only darkness and a small forest where Death waited and Evil waited and where I would soon wait with them.

The screaming ended and I didn't know why. I could hardly see a thing. Twigs snapped beneath my feet. Branches scraped my arms and tried to hold me back, tried to save me. My foot wedged beneath a root and I fell. The tire iron bounced into the darkness. The stillness among the trees carried laughter to me. It reminded me of when I was a kid at school, reminded me how everybody would point and laugh at some kid's misfortune. It took me a few seconds to realize it wasn't directed at me. Behind the laughter came soft sounds of whimpering. It was coming from a woman. I couldn't see her, but I knew how she looked. She would be bloody, her clothes torn, and her skin grazed and ripped. It made me angry. I got to my feet and continued on until I came to the small clearing.

A flashlight leaning on the ground pointed at her. She was fully dressed, bound to a thick tree by thick rope. Her blouse was ripped open, revealing a bra with a broken strap. Her clothes were dirty, like she'd been dragged some of the way here. She wasn't gagged, but she wasn't talking either.

The man had long, black, knotted hair. It covered the side of his face and looked like the kind of haircut you'd see on somebody who spent time chained to the trees they were trying to save. But he didn't have that tan—this guy's tan was comparable to a skeleton. He was a solid guy, a good six feet tall, or an extremely good five feet tall as my dad would have said. On the ground was a satchel. He crouched and unzipped it. He pulled out a knife. It scared the absolute shit out of me more than seeing Woman One step out in front of my car and Woman Two tied to a tree. Seeing that knife was like having a good dose of reality filled into a syringe and injected directly into the brain. Even though I knew I didn't have my cell phone, I still patted down my pockets looking for it. That knife was a message. It was telling me I was out of my depth. It was telling me to turn away. It was telling me as bad as everything was, there was still worse to come.

The man, who I would later learn was named Cyris, tossed the knife in the air, catching it by the blade. Then he dragged it from his fist so it sliced into him. He pumped his hand so that blood ran from the cut. Then he walked his bloody fingers over her face. It was the creepiest thing I'd ever seen; it was like watching an artist toying with his canvas. He cut her remaining bra strap and it fell away, exposing the tops of her breasts. I couldn't help myself—I spent one, perhaps two seconds staring at them. This, of course, I don't tell Jo.

I was about to move forward when he started speaking, scratching at the side of his face. He asked how she wanted it. Instead of telling him she didn't want it at all, she shook her head and tried pressing herself into the tree, tried to make herself invisible against the trunk. He grunted something that I couldn't make out, then he bent down and returned the knife to the satchel. For a moment I felt better about things, but in that same moment I was worried that he was going to pull out something even worse. Which is what he did. He pulled out a metal stake and a hammer. Immediately I had visions of the police coming here tomorrow morning, of this woman somehow nailed to a tree, of me nailed to a tree next to her. I focused on Cyris's flashlight. It looked like it might weigh about the same as the tire iron I'd lost. I could either go for it or I could stand here and watch Kathy die, or I could leave.

Cyris mumbled again before putting his hands on his hips and thrusting his pelvis forward. I felt an anger I'd never felt before building up inside of me. I wanted to hurt him. A lot. I felt like I was in some bizarre game show and up for grabs were all these prizes: heroism, fame, maybe even a movie. If I failed the fame would be unknown and short-lived, and I wouldn't even be a dead hero. I would just be dead and the game-show host wouldn't even pronounce my name correctly.

Then he started laughing. He told her she could scream all she wanted, that he wanted her to scream. He swore constantly. It was then that I heard his name. Cyris. It made me think of country singers and cowboy boots and bad haircuts.

"You need to go to the police," Jo says, and Dalí's trees disappear and Jo's remain. I look at her reflection in the window. I've lost track of how many times she's told me now. I just wish she could come up with a new angle. "You have no choice," she adds.

I think about the way the bodies were found. I think about racing through the streets of Christchurch. I think about Cyris.

"I can't," I say. "They'll think I did it."

"Why didn't you go last night as soon as you rescued the women?"

"Because of Benjamin Hyatt," I tell her.

She looks at me blankly for a few seconds, and then it comes to her. "But this isn't anything like that," she says.

"Isn't it?" I say. "He's the reason we got the hell out of that bar six months ago after I hit that guy."

She doesn't answer because she isn't sure. Benjamin Hyatt was in the news a year ago. He was a family lawyer. He was fifty-five years old. He had a wife and two children. He was an upstanding guy. A decent guy. People loved him. One night last year he worked late. He was walking through the parking garage close to midnight. In the car next to his a woman was being raped. Her clothes were lying in a heap on the concrete floor and she was crying. Hyatt didn't even think about it. He reached into that car and pulled the rapist out. They fought. But the guy's pants were down around his ankles and he didn't have great balance. Hyatt used that to his advantage. Plus Hyatt used to box a little when he was younger. So he boxed now. He boxed at the guy and knocked him out, only the guy hit his head when he went down and slipped into a coma. The following day the police charged Hyatt. It was their view that Hyatt should have only done his best to contain the rapist, and should not have continually hit him. They said that Hyatt, in a fit of rage, decided to teach the guy a lesson. They said he had created a confrontation, when all he needed to do was call the police. Then the rapist died. The charge was upgraded to murder. Hyatt went to court. The public was on his side, but the law was not. Hyatt had overstepped his boundaries. He had used his fists as weapons, and he had killed a guy. The police wanted to make a point. You couldn't go around acting like a superhero. Hyatt was sentenced to nine years in jail, and would be up for parole within five. The problem was Hyatt's boxing skills that got him into jail couldn't get him out of the many situations jail offered. He was beaten to death two days into his sentence.

"That's why we didn't go. We thought he was dead and, well, none of us was thinking straight. Did we make the wrong decision? Of course we did. But at the time Benjamin Hyatt was all I could think about. I was sure, I was so sure that if we called the police I was going to end up in jail. Or I'd be put into custody while they figured it out. And bad things happen to people in custody," I say. "We needed to think about it. We wanted to get a lawyer first."

"And now? Why don't you go now?"

"Because now they're not going to believe me."

"They're not going to put you in prison, Charlie. Not if you didn't do this."

"Won't they? Come on, Jo, if they can't find Cyris, then that only leaves me."

"So what are you saying? That you want to find Cyris?"

"I'm not saying that," I tell her, though I have been thinking that. Problem is I wouldn't know how to go about it. "But he killed each of them in their own house, and I was in both those places too. They're not going to believe me."

"You think I do?"

"Don't you?" I ask, turning toward her.

Jo looks down at her coffee cup. It's the kind of body language only a blind person could miss. Her cup is empty, but there must be something awe-inspiring in it because she doesn't look up at me for another minute.

"You don't believe me," I tell her.

"I didn't say that."

"Then say you believe me then."

"A year ago I would have believed you," she says.

"Jesus, how can you make a leap from me beating up some guy who jammed his hand up your dress to thinking I'm capable of murdering two women?"

"I'm not making that leap at all," she says, looking angry. "I'm saying that you're not completely the man I thought you were."

"I . . ."

"I don't doubt you had something to do with their deaths."

I move back to the sofa. My coffee hasn't got any warmer. *Something to do with their deaths*. I can't believe you," I say. "I can't fucking believe you would say that."

"What am I supposed to think? You've come here out of the blue, you're covered in cuts and bruises, you tell me you were with two dead women. If everything happened the way you said it happened, then you'd have gone to the police," she says, summing up problem number one. I know problem number two won't be far away. "That's what an innocent man would do. So if you really are that innocent, then why are you deliberately making the wrong choice?"

Ah yes, the Real World. A world full of ghosts and monsters—and choices. I can't go to the police because they'll think I did it. Hell, even Jo thinks I did it. Cyris drove a metal stake into Luciana's chest and then into Kathy's, he killed each of them in their own homes. Somewhere during the night his insanity rubbed off on me. I slam my coffee cup onto the table so that its cold contents splash me. Jo jumps. "Are you deaf? They'll put me in prison!"

"Calm down, Charlie."

"Calm down? I am calm!"

"If you won't call the police, I will," she says, getting up.

I put both hands out in front of me as if to ward off her suggestion. "I'm sorry, Jo, I'm sorry," I say, trying my best to sound it even though I'm not. "Please, don't call them, okay? Please, not yet. I'm just . . . fuck, I don't know. Stressed. Confused. I mean hell, everything I know I should have done I didn't do because . . . I mean . . . well, people can't know what they're going to do until they're in that situation, and last night was . . . was about as tough a situation as it can get. Please, just let me convince you."

"Of what, Charlie? That this Cyris of yours exists? That you killed him too?"

And there lies problem number two. There lies the biggest reason for her doubt. I killed Cyris. I killed him with my bare hands and somehow that didn't stop him. Didn't stop him at all. Not in the Real World because there bad things happen. In that world bad people like Cyris can come back from the dead.

Of course I'm enough of a realist to know that's not true, because the dead stay dead and that's the way it's always been and that's the way the living prefer. I didn't kill Cyris, I only wounded him, and in the process he became unconscious. I don't know. Maybe he just played possum. I wonder what the outcome would have been if that knife had gone a few inches higher or lower. Would I be sitting here with cold coffee on my hand? Would I be sitting with Kathy and Luciana instead?

"He was a monster," I tell her.

"Repeat after me, Charlie. There are no such things as monsters."

I shake my head. "I'm not saying he came back from the dead. I'm just saying he's a monster. Not the movie kind, but the real kind. Monsters are real people, Jo."

"I'm calling the police," she says.

"You can't."

"Just watch me." She heads toward the phone.

I stand up. "Don't, Jo. At least just let me walk out of here."

She turns around. Puts her hands on her hips. She stares at me, and I was married long enough to Jo to recognize when she's making a big decision. I say nothing. It takes her a few seconds, and in that time she stares hard at me before coming to her conclusion. "Okay, Charlie, you win. Just don't involve me any further."

"Come with me," I tell her.

"What? Why the hell would you suggest that?"

I go to answer, but really I don't know. It just came out.

"Leave, Charlie. Now."

"Coming here could have put you in danger," I say, and I say it as a reason for her to come with me, but when the words come out I realize they're true. "Cyris will find me, and if he finds you he'll kill you," I say, the words urgent now. "No matter what you think, he is a monster, Jo."

"Then I'm no safer with you, am I?"

"Are you going to call the police?"

"You're a mess. You've taken a beating, your hands are shaking, you keep shouting."

"I'm not shouting!"

"You are. Look," she says, "why don't you go home and we can discuss it tomorrow, okay?"

"I'm not shouting."

"Okay, okay. Please, I want you to leave."

"I'll leave, but you have to promise me you won't call the police."

Hands back on hips. Another decision process. "I won't."

"Won't promise or won't call them?"

She tilts her head and stares at me, tightening her lips into a thin line.

I hold my hands out in front of me, this time trying to ward off her anger. "Okay. Look, I'm sorry, I really am. I didn't mean to upset you. I'm going to leave."

"I think that's best."

Not knowing what else to say, I end up thanking her for the coffee, which, in the context of the evening, feels like an incredibly dumb thing to do. She walks me to the door. I stand on the doorstep and look back at her. Maybe she's right. Maybe the police would understand. But I'm picking they wouldn't. I'm picking if I walk in there and tell them what I told Jo I'll never walk back out. Everybody knows the police have a way of making people look guilty when they're not. Everybody knows innocent people go to jail, innocent people who think the justice system will work for them, innocent people who lose ten years of their life for something they didn't do.

Only running away isn't the solution either.

"Charlie?"

What I need to do is find Cyris. That's the solution. It's like what Jo said earlier. If I can do that, then the police will know what really happened. It makes sense. Perfect sense. But how?

"Charlie?"

Put an ad in the paper? Put up a blog online? Social media? And if I did find him, what then? Would I really go to the police? I think about what I did to the man who touched Jo. What would I do to the man who killed those two women?

"Charlie!"

"What?"

"If you're not going to go to the police at least get checked out by a doctor, okay? Despite everything, I'm worried about you."

Worried about me. Yeah, sure she is. Worried enough to chuck me out without helping. I rub the huge bump on my forehead and instantly regret it. I nod slowly, then, feeling incredibly alone, I walk down the driveway to my car.

# CHAPTER SIX

Feldman lives in a single-storey townhouse, twenty years old, maybe thirty, fairly similar to the place Landry lives in, really, which makes him feel sick. Not the kind of medicine sick of late, but more of a mental sickness—it's bad enough he has to breathe the same air as that lunatic let alone have something else in common with him.

Landry parks right out front. He kills the engine and steps out of the car and sucks down a few deep breaths. He needs a cigarette. Badly. His hands are shaking. He decides he needs that cigarette badly enough that he leans back into his car and pops the glove compartment. There's a brand new box in there. He bought it yesterday when he gave into the temptation, but had done well since then not to crack it open.

He lights one and leans against the car and stares at Feldman's house. There's nobody home. He can tell. Houses have a feel about them. He's never been wrong about it. And this one feels empty. The curtains are closed and there are no lights on. There's no car in the driveway. The lawns need mowing and the garden is in disrepair, but the house looks like any other on the street, well kept and reasonably tidy. Most killers have pretty average lifestyles. Steady jobs too. Sometimes they're even living the family life—white picket fence and a four-door sedan. That's what makes them so scary. They act human and they slot into society and since a young age they've known how to hide the crazy; they put it up on a shelf and only bring it out on special occasions. Like last night.

Landry can feel his lungs relaxing. His hands have stopped shaking. He gets a quarter of the way through his cigarette and decides that's enough. He decides that's a pretty good compromise considering the doctor wants him to completely give up. He drops the rest of it and uses his foot to stub it into the ground. He walks up to the front door and knocks loudly, but nobody answers. He considers asking the neighbors if they've spoken to Feldman, but doesn't want to risk them alerting Feldman that he's wanted for questioning. He walks around the house, peering through the windows, but unable to get an angle past any curtains. He pulls out the evidence bag from his pocket, the one with the piece of paper he took from the pad. He stands by the back door and uses his cell phone to dial the number from the pad. It's a landline number, not a cell. He can hear the phone inside the house ringing. After eight rings the machine picks it up. He listens to Feldman's voice. Is this the voice of a killer? Is this the voice of a man who can tear women apart? He doesn't leave a message.

The next step is to go and get a warrant. A judge would give it to him too. Plenty of evidence to suggest Feldman needs talking to, that his house needs going through. At this time of the night the only judge he would be able to find would be a severely pissed-off judge.

No point in pissing off any judges.

No point in chasing Feldman if he's not their guy.

Best for everybody, really, if Landry just makes his way inside to make sure. No harm, no foul.

He puts on a pair of latex gloves. He reaches into his pocket for a lock-pick set that he's used in the past when the occasion called for it. He's never been good at picking locks, and after fifteen minutes he still hasn't gotten anywhere. He puts the set away and walks back to his car, then returns with a crowbar that he always keeps in the trunk. He wedges it in the door by the lock and gently applies enough pressure until pieces of wood splinter away, and then he's inside, the air temperature twice as warm as outside.

He doesn't switch on any lights. He uses a flashlight. He starts in the living room, which is where the back door has led. To his right the kitchen, to his left the lounge and the hallway, which no doubt lead to bedrooms and the front door. There are photographs on the walls, a man and a woman, he assumes the man is Charlie Feldman, his instinct is to assume the woman is somebody Feldman has killed, but of course it's more likely to be a girlfriend or a wife. Only the house doesn't have any feminine touches. In fact it looks like a woman hasn't been through here since the day Feldman moved in. Everything is man-stuff, and it's something else Landry and Feldman have in common. No pet, no plants, no bright colors. The lounge has a big-screen TV and a game console in the cabinet beneath it. There's some artwork that looks generic, circles and rectangles mingling with squiggly lines and the occasional wobbly triangle. There's a couple of B-grade movie posters, aliens looking mean, damsels in distress, and these

Landry likes enough to think about taking home with him when this is all over. They remind him of the calendar at the last scene.

One bedroom is empty, another has been turned into a study, the third one is actually a bedroom. He looks through the study. There's a computer on a desk, and on that desk are more photographs of the same two he saw out in the dining room. Another B-grade movie poster, a calendar with swim-suit models, a filing cabinet. He spends a few minutes learning about Charlie Feldman. He goes through things, he switches on the computer and reads some emails. Feldman is married but separated, probably to the woman that's in the photographs. A woman by the name of Jo. Jo Feldman—who used to be Jo London, and who is possibly Jo London again. His emails from her go back eight years. That's when they met. Six months ago he moved out of their house and came here. The emails don't say why, but they refer to an incident at a bar. He writes down the date. It's something he might follow up. After Feldman moved out, there were a few emails between him and Jo over the first two weeks, then that became one a month, but the last one was three months ago. There are a few emails from Feldman's parents. Trivial stuff. Things about garden-ing, birthdays, outings, the price of food. Some jokes. Emails from friends. From work colleagues. Feldman is a high school teacher. He teaches English at a nearby school. Landry knows the school. Has arrested kids from that school over the years for shoplifting. Feldman has been working there for nearly ten years. He wasn't dating anybody new. Didn't have much of a social life. Looked like all he did was work, come home, and hang out with friends in front of his TV playing games. There are some games of golf scheduled in there, some tennis. No mention of Kathy. No mention of Luciana. No mention of his need to kill anybody. Nothing to make Charlie Feldman look guilty of anything.

He switches off the computer and goes through to the bedroom. The bed hasn't been made. There's a photograph of the woman on the bedside table. Feldman must still love his wife. In Landry's experiences, once the wife becomes an ex-wife, there's not a lot of love there. There are no women's clothes anywhere. One toothbrush in the bathroom. Nothing to suggest Feldman wasn't living anything other than alone. In the closet the hangers are mostly empty, others have been shoved to the far sides. It looks like Feldman left somewhere in a hurry.

He goes down to the kitchen and through to the laundry. The washing basket is empty. He opens the washing machine and finds a pair of shorts in there, along with a T-shirt, socks, and underwear. The wash hasn't been put on. Everything is dry. The shorts are covered in blood. The T-shirt has plenty of blood on it too. He's dealing with an idiot. At the very least Feldman should have washed these things.

The bloody clothes confirm what the pad suggested—Charlie Feldman was at the crime scenes last night. He drops the shorts and T-shirt back into the machine. He peels his own shirt away from his body, letting some air flow beneath it. He can't remember ever sweating this much. For a moment he thinks of the dead woman, of the way her body pushed at the sides of the body bag, the way the bag looked too small to fit somebody who was so full of life, somebody with dreams and memories, somebody with a husband, with friends, with a career.

His cell phone rings, the sound breaking his concentration and making him jump. He looks at the display. It's Schroder.

"How you feeling?" Schroder asks.

"Not the best. Just getting ready to go to bed. What's happening?"

"A lot's been happening," Schroder says. "We've spoken to about a hundred people. We've got more interviews scheduled for tomorrow. You're coming in?"

"I'm not sure. I hope so."

"We could really use you," Schroder says.

"I know."

A pause, and then, "Is there anything else going on? You seem a little off."

"I'm just tired," he says, staring at the washing machine as he talks. "That's all. And feeling sick. Something I ate."

"Nothing else?"

"Nothing."

"We got a report of a car speeding away around five a.m., from one of the neighbors, but she didn't see it. Just heard it."

"Anything else?"

"Not yet. But there's a lot to look at. I'm confident this time tomorrow we'll have something to work with. Hope you make it in."

"I hope so too."

Back outside Landry lights up a cigarette to help keep the demons at bay. This used to be his favorite time of the day because normally he'd be sipping a beer and watching TV. Now he's one statistic trying to solve another. In the distance a dog is barking, and a few moments later it is joined by another and another.

He gets his phone back out of his pocket. He calls the station. Ends up chatting to another detective. Detective Inspector Wilson Hutton. Hutton is the kind of guy you wouldn't want to leave with your wife, not because he'll try and sleep with her, but because he might try and eat her. He's at least a hundred pounds overweight, and Landry has often wondered how the guy is managing to keep his job. He gives Hutton the dates he learned from Charlie's emails.

"There anything reported from around that time?"

"Care to narrow it down?" Hutton asks.

"Something from a bar. A bar fight maybe?"

"Any names?"

"No."

"Has this got anything to do with the double homicide?"

"Nothing. Just curious about something, that's all."

"Give me ten minutes," he says.

He gets into his car. Feldman is on the run, but he's sure the guy will come back. Guys like that always do when they figure out they have nowhere else to go. It won't be tonight. But Landry will find him, and if he doesn't find him tomorrow, then he'll come back here every night until he does. He spends ten seconds coughing hard enough for his chest to feel like it's on fire. He flicks the cigarette—this one half-finished—out the window and is tempted to send the rest of the pack with it, but temptation gives way to sanity and he hangs on to them. For now.

He gets out his notepad. He'd jotted down the details of Feldman's parents and the wife he's separated from. He figures it's too late to ring the parents, but he gives the wife a call. She doesn't answer. He gets out a map from the glove compartment and looks up her address. It's less than ten minutes from here. He figures he can swing by her place on the way home. She might have an idea where a guy like Feldman might run.

# CHAPTER SEVEN

I get halfway into my car when I stop. With every passing second I become more and more convinced that by coming here, I've put Jo in danger. Last night was one big display of what a crazy man can do, and if nothing else, Cyris was a whole lot of crazy. Will he come looking for me?

I don't know. Maybe. I don't see how he can know who I am. Except he saw my car, he could track me down from the registration plate. Kathy had my details too. I gave her my name and phone number—what happened to that piece of paper? Could Cyris have found it? Okay—so he can figure out who I am. There's every chance he will come looking for me and, by extension, he could look for those I love. I need to warn my parents. Need to warn my friends.

I carry on walking to my car. I need to go to the police. Of course I do. Will they believe me? I stand by what I said to Jo. If they don't believe me, they'll certainly convict me. And if the evidence is there to prove Cyris exists, how long until they act on it? I could go in there and within fifteen minutes there'll be a manhunt for Cyris. Or I could go in there and sit in an interrogation room for the next twenty-four hours while Cyris is on the loose killing more people.

I need to find him. Need to stop him. Need to make him pay for what he did. And while that's happening, Jo needs to leave town for a few days. I head back to the front door.

I've known Jo eight years. We were married for six, five and a half of those happily. We're still married now, technically. She'd never betray me. She'd never turn me in. But we're in the Real World now and trust isn't a quality I can hope for. Yet it's one I cling to when I step back inside and find Jo hanging up the phone.

"What the hell?" I say, closing the door behind me, resisting the urge to slam it.

"I know what you're thinking," she says, "but it's not what you think. I was calling a friend."

"Who?"

"Somebody you don't know. I hung up before they answered."

"A boyfriend?" I ask, hearing the jealousy in my voice and annoyed at myself for it.

"It's none of your business," she says.

"You were calling the police, weren't you."

"No." I want to believe her, I really do. "You promised you'd leave," she says.

"How much did you tell the police?" I ask.

"It wasn't the police," she says. "First of all you come here and . . ."

"How much, Jo? Are they on their way?"

"Stop shouting, Charlie."

"I'm not shouting! How much did you tell them?"

"I haven't said a word. I told you nobody answered."

I move over to the phone. Jo steps back from it. I twist it so I can see the display. It's lit up because it was just in the process of being used. It shows a 1 and another 1 on the display, and then it goes dark and the 1s disappear. She was two thirds of the way to calling for help. Jo grabs at the phone, but before she can snatch it up I push her away. She stumbles into the kitchen bench and falls. When she looks up at me her eyes flash with tears and anger and as bad as I've felt all day, seeing her on the floor like that makes me feel even worse. I let the phone go so it dangles on its cord, reaching the floor.

"I'm sorry," I say, moving toward her. "I didn't mean . . ."

"Get out, you bastard. I can't believe you did that, but I guess that makes me stupid, doesn't it. I should have known."

"Yeah? Why?" I ask, but I know why. Because of that night six months ago.

"Just get out," she says.

"I'm sorry, Jo. I was just trying . . ."

"Get! Out!"

No, no, this is wrong. All wrong. I just need to convince her of that. I put my hands out in a warding-off gesture, an *I have no rabbits hidden up my sleeve* gesture. "I'm sorry, Jo, I'm stressed, that's all, I'm stressed."

"Get the hell out, Charlie."

"Jo . . ."

"I want you to leave," she says.

"Why? So you can not call the police again?"

"So what are you going to do, Charlie? Are you going to kill me too?"

Her comment isn't a physical slap, but I react as though it is. I stammer for a few seconds, trying to say something that will convince her that she's safe, but is she? "How can you think I killed them?"

"What am I supposed to think?"

"You're supposed to trust me."

She smirks at that and I don't blame her. "Trust you? You must be pretty far gone if you think I should trust you after this. So what are you going to do now? Kill me, or stay here and monitor who I call?"

"Come on, Jo, stop overreacting."

"Stop shouting. I'm sick of you shouting."

Well, I'm sick of people dying. I'm sick of seeing blood. I'm sick of being chased by Evil and spoken to by ghosts. I'm sick of guilt resting like a bowling ball in the pit of my stomach. I hate that I no longer have any control in my life. I hate this Real World, the killing hours that make up the days. I think I have the justification to scream and shout until my throat is raw.

"I'm sorry, I'm sorry, I didn't mean to shout," I say, not realizing I had been. "All I want is for you to believe me." I try to keep my voice low and steady. As if I'm talking to a woman on a ledge.

"I believe you, Charlie. Is that it? Does that make you happy enough to leave?"

"You don't believe me."

"No, I really do. It's just come to me now. So you can leave."

I reach toward her to help her up and she flinches away, and in that movement I see myself through her eyes. Suddenly she believes there are monsters in this world, and I'm one of them. I look away, unable to face her. For a moment I think of last night, the highs and the lows, of which there were both. Incredible, incredible highs. Sick, ravaging lows. One of those lows came when I finally decided to do more than just stand

and watch. I ran from the tree line to confront Cyris. I ran and the only thing I did successfully was step on the flashlight and lose my balance. Seconds after I hit the dirt, Cyris started hitting me. That was another low point. He was hitting me and telling me how stupid I was for trying to save a dead woman.

*She's like a baby*, he said, and I was trying to ward off his blows, *flying through a windshield that hasn't landed yet*. Another punch. Another struggle. He got me in the side of the head. Got me in the shoulder. *Surely you can see that*, he said, but I couldn't. I couldn't see any windshields. Any babies.

"I think you might be in danger," I tell Jo.

"You have a talent for seeing the obvious."

"You need to come with me."

"No."

"Please. He'll come for you. I know it."

"You need to leave, Charlie. You need help. Professional help."

I reach back out to help her up. This time she takes my hand. "You need to go somewhere for a few days," I tell her, "and you can't call the police."

"I'm not going anywhere," she says, "and the first thing I'm going to do is call the police. For your own benefit, Charlie. That blow to your head has done more damage than you think."

"What can I do to convince you?" I ask.

"Pushing me wasn't a good start, Charlie."

"There's nothing I can say?"

"No."

"You're sure?"

"Positive."

"In that case, I'm sorry."

"What for?" she asks.

I push her to the floor and we struggle, but I'm heavier and stronger and more determined to save her than she is to save herself. It's the only way. It makes me sick, but not as sick as if Cyris were to find her. I pull the phone cable out and use it to bind her hands and feet. She stops struggling. I gag her with a hand towel. Action Man has taken the wheel and he's steering me right past morality and into an abyss. I take a step back and look down at her shaking body. I spend the next thirty seconds almost untying her and the following thirty convincing myself this is for the best. For both of us. She isn't safe by herself. Not now. I pack a suitcase full of her clothes and dump it in the backseat of the car along with her handbag.

I try to get Jo to her feet, but she refuses to stand. I've bound her arms behind her so I pull up on her wrists and the pain in her shoulders forces her up. I cut the cord by her feet. She tries to pull away from me, knocking over a dining table chair on the way to the door. I straighten it back up. I tighten my grip and lead her out to the car.

"It'll be easier for us both if you cooperate, Jo. Otherwise I'll put you in the trunk. Come on, Jo. Help me out here, okay?"

She doesn't help me out. I force her into the trunk and tie her feet back together. I feel exhausted. I also feel like that stranger is still living in my body. I'm watching my real self in this Real World and not enjoying the ride. With the suitcase in the car it feels like we're going on holiday.

I roll down the window. The air is cooling down, but still has a warm edge to it. It's hard to imagine being in danger in the tranquility of this night. I hear banging against the roof of the trunk, but try to shut it out. I want to be with that tranquility, I want to feel it inside me, but that's not possible. It may never be possible again. It was tranquil last night too, up to a point.

I rub my fingers across the bump on my head. It was just after Cyris, his breath on my sweating face, asked me if I wanted a piece of the action that I thrust my head forward and felt his nose explode beneath my forehead. That was one of the high points.

The windshield of the car shimmers and I dig my fingers into the tears and wipe them away. From the back of the car Jo beats out a steady rhythm. We head west and pass through the central city. Monday nights have little traffic and even less foot traffic. Nobody can hear Jo making trunk music.

I pull into the parking lot of the Everblue Motel. Its design is similar to other motels that have been built where traffic is heavy and land is cheap—just two long rectangles of concrete block running perpendicular to each other. It's hard to tell in the light whether the paint on the walls has faded in areas from the sun or darkened in the opposite areas from exhaust fumes. In between, strips of brown grass run parallel with the sidewalk. The sidewalk is chipped on the edges and patches of grass bleed between the long cracks. The neon *b* in Everblue has blown out. The rooms face away from the road. I count seven cars in the parking lot and nobody around. I stop outside the office. It's lit by harsh fluorescent lights. I leave the engine running and the stereo turned up loud with the window open to help mask Jo's sounds, even though sounds coming from a trunk are to be expected in a neighborhood like this.

Pamphlets on touristy things to do in Christchurch line one wall. You can start the day by skiing and then go surfing in the afternoon. You can go skydiving or Jet Skiing or play one of thirty or forty golf courses. You can wake up one day and watch two women get killed then kidnap your ex-wife. It's all part of the Christchurch experience. Slipped in among the pamphlets are leaflets from the Jehovah's Witnesses and

Mormons and medical clinics in the area, all offering to save us from something. A strip of flypaper hangs in the corner covered in a variety of insects, a few of which are still twitching. An electric fan with a bent propeller circulates slowly, the tip of the blade pinging against the grille every half second.

I ring the bell and a man steps out from behind a greasy curtain with a piece of greasy chicken in his hands, and I'm grateful he's wearing a black T-shirt instead of a fishnet wife beater. The T-shirt has *You can never have too much duct tape* written across it. He has tiny pieces of toilet paper stuck to his neck from a recent attempt at shaving. He starts talking in short, uncomplicated words either for his benefit or mine. He gives me the hourly charge for the rooms. I tell him I'm staying the night, and then I ask for a room with two single beds.

He gives me a funny look. "You some kind of weirdo?" he asks.

"Some kind, yeah."

I give him a false name and real cash because that's all he's expecting. He glances out at the car and doesn't ask where the second person is, but a man in his position probably has a pretty good idea. His T-shirt sums it all up.

I move the car up to the room and park between an old Toyota and an even older Ford. Both are painted white. One of the side mirrors on the Toyota has been broken off, maybe from an accident, maybe from vandalism. I carry my suitcase inside then come back outside for Jo's. I head back and, making sure nobody is looking, I open the trunk. Jo doesn't make it complicated for me to help get her out. I carry her inside and sit her down on the bed. I lock the door with the cheap dead bolt and slide the chain across.

She muffles something at me. I remove the gag.

"Think about what you're doing, Charlie. It's not too late. You can take me back home and I won't tell, I promise."

She's scared now. All that came earlier, she was angry and disappointed, I frightened her in those moments, but now she's scared, scared of what I'm capable of. She genuinely sounds like she means what she's saying.

"I can't do that, Jo. You're in danger."

"Only from you."

"I just need you to spend a day with me so I can prove I'm not lying. Just a day. Then you can do what you want, okay?"

"People don't come back from the dead, Charlie."

I picture Cyris. He's a big guy. Then I think about the knife I stabbed him with. It's long and sharp. In my mind I see him standing sideways. The blade is next to him. I figure it out like one of those old-school science cartoons—*This is Joe's homicide*. The knife goes in. The tip comes out the other side. I stabbed him, but I didn't finish the job. If I had, Kathy and Luciana wouldn't be haunting me.

I stuff the gag back into Jo's mouth.

The room is small and cozy and very simple. The walls have been painted cream. There are no paintings, only a calendar from three years ago strung up on a nail bashed into the mortar between two of the concrete blocks. A door closes off a small bathroom with a small window that doesn't open. The kitchenette has utilities dating back thirty years. There's a TV, the remote to which is bolted onto the bedside dresser. The dark blue curtains are pulled shut, hiding the lack of view. The carpets are cheap and look like the bodily fluids get water blasted off them every other month. The cigarette burns in the bedspread and on the carpet match the ones on the dresser.

Jo doesn't struggle too much when I tie her to the bed. I don't tell her I would do anything to protect her because she won't believe me. All I can do is show her. I use towels to bind her arms and legs and wrap the motel's phone cord around her waist and the bed. Back on my own bed I kill the lights and wonder if I ought to be killing myself. I feel sick to my stomach and my heart is racing. I wipe an arm across my forehead and it comes away sopping wet. I lie down, but I don't think I'll ever sleep again. The neon from the sign outside flickers around the edges of the curtains and makes the room glow red. I can hear it buzzing. I reach out and roam my fingers over the sticky buttons of the remote control. I stab at them until the TV blinks into life. A menu with a blue backdrop displays a list of movies I can choose from for an extra ten dollars. Most of them are adult. I remember reading a statistic once that the average time an adult movie is on in a motel room is seven minutes. That means they watch the start and get what they need around ten percent of the way through. They don't know what happens after that. Don't know how it ends. Could be the actors all sit around drinking coffee and nobody would ever know.

I use the remote to steer away from the menu and go to the local channels. A TV evangelist appears telling us all that God's strapped for cash, and how, with our credit cards, we can help Him out of his bind. Maybe the repo guy is after Him. Maybe Jesus has racked up some gambling debts. I skip channels until I find a news broadcast. It's live from the scene. Kathy's house is swaying around because the camera has zoomed in beyond the operator's control. The police aren't saying much. The report is similar to the one I didn't want to watch earlier. Gone are rehashed interviews with family and friends. Added are pictures of a body being removed. I wish I'd never turned the TV on. I switch it back off and lie back, listening to the letters buzzing outside, all except for the *b*. The concrete block walls drown out the traffic noise, but not enough of it.

We lie there surrounded by the sounds of the night. I can hear Jo shifting her body, trying to get comfortable. I don't talk to her and she doesn't mumble through her gag. I'm unable to switch off my mind. I can't stop thinking about Kathy and Luciana and Cyris. I can't stop thinking how the shape in the body bag on TV was more than just a shape back when this day started. I can't stop thinking about Jo. Things are bad. And as Monday sets about turning to Tuesday I have a feeling they're only going to get worse.

# CHAPTER EIGHT

Landry repeats the procedure from before. He parks outside the house and leans against his car, only this time he doesn't give in to the temptation of another cigarette.

The night seems to have cooled off as far as it's going to get—somewhere around ten degrees he guesses. This same time last year the evenings were half that. He can hear the waves in the distance. The house is a few blocks from the beach. The moon is hanging out over the water and he imagines the view out there must be pretty good. He can't remember the last time he walked on a beach at night. Maybe he never has.

The house is a similar age to Feldman's, only instead of brick it's wood. Similar gardens, only more trees, and with a driveway that snakes up around the side of the house in a way that you can't see the front door. He's halfway up there when his phone rings. It's Hutton.

"I think I have what you're looking for," Hutton says.

"Shoot."

"Guy by the name of Francis Booth was found unconscious in the bathroom at a bar by the name of Popular Consensus. Hey, doesn't your brother own that bar?"

"Yeah," he says, and the story is starting to ring a bell. "So what happened?"

"The guy was taken to a hospital. Had a broken nose, broken cheekbones, a dislocated jaw. Says some guy went into the bathroom and beat the shit out of him."

"Mugging?"

"No. Guy still had his wallet on him. Said he didn't know the guy. Never seen him before. Nobody saw anything. Case is still open. You got something?"

"Maybe. Maybe not. Thanks for the info," he says, and before Hutton can ask any more questions, he hangs up.

So Feldman beat somebody up at a bar. Why? Something to do with his wife? Something to do with being jealous?

He walks the rest of the way up the driveway. Some of the cobblestones are loose beneath his feet, some of the branches from the shrubs and trees tug at his jacket. He peers through the garage window and can make out a car, but can't tell what kind. He gets the same feeling he got from the last place, that it's empty in here. He puts the theory to the test by knocking on the front door, waiting, then knocking again. Nothing.

At Feldman's house he was happy to break in, but not here. This woman is not guilty, which makes breaking into her house something quite different. And he has no reason to think Feldman has come here.

Just for the hell of it, he turns the handle to see if the door is locked. It isn't, which sets off a whole lot of warning bells. Houses have a feel when they are empty, sure, but they also have the same feel if the person inside is dead. He's not sure why his mind jumps to that conclusion, but it does—that's what twenty years of seeing bad stuff will do to you. He's suddenly feeling convinced there's a dead woman in here. The door swings open. He gets out his flashlight.

"Hello?"

Nothing. He steps inside. "Hello?"

Still nothing. He flicks on the flashlight. He's in a dining room. Nothing looks out of place. He moves further in. The headset to the phone is sitting on the floor, the cable torn from it. That same cable is a few feet away near the oven. He crouches down over it. There's a knot in the middle, and the ends have been cut by a knife or by scissors. At some point this cable was used to tie something up. Or somebody. He goes through the house, searching it room by room, feeling relief with every room that doesn't have a dead body in it. There are no signs of a struggle. The bedroom is a mess, clothes have been pulled out from the wardrobe, probably packed away into a suitcase. Did Jo run, or was she taken? The cut cable suggests the latter. But why take her and pack stuff for her?

He walks back into the dining room. Technically, he doesn't know anything bad happened here. It looks that way—but it may not be. Feldman may not be responsible for any of this. Could just be she packed some stuff and left. But the phone cord? Maybe the phone is faulty. No matter how he looks at that, the only explanation is a bad one. There's no handbag. No car keys. No purse. But there's a cell phone on the kitchen table. There's the piece of cable, and the car in the garage, and an unlocked front door. He picks up the cell phone. He goes through and finds Charlie Feldman's number. He calls it. He gets a message saying the number is no longer in service.

He walks back down to his car. He pulls his cell phone out

of his pocket. He needs to call this in. As much as he wants to get his hands on Feldman by himself, this case has now also become about Jo Feldman, and he needs the police looking for her. Only he can't do that without explaining why he was here. And anyway, he doesn't know something has happened to her.

And, if it has, then whatever has happened has happened.

He puts his phone back into his pocket. This might be about to get a lot more complicated than it should have been. He pulls away from the curb. Holding on to the evidence the way he did, well, he's already too deep now. He can't tell anybody what's happened, and he can't back away. He has to stay committed.

He'll find Feldman, he's sure of it, and if Feldman is the one who took Jo, then he'll find her too, and everything is going to be okay. That's what he tries to tell himself, but the same twenty years he's had of seeing bad stuff are now telling him that may not be the case at all.

# CHAPTER NINE

Tuesday morning and we wake up to rain. Warm rain. The type you get in summer and love to walk in. I turn on the radio and listen to a weather report. An old guy tells us to expect twenty-eight degrees. Tells us to expect more rain tonight. Tells us the twenty-eight degrees is going to drop to around ten. Tells us it's one of the warmest autumns on record. He doesn't tell us what we should do if some guy is trying to kill us. I figure he's just looking out the window and telling it like it is.

I have woken with a small headache, a dry mouth, and the flavorless dregs of a dream. There's no difficulty in separating the dream from reality—I only have to look over at Jo to know what's really going on. I have abducted her. I have stolen her away from her life and in that action Action Man is starting to become the monster Cyris is. Though my dreams were full of death and murder I was a hero, yet from the moment I stepped out of my car I was a hero doomed to fail. I don't even know what I am now.

There was a point where I thought I was going to succeed. Cyris was on top of me, the hard ground was digging into my back, the night air was still, and there were no signs of life outside of our small trio. I managed to throw my head up and crack my forehead into his nose and I used that momentum to push him backward. I got to my feet and raced for the flashlight. He knocked me off balance before I made it and my tangling legs had me back on the ground within seconds. When Cyris brought his knife down toward me his intentions were clear, and in the weak edges of the flashlight beam I knew death wasn't giving me up as a lost cause.

All I did then was react. I got my hands up and onto his wrists before he could bring the knife all the way down. I was lucky to have gotten my hands into the position without having my fingers scattered over my chest. I pushed my arms to the side to redirect his balance. The moment he began to topple I used my right palm as a hammer and nailed it into the base of his broken nose. He let go of the knife. There was no room for hesitation. I picked the blade up and plunged it ahead. The blade hit something hard before slowing down and it felt like I was pushing it through wet cement. I kept pushing until it came to a complete stop. For one moment we were frozen and then his mouth dropped open and the air that rolled out smelled like spoiled meat. He collapsed on top of me, a dead weight that I thought would get deader by the second, only I was wrong. I dragged myself from beneath him and listened as his fingers slowly tapped out a death march against the handle, and then the tapping stopped.

The silence then was complete, heavy and thick, an emptiness of sound that pushed into my ears and into my mind, crushing my thoughts. I had killed a man and it felt good. Okay—maybe *good* is the wrong word. I think what I felt in that moment was more about what I didn't feel—I didn't feel *bad*. I didn't feel any sense of guilt. If I had to choose one thing to sum it up, I would say what I felt was relief.

Of course that relief quickly changed to fear. Out of nowhere the story of what had happened to Benjamin Hyatt came to me. I had just killed a man to save two women, and for that I could go to jail. Would I? No. I couldn't see how a jury would convict me. I couldn't really see how I would be facing jail time. But of course Hyatt would have thought the same thing. Would have kept thinking it right up to the moment he got beaten so badly in jail he died.

I look over at Jo. She's staring silently at me, looking me up and down. My clothes look like I've ironed wrinkles into them. The cuts on my face are slowly starting to heal. I get up and use the bathroom then head into the kitchen. I start making coffee, hoping it will help dilute the weird feeling of waking up in a strange room and worrying about kidnapping and death. I untie Jo and take out the gag. She sits up and stares at me and continues her silence. I don't know what to say to her. I fight the urge to say sorry over and over as she uses the bathroom. She takes her suitcase in with her. I wait by the door in case she starts screaming, only she doesn't. When she comes out she's changed into a T-shirt and a pair of cargo pants.

"I'll make you some coffee," I say. She doesn't bother to thank me as I do just that. I put it in front of her then sit well back in case she throws it in my face. "Look, I know that this must seem pretty weird—"

"Weird? Jesus, Charlie, it's gone way past weird."

"Sure, maybe you're right, but—"

"Maybe? You use the word *maybe*? But what? But it's going to be okay? Is that it? You tied me up and now you want me to be your friend?"

"I wasn't going to put it like that."

"Whatever. I'm hungry. Are you going to make me starve too?"

"There isn't any food here."

"Then let's go get some."

"Why? So you can ditch me the first chance you get?"

She doesn't answer. Instead she just stares at me. Whatever she's about to say, she's given it some serious thought. I've seen the process many times over the years. She even did it when I proposed to her, which turned the whole proposal thing into a really awkward moment, but as she pointed out back then, it was better to put more thought into it than decide on the emotion of the moment. That's what she's doing now.

"I've had all night to think about it, Charlie," she says, "and I've decided to help you because I really think you could do with it. Maybe I feel like I owe you something, and maybe I'm remembering the way you used to be, or maybe I'm just as crazy as you are right now. So let's make a deal. I agree to let you show me what you need to today to convince me to stay with you, and at the end of the day it becomes my decision whether I stay or go."

"Yeah, right."

"I mean it, Charlie. I promise I won't try and get away," she says, and the thing about Jo is she's never broken a promise. The other thing about Jo is she's never been abducted before. "Just don't tie me up anymore, okay? We'll go out, get some breakfast, and then I'll help you. But only for today. At the end you have to let me go. I think you owe me that. In fact I think you owe me that at the very least. I give you my full cooperation but you give me yours when the day's over. And if I decide to go to the police at that point it's my decision, not yours. Is it a deal?"

I wish I could believe she isn't lying, because life would be a lot easier if she was with me rather than against me. "I don't know," I say, and the funny thing is I really don't. That's what wanting to believe will do to you.

"What's your plan? To keep running? Or are you going to try and find the man that did these horrible things?"

"I'm not sure," I tell her, only I am sure. I'm going to find Cyris.

"Charlie, you've been nothing but a bastard since you came around last night, but I know that's not you, I know that's not the real you, and I know that sooner or later you'll have no choice but to let me go. That means you have to start trusting me, right? For God's sake, Charlie, you might as well start now. What do you think I'm going to do? Write a note on the bill for the waitress to send help?"

It's exactly the kind of thing I thought she would do. Or she wouldn't even have to go to that effort—all she'd need to do is stand up and announce to the people there that she had been kidnapped. I want to trust her. Our lives were entwined—we were lovers, best friends, and I've kept the knot in place by kidnapping her. Only the last twelve hours I've taken all of those years we've known each other and poisoned them with paranoia and fear.

"Look, I'll bring you back some breakfast, okay? I promise. Then we'll talk."

I can't take her with me because if the police showed up at her house last night then her picture may already be circulating in the news. I can't take her with me because if I was in her situation I'd be doing what I could to escape. She doesn't resist as I tie her to the bed. I turn on the TV. It hums for a few seconds—the picture comes and goes and then settles. There's an old black-and-white movie on. It's about vampires. They're being chased by bad acting and poor directing. I recognize none of the actors, but all of the lines. I leave the TV on for Jo and hang up the *Do Not Disturb* sign on my way out.

It's eight thirty and the streets are clogged with work traffic. I think about the phone messages on my machine at home, messages which will be added to today unless I call in sick. I decide that's what I'm going to do because if everything goes well, if I find Cyris and get him to the police, then maybe I can still have a normal life for which I'd need to keep my job. The morning is warm, we're probably about halfway to what the weatherman guessed we'd get to. I walk to a nearby café. It's one of those small mom-and-pop places where Mom has put on too much weight and Pop never quite cooks the chicken properly. Most of the business likely comes from the nearby factories. It seats around twenty people inside and another seven or eight out. The smell of coffee and bacon makes the warm atmosphere inside even more appealing. I wish I could stay all morning. The rooms are painted orange and red and there's enough hardwood from the floors to the furniture to the edging around the ceiling and walls to make an ark. I'm served by a short waitress in her late forties with a haircut that should be in a museum. She smiles as she takes down my order. A name tag on her uniform says her name is Dot, but sometimes name tags lie. She brings me coffee that's on par with the cup I had at the motel. I realize I'm nervous as hell. Does anybody here know who I am? I order bacon and eggs, then I ask if I can borrow the phone, and then I call the school. I start out by apologizing for not having shown up yesterday, but I tell them I'm sick. I tell them I don't know what's wrong with me, but it's bad, and that today I'm going to a doctor. The secretary tells me to get well soon, and doesn't complain about yesterday. I return to my table and a minute later the food comes out. The bacon is slightly overcooked just the way I like it. The eggs too. I must look like a competitive food eater as I shovel them into my mouth. I buy some food to go and pick up a newspaper on the way back.

The first thing I do is untie Jo. While she eats we study the front page. The police have released more details. They mention that Luciana was found by a work colleague, Kathy by a neighbor. Both husbands have been questioned and released. Luciana's husband was in Auckland with his new partner at the time. The article mentions the pair's separation, says the husband is gay. Kathy's husband, Frank, also has a solid alibi.

The van outside Luciana's house was found with the key snapped in the ignition. Luciana's car, a dark blue Ford, hasn't been found. I read the article twice more, then I go deeper into the paper where a related article has been written by a different journalist. I read this, but don't learn anything. I go back to the front page and read the headlines again. Something in them doesn't quite gel, but I can't put my finger on it. Whatever it is, it starts gnawing at the back of my brain. I close my eyes and try to focus on it, but that only makes it worse. I look through the paper searching for any mention of Jo, but there's nothing. Then I even read my horoscope. It says forces in my life are conspiring to change my future, but isn't any more specific. The nagging feeling that I'm missing something doesn't disappear.

"I've been thinking," Jo says, "that if this Cyris guy is after you he's going to come for you at night, right? He does his thing at night, and he wouldn't risk anything during the day."

She's sitting on her bed and I'm sitting in the kitchenette

and we're both staring at the parking lot and watching the rain. I think about what she has to say. I want to find Cyris, and she's suggesting the best way to find him is by letting him find me.

"I guess that makes sense. But how is he going to find me?"

"Did he see your car?"

"Yeah. No doubt about it."

"First thing we need to do is call in sick."

"I already have."

"I need to as well."

"I'll call for you."

She doesn't look happy with the idea, but doesn't try to convince me otherwise. "It makes sense that if he's going to look for you, Charlie, he's going to start at your house. He saw your car. Maybe he took down the license plate. Or maybe he forced one of the women to tell him who you were."

I start nodding. It makes sense. "We need to stake it out."

Staking out my own house. Considering everything else that has happened this week this new development doesn't seem strange to me. "I guess it's a logical progression."

"Oh, it definitely is, for him and for us. And that has to be our plan. That, and figuring out a way to catch him when he does show up."

"How are we going to do that?"

Jo pushes away her empty plate and sips more of her bad coffee. "That's what we need to start figuring out."

# CHAPTER TEN

Another day, another dollar. And already for Detective Inspector Bill Landry it's going badly.

He didn't sleep well. In fact, he's woken up feeling more tired than before he went to bed. He got home last night with a racing mind that he tried to put at ease by having a cigarette, but halfway through the cigarette he ended up throwing up. He went to bed around one a.m., woke up at four, and has been awake since then, spending most of that time sitting at his kitchen table drinking coffee and staring at a calendar on the wall. Around seven he made himself some toast, but didn't eat it. He poured a bowl of cereal and didn't touch that either.

Around seven thirty he spent ten minutes hovering over the toilet fighting the waves of nausea the pills were bringing into his routine. Then he coughed for ten minutes, wondering what the hell the point of the pills was, too scared to cut them out of his life in case the coughing was worse. The mornings were when it was the worst. At seven forty-five smoke came from the bottom of his coffee machine, a few sparks too, and really he thought after last week's news his appliances would be the ones to outlive him. In fact there was a moment where he considered pulling it apart while it was still plugged in—it'd be a way of beating cancer on his own terms. In the end he had to settle for drinking warm water, and when you're stumbling through this world in a dozing stupor trying hard to wake up, trying hard to stay focused with both cancer and cough-fighting poison running through your system, water simply doesn't cut it. Apparently slapping yourself hard doesn't work either. He took the pills the doctor prescribed him, at one point one of them getting lodged in his throat and making him think everything might come to an end on his kitchen floor.

The morning has moved on since then. He spent a few minutes packing some clothes into a gym bag, along with some boots. He thinks he may need them later on. Right now he's having the pleasure of getting caught in traffic. Every few minutes or so he tries, but fails, to stifle a yawn. Days like this he sometimes fantasizes about climbing out of his car and picking a direction to walk in and never looking back. He saw that in a movie once. It seemed like a good idea. The button that changes station on his radio is broken, so all he can do is either listen to the same station that he's growing to hate, or nothing at all. He listens to it for a bit. There's a piece on about bringing the death penalty back to New Zealand. There's a chance it will be going to a referendum later this year—which is also an election year. The people of New Zealand are sick of the endless tide of criminals. And Feldman is just one more number added to that bunch. Listening to the radio, Landry realizes what he's planning on doing is really what the government may be planning on doing anyway—except he's just going to bring that date forward. That's all.

Still craving coffee, he stops at a gas station, pulling in behind a shiny red sports car that immediately makes him feel jealous. He goes inside, but the machine there is out of order. He wonders if it's a worldwide event. Then he wonders if it's him that's contaminating everything, if he has the Midas touch, if everything he comes into contact with is turning cancerous. He trades the idea of buying caffeine for purchasing a packet of cigarettes, even though the pack he split open last night is still mostly full.

When he gets to work somebody had taken his parking space. When he gets inside he's sure the elevator isn't going to work. He pushes the button and the doors open, but then he decides to use the stairs instead of risking getting caught between floors.

The fourth floor is in motion. Detectives are talking on phones, they're doing paperwork, they're following leads. The coffee machine works—thank God—but then he finds a crack in his mug. Of course he didn't find that crack until coffee had leaked all over his pants.

"Goddamn it," he says, fighting the temptation to throw the cup against the wall. The day has to get better, doesn't it?

"How you feeling?" Schroder asks, coming over.

"Better," he says.

"You still don't look so good."

Landry shrugs. He isn't sure what to say to that. That he's never going to look good again?

Schroder updates him on the case. They're working on the theory that the two dead women knew their killer. "He killed them in their houses," Schroder says. "The two girls have a history together, so it wasn't random. He targeted these two women for a reason."

"No idea on the reason?"

"Not yet. I'm going to run some stuff past Benson Barlow," he says.

Landry nods. Benson Barlow is a psychiatrist who has helped them on and off over the last few months.

Schroder looks at his watch. "I'm meeting him in an hour. First I'm heading to the morgue. Want to tag along?"

No, he doesn't. He wants to start looking for Charlie Feldman, and he doesn't see how going to the morgue is going to advance that search. "Why not?"

"You sure you're feeling okay? You look like you might pass out. I don't want to get you to the morgue and then have you end up staying."

"I'm fine," he says.

They take the elevator downstairs. It doesn't break down. They split up and take their own cars, Schroder leading the way. Landry puts the air-conditioning on full blast, directing it at his face, hoping it'll combat the urge he has to fall asleep. He's not sure how he's going to make it through the day.

Christchurch Hospital is undergoing a series of renovations and parts of the parking lot are cut off from the public. There are cranes and bulldozers and men breaking the ground apart with pneumatic drills. They find parking spaces and the noise is deafening until they get inside.

Landry has the overwhelming sense of wasting time as he stands in the morgue. It's a cold white room surrounded by metal tables with canvas sheets draped over them, and on those sheets are saws and pliers and forceps and knives and other tools he can't identify, all of them for cutting, cutting, cutting, all of them the kind of thing killers like Charlie Feldman would have a wet dream over. He hates being here. It's the first time he's been in a morgue since learning death was comin' a-knockin'. There's every good chance he'll be coming back in winter and those same tools will open him up and place his black organs on the same scales and into the same holding trays. He runs a finger along one of those trays. It's cold and unforgiving, just like the cancer.

"Gentlemen," a woman says, stepping into the morgue. It's one of the medical examiners. Her name is Tracey, and for some reason Tracey has a last name he can never remember no matter how many times he hears it. Attractive and athletic, Tracey is a few years younger than him. She has blond hair that was black the last time he saw her. She gives them a smile and he smiles back and over the years he's often thought she'd have made a great ex-wife.

"What have you got for us?"

"Just the obvious," she says, and she hands each of them a folder. Inside are several photographs of the wounds and lots of paragraphs and diagrams of exactly how the two women died. At the front of the folder a half-page synopsis sums up those photos and diagrams. "Cause of death was exactly how it looked," she says. "Massive heart trauma caused by metal spikes. Each one was driven in with quite some accuracy. There are some defensive wounds here, but most of what you see happened postmortem. It looks like the killer rammed these stakes into these two women, then continued to pound them in deeper with either a hammer or even his foot. Kathy McClory's right breast was removed after death," she says. "See these rough edges?" she asks, then points to the victim's chest. "Looks like it was removed with a saw of some kind."

"Any way to narrow that down, Doc?" Schroder asks.

Tracey shakes her head. "Too much of a mess," she says.

"Also, there are no hesitation marks. When the guy started cutting, there were no second thoughts. "My guess is a hacksaw, and as you guys know, there are thousands of them out there. Even if you brought the right one in I probably couldn't match it to the wounds. Sorry." She looks up at Landry. Are you okay?"

"Fine," he says. "So they suffered?"

Tracey nods, and suddenly he remembers her last name. It's Walter. Tracey Walter. "Yes. A lot. There are fingernail impressions in their palms. They were balling their hands into fists so tight their fingernails actually cut through the skin."

She spends another ten minutes going over her findings. She asks if the breast has been found and Schroder tells her it hasn't been, to which she nods and says, "Of course. Otherwise it would have been brought in already."

When they get outside they stand in the parking lot for a minute, having to yell to be heard over the sound of construction. They agree on Schroder going to talk to Benson Barlow—it will be the start of him trying to build up a profile.

"You might as well go back and revisit the crime scenes," Schroder says, which might help or it might not, but either way Landry has to start somewhere.

# CHAPTER ELEVEN

The motel smells of bacon and eggs and coffee—at least for now. During the night it smelled of depraved acts she didn't want to think about. The air is sticky and warm. The bathroom looks like it gets cleaned about as often as the place gets painted. The TV is still on, the movie that was on when Charlie left has finished, only to have been replaced by some kind of sequel that is still just as black and just as white, still with the wooden dialogue, still with the sets that look like they've been carved out of cardboard. She's desperate to get away from here. More importantly she's desperate to get away from Charlie.

Her back is sore. At some point she's hurt it, and she isn't sure if it's from the fall, the struggle, or from being tied up. It's not damage sore, but achy sore, the kind of sore you get when you've been to the gym for the first time in a year. The only good thing is that she's no longer hungry.

More than feeling sore, more than feeling angry, she feels

disappointed. She's never felt that way in a person before. A little, perhaps, six months ago when Charlie hurt that guy at the bar, but despite all that there was something in that action that was understandable. Charlie had been defending her. Only he hadn't been, not really, because it was a minute or more between the moment that guy put his hand up her dress and the moment that Charlie started hitting him. The problem was Charlie wouldn't stop. He didn't see the look in his eyes. The wild look, like that of a beast, like that of a beast that was enjoying the pain it was causing. Could she have given him another chance? She could have, and it's something she's thought about every day since they broke up, and something that had been on her mind a lot over the last few weeks. The irony is she was getting close to calling him and seeing if they could talk. There was still a future for them to be had.

Not now.

This side of Charlie is something altogether different. Much different from the man she knew, different from the man he became that night six months ago. This is a side she never thought could exist. He's not going to let her go. He says he will, and she thinks he believes what he's telling her, but his actions defy his words. In some ways it's like dealing with a stranger. A stranger who she once loved, a man who has betrayed her and hurt her, and that's why the anger and the fear are taking a backseat to the disappointment.

It's also why as much as she wants to believe in him, she can't, and that means she can't *believe* him either. She doesn't know what happened last night. All she knows is Charlie has something to do with the deaths of those two women and, really, she doesn't even know if that is true either. The only thing she knows for sure is that she has to find a way to escape.

Convincing Charlie she wants to help was easier than she'd

hoped, and she guesses that's for a few reasons. First, he has a desire to believe her so he no longer has to be alone. Second, this Charlie isn't as smart as the Charlie she was married to. That Charlie would have taken those two women to the police, despite what happened to that lawyer last year. If he had, those two women would still be alive. And all that aside, he should have gone to the police after he'd found them dead. That's what any sane person would have done.

Ergo, Charlie is no longer sane.

And the proof is in his treatment of her. Something inside him has snapped. Which means escaping should be easy. All she has to do is gain his trust. She must take baby steps, she must build up his belief that they can be a team.

That's what she needs to focus on. She needs to ignore her disappointment. She can't think about how she used to love him. She can't think about what their future might have been like if they had stayed together. Would he have killed her too?

Too?

Does she really think he killed those women? Is that what he is? A killer?

"We need to contact the police," she says.

"Unbelievable. I've already said—"

She holds up her hand in a stopping gesture. He shuts up. "I didn't say go to them. Now are you going to let me talk?"

"Get to the point."

She tries hard not to wince when he says that. Get to the point. What a bastard.

"You know things about Cyris, important things that the police don't know. You said they wouldn't know about the pasture, well, you could tell them to search there. You could tell them everything you know by writing a letter and sending it anonymously."

He thinks about her suggestion. She can see him working it out, seeing what the good points are and what the bad points are.

"It's a good idea, Charlie."

"Okay. Fine."

"There might be some stationary in the bedside drawer," she says, "though I guess it's unlikely."

He checks the drawers. Nothing. Not even a Bible.

"You put my handbag in the car, right?"

"Yeah. It's in the backseat."

"I have a pen and paper in there."

"And you're just going to sit there quietly while I go out and get it?"

"Yes, that's exactly what I'm going to do. The car is only a few yards away, Charlie. If I was going to start screaming I'd have done it already. Same thing about trying to escape. I could have gone out the bathroom window, but I didn't." Of course the reason she didn't was because the damn thing was painted shut, and even if it hadn't been she's not so sure she would have gotten through it.

"You promise to stay right there?"

She nods. She promises. He opens the door. Daylight floods in. She can see his car. She could get up and run for it, but could she outrun him? She isn't sure. He would tackle her, and things could go bad. She could land wrong. She could hit her head on the ground. There's no point in risking it. Just the fact he's gone outside without tying her up shows the baby steps she's taking are already working. At this rate she'll have talked her way out of here within the next hour or two.

Charlie comes back inside. He hands her her bag. She goes through it.

"If you're looking for your cell phone," he says, "it's at your house. I didn't want the police to be able to trace us."

"That's not what I'm looking for," she says, only it kind of was.

She finds the pad and it takes another half a minute to find a pen. When she gets out of this, she's going to throw half of this stuff out. There are receipts and tissues that have been in here for months.

He sits down on the bed and uses the bedside drawers as a writing table. He sets about going to work. She doesn't care whether he mails it—she suggested it to see if she could get him to go outside without tying her up, and to hopefully get her phone. She also suggested it hoping that by putting words on paper he may begin to realize what he's doing. If some of the old Charlie is still in there then maybe he'll see the decisions he's making are insane. Hopefully he'll take responsibility for his actions. Hopefully some of the old Charlie will start to filter back through.

"I don't really know where to begin," he says.

"The beginning seems as good a place as any," she says, concerned that that wasn't obvious to him. He rubs at the bump on his forehead and winces. Is that partly the reason he's so off the rails? A blow to the head?

He starts writing. She watches him, the pen flowing across the page, it all seems to be rushing out in a stream. She looks at the TV, at the black-and-white vampire doing what he can to get all the hot chicks. She wonders if this horror movie was on yesterday morning because it might suggest where Charlie got some of his ideas from. The news said the two women died violently. It mentioned ritualistic killings. Did they really die by being staked through the heart as Charlie said? No—surely not. Because that would be . . . what? Too horrific? She's deluding herself if she thinks horrific things don't happen on a daily basis on a global scale. So if that is how the women died, did Charlie do the staking? It depends. It depends on how guilty she thinks he is. Her loyalties now lie with two dead women she's never met. She needs to get out of here. Needs to get the police. And the vampire on TV is giving her an idea on how she can do that.

"Stakes," she says.

"What?"

"Stakes," she says, and this will test just how far Charlie has slipped into the crazy. "That's the next part of our plan," she says, glancing at the dying vampire on TV, hoping like hell the scenario she's about to pitch is going to work.

# CHAPTER TWELVE

"Stakes," Jo says.

I look up from my letter. It isn't going well. I'm up to the part where Cyris had his dead fingers curled around the handle of the knife, but I'm not sure whether to put that down. I don't bother to ask Jo because she doesn't believe I stabbed him, and looking back at it I'm starting to question it too. I didn't want to check for a pulse because I'd seen too many horror movies and knew what would happen to me if I did.

I don't add any atmosphere because I'm not writing them a story. The English teacher inside me says nothing of my shivering from being scared to death, because the police don't care about character development. I remember picking up the flashlight and pointing it at Kathy. What was it I said? That's right. I told her everything was going to be okay.

If I were to rewrite it, if I were to put things down differently, is there any way it could change what happened? I guess not. The past is definite.

"What are you talking about?" I ask.

"We make them," she says. "We use them as weapons."

In the background the TV is going. I keep glancing at it, waiting for my photograph to appear on the screen with bold words beneath it saying *Wanted for murder* and *Do not approach*. It's just a matter of time. Unless I can find Cyris.

"Why?"

"Finish your letter first," she says.

"It could take . . ."

"Just wrap things up. We don't have all day."

I don't mind that Jo is giving me orders because it means we're about to do something right, and that's going to feel good after thirty-six hours of doing everything wrong. I spend the next ten minutes wrapping things up, but don't sign it.

"Here," Jo says, and she pulls out a phone bill from her handbag. She takes it out of the envelope and hands the envelope over to me. I fold up my story and tuck it inside. I grab the phone book, get the address for the police station, and print it across the front. I mark it as urgent. All I need now is a stamp.

"When he shows up at your house," Jo says, "we'll be able to follow him home. That's the plan, right?"

"That depends on whether or not he shows up there. But yeah, so far that's the plan." And it's a good plan. Almost too good, as if a part of it surely has to fail because we're in the Real World now. Haven't I told her this? Maybe she doesn't get it. I run the scenario through my mind. Several faults stand out, but nothing stands out as being too dangerous. I try to imagine the sort of place Cyris lives in and end up picturing that big old two-storey house from Hitchcock's *Psycho*.

"So what are you saying? We hide down the road and follow him home? What do we need stakes for?"

"Wooden stakes. Think about it," she says, leaning forward, her voice picking up pace. "You said both the women—"

"They have names, Jo. Kathy and Luciana."

"Of course, you're right," she says, leaning back. "I'm sorry. You said Kathy and Luciana were staked through the chest. Why? It's a pretty unusual way to kill somebody, don't you think? Outside of a movie?"

"Maybe Cyris thought he was in a movie."

"That's almost my point. Maybe Cyris thought they were vampires, or—"

I shake my head. "No. I mean nobody is that crazy."

Jo carries on. "Or maybe he just wanted to stake them so people would think that he thought they were vampires."

Now I'm getting confused. "Why would he do that?"

"I don't know. Maybe so everything would seem a lot crazier than it really was. Think about it. The police find these two women and it looks like it was done my some madman, but maybe it wasn't, maybe it just seems that way because of the way he did it. Maybe that's why he did it that way."

I see where she's going with this. "It makes sense," I say, and then I think about it a little more. "In fact it really makes great sense."

"Or it's the opposite," she says. "Maybe he was delusional and not just acting crazy, but was crazy."

"I don't know. I still don't think people are really that crazy."

"Look at where we are, Charlie. Look at what you've done to me. Now tell me people aren't crazy."

I get her point. Only I'm not crazy. I'm just caring. I want so much to make sure nothing bad happens to her. There's no way I can explain that and have her believe me.

"I guess. But what's your point about the stakes?"

"Wooden stakes make for good weapons," she says.

"Yeah, that's true. Only his were metal."

"Does it matter?" she asks.

In vampire mythology, perhaps. In the Real World, who the hell knows? "I guess not. I'm still not seeing where you're going with this, especially if all we're doing is following him home," I say, which is true—only I'm not so sure that's all I want to do. I want to make him pay for what he did. Jo is figuring the stakes might make great weapons if we have to defend ourselves, but knives would do an even better job. Knives and a hammer.

"Do you want to catch him, or just follow him home?"

"I want to catch him," I say, but it's more than that. I don't share this with Jo.

"Then we need weapons of our own."

"So your plan isn't just to follow him, but to catch him."

"Yes," she says, and she leans forward again, "because we don't know for a fact we'll be following him home."

"Huh?"

"If he shows up at your house tonight, and we start to follow him, how do we know it's his house he's going to next? For all we know he could be going into somebody else's house to attack them. In which case we need to stop him."

"Which would put me into a similar position to last night," I say, "which means we should call the police."

She stares at me for a few seconds, then slowly nods. "You still don't have a cell phone, and you left mine behind. So we can't call for help once we start following him. Level with me," she says. "What's your plan? To call the police? Capture him? Or are you after revenge?"

"I don't know," I tell her, and it's true. "It's always changing. I woke up yesterday just wanting him caught. Last night

I wanted to capture him. Now I want him dead. I guess . . . I don't know. I guess we just follow him and see what happens."

"That's not much of a plan," she says.

I grab the remote control and turn off the TV. I get the feeling most of Jo's plan is coming from the movies that have been on this morning.

"So you believe me now," I say. "You believe that Cyris exists."

"Let's just say I don't not believe you."

"Taking stakes . . . I don't know. It just seems crazy."

"Cyris didn't think so, and anyway, isn't *crazy* our buzzword for the day?"

"We could take some knives," I say, and I think about my tire iron. Maybe it doesn't matter what we take.

"Sure, but we're playing on his terms, Charlie, and that means we have to fight the same way he fights. If he really is delusional then we have to get down and dirty and be just as delusional, and if we show up on his doorstep armed with stakes he'll not only know we mean business, but he'll freak out more."

"I don't know. It doesn't sound like a great plan. It really doesn't."

"And if you're planning on killing him," she says, "don't you want to be acting all crazy when you're doing it? People aren't going to be looking for a schoolteacher, Charlie. They're going to be looking for a madman. Come on, it's a plan. We're not going to come up with anything better."

I don't like it. "Staking out my house with stakes. I dunno. It sounds like a bad joke."

"We take hammers and stakes to threaten him and we use wire to bind him if that's all you want to do. We need to go to a hardware store, Charlie, and we also need to swap cars. We can't sit outside your house in your car. Think about it."

I am thinking about it. It's all I've been doing. "I'm still not so sure about the stake thing."

"I thought we'd moved past it."

"I wasn't even aware we'd agreed."

"Well, we'd better start agreeing on something, Charlie, because we don't have all day."

"Okay, okay, so assuming we do this. What happens?"

"First of all you have to let me come with you," she says, even though I haven't even said yet that I'm going. "We can go back to my house and get my car."

"I can get your car and I can get the tools. You stay here while I'm getting them."

We discuss it some more and I feel like I've just agreed to do something I totally don't want to do, and I have a slight feeling that this is exactly what Jo wanted. I tie her back up and head outside, then go down to the manager's office and pay for another night's accommodation. He looks at me like I'm crazy. I tell the guy not to bother cleaning the room though I don't think it was really on his to-do list. I drive to Jo's house. It's surprisingly hot, and because the air-conditioning in my car is faulty I have to roll the windows partially down. In the distance rain clouds are starting to move in. I keep my Honda below the speed limit. When I get to Jo's house I just keep on driving because the garage is open and her car is gone. Has Cyris been here? How did he know to come here? Has he been following me? No, because if he was following me, he'd have broken into our motel room last night and stabbed us a few dozen times.

I take a left and start putting distance between me and Jo's house. I turn on the radio to listen to the news. Nothing new has developed. Disappointed but not surprised I turn the radio off and stare out at this world I'm driving through.

I know this world. I live in this world. Yet it has become a stranger to me.

It's starting to rain when I pull into the parking lot of a hardware store. It's a large single-storey place made completely from concrete, the sort of one-piece slabs constructed on the spot. A line of wheelbarrows is parked out front, along with garden sheds and patio furniture. Nothing small enough to pick up and run away with. Nothing exciting enough to make an impulse buy. In the middle of a Tuesday afternoon the large store is close to empty as I make my way up and down aisles. I start in the gardening section, but the garden stakes are too big and would fill our hands with splinters. I move to different sections where I buy rope, duct tape, a craft knife, a chisel, a broom handle, and a small saw. The last thing I select is a large wooden mallet. It feels like I'm shopping at Vampires Я Us. The guy at the counter looks like he missed his calling as an undertaker. His skin is stretched tightly on his skull with black smudges of some long-suffered or soon-to-arrive illness beneath his eyes. He says, "Raining out there, huh?" in a tone that suggests it's my fault. I pay in cash and he forgets to tell me to have a nice day.

I drive back to the motel and carry the purchases into the room, first making sure nobody is around. The room is stuffy. A faint taste of perfume lingers in the air. Cheap perfume. The type of perfume you find lingering in the air in cheap motels. The earlier scent of bacon and eggs has disappeared. I close the door and untie Jo, who smiles at me. She seems to have come a small way toward forgiving me. The unsent letter in the back pocket of my pants feels warm.

"You didn't get my car?"

"It was gone," I tell her.

"Charlie . . ."

"I'm not making this shit up, Jo. It was gone. I'm not saying Cyris took it, all I'm saying is it wasn't there."

"But you think he took it, don't you."

"If he did, then . . ."

I stop talking. Jo stares at me. "Then what?" she asks.

"Then nothing."

"You're unbelievable," she says.

"What?"

"You're trying to tell me that if Cyris did steal my car, then he knew where I lived, which means you're saying you did the right thing by kidnapping me."

"I'm not saying that at all," I say, but it's what I'm thinking.

"Let's just get this done," she says.

We pull the tools out of the plastic bag and line them up on the floor. I didn't buy any top-of-the-line gear, just the basics. I lay some newspaper down for the mess, then we cut the broom handle into four pieces. On the last cut Jo slips on the saw handle. It twists and flexes and the blade snaps into half a dozen pieces.

"Sorry."

"It's not like we need it again," I say.

Jo holds the first stake on the ground while I chip away at the end with the chisel and mallet. I manage a sharp but not very sculptured point. I repeat the procedure on the second and get the same result. The third and fourth don't work out any better. I try not to think about how this must look to an outside observer.

The sawing and chiseling is hard work and soon the sawdust sticks to our wet faces and hands. I want to take a shower, but I don't want to leave Jo by herself.

"Some arsenal," she says, looking down at what we've achieved. "Can you think of anything we may be missing?"

I look at what we have. Don't see a gun. I point this out.

"What about garlic or holy water?" she asks.

I'm not sure if she's joking and I start to wonder whether she's missing the whole point here, but perhaps I'm missing it too. That's why I'm looking at four wooden stakes and a mallet. Jo sits on the edge of her bed and watches me pack up the mess.

"We should try and get a few hours' sleep," I suggest. "We don't want to fall asleep while watching my house."

Jo silently nods. "That's just what I was going to suggest."

"Um, I'm sorry, Jo, but I need to tie you up . . ." I say, my voice trailing away.

"I'm not going anywhere, Charlie."

"Yeah, I know."

"Then why do it? Don't you trust me?"

"Of course I do."

"Then you're not tying me up, okay?"

If I don't tie Jo up I won't be sleeping either. I let her use the bathroom and then she makes it easy for me by not struggling as I tie her to the bed. I lie back on my own bed. The alarm clock looks forty years old. It's big enough to think it may be powered by a mouse running on a wheel. I fiddle with the buttons and set it to give us three and a half hours. Assuming we can sleep.

My body molds into the previous outline of thousands of other people who may or may not have known what love is, but probably came here to experience a fifteen-minute imitation of it. I turn on the TV and am given the menu for porn or wholesome family TV. It seems every motel these days has religion and sex only a fingertip away. I flick channels looking for some news and come up with nothing.

On Sunday night I was a schoolteacher with a simple life and complicated students. My head is starting to throb and I raise a hand to the lump. It's still the same size as yesterday.

Maybe it's never going to go away, maybe it's going to be like a badge of honor—or in my case a badge of dishonor. I think about untying Kathy from the tree and how grateful she was for it. I think of Cyris and how dead he looked. We left him there, just a body of evil trapped inside human skin with a bad name and a poor haircut. We left him with every intent to go to the police. We left him in the dark to come back.

And that's exactly what he did.

# CHAPTER THIRTEEN

Landry goes through the drive-through of a fast-food chain and orders a burger that he knows is going to taste great, but won't feel that great in an hour or so. He becomes so convinced about how sick it's going to make him feel, that he ends up pulling over beside the next garbage bin he sees and dumps it on top without taking a single bite. He eats the fries and has the drink and drives away, and a minute later he's so hungry he's tempted to go back for the burger.

It's raining now, but not heavily, and he wonders how long it's going to last. He hates the rain. Always has. When he was a kid he often had to walk to school in the rain, then sit around in wet clothes all day. He wants to pull over somewhere and take a nap. Or go home.

He reaches Luciana Young's house. The media activity has died. In fact there are no journalists anywhere at the moment. Maybe there's been a massacre across town he hasn't been told about. He knows the media still has its uses, but he likes to think that horse shit has its uses too, as do leaches and maggots. There are still patrol cars at the scene, and some of the forensic guys are still looking around inside and out. Neighbors are being reinterviewed today.

Stomach rumbling, Landry heads into the victim's house wishing he could go into the kitchen and fix himself something to eat. The smell of death stained into the carpet quickly kills his appetite, though. The smell of death has stained his clothes too. He can smell it on himself. Or perhaps that smell is him.

He's been inside only a minute when Detective Hutton shows up. There's another guy with him. A guy who's obviously not a cop.

He approaches them. Hutton introduces the man as the dead woman's husband. They don't shake hands. The husband is here to take a look around. He's in his mid- to late thirties, with a hairline that looks as though it's been receding for at least half of that time, and a pair of designer glasses that he takes off so he can put the arm into his mouth while he studies everything. Landry follows them. They go from room to room, the husband the entire time looking like he's going to be sick. The husband's task here, Landry knows, is to see what is out of place. Has anything been taken. Has anything been added. They spend a few minutes in each room before finishing in the master bedroom.

In the end it's just the missing clothes. Pants and a shirt are missing. Feldman probably changed after getting blood on his. Landry stares at the victim's bed thinking she probably wouldn't mind if he spent three hours lying on it. It would be a reward for what he's going to do later, by finding and dealing with her killer.

Hutton leads the husband back outside. They avoid the bloody footprints along the way, prints that look like practice dance-step cutouts, which lead from the bathroom to the garage before disappearing. Landry stays in the hallway. The smell of vomit in here mingles with that of death and makes a cocktail that claws into his nose. The vomit is confusing. What person would be sick viewing their own handiwork? Guys like Feldman kill and torture and dismember for their own satisfaction—they do it because they enjoy it. It doesn't make sense to do all of that, and then throw up.

When he was here yesterday, before he went to the second crime scene, he didn't know about Charlie Feldman. Now he can look at everything from a different perspective. He goes into the lounge. There's an empty beer bottle on the coffee table that has been dusted for prints. Those same prints have been found in the bathroom—the owner of those prints took a shower here. The prints don't belong to either of the women, or the husbands.

Did Feldman make himself at home? Did he have himself a nice relaxing beer while torturing Luciana Young? There are also two wineglasses on the table. Each has been matched to one of the two dead women. So more likely the three of them sat down here at some point and shared a drink. And then what?

On the driveway the cordless phone was found in pieces. Phone records show it was used to call the police, but within seconds the line was disconnected. Fingerprints on the phone match the fingerprints on the beer bottle. The same person who drank the beer and smashed the phone also tossed a set of car keys beneath the van found parked outside. If Luciana had gotten to that phone a few seconds earlier . . . things could have been different. Life and death are often all about bad timing.

The van has been towed to the forensics lab. It will be stripped down and examined to a minute detail. This morning it was reported stolen. The key was snapped in the ignition, the rest thrown beneath it. Feldman drove the van there, then took Luciana's car.

He spends an hour at the crime scene looking for any connection to Charlie Feldman, or even Jo Feldman, and finds nothing. He can't find a connection to the school Feldman works at. The more he continues to search and find nothing, the more he becomes convinced Sunday evening was the first time these two women ever met Feldman. But why have him back here for a drink? Did they meet in a bar?

He's walking out to his car getting ready to drive back to the other crime scene when Schroder calls him.

"Finding anything new?"

Landry shakes his head out of habit, and says no.

"Well I got something. I just got a report of Luciana Young's car," Schroder says. "How about I meet you there."

"Where?"

Schroder gives him the address. "I'll see you there in ten minutes."

He's been driving for five of those ten minutes when it suddenly hits him—he's driving in the direction of Jo Feldman's house. Sure enough, the street he pulls into is only a block away. Schroder is already here, along with the Armed Offenders Squad—which consists of a dozen cops dressed in black body armor and carrying guns.

"We're canvassing the street," Schroder says. "Gotta be careful," he says, "whoever stole Luciana's car may live here."

"It's possible," Landry says, but he's thinking it would have been more possible if they had been one block over. Talking to the people on this street isn't going to be worth a damn. "Or he had another car here that he switched with. Or stole one. Or walked. So what do you want me to do?"

"Help with the canvassing," Schroder says. "Then I need you to help me start working up a list of names and addresses. Somebody here must have seen something, and we're not leaving until we've gotten in touch with somebody who did."

# CHAPTER FOURTEEN

Not only is Jo surprised that Charlie has fallen asleep, she's surprised it's happened so quickly. He never used to be like that. Whenever they went to bed he'd often lie awake for an hour or more after she'd fallen asleep, he'd read or he'd stare at the ceiling, and then he'd complain about it the following morning. To fall asleep as easily as he has shows how exhausted he is. Back then there was always something comforting about falling asleep next to him, about falling asleep first—he made her feel safe. Protected. Funny how the world can turn on a dime. The man that made her feel safe is now the man she's about to hit in the head with a wooden mallet.

She spends the next two minutes watching Charlie. She's seen it before, the way one hand rests on the pillow over his head, his shoulder looking like it's going to be disconnected. There is the rare occasion where he will go to bed first, or she'll come into the lounge to find him asleep in front of the

TV. His face is tight, there's a dream going on inside that head of his. He flinches a little, but there's nothing to indicate he's going to wake.

Breaking the hacksaw blade earlier was no accident. She stretches out her fingers, then starts maneuvering her hand closer to her body, looking for the piece of blade she hid in the folds of the bedspread while Charlie was cleaning up the stakes and tools. Ideally she'd have kept it in her hand, but that was impossible. When she lay down, she aimed to sit on it to hide it, getting her hand as close to it as she could before Charlie tied her up. Now she's starting to wonder if it was close enough. She pushes at the bedspread, stroking her fingers back and forth. The blade must be made from the same stuff as her car keys are—the kind of stuff that gets lost no matter where you put it.

Charlie grunts. His body tightens. His lips part slightly and move. She's never known him to talk in his sleep, and she pauses, waiting for it to happen now, but words don't follow the gesture. She thinks he must just be on the border of cramping up when his body relaxes, he exhales loudly, and his mouth closes back up.

Maybe this is a mistake, she thinks, still unable to find the blade. This could be fate intervening, the universe telling her to hold off from doing anything stupid. Of course if the universe worked that way, then it didn't work too well for Kathy and Luciana, and it sure as hell didn't work well for her last night. Still, she is starting to get some control back. If she manages to cut through her bindings and then Charlie catches her, she's going to undo all those baby steps. It's a gamble. This could be her only chance to escape.

Of course no matter how she looks at it, she still doesn't think he's capable of murder.

Yesterday she wouldn't have thought he was capable of kidnapping.

She gets her hand closer to her body. Her wrist hurts as she flexes her hand back toward her arm, but she gets her fingers beneath her body and is able to roll a few inches upward. After a few moments of despair she feels the edge of the blade prick against the pad of her finger. She grits her teeth and holds back the urge to swear. She slips the blade into her fingers and moves it to her fingertips. She twists her hand and touches the blade against the towel. She has to make the decision. Getting to this point has taken longer than she wanted. If she starts cutting, and doesn't get all the way through, he's going to know she tried to escape and he will lose all trust in her.

But what if this is her only chance?

She looks over at him. He's not breathing heavily. The dream he is in isn't a deep one.

She thinks about the traffic outside and is aware that any altercation out there, a car horn or the shrieking of tires, could be enough to wake him. Or the alarm Charlie set could be about to go off. She can't see it because it's angled away from her. It feels like she's been tied up for ten minutes, but it could have been twenty. Or thirty.

Her indecision suggests she's already made up her mind. That she'll hide the blade in her pocket and use it later. Only then she drags the blade across the towel. Once. Twice. Cut or not to cut? That's the question. And she needs to hurry up and make up her mind.

# CHAPTER FIFTEEN

The roads are getting thick with traffic. Landry hates traffic. Ten years ago he took his wife—no, his second wife—to London. They spent three weeks there. He didn't like it. It was too busy. You could lose hours in traffic. You could get up in the morning and drive half of the day and only have gone a dozen miles. He remembers coming back to New Zealand and vowing he'd never complain about the traffic here. Or the rain. Only both those promises were left in the dust, along with his second marriage.

He makes it in to work, and now things are working better. His parking spot has opened up. He finds himself a coffee cup that hasn't broken. He fills out a warrant. It's a standard form in which he has to fill in the blanks. He writes in the address. He writes in the person of interest. The person of interest is a guy by the name of Desmond Important Person, and they want to search Desmond's house. It's not the guy's

real name, but he had it legally changed from Desmond
Douglas seven years ago. In the years he's been known as
Desmond Important Person, he's also seen the inside of a jail
cell on three different occasions, once for burglary and twice
for stealing a car. Douglas is nowhere to be seen, and unfor-
tunately for him Luciana Young's car happened to be parked
two doors down from his house. With no other suspects on
the street, Douglas has become somebody the police need to
talk to. Landry knows it won't lead anywhere—Douglas isn't
their man—but he's happy with the distraction it will give
Schroder and the others. Once he has the warrant, he can
get back to doing what he hasn't done yet—and that's figure
out where Feldman is.

The drive to the courthouse from the police station takes
ten minutes. He hands the warrant off to a registrar. He tells
him it's urgent. The normal turnaround for a warrant can be
half a day. He tells the registrar he needs it in five minutes.
Tells him there's a woman who's missing. The registrar, a guy
in his early twenties with too much acne and not enough
hair and not enough money to buy a nice suit, tells Landry
he understands and goes off to find a judge to sign it. Landry
spends the time pacing the halls, staring at a whole bunch of
bad people who are going to be around long after he's gone. It
takes twenty minutes for the warrant to get signed.

By the time he gets back out onto the street the traffic is
so thick he actually uses his sirens just so he can clear a path
through town. He switches them back off when he's in the
suburbs. At least the speeding woke him up.

Schroder and the assault team are still where Luciana's car
was parked—only the car isn't there anymore. It's been towed
down to the station as evidence. He hands the warrant to
Schroder, and then he starts coughing, and then he notices

his hands are shaking. All of it is real. Schroder notices the same things.

"Look, Bill, you really do look like shit. Are you sure you shouldn't be home?"

"Maybe you're right," he says, coughing into his hand to press home the point.

"We'll search this guy's house," Schroder says, pointing toward Desmond Person's house. "But, to be honest, burglary and car theft is a big step away from what happened to those two women. At the most you'll find he probably stole the car and drove it here."

"His file says that's what he used to do? Steal cars and bring them home?" Landry asks.

"Well, no. But somebody brought it here."

From there Landry drives from suburb to suburb, doing what he can to avoid traffic along the way, until finally he's back at Charlie Feldman's house. It's been years since he was last on a stakeout. It was with . . . hell, it was with a guy by the name of Theodore Tate, a guy who used to be a cop, but then became a private investigator and then became a real pain in the ass before ending up in jail. For the last year Landry has been convinced Tate is the kind of guy who's done bad things for what he thinks may have been good reasons, only . . .

Only shit. That's exactly what he himself is becoming. Tate has killed people—more people than he's let on, Landry is sure of it. Maybe Tate has cancer too.

The idea of becoming Theodore Tate is a miserable one, but one he only has to deal with for six months. Maybe less. That stakeout they went on together was at least ten years ago. Normally stakeouts were boring. They were watching a clown. Quite literally. The circus had come to town, and some poor teenager had become brain dead after buying drugs from somebody that his buddy said worked at the circus. Suspect was a guy by the name of Mortimer Dicky, also known as Bee-boop the clown.

He spends a few seconds wondering if this is the right path. The Theodore Tate path. He could find and arrest Feldman and bring him into the station by himself, end his career with the people in this country loving him. And why the hell not? He deserves something other than the cancer for all his years of protecting the innocent, doesn't he? Or he sticks with the Tate path. Make Charlie Feldman simply disappear. Magic.

He's always been a fan of magic.

He reaches Feldman's house. He knocks on the front door. No answer. He goes through the back gate and to the back door, which is open exactly how he left it. He goes inside. He puts on a pair of latex gloves. The living room looks the same. So does the kitchen.

But things are different when he gets down to the other end of the house.

Very different.

The kind of different that makes him clench his fists and makes him angry. The kind of different that answers the question of what he's going to do once he finds Charlie Feldman, while at the same time dismissing the question as to whether there was any chance Feldman was innocent.

He spends ten minutes writing down every contact he can find that Feldman has. He walks back out of the house. His hands are shaking. He could probably wait inside hoping Feldman will return, but the way he can tell if a house is empty before approaching it, well, he's not the only guy on the force with that skill. Same might go for Feldman. He doesn't need any reason to scare the guy off. And if Feldman drives past and freaks, then he's going to drive on, and Landry will never even know. So he decides to wait in his car.

He's not sure if Feldman is going to come back. He must have come back during the night and he must have noticed his house had been broken into. Damn it, he should have staked the house out last night. This could have been over by now.

The day will be dark soon. He yawns again. He can't help it. He adjusts his seat, opens a packet of peanuts, and begins calling the names on his list, starting with Feldman's parents. He gets hold of the mother. No, their son isn't in trouble. Yes, they're just hoping he can assist in an investigation. No, it's not important—something to do with one of his students who's gotten into trouble. It turns out Feldman doesn't even own a cell phone. The mother has no idea where Charlie may be—normally either at school or at home. Landry thanks her for her time. He can tell she's worried. Then he hangs up.

He carries on through the address book. If he's lucky, Feldman might just return home, or somebody might have an idea where he can start looking.

# CHAPTER SIXTEEN

The ghosts are back. They're telling me this is no dream. I find it hard to believe.

I'm with Kathy and Luciana and they're alive again, but in this dream I don't even know they're supposed to be dead. Do they know? I try to ask, but the words don't come out. Kathy is leaning into me, my arm around her as I help her leave the pasture the same way we arrived—alive and in one piece. Her other arm is around my shoulders, her hand digging into my upper arm hard enough to make a line of bruises. We leave Cyris and his tools and my tire iron behind. Kathy knows Luciana is alive because I've told her, and she smiles at me knowingly and without words tells me this is soon to be a lie. I don't tell her she's wrong.

Luciana jumps from the car the moment she sees her friend and the two lock themselves in an embrace. It's the embrace of close friends and even though I don't know either of these women, I wish I was part of it. They hold each other tight and I look away, choosing to stare at my car instead, this car that I'm sick of seeing, this car that I want to trade in, but at the moment is the best damn car in the world.

The two women break their embrace to include me in it, and no, they're not ghosts, not yet—that's still to come. For now they're very much alive, alive and grateful and warm to touch, and when I open my mouth to warn them the words don't come out. I try to tell them they mustn't go back home, they mustn't take me with them, but the dream is a memory and is deciding to stick to what is true, and therefore has only one path it can take.

We pile into the car, Luciana in the back and Kathy next to me. I start driving to the police station. I make it a few hundred yards before Luciana says she'd like to go home first. Kathy agrees. They want to go home. They want to clean up. Put on some fresh clothes.

"You can't do that," I tell them. "You can't wash away the evidence."

Kathy nods. "That's true," she says. "Let's at least go back to Luciana's house and make a plan."

"A plan?"

"We need a lawyer," Kathy says.

I don't understand. "What for?"

"Her husband, Frank, is a lawyer," Luciana says.

I feel jealous at this piece of information. It's stupid. "I still don't know why we need one," I say.

"Benjamin Hyatt," Kathy says.

The name sounds familiar. It takes a few seconds for it to filter through layers of memory. "The lawyer from the news?" I say.

"Exactly."

I tell them it's not the same thing. They agree, they tell me it's different, but they also tell me the result is the same. The circumstances don't matter as much as they should when it comes to the law. We still killed somebody, but of course it was more *I* than *we*. We debate the merits of going. We debate it for only a minute when Luciana points out we can discuss it back at her house instead. She tells me she needs a drink.

She gives me directions to her house. I try to steer us toward the police station, but the world the dream is set in is set in stone, as much as I try to save their lives now, there can be no changing it. I manage to find the words to tell them they are going to die if we stay on this course. I know this because their deaths were front-page news, and what you read in the papers is true, the dream is real, the memory is real, because we are in the Real World. Even though the words come out, neither Kathy nor Luciana can hear me. It's like one of those movies where somebody takes you on a journey into the past to see what a dick you've been, and nobody can see or hear you.

We drive past thousands of shadows. The roads are empty. A few wisps of cloud float in front of the moon, which is bright white and full. My mind is buzzing. My hands are shaking. I keep being amazed that it's blood that has been coming out of me and not pure adrenaline. We make conversation, but mostly it's the two women talking, and mostly it's me just listening. Parts of the evening already don't feel like they happened. Other parts are real. Too real. About as real as you can get.

We park the car outside Luciana's home. It is a single-storey townhouse, and through the haze of a lost day and a half, the image of the house shimmers. I saw this at night and never fully took notice of it because I was too caught up in the people, not the places, so the dream struggles to fix an image.

At first the house is made from red brick, but then from white, and the roof is steel at one point, but then tiled—the blanks are being filled in by other houses I've seen that look similar. The roses in the garden shimmer, then turn to weed. Nothing here is real. Everything is real.

We lock the car because any neighborhood is a bad neighborhood when you've just fought for your life. The back door is ajar and Luciana pushes it open. The air is warm inside. The girls tell me they were abducted from their own homes. I don't see any signs of forced entry, but maybe Cyris broke in through one of the windows, or maybe the back door.

We all sit down in the lounge, and the moment we do all the conversation dries up. We spend a few seconds looking at each other, then a few more seconds looking at the floor. I have the urge to tell Luciana she has a nice house, but manage to resist it. Kathy smiles. Luciana stands up and says she's going to take a shower. I tell her that's not going to make the police happy. She tells me she's sorry, but she needs to take one. She feels dirty. If she doesn't shower, she's going to be sick.

Kathy disappears and comes back later with a bottle of beer that is cold in my hot hands. Tiny beads of condensation start to run down it. I flick the edge of the label with my fingernail. I look around me. The couch and two chairs are leather. Expensive. No claw holes in the furniture or fur on the cushions. The carpet is thick and soft, red one second, blue the next.

Kathy has also carried a bottle of wine in with her and two glasses. She fills each of them up and sips at one and pushes the other toward the chair where Luciana was sitting. It seems surreal to be drinking wine, and I wonder if sauvignon blanc is the wine of choice when you've just survived being raped and almost killed.

The dream leads me along—I can't change it, can't stop it, can only complete it. Kathy sits down next to me, her knee almost touching my knee, and she cups her glass in both hands and slowly sways her wrists, watching the way the wine climbs up the sides.

"He wanted to take us away so he could hear us scream. That was the only reason he gave. He was going to kill us by driving metal stakes through our hearts."

I sip at my beer, which I drank a lifetime ago. Casual conversation. Casual drinking.

"Crazy," I tell her.

"The world is full of crazy people," she says, and there's that buzzword again. "If you hadn't come along who knows what he might have done to me."

"I don't want to think about it," I tell her, but of course I don't need to. I would see it for real very soon.

"Nor do I," she admits.

"Does Luciana live alone?" I ask, changing the subject.

She smiles a sad smile and takes a large sip of wine. "Her husband left her for a gym instructor. Hasn't spoken to him since."

"Must have been some woman." My beer is cold and smooth and I've never felt like I've earned one so much. I'm not really a beer guy. I'm more a gin-and-tonic guy. But this may just be the best beer I've ever had.

"Some man," she says.

"Sorry?"

"The instructor. Some *man*," she says.

"Oh."

She laughs the laugh of somebody who doesn't know death has looked up her address and is en route.

"So what about you?" she asks. "You're married I see."

"Huh?"

"You're wearing a wedding ring."

I look down at my hand. I smile. I nod, then I shake my head. Then I stop smiling.

"That complicated, huh?" she asks.

"Isn't it always?"

"It's not meant to be," she says.

"It is in my case. We broke up six months ago."

"And you still wear the ring," she says.

"Yeah. I keep meaning to take it off, but you know, it just doesn't happen."

"I do know. My marriage is over, but we're still married. Does that make sense?"

"It does," I tell her.

She starts to laugh.

"What's so funny?" I ask, and take another mouthful of beer.

"You're going to murder me later on tonight, Charlie, and there's nothing I can do about it—except laugh."

I almost gag on the drink, surprised at her words, surprised that she knows death is close by, surprised she can make her laughter seem so real. That means the dream can change. That means nothing is set in stone after all.

"We have to—"

She interrupts me. "Really, it's okay, because neither of us can change it now. I'll be upset at first—and rightly so. You're going to kill Luciana too. I really wish you wouldn't."

"I'm not going to kill either of you."

"It's a done deal, Charlie. Things will change. You will change. Think of it as character development. Now, where was I? That's right, I was telling you about Luciana's husband. Charlie? Hey? Are you still with me?"

"I'm still here," I tell her.

"Charlie?"

The dream starts to fade and I call out to it because it has lied to me, lied about that conversation because it couldn't have happened. Has it lied about anything else? I cry out, desperate for the dream to continue, desperate to see what I did next, but there's nothing. I clutch my beer tightly, but can no longer feel the glass beneath my hands. The women are ghosts again, telling me to wake, to wake.

I wake as I woke yesterday, submerged in guilt and aware that the design of life is to be full of useless hopes. I feel more tired than before I fell asleep. I open my eyes and roll onto my side. Jo is staring at me.

"What's wrong?" I ask her.

"Nothing's wrong," she tells me.

"You look . . ."

"Look what?"

Guilty, I think, but I don't tell her. "Nothing," I say.

"Are you going to untie me or leave me here all day?"

I sit up a little too quickly. The world darkens and for a moment I'm back in the dream—two dead women are waiting there for me—so I grip onto this world as tightly as I can and claw myself from the blackness. I untie Jo. It isn't dark outside yet and won't be for another couple of hours. I check the clock and see the alarm would have been going off in twenty minutes. I figure we may as well leave now. We need to get to my house before Cyris does, and I'm assuming he won't get there until after sunset.

I don't bother tying Jo back up. I look outside to make sure nobody is around, then open the door and quickly load our suitcases into the car before leading Jo to the passenger seat. She doesn't struggle or complain.

The rain that came earlier has already disappeared. There are no clouds in the sky and the earlier breeze has died away too. You'd be crazy to think it had even rained. What is remaining is the dream. I can't shake it. The other thing that is back is the headache. I hang my arm out the window. Jo rolls her window down too. It just keeps getting warmer. At this rate we're on track for what the old guy on the radio said this morning.

We drive through town, and for the first time I'm able to see past the Garden City postcard image and see Christchurch for what it really is. People are getting killed here every few weeks. Last year it was the Christchurch Carver, then the Burial Killer, there have been bank robberies, revenge killings, people being thrown off roofs. It's a building statistic that everybody seems to be keeping a secret. It's becoming a part of modern-day life just like rising gas prices and global warming and terrorism, and we just sit back and accept it because nobody is showing us an alternative.

In the distance, on the Port Hills, the sun glints off house windows. Some reflect the sun and look like they're on fire. Others look as though a giant tub of glitter has been spilled over them. Teenagers go up there at night in their souped-up cars and pour diesel over the roads so they can do burnouts and impress their friends before killing and dying—these are the boy-racers of the world, our next generation, and sometimes that scares the shit out of me. Some of these kids I teach. Some of them you know are going to make something of their lives—they're going to do good, they're going to help people or change the world, provide art and love and make little people with other good people—then there are those destined to hurt, to cause pain, to end up behind bars.

Daytime and the hills are filled with mountain bikers and paragliders and the husks of incinerated stolen cars, patches of landscape cordoned off with yellow police tape where some poor kid is getting peeled off the asphalt. It happens. It happened to one of my students last year. Speeding in cars was all a bit of a laugh. His friends, other students of mine, kept saying he always wanted to die young. That he died doing what he loved. That's one of the dumbest phrases I've ever heard. He may have loved speeding, but I'm sure he didn't love his car crushing all around him, didn't love the fireball that burned flesh from bone. He didn't love screaming. He didn't die doing what he loved at all.

We reach the highway I was driving down when the Sunday night Old World collided with the Monday morning New World and created the Real World. Just after the turnoff I pull the car over by the pasture with the trees and the grass and the shallow graves that were meant to be. I kill the engine. The hot sun has burnt away most signs of the rain. We have enough light for maybe another hour.

"What are we doing here?" Jo asks. It's the first time she's spoken since we got into the car.

I nod toward the trees in the distance. "This is where it all happened."

"You want to go in there?"

There are only a few cars on the highway behind us. I could probably dig a grave a few yards from the road and nobody would notice. Or care. I wonder how much evidence has been washed away over the last few days. A strong heat wafts through the window and it smells like mown grass. My clothes are sticking to me. Out there is a patch of ground that may or may not be covered in blood. Pieces of clothing are out there too. I had come along the other night, I had been a savior, a knight in shining Honda. Cyris had offered me to join in on the fun, but I wanted a different sort of fun.

"I guess not," I tell Jo. "I just wanted to show you."

I start the car and pull away, heading for home. The conversation doesn't start back up. I slow down a little as I get nearer my street. I head to my house and pull up the driveway.

"I want you to come in with me."

"What for, Charlie? I thought we were going to sit outside and watch, and watching from the driveway isn't going to work. We need to be further down the street. Plus we're still in your car. That's not really that useful."

"I just want to check it out. I want to see if he's been here."

"Have fun."

"You're coming with me."

"Fine."

I step outside and circle the car to open her door. She climbs out and I put my hand on her shoulder. I'm expecting her to start screaming, but she doesn't. I open the gate and the first thing we see is my back door yawning wide open—splintered pieces of wood where the lock once was have twisted away. I think back to Kathy's door, then to Luciana's. Neither of theirs were forced or pried open.

"Who did this?" Jo asks.

"Who do you think?"

All the curtains inside are drawn. Did I leave them like this? The air inside isn't as stagnant as yesterday, thanks to the back door being broken open. Cyris wasn't thoughtful enough to smash the windows to let the air circulate. Apart from the door nothing seems out of place. The living room is relatively tidy and I can't see anything damaged.

"We should contact the police," Jo says, and something in her voice is more convincing than anything else she's said today, and I realize why that is—up until now she didn't believe me. "Unless . . ." she says, but doesn't finish it.

"Unless what?"

"Nothing," she says.

"You were going to say unless I did this myself, weren't you?"

"No. Of course not."

"You still don't believe me," I say, my voice raising.

"I didn't say that. You said that."

"Goddamn it," I say, shaking my head.

I lead the way into the lounge. I'm expecting to see torn curtains, the TV tipped over, the sofa and chairs shredded, but there's no evidence he even came in here. I move to the windows. The sun has nearly gone and so has the blue sky. The clouds from this morning are back. They've appeared from nowhere and in the distance they look black. Within half an hour it's going to pour down.

"You have photos of us up on the walls," Jo says.

"Yeah. I guess I do."

"Probably not the best thing to do if you're dating," she says.

"You're right," I tell her. "It'd be stupid if I was dating."

"You're still wearing your wedding ring."

I look down at my hand. Yeah, so I am. I shrug, feeling a little embarrassed.

"Charlie . . ."

"What?"

"Nothing," she says. "Just . . . just nothing."

We pass the bathroom and I think back to when I stood outside the bathroom door at Luciana's. I remember opening it and seeing the most grisly thing I'd ever seen. Of course that scene would almost repeat itself fifteen minutes later.

There are no corpses behind the bathroom door and no damage either. We check the spare bedroom and once again everything's intact. We double back and check the bedroom on the right, the room I use as a study.

And here is the evidence of vandalism I was thinking I wouldn't find. Only this is nothing as menacing as the drains blocked with rags and the faucets turned on full so the house is flooded. This is not as vulgar as large body parts drawn on the walls with paintbrushes. This is time-consuming. It has taken effort.

The computer monitor lies on the floor. Several crevices run the length of the plastic casing and there's a hole in the middle of it. It looks sad down there. The keyboard has fared no better: it has been twisted and bent and several of the keys have popped off from the pressure and are scattered like misshapen dice. My laser printer has been tossed aside. It has gouged out a hole in the wall and a black puddle of toner has spilled onto the carpet. Of the two bookcases the first has been tipped over so that it lies on an angle with books crushed beneath it, their pages and covers bent and torn. The second bookcase is upright, but the books have been removed and the covers ripped away. A pile of loose pages has been stacked next to it.

Straight ahead beneath the window in a black cabinet is a small stereo system. The covers have been removed from the speakers and the cones pushed in and ripped. The front of the stereo has been smashed in, damaged by the computer lying at the foot of the cabinet. The stereo is on and some of the lights work—most of the display doesn't. Hissing comes from the speakers, but no music, and the CD player is making a soft clicking noise over and over like a metronome. The TV I have in here is lying on its front on the floor. The antenna, twisted on the floor next to it, looks like a tool somebody would break into a car with. The remote control is next to it. Each of the rubber buttons has been stretched and torn out. The batteries have been removed and crushed with what seem to have been teeth. Behind the TV my aluminum garbage bin has had the sides and lid kicked in, denting any reflection it once offered. Its contents, only paper and plastic, have been littered over the rest of this mess. My small collection of die-cast cars, all classics from the fifties and sixties, haven't been smashed underfoot, but the doors, the bonnets, the wheels, and the trunk lids have all been removed. The cars are still on the shelves, on the drawers, on my desk, but the broken accessories are in individual piles on the floor, one for different parts, down there like confetti.

I realize I'm holding my breath. I begin to let it out as I slowly turn a complete circle in my room, spotting new damage as I do so. The DVD player beneath my TV has had the tray snapped off. The display on it has been broken and the play button pried off. A lamp is on the floor, the framework twisted and bent, the bulb shattered, the prongs on the plug wrenched sideways.

Jo waits in the hallway asking me over and over what I've done. All this destruction around me. This is my room. My personal space. If I snapped right now, if I lost my mind and went completely berserk, there'd be nothing left in here for me to break.

But I don't snap. As much as I love my books, my cars, my toys, they're nothing to what has already happened this week. In the scheme of things all this is nothing. These are just items, materials, things that can be replaced. It will cost me money, but that's all. I can move on. I cannot say the same for Kathy. I cannot say the same for Luciana. I lean down and turn off the stereo. The CD stops clicking and the hissing disappears and the room becomes eerily silent. Even Jo stops talking. I walk through the destruction back into the hallway. It's as if a localized earthquake hit my room.

I close the door on everything.

If only I had taken a different route home the other night.

I tell myself not to think this way. I try not to tell myself that Luciana may have found somebody who wasn't going to help and then kill them. I try not to tell myself any of this, but it's true. What would have happened if I hadn't come along? Would another game-show contestant have succeeded where I failed?

"If you didn't do this, Charlie, then it's time to go to the police. There has to be plenty of evidence here."

I open up the door to my bedroom. The curtains here are closed. Everything appears normal. I start to close the door. "The only evidence here is that the place has been trashed. It doesn't show by who."

"What's in the box?" Jo asks.

I push the door back open and I see it now, sitting in the center of my bed, plainly in view. I can only imagine what's inside. The box makes me uncomfortable in a way I can't describe. I know that whatever's inside it will rock my world and shatter what small hope I have left, but if I don't look then I can still hold on to the hope that it's empty. It's the Schrödinger Paradox. Schrödinger's severed head.

"Charlie?"

"I don't know what's in it."

"The hell you don't. You kept a souvenir, didn't you? What is it? A head? A heart?"

"I didn't, it's not mine, really, I . . . I . . ." I bite my lower lip hard enough to draw blood. "Let's go back to the car. He'll be back. If he looked for me last night he'll look for me again tonight."

"What is it, Charlie? What have you done?"

"Nothing. I promise you. I don't know what's in there."

"We have to call the police. It was already out of hand by the time you came to me, Charlie, and now look how much worse it's gotten. Think about where we're going to be this time tomorrow if you don't go to the police."

"Let's go," I tell her.

"To the police?"

"No. We're sticking with the plan."

"Charlie . . ."

"You said you'd give me the day," I tell her.

"Not all of it."

"I just need a little more time. An hour. Two at the most. We watch the house till midnight."

"That's almost six hours away."

"Then I let you go. I promise."

"You promise?"

"I just said I promised."

I close the house up. We head outside. Jo seems happy to leave. I'm happy to leave too. We pile into her car. I back out of the driveway. I drive fifty yards then do a U-turn and park against the curb. The shortest drive of my life. I kill the engine and we wait.

# CHAPTER SEVENTEEN

Jo is starting to believe him. Charlie is still being a bastard, and there's no excuse for what he did to her last night, but it's really looking like this Cyris fellow exists. Would Charlie have done any of that crazy shit to his own house? She doesn't think so. She doesn't think he would kill anybody. And just what in the hell was in that box?

Of course it's been six months since she last saw him. A lot can happen is six days let alone six months. He's not behaving like the Charlie she used to know. But she needs to play devil's advocate here—she needs to follow the idea for a moment that perhaps he is guilty. Saving a body part is a good way of starting up an insanity defense. Which means she's still in danger.

Either way she's in danger. Either from Charlie or from Cyris, doesn't matter whether they're the same person or not. She needs to stay calm and collect her thoughts because common sense, in theory, beats out insanity any day.

"I'm sorry I doubted you," she says, but she's not sorry, and she still might be doubting him. She isn't sure. What she is sure of is that there's an escape opportunity here. This is what she's been working toward. Thank God she didn't blow it back at the motel by trying to cut herself free. She would never have done it in time.

Charlie looks over at her and his face relaxes. "Really? Do you really mean that?"

"I'm also sorry you had to bring me here to convince me. You didn't have to hurt me, Charlie. I just wish you hadn't hurt me."

"I wish that too," he says. "I'm sorry, Jo, so sorry. I just . . ." he says, but he trails off.

"Just didn't know what to do," she says for him.

"I think I knew what to do. I just kept doing all the wrong things."

"Listen, Charlie, we agreed you'd let me go at the end of the day. That you would show me what you needed to, and—"

"I can't let you go," he says. "Don't you see? Cyris is looking for me. And he might be looking for you too."

"I'll be safe. I'll go to the police."

"And then the police will come looking for me. They're not going to believe what happened. No, we stick with the plan. And it's a good plan. It's your plan. We wait for Cyris to come back. I know he's been here already, but he won't know where else to look."

"Okay," she says. So that didn't work. She still has another angle. "So what about this. Cyris left the box behind for a reason, right?"

"I guess, but I have no idea what that reason is."

"What if he's planning on calling the police?"

"What?"

"He might be calling the police to tell them to come to your house. An anonymous tip. They'll come here, find that box, and you'll look guiltier than ever."

He shakes his head. "No, they'll see the house was broken into. They'll see all that damage. Surely they'll know it wasn't me."

"If you're that sure, then why don't you call them yourself?" she asks.

"Shit," he says again. He puts his hands on the steering wheel and tightens his grip. "So what are you saying?"

"I think you know."

"We have to go and get the head," he says.

"How . . . how do you know it's a head?" she asks.

"Jesus," he says, turning toward her. "What, now you think I'm guilty again?"

"I'm just asking."

"I don't know," he says. "That was just a guess. It could be anything."

It's a good answer. She believes him. "You need to hurry," she says. "It's already gotten dark. Cyris could show up at any minute, and so could the police."

"Me? You're not coming back inside with me?"

"No way in hell am I going back in there, not when there's a box in there with a head in it, and not when—"

"It might not be a head. In fact it's probably not. Both women had them still attached."

"He left you something, Charlie. You think it's a box full of cake?"

"No."

"Then we're in agreement."

"What am I supposed to do with it?"

"I don't know. Hide it somewhere."

"Hide it? The police are going to look everywhere."

"Well you're not bringing it back to the car."

"Goddamn it, Jo, I have to . . ."

"You'll figure it out. Now I suppose you want to tie me up, is that right?"

"Yeah. I'm sorry."

"Just hurry up," she says. "I don't want to be out here alone."

He leans into the back and pulls out some of the rope he bought earlier. "Don't make it harder than it needs to be," he says.

"I won't," she tells him.

She tightens her muscles as he wraps the rope around her body and the seat, and she bites down on the gag. He reaches into the backseat and grabs one of the stakes. A moment later he steps outside, taking the keys with him. She relaxes and feels the rope give slightly. Charlie looks back at her and shrugs a little, some kind of apologetic shrug. He crosses the road and jogs toward his house. Her hands are down by her sides. She starts stretching her fingers toward her pocket where the broken piece of blade is.

# CHAPTER EIGHTEEN

When Landry's cell phone goes off it pulls him out of a dream that involved getting his cancer news from a hot-looking nurse in a tight outfit that made the news not seem so bad. He wasn't even aware he had fallen asleep. His chin is covered in drool and his neck is stiff and he's slumped down somewhat in the car. And it's hot in here. He grabs his phone. It's Schroder. He presses the answer button.

"We found nothing useful in Douglas Person's house," Schroder says, "aside from a bedroom he's turned into a hot-house to grow maybe twenty grand's worth of cannabis. We're still looking for the guy, but I'm guessing he's gotten wind we're looking for him so is lying low. How are you feeling?"

"Not the best," Landry says, which is going to sum up every day between now and the end of days. At least the end of days for him. He feels bad about not saving Schroder some time by telling him Person is not their guy. Still, Schroder will look back at this in the future and thank Landry for saving him some problems by taking care of the trash.

"You should take tomorrow off," Schroder says, not sounding like he means it.

"I'll be there," Landry says. "I forgot to ask, but how'd you get on this morning with Benson Barlow?"

"There are so many theories floating around and the problem is most of them are sticking. The way he killed them . . . hell, I told Barlow about the scenes, he said he wouldn't even know where to begin. I'm about to talk to the second victim's husband," he says. Luciana is the first victim and Kathy is the second victim. They know that not because of time of death, which is too close to really tell them apart, but from the blood transfer between the scenes. "Everybody keeps thinking it's some kind of ritual, and I think—"

"I have to go," Landry says, "I'll call you back."

"Bill—"

"I'll call you back," he says. He hangs up the phone. Fifty yards away somebody is jogging toward him. But not toward him, toward the house. That figure goes under a streetlamp and slows down, tilts his wrist to look at his watch, and Landry gets a good view of him. It's Charlie Feldman. He recognizes him from the photographs inside the house. Landry can't tell what it is Feldman is holding in his right hand, but it looks like some kind of weapon. If Schroder hadn't called . . .

But he did call. That's all that matters.

Charlie goes through the gate. Lights come on inside the house. Landry rubs his hands at his eyes. He's never fallen asleep on a stakeout before. Never. Then again he's never been on heavy medication before either. Jesus, the day turned warm and he got sleepy. What sort of detective is he? The worst, and one who's tiring easily because he's dying.

He scrapes tiny pieces of wet gunk from the corners of his eyes. He starts the engine and slowly lets out the clutch, allowing the car to drift up the street. He stops outside the house. His anger is pulsing like a beacon in his mind as he walks over the grass verge to the sidewalk. He tucks his keys into his pocket. He can feel the adrenaline coursing through his veins and it worries him because he can't afford to lose control of his emotions. He looks up and down the street. There are lights on in most of the houses, but nobody around. People have settled in for the evening. They're watching TV and drinking coffee and the realities they face every day are different from his.

He pauses outside the house and sucks in a deep breath, then another and another. He needs to stay calm. He can't afford to make a mess of things. He straightens his tie and pats down his shirt, then wonders what in the hell he's doing. He isn't here to sell this man a jail sentence.

He clenches his fists, takes in another deep breath, then walks up the narrow sidewalk to the front door. When he reaches out to knock he notices for the first time that his hand is shaking. Excitement? Or nerves? He hopes it's one of those and not the alternative, because the alternative comes with nausea and vomiting. He turns his hands over and watches his fingers as he makes a fist then loosens it off. Something deep inside him feels different from the other times he's come to arrest people. Something he can't quite recognize. He suspects it arrived last week in his doctor's office as he watched the minute hand of the clock on the wall shift six degrees closer to the end of his life.

He reaches up and gets ready to knock.

# CHAPTER NINETEEN

The clouds look like bruised cotton candy, the lights from the street and from the city making them glow. Night has arrived and with it my fears. I have to hold my watch up to my face and twist it to get some illumination from a streetlight flooding across the hands. It's quarter past seven.

I step past the gate and climb the two steps to my back door. I carved a weapon out of a broom handle and now it's all I have to protect myself, and I point this thing ahead of me even though I know my house is empty. I'm not sure if I can get any crazier.

The first thing I do is turn on the lights. I head from room to room switching many of them on. When Cyris arrives he'll think I'm home. I try to put myself into his mind, subjecting myself to his dark thoughts. He'll figure I'm thinking it's safe to return since he's already been at my house. He'll see the lights on and he'll want to come in and check it out.

I head down to the bedroom. I look at the cardboard box and try not to feel intimidated by it—but fail. I need to check what it is. It won't be a head, because both Kathy and Luciana had their heads when I saw their bodies. The corner of a piece of paper is sticking out from under the cardboard flap. I grab it. It's covered in patches of dried blood. Written across it in Kathy's handwriting is my name and number. I'd completely forgotten about this. I don't know whether to feel relieved that it was Cyris who found it and not the police.

A car pulls up outside and a door opens, then closes. I stand motionless, a cold sweat breaking out across my forehead. I'm like some mindless bunny caught in the headlights of a car, paralyzed with confusion and fear. A few moments later knuckles are banging on my door. I tighten my grip on the stake. Would Cyris knock? No, I don't think he would. Then who is it?

I shouldn't have turned on the lights.

I step into the hallway, but I don't want to answer the door because my mortality is going to leave through it. Then the knocking comes back. I'm now Action Man, ready to defend my home and castle. I keep the weapon behind me. Cyris is here.

Only Cyris wouldn't knock. The police would knock. The police would want to know if I knew where Jo was. They wouldn't be too thrilled with the way I looked, all beaten up and bruised. They wouldn't be thrilled with the way my house looks, or with whatever is in that box.

Action Man: hold no fear. Action Man: save the world.

"Who's there?" I ask, feeling nothing like Action Man.

"Mr. Feldman?"

"Who wants to know?"

"Mr. Charlie Feldman? My name's Bill Landry," a small

pause, then, "Detective Inspector Bill Landry. With the Christchurch Police Department. Mr. Feldman, I've a few questions for you. How about you let me ask them inside?"

"I'm quite busy."

"I figured as much since you didn't come to the door straightaway."

"Sorry about that," I say, "but I didn't hear the first knock."

I put the chain on the door, unlock it, and open it enough to look at him. The man standing there looking at me is around six feet tall and heavily built. He has the same build as Cyris, but is far better groomed. He's wearing a shirt that looks like he's slept in it, and a tie that is one of those unique items of clothing that will never cycle back into fashion. He's standing on a slight angle that makes him appear as though he could pounce forward just as easily as he could jump back. He looks like he's expecting me to do something. Maybe run. Maybe attack. He has one hand behind his back, perhaps reaching for a gun, or for some handcuffs. His other hand is holding out his identification. I take a look at the photograph. A good, long look. Same buzz cut graying hair, same brown eyes, same strong jawline, same long nose. The sort of face you'd expect to see cast as the hero in some war movie. The sort of face you don't want on your doorstep behind a policeman's badge with the intent of arresting you. His lips have little or no color in the photograph, but even less in reality, just like the rest of his face. The dark smudges under his eyes make him look unhealthy and tired and remind me of the guy who sold me the broom handles. I'm pretty sure I've seen him in the background on the news. I suddenly feel like I'm going to faint.

I close the door, toss the stake into my bedroom, close that door, then take the chain off and hold the front door open, standing in the way so as to not invite him inside.

"Expecting trouble?" Landry asks.

"Huh?"

"The way you inspected my badge, it looked as though you were expecting somebody else. Or maybe you're just looking for an excuse not to let me in."

"I'm merely being cautious. Is that a crime?"

"Not at all, Mr. Feldman." His smile has about as much warmth as ice. "In fact I wish more people were as careful as you. Have you finished taking a look?"

When I nod he closes the ID and tucks it into the back of his pants.

"You look anxious, Mr. Feldman. Like you think half the world is out to get you."

"What half are you in?"

"That depends on how you answer my questions. Perhaps we can step inside?"

Before I can answer he tilts his head and gives me a direct look. "Unless of course you have something to hide?"

"Come on through," I say.

"After you," he says, and I realize he doesn't want to turn his back on me.

I walk down the hall. I can feel his eyes on me. I hear the front door close. I wonder what Jo is thinking. I lead him into the dining room. A light sweat has formed across my forehead, but I do nothing about it. I drag a seat from the table for him and sit opposite. He pulls out a notebook and rests it on the table before he sits down. He doesn't open it, just slowly taps a fingernail against the cover. I rest my right elbow on the table, cross my legs, and don't offer him a drink.

"I'm curious—if you didn't hear me the first time I knocked on your door, how did you know you were answering it after my second?"

I open my mouth to answer, but can't come up with anything. He smiles, but it seems he doesn't really want an answer. He saves me from the awkward moment by taking me into another one.

"Who hit you?" he asks.

I raise my hand to the bump on my forehead. It stings on contact. I try not to wince, but fail. Gets me every time. "Nobody hit me."

"Walked into a door, did you?"

"A tree."

"Wouldn't be the same tree that broke into your house?" The detective twists his head and points his thumb at the back door. "Who broke in?"

"I don't know. I only just got home."

"Anything taken?"

"No."

"Damaged?"

"Just the door."

"Why would a man who comes home to find his house has been broken into not call the police?"

"I was about to," I tell him, trying to figure out if he's here because of Jo, or because of Kathy and Luciana.

"Would you like me to help you look through your house?" he asks.

"No, no. That's fine," I tell him, and I know he's driving at something.

"You said you just got home. From school?"

"Yeah."

"I rang your school today, Mr. Feldman. They said you weren't in."

"I took the day off, but I had to go pick up some work."

"Where were you on Sunday night?"

"Sunday night? Umm, let me think." I run my hands through my hair trying to look like I'm trying to remember. Trying to act as though Sunday night was no different from any other night. Nothing to make it stand out. "I was at my parents'."

"Doing what?"

"Just catching up. You know what it's like."

"What time did you leave?"

I shrug. "Not sure. Maybe somewhere around eleven o'clock, give or take."

"Where did you go when you left?"

"Home."

"You came straight here."

"That's right."

"And went straight to bed."

"I had a shower first."

"Anybody see you?" he asks.

I shrug. "My shower isn't outside."

"Did you spend the night alone?"

"That's right," I say.

"You're sure you came straight home?"

"That's what I said."

"Uh huh. Well, I guess that pretty much sums it up," he says, but he doesn't make any attempt to get up. He just sits there, staring at me, maybe pissed off because I haven't offered him coffee, or because he thinks I'm a cold-blooded killer. He hasn't put his pad away.

"Good." I lean forward and start to stand.

"Just two more questions."

"Just two?"

"First, why haven't you asked me why I'm here?"

I sit back down. "What do you mean?"

"You didn't ask what I'm investigating. All these questions. It's like you already knew. You just opened the door and resigned yourself to the fact that I was here to arrest you. I've seen that look many times, Mr. Feldman. It's the look of somebody who was hoping they wouldn't get caught, but aren't surprised they have been. I saw it in your face. You didn't ask what I wanted because you thought I was here to take you into custody for murder. You didn't go through the whole routine of trying to figure out why a detective inspector would show up on your doorstep late at night wanting to ask you questions. An innocent person would have. Or a good liar. Your problem, Mr. Feldman, is that you're neither."

It's buzzword time. "That's crazy."

He stops tapping his finger and points it at me. "Have you ever heard of Camelot Drive?"

I know what's coming and can't see a way out of it.

"Mr. Feldman? Just a yes or no will do."

"No," I answer quickly.

"The body of a young woman was found there yesterday morning. But you know all about that, don't you?"

"Sure, it's been on the news. Everybody knows about it. Does that make everybody a suspect? Unless you've got—"

"Why would we think of you as a suspect?"

This guy is annoying. I have the urge to tell him to stop playing games. "That's why you're here, isn't it?"

"But you must have done something to think that we would regard you as a suspect."

"Look, if you've got a point here maybe you should get to it."

He nods. "Fair enough," he says. Then he follows that up. "You knew those women."

"No I didn't."

"So if we take your fingerprints and DNA, we're not going to get matches to those at the scenes?"

"That's right," I tell him. "I was never there," I say, thinking I should come clean. I should tell this man everything that happened. I decide not to. If Landry were sure of himself then he would be arresting me, not questioning me.

"How well did you know them?" he asks.

I shake my head. "I thought you only had two more questions for me."

"That was until you started lying. You've never seen or spoken to either woman?"

Again I shake my head. "I'm not lying," I tell him. "I don't know either of the women, I've never seen them before in my life, so if you have anything to back up what you're—"

Landry stands up and tucks his notebook into one pocket, and from another he produces a plastic ziplock bag. Inside is a small pad. He holds it toward me and I reach up to take it. "You don't need to hold it to read it," he says.

I move closer toward it. It's the pad on which Kathy wrote my details, only that isn't the page that's on the top. Sherlock Landry has used a pencil to rub over the page beneath it. My name and phone number have appeared, and with them any chance I have of talking my way out of this. The top page to that pad is in my bedroom. I try to explain this, but my mouth has gone dry and I feel as if somebody has poured glue down my throat. All I can do now is take my chances with the truth.

"I can explain," I tell him, the words coming out slowly.

"I think it's in your best interests to explain at the station, where you can have a lawyer present," Landry says.

"I, um, I . . ."

He pulls his handcuffs from behind his back. Maybe they

were clipped to his belt or inside a pocket. Then he pulls out a gun. He keeps it pointing at the ground. "Turn around, Mr. Feldman."

"You're arresting me?"

"What other choice do I have?"

"You could arrest the right person. I didn't kill anybody!"

"We'll discuss it at the station. Where you can have a lawyer present."

"No, no, this is all wrong. All wrong," I repeat.

"Come on, Mr. Feldman. Don't make this harder than it needs to be."

They're similar to the words I've been using with Jo, and on the receiving end they don't sound good at all. I put my hands out in front of me and start waving them around in tiny circles. "No, no, please, wait a second, let me explain."

He raises his gun. He points it right at my face. "Turn around, Feldman," he says, missing the Mr. "Don't make me ask you again."

I turn around and put my hands behind me. A few seconds later the cold bracelets click into place.

"What's this?" he asks.

I turn back and face him. He's holding the envelope with my story inside. "It's the truth."

He tears it open and drags the loose pages out. After a quick skim through he pushes them back into the envelope. "Unbelievable," he says. "I knew you were with those two women."

"You have to read the whole thing," I tell him. "I was trying to help them, not kill them."

He raises a finger to his lips. "No more talking, Feldman. How about you tell me about the box you have in your bedroom?"

"What? You were in my house?"

"The box," he says. "Tell me about it."

"I don't know what's in it. Cyris left it here."

"Cyris. The man from your confession."

"It's not a confession. It's an account of what happened."

"We'll see about that," he says, as if it's all up to him. "Let's go."

He pushes me ahead of him. He gets me outside and tells me to wait for a few seconds, then disappears into my bedroom. I look down toward Jo, but can't see her. I think about running, but there's no point. I wouldn't make it far. Landry comes back out. He's holding up a wooden stake.

"Want to explain this?" he asks.

"It's because—"

"Shut up, Feldman," he says.

"I thought you—"

"I said shut up."

He stays a few feet back as we walk down the hallway and out to his car. His car is an unmarked, four-door sedan. The reflections of the streetlight off the side windows look like two moons. He ushers me into the backseat, twists me sideways, undoes the handcuffs, and reattaches one cuff to the handgrip above the door. He pulls out another set of handcuffs and attaches my other hand to the same handgrip. It doesn't seem like standard protocol, but I guess that's because this isn't one of those police cars with a metal grille separating the prisoner from the driver. Plus he's alone.

He gets into the driver's seat. He needs to know about Jo.

"Listen, I need to tell you about—"

He turns around to face me. "This is quiet time," he says. "You say one more word while we're still driving I'm going to put a bullet in your head. I've seen what you've done, Feldman, and I suggest you believe me."

"But—"

He points his gun at me. "If you don't believe me, Feldman, just say one more word."

I believe him. He faces forward. He starts the car and we pull away from my house, leaving Jo tied up in my car watching for Cyris.

# CHAPTER TWENTY

It started with the notepad. Then with the bloody shorts. The confession. Feldman's wife missing. The lying. The wooden stake. There's no way of shifting all those pieces into different positions and still not getting them to match. It's undeniable. Irrefutable. It's like the cancer running through his body—it can't be forgotten.

Landry changes gear and speeds up. He wishes he could keep his mind off the cancer if only for a moment, but he can't. The cancer isn't changing how all those pieces fit into place, but it's changing how he's looking at them. It's changing the way he's looking at everything. He glances at his hands and sees them still shaking. He knows it isn't nerves. He's following through with the plan. The alternative is to take Feldman down to the station. He'll be charged. He'll go to court. He'll be found guilty, or he'll be found insane. With all that cutting and severing, insanity seems to be the way the jury will go. So Feldman will go to a psychiatric institution. He'll get pills and he'll get counseling and five or ten years after Landry has been rotting in the grave Feldman will be back on the streets.

Life is unfair. Death is unfair. Feldman will kill again. That's the way the justice system works. Nobody is saying it's perfect. They're just saying it's the best they've got. What else can they do? Execute the guy?

*Execute the guy?*

Well that's what all this is about, isn't it? It's why he kept that notepad to himself. It's why he packed his gym bag with different clothes and boots. It's why he has a shotgun in the trunk of the car. It's why he knows about Feldman and Schroder doesn't. If life was fair Feldman would be the one with a death sentence scheduled to start this winter, not him. Feldman would be the one with lost times and last thoughts flooding his mind.

He doesn't even think about doing the right thing now. He's happy to follow where his thoughts are leading. Has been happy to follow them all day. Tonight he's going to find justice for the three dead women—for Kathy, Luciana, and Jo. Because Jo is dead. He's sure of it. Not sure enough to have shot Charlie already—he'll work on that soon. After a career in the police force and living with cancer for a week he's come to realize that being a cop is all about correcting God's mistakes.

"Where are we going?" Feldman asks.

"Have you forgotten what I told you?"

"We're heading out of the city. You're not taking me to the police station, are you?"

"No," he says, and what this is leading to isn't *murder*, not really, not in the same sense of the word that Feldman is a *murderer*. It's more like an exchange. A two-for-one bargain.

He can't save Kathy or Luciana, but he can save the next girl. That can't be a bad thing. Not really. It can't be a bad thing to live with. And perhaps Jo is that next girl.

"Where are we going?" Feldman asks.

"You need to shut up," he says.

"Are you going to kill me?" Feldman asks.

"Maybe."

"I didn't do it," Feldman says, his voice panicky now. "I know you think I did, but I didn't."

"You'll get your day in court," he says.

"I thought you just said—"

Landry pulls over. Feldman shuts up. Landry turns around and points the gun at him. "One more word, Feldman, and this ends right now. Nod if you understand."

Feldman nods.

"You'll get your chance to talk," he says, "but not here and not now. But soon. When we get where we're going. You say one more word before then and your brains are going to paint the back of my car, and neither of us wants that, do we," he says, knowing how much cleaning that would take. Not from experience—but he's seen gunshot wounds to heads before and knows what can happen.

Feldman shakes his head.

"Good," he says, and he puts the gun back onto the passenger seat, puts the car into gear, and carries on driving.

# CHAPTER TWENTY-ONE

My wrists are hurting. I try to make myself more comfortable, but it's impossible. Time starts slipping by. We skirt the edges of town where property looks rough, but is usually expensive because of its location. The loop starts to get wider. We begin hitting the outer edges of suburbs. Different economic diversities. Nice homes. Nice people. Bad homes. Bad people. We keep driving. We end up going west, right out of the city. Landry's cell phone rings. He ignores it. A minute later it rings again, he looks at the display, then switches it off.

There isn't much in the way of traffic. Not much in the way of lighting. Just long, dark highways, boarded by long, dark fields full of crops and animals, all being grown so the rest of us don't go hungry. Landry said that *maybe* he's going to kill me, but I think he's already made up his mind. He said I'll get my day in court, and I think that that day is today. It's tonight. It will be a court in the middle of nowhere, one where I plead not guilty and still end up hanging from a tree. I wonder how many others he's done this to. I wonder if it's standard practice, that Landry is one of many cops who think they're doing the world a favor. And he would be—no doubt there—if he had the right guy.

I keep looking out the window, trying to figure out where we're going—as if it actually matters, as if the location is the relevant point here and not the fact that Landry is crazy. Twenty minutes pass silently. Landry keeps the same pace. I'm hoping he's using the miles we're putting between us and the city to good use, that he's thinking things over and coming to the conclusion that he needs to turn around and take me back into the city. I need a lawyer. I need my chance to explain things. The hum of the motor and the slight clinking coming from my handcuffs are the only sound. I can't lean back because the pull on my wrists is too strong. My lower back starts to get sore. The first drops of rain splash lightly on the roof, slowly at first, then it picks up until it becomes a constant thick patter. Landry turns on the wipers—*wubwud, wubwud.*

Another twenty minutes go by and all I'm looking at are black hills. My back gets sorer. I get more scared. I want to say something, but I'm convinced if I try I won't even get the trial he's planning. It may be crazy, but that trial is still the only chance I have.

We hit the hour mark. Are we ever going to stop? The rain is really heavy now. Ninety minutes and it's just long, straight roads and no car lights ahead or behind us and I desperately need to take a leak. I close my eyes and ride it out in silence. It's all I can do. The tires start bumping over a gravel road and we come to a skidding halt. Landry steps out, shifting the weight of the car so it bounces up slightly. He moves into the path of the headlights where he swings open a chain-link fence. I can hear its hinges squeak over the noise of the rain. They sound like a coffin lid being pried open. I have large, red indentations around my wrists visible under the car's interior light. As the skin swells the cuffs get tighter.

Landry comes back. There is water dripping from his jacket and ears. He glares at me, a look that suggests I'm to blame for everything that's ever gone wrong in the world. He puts his seatbelt back on. We roll forward. He doesn't close the gate behind him. The gravel peters out as the surface becomes dirt. The back wheels spin occasionally as they fail to find traction in the mud. The driveway becomes bumpier and painful because every small bounce is amplified through my wrists. We only drive five minutes before we come to another stop. He kills the engine. I can hear rain and I can hear each of us breathing. The headlights shine over the trees ahead of us. The dashboard lights shine over Landry, making his skin look orange. I peer out the window to my left. Only darkness. To my right is the same.

Landry turns off the lights. We're in complete darkness. He opens the door and the interior light comes on, making it difficult for me to look outside as my reflection continually gets in the way. He gets out and lets the door close behind him, but it doesn't latch, so the light stays on. I stare at my reflection as if it's another person who can help me, but it's only somebody else who's letting me down. Landry disappears. I keep glancing at my watch as if time is suddenly my greatest ally. My ass is sore, my back is throbbing, and my neck is stiff. My arms and legs are cramping, especially my shoulders. My headache is back. I have the urge to cry. I have the urge to scream at the world and tell it that it's not playing fair.

I wonder how far from the Garden City we've come. Out here it's just one huge garden. Miles of it. It's as if God created too many trees for Eden and dumped the surplus. Landry pops open the trunk. A jangle of keys, a few thuds and bangs, and then it's slammed shut. Then nothing for about five minutes. He's carrying a flashlight and I watch it light up the area as he's walking. There's a structure out there to the left, some kind of shack, but I can't see any detail because of the reflection inside the car. He walks up the porch steps and goes inside, and then all I can see is a glowing light from behind glass. I stare at it, but it doesn't move. He's resting the flashlight on something. I pull at the handcuffs. I pull at the handgrip they're attached to. I put my feet into the side of the door and use all my strength. It's no good.

The glow of the flashlight moves again. Landry comes back out. He opens my door, leans in, and undoes one set of handcuffs. They dangle from the handgrip. He throws the keys for the remaining cuffs at my feet.

"Don't waste my time, Feldman."

He stands a few yards from the car. Rain pours around him, but he doesn't seem to care. He has the air of a man who knows not to bother trying to stay dry because he plans on spending more time getting wet. He's watching me with the barrel of a shotgun. I'm not sure where his handgun is.

The handcuffs are difficult to unlock. My hands are sore and my fingers are shaking. Rain is blowing into the car and I blink away what to Landry must look like tears. Finally I manage to get the key into the small slot, then both hands are free. I almost faint with relief.

The shotgun touches my cheek. The barrel is steel and as cold as ice. I stop dead. My blood drains into the balls of my feet.

"Grab a cuff from the handgrip, Feldman, and put it back on."

I don't even try to argue it. It's hard undoing it, but I get there. Then I wrap one bracelet around my wrist and do it up. Then the other.

"Don't hold back now, Feldman. Make sure they're nice and tight."

I look around as I tighten the cuffs. There's no help here. I try not to grimace as the metal bites into the bones of my wrists.

"Keys?"

The barrel is still touching my face as I flick the keys to the edge of the seat. Holding the weapon in one arm he lowers himself and, keeping his eyes on me, reaches for them. I watch them disappear into a pocket and only now do I realize he's changed out of his cheap suit into jeans, a flannel shirt, and a dark jacket. He's wearing a cap that says *Kiss the Cook*. The rain hits the brim and rolls off the edges. His loafers have been replaced with hiking boots. He's also wearing leather gloves.

"Come on out and don't try anything funny, Feldman. I don't have the patience for any trouble."

I slowly climb from the car. On legs shaking from near cramp, cold, and terror, I stand and step forward. To my left I can hear a river.

"Enjoying yourself?" he asks.

"Not as much as you."

In a blistering movement I'm on the ground, my eyes swimming in their sockets, bright lights circling them. I manage to look up at Landry, but struggle to focus on him. What I can see is the shotgun in his hand, the butt facing me, and through a mind drowning in red-hot pain I slowly understand the connection. I manage to stay on my knees for a few more seconds before spilling onto my side. My jaw is throbbing. I think I'll lie here forever. Before I get the chance he drags me to my feet and props me against the car. He slaps me around the face, hard, as though this is going to help me think straight.

"Okay, Mr. Smartmouth, neither of us wants that to happen again, and it won't, as long as you cooperate and stop being such a smart prick."

My eyes are struggling to focus and it feels like I'm trying to tune his words in from far away, but yeah, I get his point. He grabs a handful of my hair and shoves my head backward.

"Do you understand?"

My ears hurt and I slowly nod, not wanting him to scream again. The motion is nearly enough to make me vomit.

He steps back and tracks me with the weapon. "Now step forward."

I stumble forward.

"Behind you is a cabin. It's probably not up to your expectations, but it won't kill you. We're going to walk over there and you're going to make your way inside. Just keep in mind that this is a Mossberg pump-action shotgun, Mr. Smartmouth. . . ." He pauses. "Can I call you Mr. Smartmouth?"

I nod and it hurts.

"Just keep thinking about the shotgun. Keep thinking about what it can do to you. Now hurry up, or are you waiting for an invitation?"

I turn around. My view shifts from the shotgun and the man behind it back to the car and the cabin beyond. Though calling it a *cabin* is a fairly generous term. It has the minimum number of walls required to hold up a ceiling and be labeled a *building*. It looks to be the size of a small one-bedroom house. The walls are warped and knotted, made from a mixture of woods. The side wall I can see is made from weatherboards, while the wall closest with the glass sliding door is constructed from plywood and fence pales and plenty of sealant. The roof is made from aluminum sheeting. Without any guttering to catch and drain the rain, a small moat has formed around the cabin. A wooden porch extends a few feet from the sliding door and the roof extends above it. The glass part of the door is covered in grime, but isn't broken or cracked. Pine needles stick to the glass all along the bottom. The metal runners have darkened with mud and rust. It's hard to imagine anybody dragging these pieces out here in their car and constructing this small home away from home. Hard to imagine some do-it-yourselfer walking through a scrap heap and coming across these bits of wood and tin and getting the final image of this cabin in his mind.

Hard to imagine anybody would go to this effort.

Yet somebody has. Perhaps the same somebody standing behind me.

I walk past the car and climb up onto the porch. It creaks beneath my weight, but I don't fall through. Inside the air is just as cold. The rain yells on the roof, but I can't see any signs of leakage. There are two rooms. We're standing in the main one. Surprisingly, the inside of the cabin has been lined, so instead of seeing the same weatherboards and the same fence pales along with some framing, it's been lined with plywood. There's a fireplace, a bench, and a couple of soft chairs that look like they may have swallowed a few animals over the years. Landry closes the sliding door, locking out the rain and any hope I have of getting out of this place alive.

"Sit down," he says, pointing me to the larger of the two chairs. Its fading pattern of yellow flowers doesn't make it look even remotely comfortable. Nor do the worn gashes with escaping foam and protruding springs. I fall into it. The broken framework pulls my body right to the back so my feet come off the ground. I rest my handcuffed hands in my lap. I can smell pine and mildew. Landry lights a match, and then in turn lights a lantern. It has a glass shell dotted with mold, but lights up the cabin a hell of a lot better than his flashlight does. Then he lights another one and puts it in the opposite corner of the cabin. Then he sits in the opposite chair. His is a checkered, brown-and-black pattern that somebody could play chess on. Next to him on the floor is a duffel bag. It's unzipped, and I can see the clothes he was wearing earlier are folded up inside it.

An oval rug in the center of the floor is stained with mud and animal hair. The open fireplace is made from brick and cinder block with a chimney that is a long metal tube not much wider than my leg. At the moment it's set with blocks of wood and yellow newspaper, but hasn't been lit. Landry either likes the cold or doesn't plan on being here long.

He rests the shotgun across his legs then sighs. No possible way can I get to him before he gets to his gun, not the way the chair is trying to eat me. I figure that's the whole point. He looks tired.

"I know what you're thinking," he says.

"I'm not so sure you do."

His hands clutch the Mossberg tightly. "Jesus, why in the hell do you have to keep on being so smart? Can't you take anything seriously?"

I shake my head. "I wasn't being smart. I'm taking this seriously. I'm just saying you don't know what I'm thinking." It's hard not to stumble over my sentences, but I manage it. I'm scared. I know it and he knows it. So far it's all we have in common. He lets go of the shotgun, leans back into his chair, and starts nodding.

"You're wondering if this is my place. You're wondering if I've brought people out here before. I'm right, aren't I?"

I nod. He's right.

"It belonged to a guy just like you. I caught him. It's a while back now."

"Did you give him a trial too?"

"Jesus, Feldman."

"You're making a big mistake. I didn't kill anybody, and if you give me the chance to—"

"Shut up, okay? Do you know how many times I've heard guys like you tell me they're innocent? I don't need to hear it from you. All I want to hear from you is a confession."

"Look, I know how you feel, I can understand—"

"You can't understand anything, Feldman, you really can't. I'm sick," he says, and slowly he shakes his head. "I'm sick of dealing with all of this. Sick of people who kill for the hell of it, just for fun. I see these people go to jail, I see them released, and then I see them reoffend. They're predators, and that will never change. They'll always be among us. Their faces change, but their thoughts never do. They live among us doing what evil men do. I thought I'd seen everything. But there will always be worse."

"Let me explain."

"This is an awful place to die," he says, and he looks around it as if he's seeing it for the first time. "This useless shack in the middle of nowhere. You want to know what it was built for?"

I don't answer him. I don't need to.

"The guy's name was Martin Rhodes. He was a pretty normal guy to everybody who knew him. Had a girlfriend he was engaged to. They owned a house together. They knew their neighbors, they had lots of friends. He was an artist. A sculptor. Used to make swans and shit out of blocks of ice for weddings. He was a pretty talented guy."

"I remember," I tell him.

"Yeah, I thought you would. He was all over the news. It's the ice sculpting thing that people remember about him more than what he actually did. They remember that before they even remember his name. It was six or seven years ago now. So this is his cabin. This is where he brought his girlfriend when she no longer wanted to be his girlfriend."

"There's another guy, his name is Cyris," I start, and he holds up his hand to stop me.

"Her name was Vicky. He tied her up and put her in the trunk of his car. That's a long drive in that condition. A real long drive. That alone could have killed her. There used to be a bath right there," he says, pointing to the far corner behind me. "No plumbing, just an old tub that suited the décor of this place. He kept her in the trunk while he carried buckets from the river that runs about a minute west of here. It had to be close enough so he wouldn't have to walk far. He filled the bathtub with freezing cold water and he held her down in it. You want to know why?"

"This is a mistake," I say, but he's off somewhere, living in the past.

"He didn't like the fact she was moving on without him. So he drowned her. And then he revived her. And drowned her again. He had her up here for six days, drowning or coming close to drowning her, and reviving her until she couldn't be revived anymore. We found him when he came back into the city. He led us here. He'd put her back in the bath. He said he was cleaning her. We took the bath away as evidence and left this cabin standing. You want to know why?"

"I understand why you think—"

"It wasn't cost-effective. That's what they said. Didn't want to pay anybody to drive up here with a sledgehammer and knock this shithole down. I haven't been here since then.

And I haven't seen anything as sick until now. So when you say you understand, that's bullshit. You don't understand anything other than how it feels to cause pain."

"I get it," I say. "I get your world-has-gone-to-shit story, and maybe you're right. Everybody hates somebody, nobody likes anybody, people fight for no reason or for every reason. It's front-page news every day. I get it. But you're making a mistake here. I haven't killed anybody."

"Q and A, Feldman. You get that? I ask, you answer. So let's start with a fairly simple one. You think you can handle that?"

I say yes and he seems happy.

"Who has the gun?" he asks.

"You do." It's a big gun. No missing it.

"Who here is the officer of the law?"

"You are," I say, though at the moment that's a rather fine distinction to make.

"Who's wearing the handcuffs?"

"I am."

"Who's on trial?"

"I am."

"So who's asking the questions?" he asks.

"You are."

"So you would be?"

I shrug. "Answering," I say.

"Are things clear enough?"

"They're way too clear," I tell him.

"Good, so you'll shut up unless I've asked you something."

He lifts the shotgun, crosses his legs, then replaces it. The barrel points at the wall. His hands are shaking slightly. We both notice this at the same time. I want to tell him he's not only drawn the wrong conclusions, but also painted an entirely wrong picture. I want to tell him he's a lunatic. I raise my left hand to my jaw—my right follows because of the handcuffs. I move slowly because I don't want Landry misinterpreting any movement as an attempt to attack him. My jaw is throbbing. I'm lucky he didn't dislocate it.

"I've brought a Bible along, Feldman. It's in my bag. I'd offer it to you to swear upon, but I think it would be pointless." His eyes narrow and he sweeps his hand through his gray hair. "I know what it's like to no longer believe in God and I can't imagine you ever did."

I'm thinking the same thing. My life seems to have gone back to that game show, only now up for grabs is the opportunity to kill me, and it seems everybody is banging on their buzzer to have a turn. I wonder who the game-show host is then realize it's my new friend Evil.

Landry crouches forward in his chair. "What do you believe in, Feldman?"

"A fair trial."

He gives what sounds like a nervous laugh, then starts picking at a stain on his right knee, but only smudges it wider. He keeps itching at it then looks up at me, expressionless.

"You're nothing more than a stain, Feldman."

He reaches into the duffel bag and rummages around beneath his clothes and pulls out a wooden stake. I recognize the craftsmanship. He must have picked it up when he went back into my bedroom. He waves it back and forth, his eyes following it as if out of all the wooden stakes he's seen this one has to be the nicest. Eventually his gaze moves back to me. There is no doubt in them. I can't imagine anything I say will make him think I'm innocent.

"Which one did you murder first?" he asks.

"Why? It doesn't matter what I say. I keep offering to tell you what happened, but the only thing you want to hear is the version you've come up with." He doesn't answer. I listen to the rain. It's still heavy. I wonder if I'll be dead before sunrise. "There's nothing I can say that doesn't make you angry."

He keeps staring at me. Then he just nods. "Okay, Feldman, you make a good point. I said you'd have a fair trial, and that's what I'm going to give you. So think of me as the prosecuting lawyer with a whole bunch of questions. So let's start with the question I asked you, and we'll see where that goes. And then we'll see what the judge has to say."

# CHAPTER TWENTY-TWO

The rain is pouring heavily on the tin roof. The inside of the cabin is damp, his skin feels clammy, his feet cold, and he feels sick at being in a place where such depravity took place. He feels sick too sitting opposite this piece of human trash.

He is starting to feel a little nauseous. When was the last time he ate? It takes him a few seconds to figure it out, which is a few seconds longer than it should have taken. It was the fries from before. He should have eaten the damn burger too. He'll pick one up on the way home later. Maybe two or three of them.

The cabin felt just as damp last time he came out here, even though that was in the middle of summer. It's amazing that after all these years his memory of the scene is so intense that he could almost close his eyes and use muscle memory to get around, his limbs knowing where to go. It just proves the worst thing you ever see will stay with you the longest. That girl in the bathtub died hard. Harder than anybody else he can think of.

Now that he's here, he has to admit to himself that there are doubts starting to creep in. He's never killed anybody before. He's wanted to. Who hasn't? As a cop, he's wanted to do it more than most people. He's had chances. There have been people he's chased down that he could have put a bullet into, but chose not to. He's annoyed that the anger that fueled him all the way out here seems to be disappearing. He needs to get it back. He thinks of the way Kathy and Luciana were cut open.

It helps.

It makes him feel once again he's on the right path. Only problem is this path is pretty close to another path, one in which he thinks he should have just taken Feldman in to the station.

All he can do now is move forward. If he shows up at the station with Feldman now he'll have to explain this little outing, and it's going to look as though he withheld evidence just in case he felt like killing the suspect. Which is exactly what happened. And exactly what he's going to have to do. Now. He could blame the pills and the cancer, but he'll still be disgraced. He'll lose his job. They'll send him home and they'll wonder how many other people he brought out here, or took to similar places. He'll pass from this world to the next under a cloud of suspicion.

He pictures the two dead women. He pictures the contents of the cardboard box. He pictures the other cases he's never been able to let go even long after they were solved. The fuel is coming back. He remembers the young woman floating facedown in the bathtub in this very cabin, her gray, wrinkled skin, her milky eyes. He thinks of other young women face down in alleyways and hallways and ditches and other bath-tubs. Feldman's as guilty as they come—he's doing the world a favor by taking him out of it.

He hates Feldman. Hates his sarcasm. In the end it'll be the smugness that'll make his transition from judge to executioner easier to bear. As soon as Feldman admits what he did then he can happily . . .

*Happily?*

That's the wrong word. There's nothing happy about this. This is the last place he wants to be. In six months when his sins are weighed up in whatever magical afterlife landscape he goes to, a large piece of him will still be back here.

He needs Feldman to confess, then he can get this over with. He needs that confession because it will come with a feeling of justice. With it, dying from the cancer will be easier to do.

Without it, he's just one more bad man doing bad deeds.

# CHAPTER TWENTY-THREE

"I didn't kill anybody," I reply, choosing to answer his question about who I killed first with the honest truth. I don't know what it is, but nobody these days is prepared to believe anything I say, and I haven't lied yet.

I try to think about things logically. Like a mathematician. Or one of those thinking-outside-of-the-box riddles: two people are in a room, one has a gun, the other is handcuffed. No wonder I never liked riddles.

"Kathy and Luciana were staked through the heart," he says.

"I didn't do it."

"I saw the bodies. And I found a stake on your bedroom floor."

"I can explain that."

"Okay. Go ahead and explain."

So I do. I go ahead and tell him how my Sunday night to

Monday morning unfolded. I tell him about driving home. About Luciana stepping out in front of the car. My trip through the woods. Finding Kathy tied up. Killing Cyris. I tell him we didn't go to the police because of what happened to Benjamin Hyatt, and how we wanted to get a lawyer first. The ghosts stay away as I tell him, but as I get closer to the end of the story, I can feel them nearby, and eventually they appear as I'm telling him about my conversation with Kathy in the lounge while Luciana was in the shower.

"Kathy was asleep when he first attacked her," I tell him, and in the front of my mind the lounge we sat in while she told me this starts to form, slowly at first, and soon I can smell the blood on my clothes and taste the last mouthful of beer. Kathy brought me into a world where evil happened and I had loaded my hands full of its treasures. I can see Landry sitting opposite me, but standing just over his left shoulder is Kathy. She's so real I could touch her. But of course she's not real. She's a figment of my imagination. Guilt manifesting itself into a form in which it can haunt me. My head is hurting from the blows it's taken lately, and I reach slowly up and to the bump from Sunday night, and Kathy fades a little as I rub it, but then comes back when I stop. A real ghost wouldn't do that. One projected by my guilt would.

"I never heard anyone come in," she says.

"I know you didn't. It wasn't your fault," I say to my guilt, hoping in a way it could be more than that, hoping it really could be Kathy I'm talking to.

"Jesus, Feldman, you've lost me," Landry says.

"I didn't know what time it was, Charlie, maybe ten thirty, and I woke up as his hand pressed down against my mouth. I wanted to scream, but couldn't. He held the tip of a knife next to my eye."

"I killed him with that knife," I say.

"Him? I'm not talking about this Cyris you're going on about. I'm talking about the women. Which one did you kill first, Feldman?"

"I didn't kill them," I say. "I really didn't kill them."

Kathy is ignoring Landry because in her world he never existed and that's the fundamental problem with homicide cops—it's already too late when you need them. Kathy stares at me with remorse and pity. She has a drink in her hand. It's the one she had before I showered to wash away the blood. She seems uninterested in the cabin. The cold doesn't affect her. The back of my neck is alive with goose bumps. She isn't a ghost. Isn't my guilt. She's a memory. Her words are the same words she told me.

"I could smell his skin. So vile. Like he hadn't bathed in days. Strange, huh? I was choking on his odor. I was sure he had plans for me, but right at that moment the smell was all I could think about."

"He broke into Kathy's bedroom and abducted her," I say.

"You killed her first?"

"He moved his knife to my throat. It trapped the smell and the taste in there. I was desperate for air and was starting to black out. Then he was promising me if I made a sound he would kill me. His eyes were so dark. So intense. I knew then that this man was pure evil. Have you ever seen pure evil, Charlie?"

"I once saw an episode of *Melrose Place*." Kathy's ghost smiles, and Landry looks at me as if I've completely lost it. Maybe I have.

"He told me his name was Cyris and I should remember it because I'd be calling it out over and over in the night. He told me to nod if I could remember that, so I nodded. I was so afraid and I thought he was going to kill me right there, but instead he backed away and tossed me some clothes. He ordered me to dress and I was happy to."

"Answer the Goddamn question," Landry says. "Who'd you kill first?"

"Cyris. He was the first one to die."

"Tell me about the women. Tell me why you killed them."

"Yes, Charlie, tell us why," Kathy says, surprising me because it means she knows about Landry, and this is turning from a memory of a conversation into an actual conversation.

I close my eyes to try and hide from her and what I see is Cyris in the trees, Cyris with the metal stake and the knife, Cyris asking me if I wanted to join him. When I open my eyes I'm expecting to see Kathy has gone, but she hasn't. She pours herself another invisible drink, then leans against a doorway that is nearly two days ago and at least sixty or so miles away.

"They weren't meant to die," I say. "Don't you see? I saved them. I saved them."

"From Cyris. Tell me what they did to make you kill them. Tell me."

"I didn't kill them."

Kathy looks down at her ghostly feet. They are bare and I wonder if she can see the floor through them like I can. "I didn't know he was going to take me away to hear me scream. I would have fought more had I known what my fate was going to be."

"He took them from their houses to torture them," I tell Landry. "He tied them to trees."

"In the pasture you wrote about."

"Things like this only happen to other people," Kathy tells me, and she starts to fade.

"He forced her into a van, and that's when she saw he had

Luciana too. She was unconscious. She said that scared her the most."

Kathy is nodding slowly, agreeing, fading quickly now.

"She said she knew at that point she was going to die."

I try to imagine the terror she must have felt as Cyris forced her to walk through those trees, the horror of having Cyris carrying her unconscious friend with them. My fear of walking through those trees in the darkness later had been nothing in comparison. What would it be like to know you were being taken to your death? How would you feel knowing the rest of your short life would be lived out in immense pain and cruelty? I shudder at the thought of putting myself into her position. This is electric-chair material. Like being taken down a corridor there is no coming back from. I look at Landry's bag and think of the Bible inside he told me was there. Could anybody in these situations really find comfort from one?

"He tied her up to a tree. He dumped Luciana on the ground. He didn't know, but she had woken during the walk. He'd dumped her at the side of the clearing they were in. He was so focused on Kathy that he didn't notice her inching away. Eventually she would run away and flag me down. As she was doing that, Cyris was telling Kathy that she was a mistress of evil. She said it was like being attacked by two different people. One moment he was calm, the next he was in a frenzy—only she was sure the frenzy was an act. She was positive he was calm the whole time."

"An act? Even if I believed another man killed them, why would I believe he was acting in a frenzy just for the sake of acting? He had no audience."

I tell him what Jo said. About an actor in a role. About him wanting the police to believe one thing when in fact it had been another. Then that scenario evolves a little. "Maybe he even only wanted to kill one of them, but by killing them both it looks more random, right? It looks like he picked two women and drove them into the woods to kill them in some ritualistic or crazed act. What if only one of them was a target? If he killed her then you would look for somebody more personal to the victim. Isn't that how it goes? This way who do you look for? Some maniac?"

"And that's what I found. You were Cyris when you killed them and you're Feldman now that you got caught. You were right about the actor."

"You're wrong."

He shakes his head. "There was a connection between the two, so I know you didn't just pick their houses at random. You followed them first. Where did you first see them? The supermarket? The movies?"

"See? This is exactly what I said before. You're not willing to hear anything that doesn't fall in line with what you think happened."

He holds his hand out and uncurls his fingers. The stake rolls out. It hits the ground and doesn't bounce. It makes me jump. It makes me think of the way Kathy and Luciana died.

"Maybe you met them at a bar. They were friends out having a quiet drink, and you were the guy who kept hitting on them. In the end they figured out you wouldn't leave them alone so they played along with you. You swapped names and numbers, only they gave you fake ones and you gave them your real one. You took it back after you followed them home and killed them."

"There was no forced entry. How do you explain that?"

"Maybe you convinced them at the bar you were a nice guy and they took you home. Maybe they were drunk and asked you for a lift. You had your bag of tools in the trunk and you just couldn't say no. They let you inside and the rest is obvious."

He reaches inside his jacket and pulls out a packet of cigarettes. He removes one with his lips, starts to put them away, then holds them out to me as if to show he isn't such a bad guy after all. I shake my head. I don't tell him that those things will kill him. He shrugs, as if not accepting one of his cigarettes is undeniable proof I must be crazy. He lights it and sucks deeply, then breathes a mouthful of smoke into the damp air. It hovers above his head, but doesn't drift.

"You cut off Kathy's breast and took it home."

"What?"

"What? You didn't think I looked in the box?"

"I had no idea. I just assumed it was a head."

Landry shakes his head. "You just don't stop trying, do you?"

I feel sick. "It still doesn't add up. You think one of them waited in the car while I killed the other?"

"You attacked one of them quickly and knocked her un-conscious, then subdued the other. You probably left her tied up in the car."

"That's not how it happened."

Kathy's ghost has gone and Luciana's arrives. She looks at me from where Kathy stood earlier, only she has no drink to hold. Instead she's holding a towel to dry her wet, ghostly hair.

"She tried to call the police, but you had to stop her, didn't you?" Landry says.

"What happened?" Luciana asks.

"I broke the phone."

"I know," they both say, but only Luciana carries on. "It was too late anyway, Charlie."

"I'm sorry."

"Did you kill Jo?"

"What? No," I say. "How do you even know about her?"

"But you abducted her."

"Yes."

"That's what I thought."

I shake my head. "No, it's not what you're thinking. I was trying to help her."

"You were helping her by abducting her."

"I know it sounds crazy, but it's the truth."

"No, I don't think you know just how crazy it really sounds. Where is she?"

"She was helping me find Cyris."

"Let me get this straight. You abduct her, and she agrees to help you."

"Like I said, I know it sounds crazy. But it's true."

"You have no idea how many times I've heard that during my career," Landry says. "People think if they lead into a conversation by saying they know how crazy it sounds, that somehow it will make what they say more believable. But it doesn't. It only makes them sound more guilty."

"Well, she was helping me."

"Bullshit."

"She was in the car," I tell him, and suddenly I realize what that means. "She saw you! She will have seen you, and she'll be able to identify you to the police. You should take me back. Don't make it worse for yourself."

"You're lying."

I shake my head. "I'm not lying. Look into my eyes and tell me I'm lying."

He looks into my eyes. "You're lying," he says.

It's been a few hours since I tied Jo up. In that time she will have managed to work herself free, or in that time somebody will have walked past the car. If she worked herself free, she will have gone into a neighbor's house to call for help. She couldn't have driven anywhere because I have the keys—unless Jo has spent time over the last six months learning how to hotwire a car. Right now the police will be looking for me. She will have told them. The only problem is she won't have told them where. And she won't be able to have told them who took me. But it's something. Knowing Landry may be found guilty of killing me isn't much comfort, but it's something.

"Tell me about Luciana," he says, and as if on cue, Luciana reappears.

She slowly shakes her head at me exactly as she did on Monday morning. She finished drying her hair and offered me fresh clothes to replace the bloody ones I was wearing. She shook her head when I told her mine weren't that bad and called me a typical male. She left me alone in the lounge to think, alone to drink my beer, and the beer had my head buzzing. Kathy was trying to call her husband. The next thing I knew darkness was my friend and in the darkness I thought about the offer Cyris had made me. I had fallen asleep. I woke to find Luciana crouching in front of me and my beer seeping into her carpet.

"She told me not to worry about it," I say.

"About what?"

"She said, 'It's perfectly okay for the man who saved our lives to stain my carpet.' She handed me a flannel and a towel and a change of clothes, then gave me directions to the bathroom."

"You showered in her bathroom," Landry says. "You showered before you killed her."

"Yeah, I showered. I wasn't going to. I wanted to show up the way I was, but . . . I don't know, there was something just too creepy about sitting around with another man's blood on me. Anyway, I figured I'd still have my clothes, and that would be enough. Kathy was still trying to get hold of her husband. She said she'd stay in the clothes she was in."

"You were a mess," Luciana says, then smiles at me, the tense of her sentence suggests she's thinking back to the past, that she's not still there living it.

I walked down her hallway and walking into the steam of her bathroom filled me with excitement. It was full of typical womanly scents—soaps and subtle perfumes that made you think of meadows and flowers. For the first time I thought of Jo. Up until that moment I hadn't given Jo, or my parents or any of my friends or my job, a moment of thought. I was in a house with two beautiful women and they were in my debt. Anything could have come from it and, as it turns out, something did.

I dropped my own clothes in a heap. I had no idea how bad I was until I looked in the mirror. I was smeared in blood and dirt; patches of my hair had been welded together with blood. The only clean parts were where my clothes and watch had been. There were clumps of dirt in my ears and my forehead had the lump it still has now. I was smiling—smiling to be alive, smiling as I thought what my students would say the next time they saw me walk into the classroom looking like I'd been hit by a car. And, truth be told, I was smiling at the thought of Kathy and Luciana joining me in the shower. Of course I was. What guy wouldn't?

The hot water hit my damaged body and stung like hell. I was in the bathroom Luciana would soon die in. I was dancing from one foot to the other, washing green shampoo through my hair, creating a red lather. Red water ran down my body, moving over sore muscles and torn skin in long stripes. It was blood and I liked the fact that most of it wasn't mine. When I returned to the lounge Kathy and Luciana were talking on the couch.

"You certainly looked uncomfortable in those clothes," Luciana says to me.

"I didn't have any underwear on."

My headache, as it is now, was thumping along nicely.

"I'm trying to be serious here, Feldman," Landry says, "and all you can tell me is you weren't wearing underwear in the shower? Why the hell would you?"

"Ignore him, Charlie," Luciana tells me. "We should have gone to the police. That's what you wanted to do. We sat down and talked about it. You wanted to go. I wasn't sure. But Kathy wanted to get hold of her husband. She said her husband used to tell her all the time where people messed up was by not having a lawyer. She said the common mistake innocent people made was to assume the police would think that innocent people were innocent. You wanted to go and she wanted to stay, and I sided with my friend. Of course I did. If I'd agreed with you . . ." she says, and doesn't need to finish the sentence.

"Cyris was dead," I say, to both Luciana and Landry. "So we decided to wait until we could get hold of Kathy's husband. We would then go in together. We were all too upset and exhausted, and that was a recipe for saying the wrong thing during questioning. We planned to go first thing."

"Why did you shower?"

"I told you already. I was a mess," I tell him. "I was covered with Cyris's blood and I know it's dumb, but I kept feeling like it was going to seep into the pores of my skin and make me sick."

"Your playacting alter ego."

"Think about it," I say. "Why would I shower before killing

two people? Why would I shower if I was going to get covered in blood anyway?"

"Because you showered after you killed them, not before," Landry says. "Tell me again why you killed Jo."

"I didn't kill Jo. She was helping me." I look at his *Kiss the Cook* cap and I wonder what state of mind he was in when he bought it. It's hard to imagine him out shopping, just cruising the mall and walking into a clothes shop and finding that hat on a shelf. Did he make pleasant conversation with the sales girl while she rang up the sale and put the hat in a bag? Did they flirt? Talk about the weather? Did he wear it out of the store? Did he know then that one day he would wear it while taking another man's life? Or was it a gift? He's not wearing a wedding ring, but aren't cops with tough-guy attitudes often divorced? Maybe he has children, maybe the hat is a father's day present.

Luciana is starting to fade, following Kathy back to the world where they live now. She's wearing the robe she died in, but the towel she had wrapped around her hair when she woke me is gone. The night was winding down and since we weren't going to the police it was time to go home. Since they would end up dead in their own houses the first thing I needed to do was separate them. I sat wearily on the arm of the couch—Monday morning was draining me. It was at that moment I learned Kathy was married.

"You were jealous, weren't you?" Luciana says.

"How many victims?" Landry repeats.

"I wasn't jealous," I say, but I was and Luciana knows it. Jealous that Kathy was married. It was stupid. At least she was married to a man who would help us. I had killed a man and I needed representation. I didn't want to be the next Benjamin Hyatt. I didn't want to be the next guy the country felt sorry for, then read about in the newspapers having been beaten in jail. In the end we agreed to get together in the morning. I grabbed my bloodstained clothes and I left, taking Kathy with me.

"We should have stayed together," Luciana says. "But he was dead. You told us he was dead."

I look away. I can't face her. She's right. I told them he was dead and he wasn't.

"Jealous? Are you on something, Feldman? Is that the problem?"

"Among other things," I say, and Luciana fades away and life, as it is out here at gunpoint, returns to normal.

# CHAPTER TWENTY-FOUR

Landry is confused. It's like Feldman is having a conversation with somebody who isn't here. Feldman understands this is a trial—is he trying some sort of insanity defense? Perhaps he's not trying one—perhaps he really is just that insane. Would it make a difference?

It would. If Feldman wasn't in control, if there really is something in his brain that isn't wired up right, then the guy cannot be held accountable. If he had arrested him and not brought him out here instead, then over the following days they would look into his life and see if there was any history of being mentally unstable.

That's not what is going on here. Feldman is in control of his actions. Of course he is. He's a psychopath. Only that word doesn't come close to describing Feldman. He doesn't know what word does. It would probably take a combination of words. A string of them. Long-lettered terms that only doctors with diplomas would know how to pronounce. Landry has never dealt with anybody so messed up, and in a way this actually helps. It helps that with each sentence that comes out of Feldman's mouth Landry knows his decision to bring the man out here is the right one. Hell, it's even cost-effective.

He adjusts the gun across his knees, shrugs his shoulders back to offset the beginning cramp, and shifts further into the chair. Not much longer to go. So far the only thing that Feldman has said that may be remotely true is what he said about his wife. There was something in his words that frightened Landry. Something that suggested perhaps she has been helping. If that's the case, then she'll have called the police by now. It means there's no going back. Not that it matters. He's a dead man anyway.

"You just said you weren't jealous. Weren't jealous of who? Jo?"

"I liked Kathy, that's all. Is that a crime?"

"The way you liked her it sure as hell was. Why'd you kill Luciana in the bathroom?" he asks, catching himself using the victim's first name. How long has he been doing that? It means he's personalized them; it means this has become more than just a case. But why the hell not? If he's going to kill a man it ought to be over somebody with a first name. They deserve to be personalized. They deserve justice. *Revenge? Do they deserve revenge?* Of course they do. That's why he's out here.

*Is it? You're not out here for yourself?*

He decides not to answer that.

"Why not the bedroom? You said she'd already showered, so why take her back in there?"

"I don't know why," Feldman says, and Landry has heard that same answer before from dozens of men unable to explain why they killed dozens of women.

"She was still alive, Feldman, when you rammed that stake into her heart." He leans forward and tightens his grip on the shotgun. "We know that because of the blood splatter. Her heart pumped all that blood out into the bathtub."

"Answer me this," Feldman says. "The phone call to the police. How did the phone get outside if I burst into her house when they arrived home?"

"Because Luciana made it outside. You took the phone off her and broke it before dragging her back inside."

"Yeah? She made it all the way out there and didn't scream for help?"

"You got to her before she could."

"Why would I snap the keys off in the ignition of the van?"

"You broke the keys because the van was stolen and you had use of the victim's car."

"Come on, that doesn't even make sense. What would be the point? Even if I was using the victim's car, what reason would I have to break off the key?"

"Because it was an accident."

"An accident? Do you know anybody who's ever accidently done that?" Feldman shakes his head. "You have all the answers, don't you. Doesn't matter that they don't make sense. The craziest thing of all is that you think I'm the crazy one."

Landry jumps to his feet, frustrated that a man like this can label him anything, let alone *crazy*. He moves quickly across the room, wanting to strike him hard with the shotgun, but when he takes aim and Feldman twists away he realizes this sick son of a bitch probably isn't that far off in his assessment. Of course he's crazy. No sane police detective would have brought a suspect out here with the pretense of a trial. He lowers the gun and steps back. Feldman turns toward him and opens his eyes, his body relaxing with relief.

"The cars don't make sense," Feldman says. "How can my car have been there, Luciana's disappear, and me also having used the van? How can I have stolen Luciana's car, and driven mine away at the same time?"

"Because your car wasn't there."

"It was. I was driving it."

"No. You left your car near your wife's house. You then stole a van. You drove to Luciana's house and for some reason you snapped the keys in the ignition. You then stole her car. You drove to Kathy's house and killed her. Then you drove back to your car and swapped them back over. Then you abducted your wife." He sucks in another breath of cigarette smoke. *Good, sweet smoke. Help me get through this.* "Why did you keep her breast?"

"I'm innocent," Feldman says.

The pieces all fit together nicely without worrying about Feldman being innocent. The stake in Feldman's home. The severed breast. The bloody clothes. The letter he wrote. The cuts and bruises on his skin. His ramblings during their interview. His lying at the start of the evening. The bloodstained notepad with his name on it. Kidnapping his wife. What more does he need?

Nothing. He already has more than any jury would need to convict.

*Are you sure? Are you really that sure? Or are the pills fucking with you?*

He flicks his cigarette butt toward the fireplace, only managing to get half the distance required. He pulls out the packet and lights another. He's sick of this. He wants to go home. Wants to retire. Wants never to have heard of Charlie Feldman. "I want to hear it in your own words."

"Hear what?"

He sucks in a deep breath. The air is cold and tastes of mildew and cigarette smoke. "Just tell me the truth. Things'll be easier on both of us. We can get this over with."

"I've been telling you the truth."

"Which one of them did it to you, Feldman? Which woman was the lucky one to give you that nice bruise on your forehead?"

"Look, Detective, what you're doing is crazy. Think about it. You've brought me—"

"Shut up, Feldman," he says.

"Just think about what—"

"Are you deaf? The comic deaf man? Is that it?"

Jesus, why is he even bothering looking for a confession? He ought to just do what he came out here to do. Go home. Get drunk. Sleep it off. Get drunk again in the morning. Get drunk every morning between now and the end. Staying drunk might turn all of this into a very bad dream.

"What about the door to my house?" Feldman asks. "You know somebody broke in. You know somebody trashed my room. Why would I cut her breast off and leave it on my bed? Why would I let you inside knowing that? If I was going to kill somebody I'd hide all the evidence."

"I'm the one who broke into your house, Feldman."

Feldman cocks his head and pulls back a little. "What? You did all that?"

"I broke in last night. Your house was fine. You must have come back after then and done all that damage. And you wanted a souvenir, Feldman. Your type always does. And your type is always so Goddamn cocky you never think we're going to show up."

"Why would I trash my own house?"

"Because you knew we would find you. You trashed it in an

effort to draw attention away from yourself. You think by saying all this nonsense it diverts suspicion away from you. That's
what you were counting on if you ever got caught. Come on,
Feldman, I'm getting sick and tired of your bullshit."

"You're saying—"

"Here's what I know, Feldman. I know you've lied to me.
You told me you didn't know these two women when you did.
You told me you weren't at their homes when you were. You
have a stake similar to the kind used on them. You have a
body part in your house. Your clothes were covered in blood.
You admitted that you kidnapped your wife. Your name and
phone number was found on a notepad next to one of the
victims. Only they weren't victims, were they, Feldman? They
deserved it. They mocked you or rejected you or looked at you
funny. Or did they simply forget to smile when you stood in
line behind them at the supermarket?"

"It doesn't matter, does it?"

"What?"

"You keep saying you'll hear me out, but you won't. You
have your mind made up."

"I said I'd hear you out, and I have. I didn't say I was going
to believe whatever bullshit you came up with."

"I'm not going to confess to something I didn't do," Feldman says, "and that's what you want to hear, isn't it, so you
don't have to feel so guilty about shooting me. It's not going
to happen. I didn't hurt those women. My wife is safe. If you're
waiting for me to tell you what you want to hear, then you're
wasting your time. I'm not playing your game anymore. You
may as well go ahead and do whatever it is you came out here
to do."

"Fair enough," he says. He stands up and points the shotgun
at Feldman. *Think, Goddamn it, think. You're a police officer,*

*your job is to uphold the law. Is that what you're doing? It is? Well, why don't you take a look at yourself?*

Keeping the shotgun level he moves to the door and slides it open. The cold wind sweeps into the cabin, chilling Landry to the bone. It chills his mind too, and in these few frozen seconds he hates himself for what he's going to do before the night is over.

No. No, no, no. He's gone through this already, he's gone through this and justified it.

*Sure you've justified it. But you're hiding something too, aren't you? The change of clothes. The Bible. You knew where tonight was always going to go. It's not that you came out here with no plan. You came out here with a bad one.*

He looks over at Feldman. The anger is starting to return, but not all of it is directed at this murderer, yet to direct some of it at himself is detrimental. He hates Feldman. He hates Feldman because all of this is his fault. He hates Feldman for forcing him to do this.

Worst of all, he hates himself.

# CHAPTER TWENTY-FIVE

There's no blood on my chair or on any of the walls or on the pine-needle stained glass door, so maybe Landry was telling the truth when he said he hasn't been out here since finding the dead girl in the bathtub. Or maybe he's lying and isn't in the habit of shooting people indoors. Things would be easier for him if he took me for a walk in the woods.

"You're going to feel empty when Cyris is found," I say, looking up at him. "You'll never be able to forgive yourself for killing an innocent man. Will you turn yourself in when that happens?"

He doesn't answer me, just stands next to the door with both hands on the shotgun. The look on his face suggests he doesn't want to be out here either. The gun reminds me that I'm just a homicide in progress, tomorrow's statistic, I'll be a story in the news. Read all about me. My heart is pumping so loudly I can barely hear the rain. My stomach is so weak the fluids inside have created a cesspool of fear that makes me want to throw up and soil myself at the same time.

I'm going to die.

It's the worst knowledge anybody can ever have, even though we know it all our lives. We just don't know when— but when you do know when it's a lot worse. Especially when that time is only a few minutes away.

"Come on, Feldman. It's time to go," he says, and he's the one who sounds as if he's been defeated.

I try to get to my feet, but the angle of the chair and the way I'm buried in it makes things difficult, as do the handcuffs. The springs in the chair cut into me as I wiggle forward. I fall back into the chair on the first attempt, and I look up at Landry expecting him to either be laughing, or be mad, but he's neither. He's just staring at me the way people stare at movie credits they're not really reading. When I finally get to my feet I'm puffing, but it's too cold in here to sweat. He gestures me toward the door where I pause looking out at what Mother Nature has to offer me on my final night, which isn't much. The wind is racing in and gripping us both tightly. My legs are shaking from fear and cold and my teeth are starting to chatter.

"No jacket?" I ask.

"I'm sure you can survive without one."

"I thought I was supposed to be the funny one."

He thinks about what he's just said, then shakes his head. "I wasn't trying to be funny."

"Can I at least make an appeal?"

"Yes."

"Then I want to say—"

"Appeal denied," he says. He reaches into his pocket for his cigarettes. He offers me one.

I didn't say it before, but I say it now. "Those things will kill you."

He smirks at my comment, then slowly shakes his head. "Goddamn it, Feldman, don't you ever shut up?"

"I can't help it," I hear myself saying, and I really can't. "But I guess now's as good a time as any to try one."

He tosses me a cigarette and I hurt my wrists plucking it from the air. I'll smoke the whole lot if it will buy me some time. "Light?"

He throws the lighter. This guy is taking no chances. He's not going to get anywhere near me. Early in the evening I was intimidated by his authority. Now it's the gun that demands my respect. I hold the cigarette tightly between my lips, raise the blue lighter, fumble with the catch, then light the end. The flame works, but the cigarette doesn't.

"You need to breathe in," he says, and he almost sounds compassionate, as if teaching a five-year-old how to ride a bike. Or a five-year-old how to smoke.

I don't know exactly what to expect, but my mouth is quickly filled with thick smoke. It catches in my throat as if I've just swallowed a wad of tissues. I start gagging. Smoke is drawn into my lungs where it burns them, and smoke and snot gush from my nose. The cigarette falls from my mouth, but clings to my lower lip. I brush it onto the ground. A small tentacle of smoke whispers from the end.

Landry is motionless, watching me with that same credit-rolling emptiness in his eyes that suggests nobody is home. Nothing here, it seems, amuses or angers him. He looks lost.

"You don't have to do this," I tell him.

"I'm almost sorry I have to kill you."

"*You're* sorry?"

Suddenly he seems to snap out of whatever daze he's in.

"I was right about you, Feldman. You're a real smart-ass." He waves the gun at me. "Now tidy up that mess."

I pick up the cigarette and flick it toward the fireplace. I pause, trying to think of an action or a word that will help me, but he pushes me onto the small porch by jabbing me with the shotgun. I put one foot forward and start walking. When I step down onto the mud it feels like I'm being acupunctured with needles that have been kept in the freezer overnight. The cold wind drives those needles deep into my flesh. My wet clothes flap against my skin. It's the coldest I've ever been in my life, and the realization I will never be warm again makes me want to cry, but I hang on to those tears. I don't want Landry to see them. Fuck him.

He orders me forward by prodding me again then turns on the flashlight and tosses it to me. I miss the catch, and have to stoop down to pick it up. I think of it as a weapon. A useless one, but a weapon all the same. He directs me into the belt of trees. Damn trees. I've seen more trees this week than in my entire life. I can't see exactly where I'm supposed to be heading.

"Stop stalling, Feldman, I'm sure you can find a path in there."

I point the flashlight into the inky blackness, spotlighting branches and leaves, but not a whole lot more—certainly no dirt path. I head forward anyway, figuring Landry will stop me if I'm too far off the track. I step between a couple of birch trees, struggling to cover my face from the branches that claw at me like dirty fingers. I manage two steps before becoming lost. Can't see the forest for the trees. Well, in this case I can't see the forest for the dark. The ground turns from mud to hard-packed dirt and roots. I move the flashlight around and start to walk slower, not to preserve time, but in order to concentrate on each footstep.

"You've got the wrong man, Landry."

"I doubt that."

"Shouldn't you at least hold off killing me?"

"I'm a busy man."

"You could just tie me up. At least until you have a few more facts."

"I've all the facts I need."

"You're wrong. Tie me up and when you find you're wrong I promise not to tell anybody." I really do promise it. The river nearby is getting louder. "Think about what you're doing."

"I am thinking. I'm thinking about your next victim."

I don't know how far we've come. Obviously Landry doesn't want my body found near the cabin. I'm thinking he has a nice location out here for me. Maybe a big hole. The colder I get the more I lose any comprehension of time. It could have been ten minutes now. Or fifteen. We could have walked a couple of miles. Kathy told me that time and distance slip away when you're being marched through a bunch of trees toward your death. Well, she was right.

"I was right about a lot of things, wasn't I, Charlie?" Kathy asks, and she's walking along with me now, gliding easily through the trees. She's wearing shoes that stay clean. It's a neat trick.

"You were right," I admit, keeping my voice low so Landry doesn't hear me. She starts to nod.

"Do you remember what I told you?" she asks.

I remember. "You told me you owed me everything. We were heading away from Luciana's house. It couldn't have been long before she died."

"Oh, it wasn't that quick, Charlie. You dropped me off home before she died. Do you remember what we were discussing?"

"We were heading toward your house, we were talking about going to the police. I remember driving past the pasture and you pointing out the black van parked opposite. Seeing it gave me the creeps. We both looked toward the trees as we went by."

"Dalí's trees," she says.

"Dalí's trees."

"What the hell are you on about?" Landry asks, but I don't answer. I keep walking, scraping my hands and arms on the branches, shivering hard.

My mind tries drifting to a time where the world was safe and we didn't know that Evil was a time bomb waiting for us. Then it drifts far enough so I'm no longer walking through the trees, but turning left into Tranquility Drive and Kathy is no longer a ghost, but flesh and blood that was warm to touch. Flesh and blood that wore the same clothes she was attacked in, flesh and blood that hadn't showered. All I knew about Tranquility Drive was I couldn't afford to live there.

Looking at her house, I knew Kathy was rich. That was fine by me. The house was a two-storey place, a tad more mansion than town house. Maybe ten years old. Dozens of shrubs dotted the front section and because of the lingering summer there were still lots of flowers in bloom. At that time of night they were black flowers. The trees were black too. Like the birds sitting in them.

This is the house I wanted to live in, with Kathy. All my life I had imagined backing out of my driveway into a neighborhood where Mercedes cars littered the street like cheap Toyotas. Kathy was the woman I wanted to be kissing goodbye as I left for work in the morning on my way to being a brain surgeon or an astronaut instead of an underpaid high school teacher who is the enemy of dysfunctional teenagers. Only it wasn't really Kathy I wanted to be kissing goodbye to, it was Jo, but Jo was no longer around.

I walked her inside. She never did get hold of her husband.

"He was off screwing some bimbo," her ghost says, "and I told you he would be back at some point for some fresh clothes before work. You were glad to hear I was having marital difficulties."

"Yeah, sorry about that," I say, but something about it bugs me. The same something that bugged me when I read the newspaper this morning.

"It wasn't your fault. You helped me check the house and it was nearly five o'clock when I walked you outside. I wrote your name and number down. You left then, and I was dead."

"You weren't dead."

"And you're splitting hairs."

I walked backward down the driveway to my car, watching her watching me. We waved then she stepped inside. I heard the door lock and I would never again see her alive. I climbed into my car. I was yawning and dozing, just driving along with the windows down and the breeze coming through, and I had this feeling of normality that made me feel ill. When I drove past the pasture I already had an expectation of what I would see—Cyris stalking through the grass toward the road.

What I saw was worse. When I drove past the pasture . . .

"The van was gone," Kathy finishes, and then she's gone too.

I break between two trees and see the flashing movement of the river flowing quickly over and around large round boulders, the water white and violent. The rain is hard here, unsheltered by the trees. Huge drops pluck the dirt next to the river, sending out small splashes of mud. It hammers on my head and shoulders and drives those angry needles of ice deeper into my soul. Landry's footsteps are loud behind me, and each time I wonder if I will hear another. It would have been warmer had he just shot me back at the cabin. All this would be over and I wouldn't have to be scared or talk to ghosts.

"Hold it there," Landry says. I stop walking and study the landscape. Black trees, black ground, black water, black sky. This is what color the end must be. "Turn around slowly."

I turn. The rain lands on his *Kiss the Cook* cap and runs off the brim. Does he have the apron to match? I can't stop shaking. Water runs down my face. I don't bother wiping it from my eyes. "Nice place," I say, quietly. Too cold to be loud. Too scared to be funny.

He comes forward. "We're nearly there, you know?"

"Where?"

"The end of the line. You want to know how I know about this place? Not about the cabin, you already know that, but about this place right here."

"You walked the crime scene?"

"Yeah, but we wouldn't have come this far. Only we had to. Because the girl in the bathtub wasn't our man's first victim. She was his second. He'd killed his first years ago. This land had been in his family for generations. He led us here. We found his first in the caves behind you."

I don't like the idea of taking my eyes off the weapon, but I follow his gaze and aim the flashlight where he's pointing. The beam is swallowed up by the mouth of a cave that's been there forever.

"Holes in there are so deep you can drop a stone and never hear it land."

"And a body?" I ask.

"It took us two days to find her and that was only because we were looking. Nobody will ever look for you. Not out here. Right now you have a choice. Do you want to meet your maker with a clear conscience or a guilty one?"

He takes aim. I can hear my heart beating, my stomach rumbling. My jaw throbs. My neck aches. I can hear the river and the rain. My bowels are clenching. My bladder is trying to let itself go. I feel like I want to yawn, scream, run, do a thousand push-ups. I suddenly have all this energy that deserves to have a chance of release. I deserve the chance to be a better person, to be somebody who will be missed.

And even though I knew he was bringing me out here to die, I never knew it, not really, I always thought something would happen. Some kind of intervention, divine or otherwise. I picture my cold, dead body lying on this cold, dead ground, and that's exactly what's going to happen in five or ten seconds. Jo will go to the police and maybe they'll figure out what happened to me, or maybe they won't. In which case I'll have a funeral with an empty coffin. I want people to say they miss me. I want a community in shock. I want the kids I teach to be disappointed I can teach them no more.

I think about my parents. About my friends. This is going to be hard on them.

I think of Jo and wish I could tell her how I feel about her. I wish I could say I regret what happened last night, that I regret what happened six months ago.

I'm standing in the rain beneath a storm-clouded sky, among the trees and the mud and the rocks, and this is no place to die.

I point the flashlight at his face, but the bright light doesn't blind him.

"Goddamn you, Feldman. And God forgive me."

I close my eyes. "Go to hell," I tell him. I can feel my legs giving way. It'll be a race between me collapsing and him shooting me.

He pulls the trigger and the gunshot is like thunder and I start to scream.

# CHAPTER TWENTY-SIX

The wet ground vibrates waves of cold into my spine as I lie on my back, looking up at the dark clouds as water flicks into my eyes. Death has chilled me. I can hear myself screaming. I clutch my hands to my chest and can feel the blood soaking upward, warm blood. It oozes between my fingers like water and slips down the sides of my chest like water, and several seconds later I realize it actually *is* water, and at the same moment I realize it isn't me screaming. I sit up and point the flashlight ahead of me. Landry is swaying back and forth, trying to keep his balance. The shotgun is in his right hand, the barrel pointing to the ground. His left hand is reaching around to the back of his head. Something moves behind him.

Or someone.

I dig my feet and hands into the slippery ground and push upward. I stand and run as hard as I can at Landry. He sees me, raises the gun, and pulls the trigger. My eyes flare red as the blood I'm about to lose surges past my brain, but the gun only clicks because it hasn't followed the sound of a double crunch. That means even though there's still ammo in the shotgun there's no shell in the chamber—I've seen enough movies to know this. So nothing happens except this small clicking noise, which is the sweetest sound in the whole world. I hit him at full speed, first lowering my head and shoulder to make the most of the impact. I connect with his chest; the flashlight pops from my hands as the gun pops from his. My momentum drives him into a tree. His head snaps back into it.

I push myself away. The flashlight shines in my eyes for a few seconds before moving over to Landry. He looks totally out of it. If he's really lucky I won't turn the shotgun on him. If he's really lucky we won't leave him out here to freeze to death.

"I've never been so happy to see you," I say, turning toward Jo.

"Don't get happy yet," she says, crunching the shotgun and pointing it at me. It wobbles in the air as she tries to control it. She's never held a shotgun before, but the mechanics are simple enough to figure out—pump, point, and shoot. She bends down and picks up the flashlight, which was sitting next to the rock she hit Landry with. She moves the beam onto my face, making it difficult for me to see her. I want to hug her, but I can't because of the handcuffs. And she'd probably shoot me.

She turns the flashlight back to Landry. Blood is running down the side of his neck and down the left side of his forehead. He's trying to lift a hand up to his head, but it keeps flopping back down to his side.

"We need to help him," she says.

"Do we?"

"Who is he?" she asks.

"His name is Detective Inspector Landry," I say, "and Detective Inspector is a man who has finally seen too much in this world and wanted to put it right. Except in this case he got it all wrong."

Landry sags a little more, tips onto his side, and ends up with his face in the dirt. I don't know how calm I'm sounding, but Jo is looking at me as if I'm the one who's got it all wrong. Perhaps I sound flippant, even dismissive. Yeah, just another trip into the woods. Yeah, just another psycho.

"He must have been really sure you did it to have brought you out here," she says.

"Is there something you want to ask me?"

"Tell me again that you're innocent."

"I'm innocent."

"Tell me why Detective Inspector Landry didn't think so."

"Because he's a madman," I say. I look down at him. He looks blankly back at me, still trying to hold on to consciousness. Water and mud are splashing over his cheeks.

"Thanks for following," I say, looking back to Jo. "And thanks for saving my life. How did you get free?"

"Does it matter? You're just lucky I decided to follow you to the police station."

"Some police station," I say, looking around.

"Lucky I followed anyway, huh? You'd be dead right now if I hadn't. It was pretty obvious what was going on. Problem is I didn't have my phone. I had no choice but to follow."

"You had a choice," I tell her.

"Don't make me regret it. Come on, let's get him onto his feet before he ends up dying out here and then I'm in the same situation you thought you were in."

The gun moves around in her hands; she's either shaking from the cold or from the shock of saving my life. I check

Landry's pocket where I saw him put the keys. So far he's had nothing to say since being struck twice in the head. I like him this way.

The lock seems smaller than the key as I try to work the handcuffs. My hands are shaking so much that the tip of the key keeps chattering against the bracelet. Jo isn't offering to help. I slide the key around until finally it fits into place. Then I go through the same drama with the second bracelet. When I'm free I snap them onto Landry's wrists. He doesn't complain. He's starting to groan. He folds his hands over the top of his head. He seems to have forgotten where he is, either that or he doesn't care anymore. He stares past me at the cave where it took a team of people two days to find a dead girl. I put the keys into my pocket.

"We need to get him some help," Jo says.

"This guy just tried to kill me. I'm not taking him anywhere."

"We're taking him to a hospital, Charlie, and then we're going to the police."

I look at her face and then at the gun and I like this combination a hell of a lot better than the last one. "I'll be charged with murder."

"If you're innocent you won't be. Anyway what sort of murderer would bring a policeman to a hospital under these circumstances?"

"So you believe me."

"Let's just say I'm more open to strange things happening."

"Glad you're on my side," I say.

"I'm not, but if we leave him here he'll die."

Then we should leave him here. I start to help him to his feet, but his legs are like jelly. He can't take any of his own weight and I can't take all of it. I'm weak from the cold and it's going to be hell carrying him back to the cabin. If he dies on the way I'll dump him where he lands and hope Jo doesn't shoot me for it.

"You're sure you don't want to carry him?" I ask.

Jo doesn't answer.

"Jo?" I hoist Landry onto my shoulders. I stagger at first, trying not to slip across the wet ground. My thighs start to burn. Landry has to be at least ninety kilograms. If lifting him is this hard, carrying him will be impossible. It's time to revisit this whole idea. Landry made his bed, he can sleep in it. It's not my fault the sleeping will be in the middle of the woods.

"I'm not sure I can do this," I say, speaking louder as I turn around.

"You've got that right, partner," the tall figure says. He's wearing black clothing, has dirty skin, long black hair, a scraggly beard, bushy sideburns, and he's standing next to Jo.

This is the man who I thought I had killed.

This is the monster in a world that, according to Jo, doesn't have monsters.

Jo doesn't have the gun anymore. Instead now it's pointing at her.

# CHAPTER TWENTY-SEVEN

Watching, watching, Cyris is waiting and watching, yeah, yeah, things are working out well, really well, and the rain keeps on falling in the forest, but he doesn't mind the rain, he loves the rain, the rain is very cool, except for when it's not. He thinks of a time when he went swimming and saw a dog drown, his dog, the damn thing was old and couldn't swim worth a damn, but she sure could sink like a motherfucker. Thinking of the wet fur makes him start to itch. He can't stop wondering what color the inside of his soul would be—then wonders if he has one at all. Would it be blue or gray?

He thinks about how that wet dog felt beneath his fingers as he held it down. If the dog could talk it would tell him to look out for other dogs because sometimes they can be rabid, sometimes they can really tear you apart. Thinking of the wet dog reminds him that it's raining. He hates the rain. He's wet and he's hungry, but this doesn't worry him because he's entertained, yeah, yeah, entertained by this hilarity, because all of this is nothing but funny. It wasn't supposed to be, it was supposed to be simple, nice and easy, and it has become nothing but. People say if you don't laugh you'd cry. In his case he likes to laugh and make other people cry. Then he likes to do worse to them. The shotgun is in his hands and it has a nice weight too, what he used to think of back in the army as a *life-ending weight*. Whether he uses it or not is up to the weatherman. Everything is up to the weatherman and that makes Cyris jealous. It makes him angry because the ability to choose who lives and dies should be up to him.

Killing out here where nobody can see him is the perfect way to end all of this, but it's also a cheap way. His mind races for another solution, a solution that equals gain, a solution that isn't so cheap or slippery, and if it weren't for the Goddamn pain and medication that's twisting his thoughts every which way, he'd be able to figure it out. He's lucky that he at least recognizes the fact he's not himself. Hell, he hasn't even thought of that stupid dog in ten years. He hasn't been right since that son of a bitch stabbed him the other night.

He's aware he's just stood on a hedgehog, but it wasn't really his fault.

Not really, not when it's so dark out here.

He starts to laugh. Stupid hedgehog. Stupid thing deserved to die.

He's angry. He can't help it. The hedgehog was innocent, but maybe it died happy, so he starts to laugh again. He laughs and starts to think of the two dead women. He thinks back to Monday morning and things were going fine, so fine, and the night was nicer than this, there was no rain and plenty of night, plenty that couldn't go wrong, but seemed to anyway, and Monday came before the drugs could take away the pain

of it all. Two pills a day became two an hour, then he started
to lose track, then he broke into his wife's morphine supply,
which is something he swore he'd never do. He also found
some stuff a buddy of his gave him years ago, stuff they used to
refer to as "*the good shit*" back in the day. So there's that, the
morphine, and whatever the hell else he's been able to get his
hands on. They're damaging his mind, no doubt there. He pictures his mind working like a washing machine, the thoughts
tumbling, no, *spinning*—it's the dryer that tumbles—and then
Charlie Feldman came along and ruined everything. Things
will work out in the end. That's not true of everything, but
it will be true of this. He's proving that. Right now things
couldn't really be any better. It would be better if he could
remember what star sign he is and this bothers him more than
anything else. His stomach hurts too. Cancer?

No. Gemini.

*You are in control*, he tells himself, *you are in control, buddy,
so now what?* He counts one policeman here who needs to die
so maybe he ought to start there because there's no use for the
policeman. In fact the exact opposite is true because there
are several uses for a dead policeman. He looks at Charlie
and he looks at the woman and he smiles his smile of relief.
Everything's under control, everything's going to work out
fine, but he should never have doubted that, and he never
will doubt it again, and his stomach is throbbing, and he can
feel the duct tape across his skin and the duct tape is gray,
but it's red too because of the blood. Thinking about things
he shouldn't doubt lead to him thinking of things he should
do—which immediately makes him think of all the drugs he's
taking. Some would say it's a miracle he's even functioning.
He doesn't believe in miracles.

He tightens his grip on the shotgun. He uses it to push the

woman toward Feldman. He doesn't know the brand of the shotgun and doesn't care. It could be Russian or American, but they all do the same thing at this range. He doesn't pull the trigger because he wants to gain something, though he doesn't know what it is, even though a few minutes ago he did. It came back to him when he read the piece of paper in his pocket. On that paper is the reason he's doing all of this. He wrote it down when he figured out his thoughts aren't what they ought to be. He wrote it on Monday afternoon. He wants to get it out and read it, but the rain will soak it. He needs to think. He needs to remember. Having ink running down his fingers won't help at all.

He covers the three people with the shotgun and the police-man doesn't look that healthy. Perhaps the painkillers Cyris has been taking would help the policeman, but Cyris only wants to help himself, and there's not enough to go around. He keeps trying to tell himself to think things through, to think things through, to think about a gain, a goal, and a small voice in his mind tells him to look at the note, but then it comes to him anyway—he's doing this for the money. Isn't that why people do anything? Love and money. Well, he sure loves getting paid.

He needs to focus on that right now.

"For the money," he shouts, and he thinks that if he keeps saying it out loud more often, it'll stick with him. That, or he should stop taking the drugs. He should write that one down too.

The cop, Feldman, his bitch wife—they're all staring up at him. The bitch wife is a surprise. He learned about her when he went through Feldman's house, but he wasn't expecting her to be helping him. When he arrived at Feldman's tonight, he was in time to see the man arrested. Before he could start following the guy, another car pulled out from the curb and began following them first. So he followed the follower. It turned out to be the same woman in the photos in Feldman's house.

They're waiting for him to say something else, and he guesses his comment is out of context for them. He should have shouted *You fucked up my plans*. Actually, that's not bad. He opens his mouth to say that and cold air rushes down his throat and for a few seconds his mind starts to focus. He has to concentrate now so he can form the words, but maybe he ought to just shoot everybody instead.

# CHAPTER TWENTY-EIGHT

Cold rain. Cold wind. One psycho with a gun. Then another psycho with a gun.

Is there something here I'm missing?

"You fucked up my plans!" Cyris shouts, which at least makes more sense than his *For the money* comment a few seconds earlier.

I don't answer him. Nor does Jo. I don't even look at Landry to see what he's doing. Probably not getting ready to apologize, I imagine.

"You remember me, part . . . partner?" Cyris asks, moving his aim from Jo to me.

I remember everything while saying nothing.

"What a show," he says. "I would clap, but my hands are blue."

He looks at the man I'm carrying and all I can think about are his blue hands. He must mean they're cold. I guess.

"Caught yourself a pig?" he asks.

Landry starts to moan.

"Put . . . down, put him down, down, down," Cyris says.

I get the point, but I spend a few seconds wondering if I could use Landry as a shield and just run straight at Cyris. I was somewhat successful the other night. Might be the same tonight. Mind reading must be one of his new abilities, because he says "Don't even think about it." Then he points the shotgun at Jo.

I crouch and hoist Landry over my head so he lands in front of me, my lower back protesting at the effort. I don't really try to be gentle, but I make sure he doesn't land on his head. He might come in useful. I've gone from thinking I was going to die, to surviving, to thinking I'm going to die again. If I had to sum it up, I'd say it's a pretty shitty feeling.

I stand up, but don't back away. Instead I slowly move toward Jo. Cyris doesn't ask me to stop. He seems to be enjoying himself. Why wouldn't he? I'm the only guy out here tonight who hasn't actually been armed.

When I'm next to Jo he scampers over to the cop and kneels next to him.

"Funny, isn't it?" he says to Landry. "Funny hah, hah, funny you brought him out here into the summer, funny because you forgot me, forgot all about me."

"Cyris," Landry says, and it's all he can manage, but he says it with a gravelly voice and with conviction, like it's an accusation.

Jo looks over at me and I can see a whole bunch of things in her eyes. Confusion, sure, there's plenty of that, and regret too. Regret for not believing me. Sure, she came along for the ride because I dragged her, sure she met me halfway in the Real World of what's real and what's make believe, but if she had committed to me, if she had just taken my hand and helped, then things could be different right now. Could be better. Could be worse. I don't know. Just different. So there's the confusion and regret, but there's also regret for hitting Landry so hard because around now he could have been helping us. I feel like she's just forgiven me, but it will last only until she dies alongside me, which, I figure, will be in only a few seconds. I hope she can forgive me for that too. She aims the flashlight at Landry's eyes. They're red. He doesn't look well at all.

Cyris laughs again, then raises his gun, tracks the barrel up and down Landry's body, and hovers it over his leg. He narrows the distance, resting the barrel on Landry's right ankle.

"Pick a limb, pick one, a limb, a limb."

Landry tries to pull his leg away, but Cyris stands on his foot, then repositions the gun so it touches the policeman's head. Landry stops moving. The rain is pouring heavily down in our little neck of the woods and small droplets of mud splash onto Landry's face. They look like chocolate tears. Cyris moves the gun a few inches away from Landry's head and fires it into the ground.

None of us are expecting the shot, except Cyris, so Cyris is the only one who doesn't jump. The mouth of the cave seems to swallow a lot of it, but the sound is still enough to feel like my ears are going to start bleeding. Landry starts rolling around, the handcuffs making it difficult for him to push his hands against his ears. He can manage to cover only one ear. The other he pushes into the ground, but to his credit he doesn't make any sound.

But that's all about to change. Cyris pumps the shotgun and pushes the barrel into Landry's leg right behind the kneecap.

"Wait," I shout out, which is stupid because I don't owe

Landry anything, but at the same time I can't stand here and watch him get taken apart.

Cyris doesn't wait. This time when he pulls the trigger, Landry starts screaming right away. The gunshot and his pain echo around us, the gunshot is high-pitched and slowly starts to fade, but the screaming doesn't. The screaming sounds like it could go on forever. Landry tries to sit up, tries bringing his knee into his belly so he can curl his arms around his leg, but the leg won't bend because the knee joint is a pile of raw nerves and slivers of bone. I can't help it, but I stagger back, crouch over, and start to gag. Jo is doing the same thing.

Landry's concussion has become the least of his worries.

His fate is the least of ours.

Cyris says something, but I can't hear. The rain steals away his words and my ears are ringing from the gunshot and, aside from that, Landry is still screaming, still pushing his hands against his wounded leg. I feel bad for him. Bad that he's seen so much in his life and has now become victim to it. He's become victim to his own anger, but it's his anger that brought us all out here, so sure, I feel sorry for the guy—but I hate him even more than I feel sorry for him. His screams grate at my eardrums. I wish Cyris would just finish him off. He's going to—there's no way any of us is getting out of here alive—so the best we can hope for is a quick death. If anybody wants to be heard over Landry's screams, they're going to need to yell at the top of their lungs.

Cyris seems to realize this and he walks over. I stop gagging. So does Jo.

"Who's next? Which one of you isn't really real? Huh? I want to know."

God, he's crazier than I thought. "Leave her out of it," I shout.

"Why? She's the meat and potatoes," Cyris says.

He moves toward Landry, walking backward so he can keep his eyes on us.

I look at Jo and she looks back. "I'm sorry," I say. It doesn't seem enough to offer her, but it's all I have. I reach out for her hand. She takes it. Her hand is cold and it's the first time we've held hands in a long time, not just six months, but longer than that.

"I figured you would be," she says. "For what it's worth, I'm sorry too. It doesn't help, though, does it?"

Cyris returns his attention to the detective. I take the flashlight from Jo and point it into the cave. We could attempt an escape through there, but soon the batteries would die and we would become lost, navigating our way through the darkness either deeper into the earth or simply in circles around it. Behind us is only a bank of rocks and then the river stretching away. Ahead of us one lunatic looking down at another lunatic. Further to the right is the same path we followed, but there's no way we could run through there keeping ahead of the shotgun.

It's the river or nothing.

Though it's not really nothing. It's the river, or get shot where we're standing.

Hell, chances are we get shot going for the river anyway. But it's something.

Landry's movements have slowed down, and finally, thank God, his screams die off. He's lying on his side, attempting to hold his wounded knee with blood-covered hands. He holds his palms against it, trying to push everything back together, trying to help it heal with a grim determination that is about two surgeons and a lot of medical instruments short of being any good. He looks over at us and in his agony I can see him pleading for help. I can't help him. He has dug his own grave and I hate him for putting us in there with him. His face and clothes are saturated in blood. There's so much the rain can't even start to move it.

Cyris points the shotgun at him and at the same time starts grinding his heel into the wounded knee. Landry's eyes roll back in his head, but he keeps thrashing around, unable to pass out. I'm too afraid to move, too scared to take my eyes from this grisly display, too much of a coward to try and help. Jo's grip on my hand tightens.

I step back, taking Jo with me.

Cyris looks over and yells something. It's indistinguishable over the loud rain, so heavy now it almost feels like hail. He points the gun at us, his mind-reading skills on full display here. Though it's not that great a trick because trying to run is the only option worth looking at. He steps over Landry toward us. We back away, getting closer to the river. We're going to have to jump for it. We're going to have to climb into the freezing cold water and do whatever we can to avoid rocks and drowning and pneumonia and gunshots. I don't know if Jo has come up with the same plan. I know she hates water and I know she can't swim. I also know she isn't bulletproof. What she needs to do is choose one plan over the other, and really it can be simplified down to two choices: dying right now, or perhaps dying on our way into the water, or perhaps dying a minute or two down the line. Living is turning out to be a hell of a lot of work and the alternative is starting to look tempting. Giving up would sure be easier.

Cyris is grinning because that's what guys like him do. The gun sways slightly as the wind pushes at him. The shotgun means he doesn't need to be accurate—he can fire in our general direction and still nail us. I can't see any way that he won't pull the trigger before we're in the water. I look down at Landry. He's starting to move, but barely. But he's looking up at me. The look on his face has changed. He's no longer wearing the look of a man who is desperate for help. In fact it's the opposite. He's wearing the face of a man who's angry. His jaw is clenched. He stares at me, and then he nods. A single nod that conveys his apology and an instruction. Like Cyris, he knows what I'm planning.

I nod back at him, knowing what it is he's about to do.

He's about to try and repent.

Cyris pumps the shotgun and we get ready to jump.

# CHAPTER TWENTY-NINE

Well, fuck it. So this is the way it's going to be. The cancer . . .
Christ, none of it even matters in the end. Coffin shopping
and picking out a suit—it's no longer his problem. This is
the moment of truth. The moment where he gets to meet his
maker and ask him the big question—what the fuck?

The pain in Landry's leg is so raw, so intense, that at this
point he's actually welcoming death. Can't be worse than this.
His throat is burning from all the screaming, it feels like he's
swallowed gasoline with a Zippo chaser. The gunfire has left
a high-pitched whine in his ears, which has eaten through to
the core of his brain and is now eating its way back out. He
can feel his heart slowing down. He's losing it.

He doesn't want to die. He's made the biggest mistake of his
life by coming out here tonight, and he's going to pay for it in
the biggest way possible. There is no going back. No do-overs.
This is far from the justice he pictured hours ago, but in a way

it's justice nonetheless. He came out here with the thought that he was doing humanity a service. All he was doing was making a mockery of everything he believed in.

What a mistake.

How can he have been so stupid?

The cancer? The pills?

No. That's just a bullshit excuse. It was the anger. That's what made him stupid. He's angry at the city because the Christchurch he grew up in isn't the same Christchurch he's been living in for the last five or ten years, and it's certainly a far cry from the Christchurch he's going to die in. So yeah, he's angry—he's angry because he has to see the depravity others don't have to see. He got to see the dirty mechanics of the world, and now he's gotten caught up in the gears.

He has wasted the last week of his life. He's spent it dying when he should have focused on living. Of course none of that matters now, not out here, not in this shithole of a forest where years ago one of God's assholes brought a woman out here to die, only to do it again a few years later.

His eyes are filling with blood. At least that's what he thinks is happening. Maybe it's the blow to the head he took earlier. Maybe the fall. There are shapes moving in front of him, and these shapes turn as red as the landscape he sees them moving across. Everything is wet. The gunshot wound isn't enough to kill him, but the blood loss is. Trained paramedics couldn't save him now. There's no hope. Not for him. Maybe for Feldman and the girl.

He digs his fingers into the damp ground and twists himself toward Cyris. His killer is facing Feldman and the woman, the shotgun firmly in his hands. Landry uses his arms and his good leg to crawl forward. He starts to close the distance.

One of those shapes in the red landscape is Charlie. He

grins. He guesses he's on a first-name basis with the guy, now that he's about to save his life. When he wanted to kill him, it was Feldman. Now it's Charlie. He nods at Charlie, and Charlie nods back. Message received. He reaches into his right pocket. Charlie took the keys to the handcuffs, but not both sets. For as long as he's been a cop he's always carried a spare handcuff key in case his own cuffs were used against him. It's a trick that Theodore Tate taught him. Of all people, Tate is the last person he wants to be thinking of right now. He curls his fingers around the key and pulls it out.

Unbelievably, his hands are steady. The key slots in on the first attempt. He undoes the left bracelet and leaves the right one attached.

He crawls closer to Cyris knowing this is the last thing he will ever do.

# CHAPTER THIRTY

Cyris is shouting at them and Jo can't make out the words. She's too cold, too confused, and she's pretty sure her hearing may be permanently shot. You never see that in the movies—you don't see bank robbers and homicide artists getting doctor's appointments to have hearing aids fitted. She glances at the river, but knows only drowning waits for her there. It looks black and cold enough to stop her heart, assuming it's still beating when she hits the surface—which at this point is a big assumption. She should have trusted Charlie. Should have trusted herself because she wanted to believe him.

The policeman is crawling toward Cyris. He has nodded at Charlie, and Charlie has nodded back, and she's pretty sure something is about to happen, and she's pretty sure she's too cold and scared to go along with the plan, but she'll do her best. The policeman's leg is a mess.

One day, when she was a kid, her dad was driving off to

work and she was standing in the driveway waving goodbye. There was a rabbit behind the car. They didn't live on a farm, but in suburbia, so the rabbit must have been somebody's pet. The damn thing didn't move, it just stayed still, and by the time Jo saw it and screamed at her dad to stop, it was too late. He backed over it. The resulting mess, the insides of that rabbit, the way its innards seemed to take up more room on the outside than when on the inside, well, that's where her mind went when she saw the policeman's knee. It looked just like that. Except where there was fur all those years ago, there is a shredded pair of pants. She cried for days back when she was a kid. She'll cry for days now too if she's given the chance.

The policeman drags his leg, the raw wound of meat— that's how she thinks of it now—behind him. He's managed to unlock one of the cuffs. She knows what he's going to try, but what she doesn't know is if it'll work. He makes his last lurch forward and latches the empty cuff around Cyris's ankle. Both men yell out at the same time: Cyris in a loud "No," and Landry in an even louder "Run." Cyris stamps hard on the policeman's hand. She sees the fingers buckle beneath his boots, and when Cyris steps away, the splintered fingers are splayed out like road signs pointing in all the wrong directions, but the handcuffs keep the two men joined. With his other hand the policeman throws the key into the darkness.

Cyris levels the shotgun down to the back of Landry's head.

"Come on," Charlie says, tugging her hand. She turns toward him. He doesn't need to tell her what they need to do. They switch hands and step toward the river. There's no hesitation. The shotgun explodes behind her, but she doesn't look back to see what has happened. She stares into the water and a second later they're falling into it.

She sinks as if a large stone has been shackled to her ankles, but the only extra weight she has is Charlie. She clings tightly to his hand as her nose and mouth fill with water that is far colder than she thought water could ever be. So cold it burns her eyes, and for all her efforts all she can see is nothing. This is complete and utter lack of any light. It feels heavy, almost appealing. For a moment—a long moment, impossibly longer than it ought to be, her heart stops. She's sure of it. Doctors might disagree, but for a second or two the cold is enough to stop it beating, but then the shock of adrenaline starts it back up. She kicks upward, but it feels like she's kicking at nothing. The current is moving them, but to where she doesn't know. Maybe only deeper. Maybe nowhere at all. Maybe right back to Cyris. All three of those things panic her, but then, strangely, after a few more seconds, none of them do. She feels calm. It's peaceful beneath the water. Quiet. And the prospect of drowning isn't really that scary. In fact it's almost . . . almost what?

The answer is *relaxing*. Drowning is almost relaxing, and hadn't she heard that somewhere before? Or read it?

Her feet hit something and she automatically pushes off from it, her survival instinct kicking in. Charlie moves in the same direction and she guesses his feet hit the same thing. The current twisting them, moving them through a corridor of no light, no sound. The relaxing feeling has disappeared. That panic from a few seconds ago takes hold, its hold so tight it makes her lungs burn.

They break the surface. It's so quick she barely manages to suck in some air before being dragged back under. Charlie pulls her tighter toward him, then she feels part of him hitting something, but she can't tell what. Her head hits something, something soft that she's sure is part of Charlie. The pain is warm and reminds her all is not lost, but she's not sure if Charlie will be feeling the same way. She manages to get above the surface again, but only for a moment, just enough to see the water angry around her. Charlie is pinned to a boulder, his back spread evenly across it, and the current is pushing her into him. He's still holding the flashlight, only it's not going anymore. The angle of the stream, the strength of the current, she's not sure they're going to be going anywhere either. She sucks in a deep breath and isn't sure how much longer she can fight before the water pulls her back down.

# CHAPTER THIRTY-ONE

*You're shooting at nothing, Cyris, shooting at nothing.*

The boulders he hits are laughing at him, and inside the laughter he can hear them telling him things he doesn't want to hear. He shuts them up by firing the gun again and again, and his fingers feel heavy against the trigger.

Charlie and his girlfriend have gone, gone into the river and gone from sight, and maybe forever. He's left out here in the darkness. Oh God, it's so dark. The moon is up there, but it's covered by cloud, and all he can see is absolutely nothing. He hates the black moon. He wants to kick it, but has to settle for screaming.

He moves away from the river. The handcuff is still attached to his ankle, the other cuff has flesh and blood scorched against it because his first shot after Charlie and the bitch woman jumped into the water was into the policeman's hand.

It blew apart into a pulpy mist. He walks back over to that policeman now. He points the shotgun at the cop's head.

"Where's the key?" he asks, but he already knows the answer. The key will be somewhere in the forest, out there making friends with the hedgehog he stood on earlier.

The cop doesn't answer. His answering days are in the past, back there with days of breathing and thinking. This guy ain't living no more. And now he has a stupid set of handcuffs hanging from his ankle. No way to shoot them off without shooting himself in the foot.

He searches the policeman for a flashlight, but finds only a packet of matches. He lights the first match and the rain puts it out, and the second, and the third, and suddenly he's out of matches, just like that. The only thing he can think of that might help is to throw the dead cop into the river, which he does, only it doesn't help at all. It was stupid to think that it even would. It does make him feel better, though—mentally, at least, but picking that bastard up has hurt his stomach. He presses his hand against his wound as he walks in the direction he thinks he came from. Then he digs his heavy fingers into his wet pocket and pulls out the bottle with the twist-off cap, but the cap won't move, not at first, but in the end it does, and he swallows two pills, maybe three—he loses count. What he needs is the shit his buddy gave him years ago, but that's all used up. He doesn't know if he can get more. There's his wife's morphine—but he vowed never to touch that. Shit—has he touched it already?

He tries to remember how long he walked earlier, and for some reason his mind goes back to the other night. He cut one of the breasts off one of those women, and then he put it in a cardboard box, and then he left it in Charlie Feldman's house. Why the fuck did he do that? He's never done anything like

that before and, come to think of it, he's not even real sure
he did that the other night. There'd be no reason to. Unless
doing random shit is a good reason.

He looks for a track, but the black moon keeps it hidden.
He wishes he had a flashlight, then remembers that he does—
it's the same flashlight he used earlier to read the note in his
pocket. It's only a small one, but it will do the job so he pulls
it from his pocket and turns it on. He walks further from the
cave and river, and he keeps on walking, following the sound
of the water because he seems to remember hearing it on the
way here, but this time he keeps it on his right. His stomach
hurts. Hurts like a bitch.

A moment later vomit erupts from him, and his thoughts
seem to focus for a few seconds as the drugs leave his stomach,
but surely they're in his system by now, aren't they? He wishes
he knew. For a few seconds things are clear and he knows the
painkillers are killing much more than the pain. They're killing his ability to think. He knows the shotgun is empty and
knows there has to be more to all of this than just killing.

He continues to walk. He's passing branches that have
snapped. Somebody came this way. Suddenly there's a lull in
the storm and another flash of clarity comes to him, and he
knows what's happening. He reaches into his pocket for the
painkillers, then throws them as far as he can into the trees.
He hears them rattling as they fly through the air, then they
are gone forever and already he misses them. He pushes ahead.
He can see shapes—no light, but shapes—and he realizes that
some of the branches here are pushed back so perhaps this is
a track, a track after all. He smiles and laughs, then stops and
rests a hand across his throbbing stomach. He sucks in a deep
breath and the duct tape holding the wound closed feels hard
beneath his fingers. He reaches into his pocket for the pain-

killers, but can't find them, then searches his other pockets, but they're not there either. Must have left them at home. Stupid, stupid, stupid.

He carries on walking, yeah, yeah, and his body is cold, so cold, but at least he's wearing a jacket, and at least he's not the one in the water. He wonders if good old Charles is dead yet. He scratches a hand across his face and buries his fingers beneath his beard, then flicks the nails over his skin and draws blood. He needs to think. Thinking and walking, that's all he has to do, and he does this as he moves deeper into the darkness, hoping he won't be lost forever—and forever started around nine o'clock the previous night.

"Into the realm of dark never he traveled," he says, wondering what he's talking about, if he's even spoken. Hopefully Charlie will survive the river. The woman too. Because he's just remembered he's doing this for the money. And going through all of this has to have been worth something.

# CHAPTER THIRTY-TWO

I'm stuck.

I'm pressed against a boulder and I don't have the strength to roll myself away. One moment I can breathe, the next I can't as water splashes into my mouth. Jo is against me, her head pressing into my chest.

If I drown right here and now, will the current keep me pressed against this boulder? Probably. Yes. At least until the rain eases off and the river calms down—if that can even happen. Maybe the river is always like this.

My strength is gone. Drained by the efforts of the night, the efforts of the week, drained by the lack of oxygen. If I can just get a deeper breath, then maybe . . . maybe I can fight back.

My hands are becoming numb. I have never been in water so cold. Somehow I'm still holding the flashlight, and somehow I manage to unscrew the base. The batteries drop into the water and I can't feel my body enough to know if they hit me on their way past, off to wherever it is that batteries go underwater. I unscrew the top of the flashlight and let it go the way of the battery. I'm left with a tube. I lift one end above the water and hold the other end to my mouth. The air above is cool and I drink it in and my energy returns, not quickly, but at least it's something. I put the tube in Jo's mouth and she gets the concept quickly, and we're able to climb a few more inches.

"We need to roll away at the same time," I tell her.

"What?"

"We need to roll away at the same time!"

"We should roll away at the same time!" she says.

In other circumstances I'd roll my eyes at that. But not these circumstances.

"On three," I tell her. "We go left."

"Your left?" she shouts.

"My left. One. Two. Three!" With renewed yet frozen energy I push away at the rock, Jo pushing with me, and we twist out into the current. Nothing at first, it seems we're dead in the water, then suddenly something hits us hard, and it takes me a second or two to realize it's a body. It's Landry. The impact gets us free from the rock, and suddenly we're traveling down the river with the dead man, gasping for air as we bob up and down, breathing in cold water, cold air, cold rain. I have nothing to hold on to except the wet darkness and Jo. As I fumble against the water, I sense more than see the branches that jut from the bank toward us like spears. They try to stab and skewer as we rush by, try to hold us with wooden fingers beneath the surface. I stay in front of Jo, trying to take the impacts away from her, Landry only a few feet or so ahead of me, not trying to do anything. When a bright orange flare lights up the night sky I genuinely believe help has arrived, but soon realize the glow is inside my head, ignited by the back of my skull cracking into a boulder. When it happens again only a few moments later the flare is gray.

Floating or drowning—I can't tell the difference now and don't think it matters. My grip on Jo weakens with each knock I take and I'm so cold I can't tell if her fingers are still clutching me.

As the water pulls us down for seconds at a time, I drift and so does my perception of time. More boulders, and I slam into them, but there's no pain. I wonder if death will have feeling. My eyes close and open, but there's darkness either way. I hardly feel a thing when my cold body comes to rest against a fallen tree. Thick dead branches cradle me above the water as my feet dangle in the current ahead. The tree bridges the width of the river. Jo is trying to claw herself from the water. I lean my face against the tree, scratching it on the bark. I watch as Jo comes toward me. Her arms reach for my arms. I kick at the water while she tries to pull me from it, and when I'm closer I clutch at branches and bark and pull myself along as though climbing a sideways ladder. This woman I kidnapped, this woman I've nearly killed, is trying to save me. Maybe this is why I love her.

The current swirls around my legs, begging me to join it, but it had its chance and lost. My feet touch the riverbed and I continue forward, and soon the water is only up to my waist, my thighs, my knees. When it's around my ankles I collapse, my body slapping into the muddy bank. I look back at the water. Landry is pinned against the tree, but it's too dark to tell which way he is facing.

I roll onto my back. The rain drums against my eyelids. I think about my warm bed—lying in it with a hot water bottle between my feet and another behind my back. All I want to do now is go to sleep. I start thinking of a Friday or a Saturday night, so I can sleep all day and then the next. I close my eyes. Something touches my face. It's frightening away my sleep. I open my eyes to see Jo slapping me. Only I can't feel it. I can see it, but that's all.

"Come on, Charlie, wake up."

I am awake. Can't she see that? I try to tell her, but it's hard since my lips and tongue no longer work. Somebody must have removed them.

"Charlie!"

She slaps me hard and again I open my eyes. Does she really think this kind of tough love is going to work? I brace my elbows against the ground and try to tilt my body upward.

"Charlie!" Jo's slapping me again and I open my eyes again. I know she's angry at me, but this is all too much. I'm no longer propped up. She needs to save herself rather than hanging around just to abuse me.

I explain this in careful detail. "Juss wev'm ere."

"You got me into this mess, Charlie. You can help get us out of it."

She stands and grabs the front of my wet shirt. My body bows forward as she pulls. I reach up weakly and grab hold of her arms. My mind is still a maze of confusion. My right eye is aching—it feels as though somebody has stapled it directly into the socket, only backward. The inside of my head is pounding, over and over, over and over. I manage to sit up and with more of Jo's encouragement I force myself onto my knees, then onto my feet. I hang on to the nearest tree to get balanced and then on to Jo as we make the first steps. And I'm exhausted. We rest against a tree. Now we have to pick a direction.

"How far do you think we've traveled?" I ask. I stutter the sentence out. My teeth keep chattering. Any harder and they're going to break.

Jo shrugs. "What time does your watch say? Mine isn't waterproof."

I look at my watch, but can't make anything out. I hold it up to my eyes and try to focus, but it's no good—it's just a blur of hands and dashes. Jo seizes my wrist and holds it in front of her face.

"It's two sixteen," she says.

"Late."

"My watch says two ten."

"It's a cheap watch."

"Exactly. It would have stopped when we dived in the water. We've been on the bank for probably four minutes. That means two minutes in the water."

Two minutes in the water. The river was close to the cabin, but so what? There was a track we took that was barely a track and we walked it for maybe ten minutes. Easy to find if you know where it is. And when it's daylight. And dry. I think harder, then realize some of what she's trying to get at. We've come downstream toward the cabin. We've crossed the distance much quicker than if we'd walked.

"How far can you go?" she asks.

"Further than you."

We both doubt it, but say nothing.

We carry on, but it's barely a minute before we're hit with a gradual slope. We struggle against it, often supporting ourselves against trees and each other. Some feeling begins to return to my legs and arms, but not my feet or hands. The slope becomes steeper as we walk further. I'm hoping, when the slope levels out, that we'll be near the makeshift track. Then all we have to do is turn right and we'll find the cabin. Or left.

My feet have gone, but my toes remain—ten individual spears of pain ready to be snapped off. This little piggy went to market. This little piggy drowned. And this little piggy caught pneumonia and died. I remember Landry telling me the cabin was a minute from the river, but I don't know how much that's going to help. The trees form a tent that keeps the rain off our faces, but not the wind. If we don't get out of our wet clothes and find somewhere warm we're going to die. It's that simple. With each passing second we're slowing down. Jo's wrist tells us time has stopped. My watch suggests differently. I don't know which one to believe. My jeans are so wet I can hardly bend my legs.

I quickly explain what Landry told me.

"Then we follow the river," she says.

"Yeah, but which way?"

"Which way do you think?"

"I don't know. If we go left we might end up where we started. We should go right first at least for a bit. We can always turn back."

She looks at me long and hard, knowing we don't have the energy to turn back if we go the wrong way, and in the end decides to follow my advice. I'm not sure why. Maybe it's because I've fucked up everything I've done this week so I'm due for some decent luck. We turn right and start moving, doing our best to stay parallel to the water, using only its sound as a guide. The trees get thinner and closer together. I want to turn them into firewood, want to burn down the whole lot. We stumble between them, breaking our way forward. It looks similar to the track we're looking for. Lots of black. Lots of trees. Lots of roots. We carry on in silence, watched by the night and the small, wet, unhelpful creatures living in it. Kathy and Luciana are watching me too. I can feel them, but that's all.

My foot snags on a root, and as in the early minutes of Monday morning I fall onto my hands and knees, only this time I don't lose hold of a tire iron. I roll onto my back and look up at the trees. Jo kneels down next to me. She rests her head on my chest and I can hear her labored breathing. I want to put my arms around her and think back to better times, but those times have gone, they are gone and the forest is here replacing them and the killing hour has arrived.

I close my eyes and look for Kathy and Luciana and hope that Landry isn't there too.

# CHAPTER THIRTY-THREE

Darkness and death aren't as scary as I thought. No Heaven, no Hell, just a place with no feeling or time or emotion. A dark place with a soft sound and cool air and, best of all, it doesn't hurt.

"Wake up, Charlie."

I was wrong to be frightened. Wrong to think that death was going to be an eternity of torture and mayhem. Wrong to think that I wasn't going to like it. Hell, it isn't even boring. Had I known this before, I never would have struggled.

"Charlie."

I roll over. Jo is next to me. This isn't death. I can't tell if she's on her knees or not. Pine needles have created a blanket for us to rest on, but not one to crawl under and get warm. Branches rustle and leaves tear from their stems above us. Cones fall to the earth and pine needles fly through the wind.

"I'm awake."

"And shivering," she says.

"I can't stop."

"It's a good thing," she says. "It means hypothermia hasn't started."

I have no idea if that's true. All I know is it doesn't feel good.

She forces herself up, pressing against my stomach to raise herself. "I think there's a light in the distance, perhaps only thirty yards away. If we can make it, promise me we'll go to the police."

"I promise." I don't want her help in getting up, but I need it. When I'm on my feet we stagger forward.

*Head toward the light.*

If this is the trail we took earlier and the cabin is ahead of us, then that makes Cyris . . . where? Anywhere? Lost? Or here? We break through the trees into the clearing. Seeing Landry's car is awful. It makes me realize that life goes on, no matter who is no longer in it. In ten years the car will still be here. The paint job will have cracked in the heat, the metal will have rusted in the rain, the tires will be flat, the rims of the wheels will have cut through them and made impressions in the ground. The whole thing will be covered in mold. The car is a slice of life waiting for the return of its owner, but it will never happen—its owner is pinned against a fallen tree, its owner will decay over the following weeks and break apart.

The cabin looks like a palace. Limping forward, I reach the porch. I can't climb up onto it so I sit on the edge and roll myself on. Jo does the same.

I can't clutch the door with my frozen hands, but Jo has more movement so she nudges me aside. The cabin was cold before, but it's warmer and drier than outside. The wind ushers us inside and we close the door behind us.

"We can't stay here," I say.

"I know, I know," she answers. "But I know I can't drive either. What about you?"

I want to say I can. But I can't. Put me behind the wheel of a car and I don't even know if I'll have the strength to change gears. And if I do, I'm only going to drive a few feet before hitting any one of a number of trees. "Not yet. What are we going to do?"

"Stay here," she says.

"But we can't."

"Just a bit," she says, rubbing her hands together in an attempt to get the process started. "Just long enough to warm up."

"That could take hours. Let's just warm up in the car."

"This will be quicker," she says. "I know it's tough to do, but we have to hold out hope that Cyris is lost."

"Yeah, but he may not be. He might be right outside."

"If we try driving we're going to crash. Then what? Start walking back to the city?"

"So what do you want to do?"

"Two minutes," she says. "We spend two minutes warming up and then we leave."

Two minutes isn't a lot of time. In two minutes I'm probably going to be colder than I am now. She moves over to one of the lanterns. She picks it up, hooking it as if she has a claw. Plenty of dry kindling has been set in lots of old newspaper in the fireplace. Jo tries removing the glass top of the lantern, but her hands are too cold, then comes up with a more practical way. She throws her lantern into the fireplace. The glass breaks. A flame is released. The brittle paper lights up like an inferno.

We lower ourselves to the fire. The wood crackles, but gives off little warmth. It doesn't take long for smoke to start flooding back into the cabin. The chimney must be partially blocked by a bird's nest or leaves. My lungs are too full of water to make room for the smoke. Jo strips down and starts ringing the water out of her clothes. I can hardly move, but I manage to kick my shoes off. Nothing else.

Jo takes my shirt and helps me with my jeans. I look down at my body. It's gray and covered in bruises and lumps and scrapes. We're both in our underwear. I don't want to strip any further—not because of Jo, but because if Cyris comes back in I don't want to die naked. Side by side we sit, clutching each other for warmth though we're so cold that hugging achieves nothing. Cyris could burst in and kill us, but if we step back outside the cold will do the same thing. Only fire can help us. Jo puts two more logs onto it.

I glance at my watch. The two minutes have already passed. We're heading up to three.

I nod toward the bag in the center of the room. "There are clothes in there."

Jo stands and grabs it. It's difficult opening the bag, but we rescue the clothes Landry had been wearing. Beneath them is a towel. He came prepared to get wet. Or bloody. Either way he was right. Jo towels herself down, then I follow suit. I'm still freezing and my body hasn't given up shaking. I can feel the heat from the fire, but it is only warming up my skin. It's my core that's chilled. I pull on Landry's shirt. I give the pants and jacket to Jo.

"You take the jacket," she says, handing it back to me.

"I'm fine," I tell her.

"No, really, Charlie, you're not. Take the jacket."

I shake my head, which is a mistake for anybody sporting

the kind of headache I'm sporting. I almost pass out. "No," I tell her.

She pulls on the pants and puts on the jacket. She does the jacket up. It's not a great fit. Then she finds the envelope with my account of what happened in one of the pockets. She tosses it onto the fire. "We don't need it," she says. "Let's just go to the police and tell them."

"Can we get a lawyer first?"

"Are you kidding?"

"I'm not sure. Anyway, we have to go," I say, happy I can now feel the words coming from my mouth. She nods. Rags of smoke are hanging lower in the air. I could reach up and my hand would disappear into them.

"I know," Jo says. She hooks out the two logs she just put into the fire and puts them into the duffel bag, which smothers the flames. She pushes the bag into my chest.

"Hug this," she says. "It isn't much, but it's something."

The bag feels like a lumpy hot water bottle.

She picks up her wet pants and hunts through them for the keys.

"How did you drive my car?" I ask. "I had the keys."

"Like this," she says, and she pulls her own keys out of her pocket. "They were still in my handbag," she says, "and I never took off the spare for your car."

It makes me feel good to know she never got rid of the key, as if by keeping it she was also keeping the chance that somehow we would get back together.

We scoop up our wet clothes. I carry the duffel bag and Jo carries the clothes and we step outside. Landry's shoes are too big for me, but they do the job. The ground plucks at them as we run toward the cars. Cyris doesn't jump out from the trees and shoot at us so I figure things are picking up. The rain hasn't eased off and perhaps it never will. My arms and legs feel warm, but my stomach and chest are cold. Landry's car is right out front, but I can't see my car or Cyris's.

"Where's the car?" I ask.

"About twenty yards that way," she says, and I follow.

I keep hugging the duffel bag even though it has cooled somewhat. We reach my car and dump the clothes into the back. There are still two stakes in the backseat. I take one out for protection.

Jo climbs into the car. I tell her to wait for me, and I run over to Landry's car. It's unlocked, and I pop the hood and grab hold of the cords going to the spark plugs, and I tug on them as hard as I can until two of them snap off. I carry them back to my car and climb in. I'm not sure how much time we've wasted. Five minutes, I guess. Ten at the most. I turn the key and the motor kicks into life. So does the heater. I turn it to high and it blasts cold air at us that is warmer than we are. It starts to warm up. So do we.

"Cyris followed you, right?"

"Must have," Jo replies.

"Where's his car?"

"Maybe he parked further away so he could sneak up."

Makes perfect sense. A guy like Cyris isn't going to drive right up to the cabin.

"Just like you did," I say.

She flashes me her first genuine smile since I tied her up and kidnapped her. "Exactly."

I gun the engine, put the duffel bag in my lap, and start my three-point turn. It takes me around six or seven points to do it. We head back up the track and come across Cyris's car. It's blocking the road and there's no way around it. Only it's not his car, it's Jo's car. Jo gasps when she sees it. It makes her realize that Cyris has been to her house.

"If he'd followed you to my place," she says, "wouldn't he have just come inside?"

"I imagine so."

"Which means he didn't follow you there, did he?"

"No."

"Which means he found my address at your house, figured out the connection, and came looking for me."

"Yes."

"Why?"

"I don't know," I tell her.

"So if you hadn't come around . . ."

"But I did. That's all that matters."

"You saved my life," she says.

"No. All I did was put it in danger by not going to the police when I could have."

"If you'd gone to the police, they wouldn't have sent somebody to protect me."

"I know. You realize I'll probably end up in jail," I tell her.

"Let's hope not."

I try to imagine Cyris's state of mind when he saw me being arrested. Was he happy or pissed off? I don't know. I don't even know if Cyris has a state of mind. What I do know is his plans were altered. With nothing else to do he followed.

"What if he's in there?" I ask, nodding toward her car.

"He won't be in there. If he'd made it back he would have come to the cabin."

I separate her keys from mine, so mine stays in the ignition and the car stays running. "I guess," I tell her. I open my door. "Lock up behind me. And if there's any problems, get the hell out of here."

"Charlie?"

I lean down and look back in. "Yeah?"

"Don't forget what we discussed earlier."

"The police. Right. We'll go right there. I promise. I'll just move it and be right back."

The rain starts to soak me, but I don't care. I pause and look back to make sure she's locking her doors. She is. The headlights blind me, leaving colored flashes streaking across my vision. I rub my eyes with my fingers, trying to arrange the colors back into some type of sensible order. There's a key in the ignition. Not her key, but some kind of generic key that isn't really a key, but looks more like the handle of a screwdriver.

I twist it. It works. I turn the lights on, shining them at Jo. Hers are shining right back. I turn my heater on high, aiming the air at my feet and face. I try to get into reverse gear, but my hand is wet and it slips off. I wipe it across the passenger seat, then try again. This time it works. I twist around to look out the back window.

At the same time Cyris pops the backseat down and crawls out of the trunk.

# CHAPTER THIRTY-FOUR

Money makes the world go round. It makes it, yeah, it makes it, yes it does, but revenge is why he's out here, not money—he knows because he checked the note in his pocket. Somehow he thought it was about the money, and in thinking that it has become that, because now he can use Feldman and his wife to earn some quick cash. And he loves cash. He loves it about the same as he loves revenge.

His head hurts, the world spins quicker than he can, and his stomach throbs. The duct tape pulls at the skin and he wonders if he's infected, yeah, infected, and he needs to take the medication, but the medication is . . . The medication is somewhere, but it only helps to numb the pain. It doesn't heal the wound, it doesn't cure him or make last Monday go away. He wants revenge, revenge and money, and it's hard to know which he wants more.

"Start driving," he says, and pushes the gun toward Charlie.

His head seems to be clearing. Not much, but enough to know this isn't all about killing people. He knows he's capable of speech, capable of command, knows that with the shotgun he has the power to get exactly what he wants.

"I said start driving, asshole."

He hid in the back of the car like a bug, out of sight, with the shotgun, and boy, what a good plan, a great plan, and he's so pleased with himself he's smiling and starting to laugh, but he must hold back the laughter, must cling to the excitement, but not let it take him over.

Charlie starts to nod and he wonders what sort of mess he would make inside the car if he were to start shooting people. People? There's only Charlie. Anyway, the shotgun won't shoot anything in its current condition. It's empty.

Something digs into the side of his hip. He adjusts his position and digs his fingers into his pocket. Bracelets? Metal ones. With a chain running between them. And blood all over them. A key is sitting in one of the locks. A key that was in his satchel that he'd left on the passenger seat.

He thinks about the money. He wonders what a suitcase full of money would look like if he were to shoot a hole in the middle of it. Would it turn into confetti? Would it turn into loose change? A suitcase of money. Just think . . . just think how it would feel to run his fingers through all those loose bills. . . .

And then he remembers! Money. He has a suitcase full of money at home! No, no he doesn't, but he does have a suitcase full of money owing to him. Or maybe a briefcase. All of this was for money. Money is the reason he got stabbed, it's the reason he wants revenge. In his mind he can picture part of the note he wrote to himself and he remembers that killing Feldman is about revenge, but picking up the money he's owed is for the job he did the other night. Things may have gotten fucked up along the way, but he still got that woman killed, so really he doesn't need Charlie at all.

Charlie is reversing now and he finds a spot where he can turn the car around.

"Don't try anything," Cyris says, and Charlie shakes his head. Does that mean he doesn't understand? Or that he disagrees? Or that he won't try anything?

When they reach the highway he tells Charlie to put his foot to the pedal.

"What's the hurry?"

"You'll learn soon enough," he says, glancing into the mirror and seeing that the bitch is close behind them. "We'll all learn soon enough."

# CHAPTER THIRTY-FIVE

What's a night without two homicidal maniacs? A boring night, that's what. So right now I am, as they say, pretty fucking far from bored.

I don't remember Cyris sounding this crazy, but that could be because we didn't talk much when we first met. The only thing I can think to do is crash the car into something solid in the hope Jo can get away, but that plan has a huge drawback—she will come to help. Cyris might still be alive and I might not. Who will protect her then?

*Who's protected her so far?*

Hopefully she's already figured out something was wrong. The plan was for me to move the car, not keep driving it.

"What do you want?" I strain to keep my voice controlled.

"Shut up and drive."

The wipers roam across the windshield, smearing the rain from side to side. I shut up and drive. No point in arguing. I try to think of a way I can signal Jo—Morse code with the brake lights or something.

"The box, what's in the box? You saw the box? It was a present. I hope you liked it."

"How's the stomach?" I ask.

"Whose stomach?" he asks.

"Your stomach."

"I'll live."

"That's a real shame."

He pushes the gun into my ribs. "Why don't you concentrate on driving."

I do just that, again following the orders of the man with the gun. Common practice. And I've been practicing a lot. When I flick the headlights to high beam the rain looks thicker. There's no other traffic on this road in the middle of nowhere. I feel like taking my hands off the wheel and seeing where fate steers my car. I've had enough. Enough guilt. Enough pain. Enough of people dying around me. I've become a catalyst for death and I don't like it. The heater is combining with my rage to warm me up. I'm thinking it might be like drinking alcohol when you're suffering from hypothermia. You feel warmer, but you're not. Your body's fooling you. And you die. End of story.

Is that to be my story?

The rain begins to ease off. I slow the windshield wipers so that every second they sweep across and show me the dark night ahead. I watch the road and concentrate on driving over the wet asphalt. My knuckles are sore from squeezing the steering wheel. My fingers are white. Slowly I unclench them. The joints pop.

"You look tense, partner," Cyris says.

Yeah, that's right.

"Money, Feldman," he says. "How much of it do you have?"

This question surprises me. I think about it. "I'm not sure. It's all wet, anyway."

"Wet? Wet, how? How did . . . no, no, no, not the money in your pockets, the money in your bank. How many dollars do you have?"

"Nothing."

He pushes the gun in harder. I glance at him in the mirror. He's blinking rapidly. "That's a lie. You're lying, lying, and lying people catch on fire. I know you have money. I've seen your house, I looked at your money statements."

"I'm a schoolteacher, not a doctor. I have a mortgage. Do you know what that means?"

"I know you're a teacher, I know this, I know, and I'm not a moron."

"The bank owns my house, not me."

He draws the gun back, then pushes it in harder still.

I jerk away. The car swerves across the road. I tug at the wheel, shift down a couple of gears, and the car swerves right, then straightens. My reactions defy my thoughts of crashing. Surely Jo must know now that I'm in trouble.

"How much you got?" Cyris asks as if nothing just happened. I glance into the rearview mirror. Jo is still behind us, but much further back now. Can money get us out of this?

"Not much."

"You owe me forty grand."

"What?"

"I could do with some money, partner. Forty grand sounds pretty sweet."

Forty grand. I have a strong feeling why he picked that amount. "Get a job."

"I have a job."

Things that didn't make sense on Monday are making some sense now. Things seem clearer since I talked to Landry. One of the world's biggest motives to kill, after revenge, is money. That's exactly what Cyris is asking for now. I know he likes money. He shouted it out half an hour ago. He wants money. Was that his goal on Monday? Was he being paid?

Yes. Of course he was. The theory Jo came up with, the theory I came up with when talking to Landry, it all makes perfect sense. To kill one woman would make the police look at obvious reasons, then obvious suspects. To kill them both in a horrific and brutal way makes the entire thing look ritualistic. It makes it look like she died for an entirely different set of reasons. Like some random madman dragged them both from their homes and committed madman atrocities on them, rather than being paid for it.

Cyris is more than a mere monster. He's a paid killer. A man who takes his job seriously enough to take on a completely different role. As horrid as it is, I can appreciate the cleverness in his process. The police are looking for some deranged lunatic because Cyris *was* a deranged lunatic in those early Monday hours.

What role is he trapped in now?

We pass a reflective sign extended out over the highway from a large white pole. Christchurch is only forty-five miles away. We'll be there in well under an hour. I slide the heater control to the little picture of feet. I've thawed out slightly. The ice in my veins is melting. The fear isn't.

"What are you thinking about?"

"Nothing." I keep on driving.

"You've got two days," he says.

"What?"

"Didn't I make myself clear? Are you an idiot?"

"Humor me."

"Two days. Forty grand. I'm sure you can arrange that."

"Sure."

"Speed up, I don't want to be out here all night."

I speed up and the headlights in my mirror get smaller.

"Faster!" he shouts.

I push my foot down and Jo's headlights soon disappear. Ahead of us the two eastbound lanes of the highway narrow into one. The road winds around a bit, but the view doesn't change—just pastures and more pastures. When Cyris tells me to pull over I do the opposite. I speed up and I switch off the headlights. We're going to crash, but if I'm lucky Jo will drive right on past.

Cyris smashes me in the head with something, and as the world goes darker, he begins tugging at the wheel. He's leaning over the backseat and I'm too woozy to try and stop him. He puts the gearshift in neutral. My foot is still on the accelerator, but only revving now. He hits me again. The colors flare behind my eyes for maybe the hundredth time this week and I'm left to wonder if those colors will ever go away. He keeps steering the car. It's slowing down. He reaches around me and pulls out the screwdriver key. When the colors behind my eyes dissolve I start looking for Cyris. He's already outside, slamming the passenger door closed. I go to open my door and my right arm stops painfully short. Handcuffs hold me to the steering wheel.

Landry's cuffs.

Christ. I'm living in a world of déjà vu.

Cyris taps on the window with the barrel of his gun. I look out and see him waving my keys at me. His scraggly beard moves as he grins. I swear at the windshield, spraying a fine mist of obscenities across the glass. At the same time I tug on the handcuffs, going through the same motions I went through earlier tonight and getting the same results. My wrist is already swelling.

I unclip the seatbelt and reach for the door handle with my left arm, pulling on it, then push the door with my foot. I turn my body so I can stand. My right arm stays inside the car, the handcuffs stopping me from standing straight. Cyris is moving off the opposite side of the road just as Jo comes around the bend. Past the shoulder is some long grass that he ducks behind. I stand as tall as I can, the handcuffs pulling my skin and hurting the bone, and I wave erratically at her so she knows there's trouble. But she's thinking maybe flat-tire trouble, or engine trouble. Just not Cyris trouble. But then Cyris steps out into the road and levels the shotgun at her. There must be a moment where she thinks she might be able to run him down before he can open fire, but then she must dismiss it because she pulls over and stops.

Cyris signals for her to get out of the car. She does.

"Looks like we're having ourselves a reunion," he shouts. He moves slowly toward us, then stops between the headlights of the car I'm driving. "Your husband here owes me money," he says. "Forty grand to be specific. He said I could look after you until he can get it. It's like layaway." He takes a few steps toward me. "Isn't that right?"

I don't answer him. Jo says nothing. He turns the barrel of Landry's shotgun so it's pointing at her face. She doesn't look scared or intimidated, but I don't doubt that she is.

"The plan's simple," he says. "You give me the money and she gets to live. You take too long with the funds, I teach her about suffering. You get my point?"

I want to kill him so badly that it hurts. I grit my teeth and my eyes are burning and I see a shade of red that can only be blood. I want to take the gun from his hands and use it to club his head into the highway. I want to run over his twitching corpse.

"For forty grand," Cyris continues, "you can have her back. It's the money you owe me, partner, for screwing me the other night."

"I'll get it, okay? You can let her go and take me instead. We can go to the bank in the morning and I can get you the cash," I say, knowing how stupid it sounds.

"No can do, partner. She comes with me."

"You don't need her."

"Oh, but I do, I do, yeah. I get lonely during the day."

"I can get the money first thing! Please! By ten o'clock everything can be settled."

"Sorry. I'll be sleeping like a baby."

"What about in the afternoon? Come on, give me a break here."

"Don't sound so desperate, little Charlie, little, little. The day's no good for me. The night's no good for me either. I've got me some important plans."

I don't want him alone with Jo for two whole days. I don't want that at all. "No deal."

He reaches out and shoves Jo against the car, then points the gun at her. "Pick a limb, partner."

I raise my free hand. "I can get you the money. But two days? Jesus, surely you can see my problem with this."

"And that's just it. It's your problem, not mine, yours." He laughs. "Partner, if you're unhappy we can cancel the whole transaction. Is that how you want it?"

I shake my head. I've seen how he cancels transactions.

"Good. I'll ring you at home at nine o'clock tonight. Be there."

"If you touch her . . ."

"You'll what? Huh? Kill me? Don't worry, partner. I don't damage my investments."

He pushes her into the driver's seat of my car and slams the door. Clutching his stomach, he moves around to the passenger side. I stare through the side window at Jo. She stares back and attempts a smile that says, *Don't worry, things will be fine*. I attempt the same smile, but who are we kidding?

I meet Cyris's eyes. I want them to be dead, reflecting only a vacant mind, but they're alive and brimming with ideas. Half a minute goes by, then Jo puts the car into gear and slowly pulls away. She goes only ten yards before the brake lights come on. Her arm appears out the window and she tosses out the handcuff key and the modified car key. They land in the middle of the road. Then the red brake lights die and the car rolls forward.

By trying to be a hero on Monday I've signed Jo's life away. I rest my head against the door. The headache is back. I can taste failure in the back of my throat. I could have driven into a tree. I could have fought Cyris while he was behind me in the car. I look down the road. The taillights are two distant red specks riding toward infinity. They look like eyes—demon eyes. They disappear around a distant bend.

They disappear and I am alone.

# CHAPTER THIRTY-SIX

The rain cannot wash away the rage or the fear that leaves me standing motionless next to my car. Hope and despair have both reached out for me, but hope couldn't get a grip. And why would it? I'm standing in Landry's shirt, his socks and shoes, and my underwear. My mind has recognized defeat and is slowly shutting down. Jo is dead even though she's behind the wheel of my car and speeding toward the city.

I lean into the car and release the hand brake. I push against the door frame with my left arm, my right beneath my left armpit because of the handcuffs. My legs try to tangle as I gain more speed, and when my left leg clips the edge of the car I lose my balance. My hand slips from the door frame and I fall, my right knee hitting the asphalt hard. I pull myself into a sitting position and get onto my feet. I look down at my knee and can see it bleeding.

I tighten my grip on the car and start over. The car builds

speed once again, and when I can tell momentum will take me to the keys, I limbo into the car and put both hands on the wheel. I can't steer because the steering wheel has locked, but I pull the hand brake when I reach the keys. I twist my body and lean out. The keys are closer to the other side of the car, out of reach. I look for something to help and find it when I look up and see the antenna. I pull it upward and when it's at its longest I bend it back and forth until it snaps off. I lean down and start fishing. It only takes a few moments to hook the handcuff key. I undo the cuffs and drop them onto the passenger seat. I lean under the car and grab the screwdriver.

Racing toward the city, I search for the taillights of my Honda, but can't find them. When I enter the city I drive aimlessly around, but it's pointless. They're gone. Jo is gone. And there's nothing I can do until I pay to get her back.

I head home. I never liked driving Jo's car, and I like it even less now. The seats are low and I often hurt my back getting in and out of it. It's not the kind of car you can use if you have kids—you'd break your back getting a child in and out of a car seat. I smile thinking about that, I smile thinking of the children we didn't have, but used to talk about having. We never named them, we thought it weird to name somebody until you'd met them. I don't know why I'm suddenly thinking about them, and even though they bring a smile to my face, I'm actually feeling sad for their loss. These kids will never exist. They died six months ago in the bar. No matter what happens, even if I get Jo back, she'll never want to see me again.

I park up the driveway and leave the screwdriver in the car and walk around the gate and swing open my busted back door. I stare at the phone and even take two steps toward it, knowing I need to call the police and knowing just as well that I can't. Cyris will kill Jo if I do. He may kill her anyway. The time to call the police is over and, anyway, it's not like my experience with them is one I want to risk repeating.

I walk down the hallway. Last time I made this walk I was in cuffs and had a gun pointed at me. When was that? It feels like a few days ago, but it's only been a matter of hours, maybe five or six of them. I look at my watch, but I can't figure it out, and really it doesn't matter. I stand in the bedroom doorway and stare at the cardboard box. I have to get rid of it. I can't sleep in my house with the body part of a woman I failed to save. I don't look inside it because Landry told me what was in there. Kathy deserves to be buried in one piece, but I can't return the box to the crime scene. I can't take it to the morgue. Can't put a stamp on it and mail it in.

These thoughts disgust me, but they're there, just logical progressions really, like a mechanic figuring out how to take a car apart, or an accountant carrying the one. Kathy is dead and for her to rest in peace her death needs to be avenged. That's all. It doesn't matter where her body ends up. I grab a garbage bag out of the laundry and put the box inside. I put my bloody shorts in there too. Then, turning the lights off, I stumble through the house and into the garage. I find a shovel.

My house is on the corner of a cul-de-sac. My backyard borders another house, but behind that are huge pastures. To get there I have to walk into the street and to a dirt driveway angled up between two homes. It's nearly five o'clock in the morning, but I still pause to scan the neighborhood. No people. No lights. Nobody to care what's happening to me. I head up the driveway. The wet ground sucks at my shoes.

I've been walking two minutes when I realize why I'm doing this. I need to bury this piece of Kathy, not just for her, but for me. It could help. It could make the ghosts go away.

The pasture is broken up into sections, different vegetables growing in each. Wire fences run between them as if the owners are worried the cabbages are going to mingle with the potatoes and create some hybrid vegetable nobody would like. Long dirt roads trail off into the distance. Dozens of irrigation pipes create a maze that leads to the nearby river. Iron sheds with spots of rust on them house farm equipment. The ruts in the dirt formed by tractors going back and forth are filled to the brim with water.

I decide not to bury the box anywhere in the pasture. The dirt is turned over all the time. Crops are planted then reaped. Tractors dragging large plows bite into the ground. One day it's pulling up carrots. The next it's decomposing flesh.

The dirt road I'm following keeps the pastures to my right. To my left the land is bordered by a long ditch with a small creek running through it. A dozen or so trees space out the distance. I walk for ten minutes, the rain no longer feeling cold against my skin. I'm numb inside, but not because of the weather. I pass more trees, and I wonder what could be buried beneath them. Just before the creek sweeps into the river, where the road turns right to move along the top end of the pasture, there's a small bank. I climb down and stand a few feet from the creek. I figure this is as good a place as any.

I start digging. My cold fingers send slivers of pain up my arms, but I like the pain—I deserve it, and when I think of Jo and what may be happening to her, I dig faster. I try to concentrate as the hole starts to grow. I dig down two feet before taking a break, standing in the hole up to my knees, sweating and shivering. The rain is becoming heavier again. A shaft of lightning hums across the sky. It lights up the hole and the creek and the plastic bag beside me, and it lights up my body. I'm covered in dirt and I'm digging a grave. I must be insane.

I've come into the night only an hour or two before dawn, carrying a body part and a tool with which to hide it.

I lean on the shovel and look into the creek as the following thunder chases the lightning. I suddenly realize that I'm not alone. I can sense her watching, but she says nothing as I slowly push back off my shovel and continue to dig. I last less than a minute before I sit down on the edge of the hole, close to tears.

"I'm sorry. I'm really, really sorry."

"What are you doing, Charlie?" Kathy asks.

"I've no idea. Things have got out of hand. I'm even seeing ghosts."

"Is that what I am?"

I shake the water from my hair and wipe a muddy palm back through it. "I don't know. Are you?"

"Don't bury me, Charlie. Go to the police."

I stand up again and dig some more. All I'm doing is throwing mud to one side while more mud runs back in. "Is he going to hurt Jo?"

"I can't know that."

"Because you're not real." More lightning, more thunder, and it sounds like I have angered some vengeful god. As the sound rolls across the pasture the walls to my hole—and my sanity—start to cave in. I decide the hole is deep enough. I struggle out. Kathy takes a step back as I pick up the bag.

"Is this really the way to go?" she asks.

"You're not really here," I say, and she isn't. She's only in my decaying mind. Ghosts aren't real, they don't exist, and I don't need Kathy to deny this. In this moment, in the Real World, I'm suddenly unsure of what is real. God, life, death, misery—does any of it matter? Of course it does. Sometimes it's just difficult to see how.

Tears dissolve on my face. I wipe them away with muddy fingers. I take the box out of the plastic bag and ball the bag up into my pocket. I gently lower the box into the hole. I figure the cardboard, the breast, hell, even my shorts will decompose after a while.

"Why did you let us die?"

"You don't believe that," I say.

"What do you believe, Charlie?"

"I believe that bad things happen for no reason. I really tried to save you."

"It's hard to believe anything when you're dead."

I close my eyes and grab hold of the moment on Monday morning when I drove past the pasture and found Cyris's van missing. I knew he had to be heading to a hospital or a morgue. Both would ask questions so maybe he would head straight home. I told myself this over and over, but I knew I was lying because I put my foot to the pedal. I was lucky because there were few cars on the roads. Yeah, Monday was all about luck. It must have been, because in the end I found the missing van. The only problem was where I found it. It was parked outside Luciana's house.

"Don't do this, Charlie."

I start filling in the hole.

"I have no choice," I say, and when the hole is filled in I turn back and find Kathy has gone. Perhaps burying that part of her has worked like I hoped. I climb up the bank, dragging my shovel behind me.

No more lightning now. No more thunder. I stop at the top of the bank and look down to her resting place. Was this the right thing to have done? Of course not. Not for her. Her ghost told me that. I don't know any prayers, only apologies, and I offer them to her.

I turn my back and start walking. Dawn is approaching, bringing the killing hour along with it. The sky lightens, turning purple, but the purple hours of my life have brought only death to me over the last few days. I break into a jog, eager to be away from here, eager to escape the hell this light will show me. The trees, the grass, the muddy banks—they all reflect this dark Evil who has entered my life.

By the time I make it home my chest and throat are burning. After all that's happened, I'm probably going to wake up with the flu. I take the time to strip off my clothes outside. I smear the mud off my skin and flick it onto the concrete.

I make my way stiffly into the bathroom and turn on the shower. I don't need to wait for it to warm up because the cold water is still warmer than me. I climb in and grit my teeth as my skin stings. I reach up and grab onto the showerhead. It's all I can do to force myself to stay. All my nerve endings are tingling. I keep my head down and my eyes closed and the pain starts to fade. Five minutes later it's gone. I turn the shower dial up and make it hotter. The pain returns, but I deserve it. I watch the water go from brown to red to clear as it runs down my body.

I step out of the shower after maybe an hour, dry myself down, fill up a hot water bottle and make my way to bed. I sit on the edge of the bed holding a wedding photo and I start to cry. I've never cried so hard. I can't bear to think about what is happening to Jo, even though my imagination is filling in all the blanks. Rape. Torture. Mutilation. It's all there, my mind unable to get away from it. There are fates worse than death, and I'm pretty sure Cyris knows how to inflict them. I make a vow that no matter what the outcome, I'm going to kill the bastard.

Before climbing beneath the covers I head to the back door

and wedge a chair beneath the handle so it can't be opened. I don't know if it's worth the effort, but figure it's one of those things I could wake up to regret if I hadn't done it.

The killing hour is gone now, but there will be another arriving tomorrow. I try going to sleep. I keep asking myself how this happened even though I know the answer. My eyes close and the events of the night catch up with me before I can answer why Cyris took Kathy and Luciana to a clump of trees within the city and not to a similar place to where Landry took me. I want to answer it because I feel it's important, but at the moment I can't see how. Falling asleep with near hypothermia and a possible concussion probably isn't the best thing I could do right now, but I figure it isn't exactly the worst. I let it happen.

# CHAPTER THIRTY-SEVEN

The smell makes Jo think of ground-up moths. It's an earthy smell, certainly nothing like life, and it reminds her of the time her grandmother died and they found a box of her clothes that had been hidden in her attic for twenty years. Tied up and gagged, locked down here in this basement, it's easy to think of people who have died, and easy to think she'll be seeing them soon. Her mother died the same year she met Charlie. In fact she met Charlie about two weeks before her mom passed away from one of the many random ailments of life—this one taking the form of a brain tumor. Charlie had been a patient of Jo's—or, more accurately, his cat had been. Charlie had brought the cat in. Its name was The Wolf, and though Jo hadn't dealt with pets before whose names had been prefixed by *The*, in this case she could see where the cat got its name—it was one of the biggest domestic cats she'd ever seen. It wasn't well, and there wasn't a lot Jo could do for it, and Charlie had been forced to make the decision to have The Wolf put down.

It's weird to think that a relationship can evolve from the euthanization of a cat, especially in a time of her life when her own mother was slipping away, but these things happen. She'd been single for over a year, her last boyfriend choosing a drinking habit over her, and she was happy to see the back of him and his drinking and the way it turned him from a pretty good guy into a complete asshole whenever they were at a bar. Charlie was opening a new chapter to her life—and back then, though he doesn't know it, she used to call him Charlie Chapter to her friends. The chapter started when Charlie came into her work with flowers to thank her for her efforts to try and save The Wolf. It was her day off. She called him the next day at home to thank him. She asked if he would get another cat. He said he wasn't sure. He asked if she had pets. She said she did—a cat named Bing Bong. He laughed. He asked if she wanted to grab coffee sometime. She said yes. Three months later they were living together. In that time she lost her mother, and then Bing Bong got hit by a car, but she had Charlie Chapter.

Then six months ago that chapter closed, and she was an idiot for letting that happen.

Now a new chapter is opening. If she was out with her friends or coworkers having a few glasses of wine, maybe she would refer to Cyris as Cyris Chapter. Though that doesn't have the same ring to it. Plus she's kidding herself—she's never going to see her friends again. Or Charlie, for that matter. Why the hell couldn't she have believed him?

If she had, would things have turned out different?

She fights uselessly with the ropes. They rub into her skin, rubbing it raw, and if she keeps fighting then soon she'll start bleeding. She stops struggling. The rag in her mouth tastes of vanilla and she wonders what it was last used on. Or who. Cyris said little on the ride here. In the end, either he had forgotten the way to his house or he had enjoyed driving in large, out-of-the-way circles for over an hour. She had considered speeding into a lamppost because surely death was better than letting Cyris do what he wanted to her, but she was too pissed off with Cyris to let herself die because of him. Pissed off with Charlie too.

Sometimes Cyris makes sense, but it's the random comments that frighten her most. When he asked if she knew how his hedgehog was feeling she had sat silently, confident that any reply would be the wrong one. Occasionally he would clutch at his stomach, and she wondered if there was a chance of grabbing the gun off him, but if she tried and failed then failure around a guy like this was certainly going to be unpleasant. He is sick, wounded—Charlie was sure he'd stabbed him, and the way Cyris has been clutching himself is evidence of that. Is he doped up? His eyes are bloodshot and his hands have been shaking a lot. If he's on medication it might mean he's ready to snap at any moment, but it might also mean he could forget he has her locked up in his basement.

The house she's tied up in, the house she could die in, isn't the run-down hellhole she'd thought it would be. She'd conjured up images of a Unabomber shack, a dilapidated slum property with flaking paint, holes in the plaster, and the windows boarded up—a more domestic, suburban version of the cabin in the woods. There would be the smell of death and decay and of countless others who had breathed hard from fear near the end. That's what the house would be like—and she's frightened that it isn't. Frightened to find normality in a home that's five years old at the most. Coming through the house looking at the carpets and the walls and the general décor she could see it had a woman's touch. A few nice paintings. Small knickknacks. And everything was tidy, like a show home. There was a TV going in one of the bedrooms, she could see the light coming into the hall, but couldn't hear anything. Is it possible Cyris doesn't live alone? It would explain why he wanted her to be so quiet. Or maybe he has women tied up in all of the rooms. Or perhaps this isn't even his house.

The basement is cold—the concrete floor is uncarpeted. She's resting in the corner with her hands tied behind her and her feet tied ahead of her. There's a coil of rope wrapped around her body. It holds her against a large drum that she prays isn't full of human body parts or the acid to dissolve them. Maybe that's the smell she can't identify. Tossed over her is a blanket from which she can draw no warmth.

She starts struggling again, twisting her hands and wrists, the rope biting into them. She can feel blood. Are there any rats down here with her? The scent of her blood will have them creeping along, creeping along, their noses twitching and their tiny paws scratching at the concrete. Any second now whiskers are going to brush against her hands, little claws will dig into her legs, small teeth will chew at her fingers, gnawing away skin, tearing through flesh. . . .

No. There are no rats down here. The house is too modern. The garage too tidy. The only messy thing down here is her. She's still wearing Landry's jacket and Landry's pants, and her underwear is still a little damp, but it did dry out a bit in the car. She squeezes her eyes shut, she forces herself to think of Charlie, to forget about the rats, to forget about Cyris.

She focuses on the ropes. She tries not to focus on what may happen over the next few hours. She keeps twisting her wrists and tries not to think about the blood and the pain as the tiredness and exhaustion start to creep in.

# CHAPTER THIRTY-EIGHT

I wake up in the afternoon into a dark world full of sunshine and without the aid of ghosts. My room is stuffy with stale air and my head is full of bad dreams. I can't believe I've slept so long. There is a second—maybe even two—where everything is as it should be. That honeymoon moment where you wake up and all the bad shit doesn't exist, and then the honeymoon ends and you remember your wife has been kidnapped, you saw a man shot apart the night before by a shotgun, a cop tried to kill you, and you spent an hour burying a dead woman's breast while talking to a ghost that isn't really a ghost, but a manifestation of your guilt.

I climb from beneath the blankets. The cold hot water bottle is on the floor. I have slept on a bed that less than a day ago held a body part. The storm has passed and when I look out my window it's as though it never happened. I wish I could say the same thing about everything else in my life. I stare out at the warm day and wonder how much longer summer can really last. Maybe we can bypass autumn and go straight to winter. For that matter, maybe we can bypass winter too. And spring.

My body feels okay until I try to walk. When I do, my jaw starts throbbing. I can barely turn my head, my neck is so stiff. Yesterday I looked and felt like I'd been hit by a car. Now it feels like I've been hit by a bus that has reversed back to hit me again. Every muscle in my arms, legs, and chest is tender. I turn on the radio and tune in to a news bulletin. Some woman talks about the police investigation, but she says nothing new. The same old guy who gave yesterday's weather report comes on and says it will be fine all day. I wonder what he means.

I stagger through the house and head for the bathroom. I stand in the shower for twenty minutes trying to loosen up. I've been spending way too much time lately showering. Too much time in the woods. Too much time bitching about why life can't be better, why the Real World must be so Goddamn real. I study myself in the mirror when I get out. My jaw is puffed up and swollen. My neck is dark blue on the left. My eyes are bloodshot. The bump on my forehead isn't looking any smaller. I study the back of my head with my fingers. Several valleys and mountains there from my journey down Cold River. It's like following a map to hell.

I'm looking at a man who has been both beaten up and beaten, but enough is enough, and that's where I am right now. Somewhere deep inside I've just pulled a giant lever, not so much an on and off switch as a one-armed bandit and five bars with the word *hate* have all landed in a row. I hate that I can never be the same Charlie I was a week ago, and that saddens and scares me. I hate Cyris, and I wonder what I'm capable of doing about that. Murder? I close my eyes and pull the giant lever inside my mind. Bells and whistles and alarms all start going off inside of me. Yeah, murder is now within my capabilities. Murder will be as easy as riding a bike. I sense other things are within my ability now too, but I'm too scared to keep pulling on that lever to find out.

The beaten man stares back at me and what seems like pity fills his eyes. The man looks like he isn't sure what I'm going to do. He looks concerned for me as though he's worried I might start screaming and take my rage out on the world. He offers no answers, but he looks ready to start laying blame.

"I'm no longer going to be the victim," I tell him.

He nods. He must think that's a good thing.

I get dressed. I walk through the house, opening up the rooms and staring out windows as if all the answers lie outside in the fresh air and warm sun. My study is still a mess, broken parts still forming piles around the room. Ideas of what to do next start firing at me from dark corners of my mind. I keep following them, one in particular is starting to take shape. More than one, actually. Each minute that goes by is a minute Jo has to spend with Cyris. Each minute that goes by is another one in which she could be dying.

Beneath my computer desk is a small set of drawers, three in total, all still intact. The bottom is a filing drawer. I pull it open and start flicking through the partitions. It takes some time to find the one for my bank. They're all out of order. Cyris has gone through them as I figured he had: this is where he got the idea of the forty thousand dollars from.

The whole concept of a revolving mortgage is simple. It's basically an overdraft where you can draw out the money you've paid in. I've paid forty thousand dollars off my mortgage and that's how much I can now access. I bought this house ten years ago. When I met Jo and we began living together, I kept my house and put it up for rent. I had one family living here for five years until they moved out, and another family was here for two years until I asked them to move out because I needed to move in.

I push the statements aside. It doesn't matter how much money I have. Money can't buy you happiness. It can't buy life. And no amount will stop me from killing the son of a bitch.

It is after three o'clock and the sun has peaked in the sky and is starting its long, slow spiral down toward a new day on the other side of the world. Ideally I'd like to be there to see it, there with Jo.

Okay, Action Man, it's time to act.

I find my wallet and everything inside it is wet. I take out my credit cards and my driver's license. I use a hand towel to dry them, then leave them on the bench in the sun. I go into the bathroom and do what I can to turn the broken Charlie Feldman into one who will fit back into society. I smile a pained smile then add some cologne and some hair gel. I load my wallet back up and head outside.

The day is even better now that I'm out in it. I think that Landry probably would have liked it. I wonder what he'd be doing right now if he weren't dead and pinned up against a log in the river, and then I feel a pang of guilt thinking about his last act, which was to save us. It's possible he wasn't such a bad guy. Possible under other circumstances I might have liked him. And probable he'd still be alive if I'd taken care of Cyris on Monday morning. Landry would have liked today. I'm sure of it. The bright sun, the warm wind, the essence of calm. Barely any traces of cloud adorn the sky. Long twin white lines float a few thousand feet high above me from a fast-moving jet. It's a great day, the type you always want to wake up to. At least it would be if I'd stabbed Cyris in the heart and not the stomach.

The handcuffs are still on the seat of my car. I hide them in the glove box. I still have a spare key for Jo's car, and I try it in the ignition, but the lock is too badly damaged for it to fit snuggly. The screwdriver still works. At least I can still use the keys to lock and unlock the car. Being in Jo's car mingling with other traffic is surreal. I look at drivers and pedestrians and I wonder what they think of me. Can they see who I am? Can they see what I've become? What I'm now fighting for? Then those thoughts are reversed as I look at their faces. Who are these people? I don't know any of them. I don't know what they're capable of. Murder? Sure, statistically some of them have to be capable of that. But how do you know which ones?

The trip to the bank takes me past flooded gardens and lawns with new swimming pools that suggest the sun hasn't been out all day. The streets are bone-dry and make for safe driving. There's no consensus about what to wear—some people are out in shorts and T-shirts, others in raincoats carrying umbrellas. I figure they're all right. I park next to a beaten-up Holden with half of its hubcaps missing.

The bank is a plain-looking building in a row of other plain-looking buildings in the middle of town, a few blocks from the police department and a few hundred yards away from the Christchurch Cathedral, a touristy church right in the middle of town. There's a guy out front of the bank handing out sandwich vouchers. He hands one to me and it makes me feel hungry, almost hungry enough to eat the voucher. The glass doors open with a hissing sound. Potted palm trees guarding the entranceway almost reach the ceiling. A whole lot more potted plants are scattered around inside. Maybe it's supposed to make the fee-paying customers feel more at ease.

Me, I feel like I'm back in a forest. I look around for a river, but the closest thing is a water cooler in the corner. It has an out-of-order sign because somebody has broken the plastic tap. I wait in line. Earlier this summer, just before Christmas, this bank was held up. People were waiting in line then just like they are now. People were shot and killed. I look at everybody closely in case there are those in here who think holding up banks is a pretty good idea.

It takes five minutes to get to the counter. I present my withdrawal slip to an old guy named George who will surely die before he retires, and even then still try to show up for work. His wrinkled face takes on a puzzled expression when he reads the amount on the slip, and he adjusts his bifocals to make sure he's read the amount correctly as if the thick lenses have added an extra zero. Then he adjusts them again to make sure he's seeing me correctly, as if the thick lenses have added an extra bruise. He asks me to step aside while he wanders off to chat to a few people, and a minute later a woman around my age comes from somewhere deep within the bank and leads me down a carpeted corridor into a small office.

Her name is Erica, and Erica is the sort of woman I would be flirting with if I didn't appear and feel half-dead and think the woman I possibly still love might be dead. The small cream office has no window so the only view is the single door we came through, an aerial photo of Christchurch hanging on the wall and a vase filled with plastic roses. I look at the photo and wonder where I was when it was taken. More people were alive then. On the opposite wall is a photo of a guy in his forties or fifties. It has his name and two years listed beneath him, one must be his year of birth, the other is last year—it must be the bank manager who was killed during the robbery.

A long desk with a computer and stacks of paper and office

clutter sits close to the middle of the room with a chair on each side. It feels like an interrogation room, and when she starts asking me questions to prove my identity I look around for two-way mirrors. I wait for her to ask where I was on Sunday night, but she doesn't. I can see her desire to inquire about my bruises and cuts, but she can't bring herself to do so. She keeps brushing her hair back behind her right ear in a nervous way. She knows something isn't right, but what can she do? She can think and she can suspect. But it's my money. A small necklace with a silver crucifix hangs around her neck. I feel like letting her in on the big secret.

After fifteen minutes of signing papers Erica agrees to hand over my money. It takes the staff another fifteen minutes to get the cash from their vault, and they count it out in front of me in a timid way that makes me think that they think I might be one bad-hair day away from shooting them all. They pack it into a small linen bag. I look for the huge dollar sign on the side to make it more obvious, but don't see one. I thank Erica, then before leaving, I take out the wads of notes and stuff them inside my jacket and pants pockets. It's a tight fit.

I walk a few blocks to the north, skirting around a crane and some cement mixers and several workmen who don't appear to be doing anything. In Christchurch there are always workmen working on shops. All the time. I do what I should have done six months ago, and buy a prepay cell phone. Then I walk to a nearby army surplus store. The walls are painted camouflage green, which makes the building stick out more. Mannequins in the window are wearing desert and jungle uniforms. Plastic people off to war. I walk inside. The lighting is dim and the air is warm. Uniforms and outfits are hanging from wire coat hangers. Stacked all over the place are army storage containers with yellow and white lettering stenciled on them. Old medals in glass cases. Old gas masks. Old everything. I look at a counter full of knives. I find a hunting knife with a sharp blade and with ridges along the top.

The guy behind the counter stands around six and a half feet and has large, flabby arms covered in White Power tattoos. He wears a black leather vest with a black T-shirt beneath it. The T-shirt says *Guns don't kill people. Grenades do*. His head is shaved and he has a long, gray beard. A name badge attached to his vest says *Floyd* and it looks out of place on his huge chest. He tells me the knife is called a KA-BAR.

I put the knife aside and keep looking. Floyd follows me around. It makes me feel uncomfortable. He asks if he can help. I tell him I'm after some fatigue gear. He shows me where it is. It's new, not like most of the stuff in here. I wonder if anybody died in any of these uniforms. I pick up a vest with lots of pockets and army pants and an army jacket and boots too. I grab a pair of compact 8 x 20 binoculars that can fit in one of the many pockets in the vest.

I put them with the knife then look through a small display of Swiss Army knives. I point to one that looks like it could do everything from repairing sunglasses to gutting a fish. He pulls it out and puts it next to the KA-BAR. The KA-BAR looks massive in comparison. I pull out my wallet. Floyd says nothing as he looks me up and down. He looks like he could break every bone in my body so I smile at him and make no conversation.

"You going hunting?" he asks.

"Yep."

"What you hunting for?"

"Deer."

"Uh huh. The two-legged type?"

I pay for the gear. He gives me my change.

"No. The four-legged type."

"Okay," he says.

"I'm thinking," I tell him, "that it may be easier to shoot deer than stab them. Is that right?"

"What kind of trouble are you in, mister?"

I hand him five hundred dollars. "The kind that needs a gun. Where can I get one?"

He stares at the money. Then he stares at me. "You're about halfway to me telling you how that can be done."

I count out another five hundred and put it on the counter next to the first five hundred. He sweeps his hands across it and it all disappears. Then he gives me a name, tells me to go and see this guy tomorrow.

"Not today?" I ask.

"You need to go shooting deer today?"

"No," I tell him.

"Then tomorrow will be fine then, won't it."

He puts my purchases into a plastic supermarket bag. I thank him and leave.

I get back to my car just as a traffic cop is about to give me a ticket. He's a guy in his thirties who looks like he's spent twenty of those years either lifting heavy weights or doing hard time. He looks up at me and before I can say anything, he says "Looks like you've had a tough day."

"Yeah."

"How about I don't make it any tougher for you? Next time put enough coins in the meter, okay?"

I almost feel like hugging him, and it restores some of my faith in the city.

I drive out to the airport and pull into medium-term parking, where Jo's car can stay for the next few days, or where the police will eventually find it after I'm dead. The walls of the rental agency I choose are painted bright orange with blue racing stripes around the middle. The windows and glass sliding doors are covered in stickers and decals. I step inside and an assistant high on caffeine goes through the paperwork with me as I rent a late-model Holden, similar to the one I saw outside the bank. I figure driving around in my own car is a pretty dumb thing to do since Cyris knows it so well.

I show the guy my driver's license and he looks at me and then at the photo. I shrug. "Car accident," I tell him.

"Car had fists, did it?"

"Something like that."

"You should take out the insurance," he says.

So I take out the insurance. I sign the credit-card form and the guy tells me to keep the pen. I add the car key to my others.

The Holden is a much nicer drive than my Honda and Jo's Mazda, but it doesn't make the situation seem any better. Just more comfortable. I throw my free pen in the glove box where it sits next to a map and a box of tissues and an instruction booklet. Back home I charge the cell phone. I change the outgoing message on my answering machine so it includes my new cell number.

I'm about to make something to eat when suddenly I realize I don't want to touch any of the food that's in my house since both Cyris and Landry have been in here. Problem is I'm starving. I get back into my car and drive a few minutes to some local shops and spend a few minutes buying some food. I'm driving back home when the answer to one of my questions hits me. I've been wondering why Cyris didn't take his two victims into the middle of nowhere. It's because he wanted them found. He didn't want them found at home, but he didn't want them to be missing forever. He wanted them found side by side in a pasture by a common highway. He would have left the stolen van there with blood in it. Maybe he'd have left other stuff on the sidewalk, like some sliced up clothes. The cops would have searched the area. This way the motivation for the abductions and murders looks obvious—it looks like a sick bastard doing what he enjoys most. Cyris wanted them found.

But not at home.

Why?

Jo would be able to figure it out.

I get home. I carry the sandwich I bought through to the table and sit down. It's chicken and cranberry and should taste great, but it doesn't. I eat it simply because I need the fuel. There is something to all of this, something to the fact Cyris didn't want them found at home. Why? Didn't he want their husbands to come home and . . .

Suddenly I realize what didn't fit well with the newspaper article I read yesterday! I stand up quickly and almost choke on my sandwich. The newspaper said Kathy's body was found by her neighbor, but Kathy had told me her cheating husband Frank would be home before the morning to get fresh clothes. She seemed sure of it. If he did come home, why wouldn't he have called the police?

I drag this chain of questions around the dining room as I pace it. Is it reasonable to think her husband came home expecting to find her missing, and not dead? Just because he was due home and never called the police? It's possible, but it's equally possible he never made it home, that he stayed where he was and cheated some more on Kathy.

Okay, so there are a few possibilities, but with nothing else to work with, I try to make these possibilities fit around the answer I want. And it's not difficult. There was no forced entry. Cyris wants money. He even yelled out *For the money*. Kathy was supposed to be missing, not dead. I think he knew his wife was going to die that night. I think he came home prepared to call the police that she was missing, and when he found her sliced up in the master bedroom he didn't know what to do. So he ran.

I think back to what I told Landry about Cyris putting himself into a role to kill the two women. The police come along, they find the hammer and stake, and they think madman. They don't think cheating husband. They think psychopath. They don't think messy divorce.

At six thirty I dress in my new fatigue gear. What I see in the mirror scares me. I slip the cell into one of the many pockets, the binoculars and KA-BAR and Swiss Army knife into others. The sun is low, its casual slide into the night almost complete. It's now just a bright, blurry orange blob. Dressed like I'm about to go to war, and feeling it too, I walk to my car, pull down the sun visor and head toward the battlefield.

# CHAPTER THIRTY-NINE

The sun sinks and my anguish rises.

I stop at a supermarket and ignore the looks. A person dressed in fatigues is a common enough sight. People who have been beaten up are also common enough. It's not often the two are combined. Normally the guy in the fatigues has given the beating. Stopping at the supermarket has never been so weird. It's as if I've evolved beyond walking up and down aisles looking for pastas and cereals and bread. This kind of mundane day-to-day living is behind me. This isn't where people go when death is all around them. I grab chips, doughnuts, a packet of cheese slices, and two drinks. I roll out a hundred-dollar note and the looks on the faces around me change. The girl working the checkout takes a small step back. She's thinking I just mugged somebody. Or killed them.

I pull past Kathy's house at six fifty in my shiny, rented Holden and park six houses further down. There are no police cars. No police tape. Life has moved on. Death hasn't, though. I can feel it waiting in the street watching me. The Mercedes I saw parked outside one of the neighboring houses is still parked in the same place. Maybe it's broken down. The street is pretty quiet. I start waiting.

I flick through the newspaper I bought with my snacks. The murders are still front-page news. No mention of Landry. I figure it's too soon. The cops will be concerned. I'm sure Landry kept any information about me to himself. Had to, so he could execute me without fear of being caught. At least that's something in my favor, I guess. I try to think if anything connects me to Landry's death. My fingerprints are all over the cabin, which will match those at Kathy's and Luciana's houses. What else is there? Oh shit. There's the piece of paper he showed me with my name and phone number surrounded by rubbed pencil. If Landry's body is found the note will be discovered. But maybe it's gotten so battered by the river it's now useless. Or maybe it wasn't in those clothes, but in the pocket of his jacket or pants, which Jo is now wearing. If she's even wearing anything.

My stomach tightens at that thought. The harder I try not to imagine her naked and pinned beneath Cyris, the more visual it becomes. I start sweating. I look for a distraction. I read the rest of the newspaper. I start on the crossword puzzle and can only manage to solve a third of it. The day goes from being light to dim to dark. The streetlights come on. An hour into my wait a dark Mercedes pulls into a driveway six houses ahead of me. Into Kathy's house. I put the binoculars to my eyes and manage only a glimpse of the car before it rolls out of sight. I start the car and move up to pull in behind the silver Mercedes. Does everybody on this street own one? I kill the engine. Wait patiently.

I can see the right front of the house and the back of the

Mercedes. I can't see any movement inside the house or the car. There's not much more I can do. I came prepared to wait for hours and now it seems I may just be doing that. I have to remain focused. Remain sharp. I have to trust everything is okay. If I believed otherwise I'd be believing there's no point in carrying on.

I start to grow restless, fidgety. The minutes slip by like lost nights. This is the first evening Landry has ever missed since being born. A few people are out and about. Some are walking dogs. Others are power walking, thrusting their arms in front of them in self-defense movements to stay fit. Nobody pays any attention to me. I probably look like a reporter. Or a cop. Both would have perfect justification to be sitting here. Both wouldn't look out of place with cuts and bruises on their faces. I consider reading the newspaper again, but it's too dark now. I want to get out and stretch a few of my aching muscles. I adjust my position in the seat. I look into the rearview mirror. My jaw where Landry hit me is getting darker. The swelling has gone down and the bruising has darkened. I run my finger along the line of the bruise. It feels soft, like a small balloon of water is trapped underneath.

I look up at the sky and wonder if it will rain tonight. When my cell phone rings I can't find it. I fumble through my vest pockets, forgetting which one I put it in, swearing every time my fingers come up empty. When I get to it I check the display. The number is blocked. I flip it open and answer it.

"Why aren't you at home, partner?" Cyris's voice crackles through the earpiece.

"Didn't want you changing your mind and deciding to kill me instead."

Cyris says nothing as he thinks about it. So I say nothing. A minute goes by in which it seems we're setting a trend.

"You got the money?" he asks.

"I got it."

"Fifty grand."

"What?"

"You're pissing me off, buddy. It's fifty grand now. It's not free to dial a cell phone."

No, but it doesn't cost ten thousand dollars either. "I only have forty."

"Forty will only get you eighty percent of her, and I decide which eighty."

At least he's sharpening up. "Fine," I finally say. "Fifty grand." This isn't going to come down to money. It's going to come down to me killing him.

"Meet me back out at the cabin."

"No way."

"What?"

"We three go out there and only you come back. Tell me if I'm wrong. It has to be somewhere more public." I've been giving it some thought. "The pier. New Brighton."

It seems like a good location. Not too many people, but enough so Cyris won't try anything. He says nothing as he thinks this through. Jo could already be dead and he just wants the money. Or she could be alive and he's thinking about the location, about how he has to change his plans. He's thinking that maybe he won't be getting the chance to kill us tomorrow night after all. So he's still saying nothing. But now he's realizing he knows my address, my details. He's figuring he can kill me later on. In his own time. At his own leisure. He can afford to drive on over one night after mowing his lawn, rip me apart, and pick up dinner on the way back. So the idea of a public place isn't looking too bad. In a public place I can't try anything against him. In a public place we all walk away alive.

"Midnight," he says.

Only he's wrong. I'm happy to try something in a public place. I have more to lose than him. Everything to gain.

"Ten o'clock," I counter. "More people."

I wince as I wait for a reply or for the phone to hang up.

"Don't forget the money, asshole. I'll cut her pretty little head off no matter how many people are around."

"Let me talk to Jo."

"She's busy."

"I need to know she's okay."

"She's okay, asshole."

"I need proof of life," I say, which is something I've heard people say in movies and documentaries.

"I'm going to give you proof of death instead, partner," he says, and with that he hangs up.

# CHAPTER FORTY

Agitated. He knows he's agitated, and the phone call hasn't helped. His stomach hurts, but so does his head and he wants to lash out, wants to strike out at everything and anything. He grips his stomach and wonders why he ever threw away those painkillers. He contemplates smashing the phone against the edge of the desk, but that would accomplish nothing.

At least he sure as shit feels better today than he did yesterday.

The last few days have been hell. He was taught in the army that there would be days like this. Weeks. Months. He never saw combat, but he was trained for it. He knew how to kill people. His wife knew how to kill people too. It's where he met her. They trained together. They socialized. They fell in love. That was ten years ago. Then five years ago they got married. Then four and a half years ago there was a training accident and now his wife is a former shell of the person she used to be. It was a helicopter accident. The thing about helicopters is that at the best of times they fly, and at any other time they don't. They're not like planes. Planes can get into trouble and they can glide. Planes have a chance of landing. They can stay level enough to jump out of with a chute. Helicopters don't glide. They fall. They crash. The pilot was killed. Two corporals were killed. Macy, his wife, ended up losing both of her legs, her left one just above the knee, her right one just below.

So she was given a medical discharge. It was going to be a new life. She went through multiple surgeries. She spent weeks where she would just cry. It was three months until he could bring her home. Things got better. They got worse. They got better again. She got counseling. She was going great. Then she tried to kill herself. He had gone to work. She tied a rope around a beam in the garage and tied the other end around her neck. She got out of her wheelchair and sat herself up on a workbench. Then she jumped. The wheelchair fell over. Then Cyris came home. He'd forgotten his sunglasses. He found her in the garage. Her jaw had clamped. She'd bitten off a chunk of her tongue and blood was running down her neck. He cut her down. He called an ambulance. He got her jaw open, but her mouth kept filling with blood from her severed tongue. He tried to resuscitate her, but there was too much blood. The ambulance arrived. They were lucky—there had been a false call two blocks away so there was an ambulance at his house within ninety seconds of him calling. The paramedics took over.

Everybody thought she was going to die. The doctors guessed she must have been hanging between two and three minutes. Her brain had been starved of oxygen. They resuscitated her, but there was brain damage. She would never be

functional. That was the word the doctor used. *Functional.*
Like she was the remote control to his TV. There were pay-
ments from the army to help with her rehabilitation from
her severed legs, but there was nothing extra for the brain
damage. Insurance wouldn't cover the costs. She had tried
to kill herself. They weren't in the business of helping people
who had tried to die. She needed full-time care. The army
helped for four years because of her legs, then a year ago they
stopped paying. It was cutbacks. Everywhere had cutbacks.
The economy was in the toilet.

He walks through to his wife. She's lying in bed watching
the TV. She likes cartoons. She's seen this particular one well
over a thousand times. It's on a DVD and it's on repeat and he
knows every word, every sound effect, and at night he leaves
the TV running for her and the volume off. She looks up at
him and smiles. "Side Russ," she says. That's his name now,
thanks to about a quarter of her tongue hitting the garage
floor.

"Hey, babe," he says. Sometimes, when he's feeling at his
worst, he likes to tell her.

"I'm hungry," she says.

"I'll get you something in a minute," he says, knowing that
if he doesn't, she'll forget that she's hungry anyway.

"Ooo have a beard," she says.

He reaches up and tugs on his beard. He's had it for a few
weeks now, and he hates it. When this is all over he'll shave
it off.

"Side Russ," she says. "Are thoo okay?"

"My stomach hurts," he tells her. "I was stabbed." He lifts
up his T-shirt and shows her his stomach. There's duct tape
holding the wound closed.

"What ha-hend?"

"A bad man stabbed me," he says, and then he tells her about it.

She starts to cry. And then she gets distracted by the cartoon on the TV. Then she starts to laugh. And then she looks over at him. "Side Russ," she says. "Are thoo okay?"

"I'm fine," he tells her. "Let me get you something to eat."

He goes through to the bathroom. He soaks his hands in water, then raises them to his face. He wipes at it, wipes and wipes and his skin is sore, yeah, and he's careful to avoid his broken nose. It's swollen and raw and there's bruising around it. Then he wipes those same hands at the mirror. The image remains and he can't get rid of the pain. From nowhere one of the headaches strikes, and he has to lower himself and sit on the edge of the bath. Christ. When it passes he opens the medicine cabinet, but nothing lives in there except aspirin, so he grabs hold of a few, even though they will do little to help. Clenching his fists, he sits back on the side of the bath and lifts his shirt. He's going to need to get some more stuff from his buddy, Derek, the guy that fixed him up years ago with *the good shit*. His buddy is the same guy that fixed him up with this gig. Derek is one of those guys who knows people. He's one of those guys who introduces people to people who need things done. He's also Macy's brother. Derek has hooked him up with other people in the past. Others that needed to die. Not many. Just a few. He's not proud of what he does, but he needs the money. He needs it to look after Macy.

The duct tape across his stomach is covered in dried blood. He chews the aspirin and the taste makes his head spin, but at least he's focused now on the job at hand, and from his back pocket he takes out the piece of paper with his instructions, with his goals, and the piece of paper helps to remind him that tonight he's going to be a wealthy man. A wealthy man. Oh yeah.

He tugs at the edge of the duct tape, but it's fastened down, and he wishes he had put some padding beneath it first because now the wound will smile open when he pulls the tape away. He squeezes his hands across his ears. Never in his life has he suffered from headaches, not until Monday. Feldman will have to pay. He's going to pay in more ways than one.

Cyris pushes himself up from the bath and moves down the hallway. He wonders how Macy would react if he were to take her into the basement and show her his investment. He wonders how both women would react. Of course Macy would forget all about it after a little while. He reaches the doorway to the basement. He's light-headed and the walls and the door are spinning in time with his mind, but in the opposite direction. He reaches out and balances himself. The room starts to spin faster. He holds his breath and the need to vomit slowly fades.

He thinks of Charlie. He thinks of Charlie plunging the knife into him, and at the same time the pain in his stomach flares up as though the knife is back in there, twisting around and around. He doubles over and collapses to his knees. No amount of money is worth this. When he gets back to his feet he unlocks the basement door and heads downstairs. The woman looks up at him and he can see she's been crying. He hates it when women cry. It's their way of making men feel guilty. It's a weapon they use to make men feel like crap. Macy never did that to him. Macy was an army chick. She was tough.

He hates Charlie Feldman for being such an asshole.

He hates the world for being the way it is.

From the bench nearby he picks up a knife and moves toward Feldman's wife.

# CHAPTER FORTY-ONE

I stare at the phone, looking to take back the words I just said to Cyris, wanting to reach through the dead air and pull them back, but they're no longer mine, they're his, and he's going to do with them what he wants to. That's the thing about Cyris. He's all about setting the rules.

The car windows are slightly fogged over from my heavy breathing. It feels like fifty degrees in here and the air tastes stale. I wipe a hand over the glass, smudging a path through the moisture and creating a gateway to the outside. Kathy and Luciana are standing only a few yards from my door. I stare at them, waiting for Jo to appear, but she doesn't, and perhaps she won't until I know for a fact that my words have killed her.

I squeeze my eyes shut, hold them closed for a few seconds to give the two girls a chance to disappear, and when I open them back up and see them still there I start to doubt that they're only in my mind. They look happier since I saw them last, as if somehow at peace. My skin tingles as my arms break out in goose bumps. A cold chill blasts its way down the back of my neck as if the air-conditioning in the Holden has just been cranked to some mystery arctic setting. I try to open the door, but my arms won't move. I can barely breathe. The world sways and I can hardly stay conscious.

Kathy is wearing a long, white dress, shoulderless, the material thin and whispery. Luciana is wearing a summer dress covered in small, red roses and yellow daffodils. She's wearing a hat too. She looks tanned. None of these clothes I saw them wearing, so why would I see them dressed like this now? They're holding hands as they stand there smiling at me. I get my arms moving jerkily and manage to roll down the window. Their mouths open and close, but I can't hear what they're saying. Kathy takes a step forward. Her hair is blowing in some invisible breeze. Luciana follows. My eyes are starting to sting, but I'm too frightened to blink, too frightened that in that split second they will disappear. Something is going on here that can't be controlled by either my imagination or my conscience.

That's when Jo appears. She fades into view, like somebody sneaking out of the shadows. She's wearing the same dress she wore on our first date. She offers a sad smile, the kind of sympathetic smile you have when you've just found out one of your friends has been hurt by bad news.

"Jo," I say, and seeing her is confirmation that I fucked up, that my words have killed her.

"It's okay, Charlie," she says.

I tell her I'm sorry. I try the door handle and just then the phone rings. I glance at it. In that instant Kathy is gone, Luciana has gone with her, they've taken Jo, and I'm alone in my car looking back at an empty street. My window is still rolled up, the smear mark on the glass from my hand is still clear. My face is covered in a film of sweat and the lump on my forehead is throbbing. As I scramble for the phone it slips in my fingers and bounces off the passenger seat onto the floor. I reach down, grab it, and open it while I'm still hunched over the gearshift.

"Cyris?"

"Charlie, it's me."

"Jo!" I say, and hearing her voice serves not only to make me feel relieved she is still alive, but also proves the ghosts are not ghosts at all.

"I'm okay, Charlie."

Thank God. Thank you, God. "Has he hurt you?"

"I'm okay. He wants me to tell you he'll see you tomorrow night."

"I know."

"He says don't try anything, Charlie."

"I won't."

"He'll let us go."

"You don't believe that, do you?"

She hesitates, and then, "I have to go. Be careful, Charlie. Promise me that."

"Jo," I say, but I'm already talking into a broken connection.

Jo is alive and so is my hope. I will either die in hope or live in despair. I drop the phone onto the seat and get back to the very business I came here to do, which is waiting. Waiting to see what Kathy's husband does.

Cyris told me he was busy tonight. I know from experience he's been busy the last few nights so I'm thinking if there's a payoff to take place there's a chance it's tonight.

I stare out the window as the minutes pass. The night gets darker. The number of people walking by thins out and then

there are none. Lights are turned on as people settle in for
the evening. An hour passes. Two hours. I'm starting to need
a bathroom. Lights start to turn off. People are going to bed.
I have nothing to do but run my theory over and over in my
head. The problem is it looks bad. Looks worse every time I
glance at my watch and see another block of time has gone by.
I was wrong to think the payment would be tonight and the
passing minutes prove this to me. Wrong to think the husband
is involved.

Wrong about everything.

I reach toward the ignition. I'm going to have to pay Cyris
and hope for the best. Resort to Plan B, which I'm still working on. I hear a car start before I start my own. I let go of the
keys and lean forward. Could this be it? I wait and watch as
the Mercedes reverses down the driveway and onto the street.
Frank. Frank the cheating husband. The car straightens and
heads away from me.

I start the Holden and begin following. I don't turn my
headlights on. When he turns the corner I keep fifty yards
behind him. The full moon and streetlights provide more than
enough light to drive by, turning the roads pale blue except
for the road markings, which glow white. Stars twinkle in the
sky, their light coming from millions of miles away and centu-
ries ago. I wonder if people like Cyris lived on those long-lost
worlds. A few people coming toward me flash their lights, but
Frank the cheating husband can't see that, not from fifty yards
ahead. Before I take the next corner, I turn on my lights.

The theory I've been playing with is once again starting to
look good. I wonder how much money exchanged hands to
end two women's lives. In a fair world I should be getting a
cut of those funds. Was money the motive? I've seen Frank's
house. I've seen his car. He was cheating on his wife. He

wanted a divorce and didn't want to give her half of everything. Instead he took everything she ever had.

Of course this is all guesswork. He could just be heading out for a hamburger.

We turn right at a set of lights and my fear that he's meeting Cyris outside the city is quashed when Frank's brake lights come on and he signals before pulling into a dead-end side street next to a shopping mall. I continue ahead and park on the road opposite. I kill the engine and pull up the hand brake. I pull the lens caps off the binoculars and watch him eight times bigger than normal life as he pulls into the entrance to the parking lot to his left. He pulls into it and kills his lights, but keeps on driving, making it difficult to follow him through my narrow field of vision. He turns right, goes straight for a bit, then turns left and out of sight. I pull the binoculars away and tuck them back into my pocket. I know this mall: he can't have gone far.

The dashboard clock reads eleven fifty. If Frank is making a payoff it makes sense it's going to happen at midnight. That gives me ten minutes to wait. Ten minutes to consider where things can go wrong. Ten minutes to figure what I can do about it.

I suck in a deep breath and, checking there's no other traffic, I leave my car and run across the road. Spur-of-the-moment decisions haven't been working out for me well this week, but I figure one has to go right. It's like continually doubling down on red at the roulette table, chasing your losses and knowing it can't keep on coming up black. Statistically it's impossible that you can roll the wheel for the next fifty years and never get it to go your way.

Only at the end of the day the house always wins.

I vault the low railing that separates the parking lot from

the sidewalk and land without the embarrassment of trip-
ping. I break into a jog. Like town this afternoon, there
are diggers and cranes and other building equipment lying
around. Skeletons of more parking lots and more shops to
come look like macabre playground equipment. Mounds of
shingle and dirt form small hills. It takes me half a minute
to reach the turn where the car disappeared. I crouch down
and peer around the corner. I can see Frank's car but no
Frank. The car has its headlights facing me, but they're not
on. I keep watching and a few moments later Frank appears
from behind his car. He climbs into his seat, pulls the door
shut and, keeping the lights off, begins rolling forward. With
nowhere to run I lie flat against the ground and watch the
car arc around at least fifteen yards away from me so I'm
out of sight. My army fatigues do what they're designed for,
and he doesn't see me. He passes and accelerates away. The
headlights flick on. He leaves the parking lot and pulls out
onto the street.

I count to ten, eager to rush out there but not stupid
enough. Then I count to ten again just to be sure. I make my
way to where the car was parked. I turn in a slow circle. Ahead
the neon letters of the supermarket have been switched off to
save power. To my left the wall of the mall has been freshly
painted, covering up a recent attack by graffiti artists—if you
can call somebody who scrawls capital letters across a wall
with spray paint an artist. To my right at the end of the parking lot is a neighboring fence. The supermarket runs almost
the entire distance from the mall wall to that fence, except
for a service alley at the far end. None of this inlet can be
seen from the road. I walk up to the large glass doors of the
supermarket. Hundreds of shopping carts are parked inside,
boxes and bags, the sort of stuff you should see when you look

through supermarket windows. Frank got out of his car, moved behind it, and came over here. Somewhere.

It only takes me a minute to find the briefcase. It's sitting in a garbage bin that's bolted to the ground a few yards to the left of the supermarket doors. I don't bother opening it, but carry it back to my car, running the entire way. I get into the driver's seat and pop the lid open and stare at bundles of cash. Lots of fresh brand-new bills. A lot of money looks great. It makes you feel rich, like you've achieved something. Even if you haven't. So that's how I'm feeling. I'm feeling rich for achieving little. I'm feeling rich for achieving a lot of fuckups over the last few days. I'm also feeling smarter than Cyris and maybe that's dangerous. Maybe for once the house isn't going to win.

But I'm also feeling angry, more at Frank than at Cyris right now. Frank is the reason the two girls died, and therefore the reason that Jo has been kidnapped. He's also the reason Landry got himself shot up and thrown into a river. It all stems from him squirreling away this pile of cash and saving it up so his wife could be sliced up and killed. I feel like driving after Frank and running him off the road. Feel like punching and kicking and even stabbing him, over and over and over till he's dead, at the same time asking him how it feels. What a bastard. What a piece of trash. I can feel myself burning up. I wonder if this is the full amount, or if it was one of those *half now half and half after* kind of jobs. I wonder why Frank didn't pay Cyris earlier, then realize he probably couldn't—he needed a day or two for things to die down. Making a payment the same day his wife was murdered wouldn't look too good.

Action Man is angry. And, like I thought earlier, Action Man is no longer a victim.

I spill the cash onto the floor well in front of the passenger seat, creating a pile of cash in different denominations. I pop the glove box and grab hold of the pen the car rental agency guy gave me. Withdrawing a single hundred-dollar note from the pile of cash, I write on it, having to go over the same lines a few times to make the letters dark enough. Then I place it inside the briefcase. I close the lid and click both latches closed. It's much lighter now.

Still no traffic so I run across the road and this time, instead of vaulting the barrier, I hurdle it. I land running, pumping my legs hard, holding the briefcase in front of me. I round the corner. Same supermarket, same view of shopping carts behind windows, same garbage bin. I put the briefcase where I found it. Before I can head back, tires shriek into the parking lot and headlights wash across the neighboring fence, sweeping toward me. My only chance is the service alley. I dive just as the light behind me comes into view. I hit the ground hard and come to a stop against a chain-link gate that rattles but not loudly enough for Cyris to have heard over the car. My car. I twist around and, staying low, peer around the corner.

Instead of turning the car around as Frank had, Cyris keeps my Honda pointing directly at the garbage bin. He climbs out of the car and doesn't look in my direction. He looks exactly the same as last night from the scruffy facial hair to the black clothes. The only difference is a pair of sunglasses over his eyes. It really pisses me off seeing him driving my car in such a way that when this is all over and I've killed the son of a bitch, I'm going to be buying a new car. He walks to the bin, walking with a slight limp and with one hand against this stomach. He reaches it and grabs the briefcase. He rests it over the edges of the bin, tilts it toward him, and pops it open with his thumbs. The angle is wrong for me to study his expression, but not wrong enough to watch him stand there for a full minute, still and silent. He closes the case, turns it around in his hands, sets it back down, and opens it again, as if he's the victim of a parlor trick. Then he turns from the garbage bin and carries the hundred-dollar note to the front of the car. Carefully he examines it under the headlights, turning it over so he can read the note I wrote for him. In the end he screws the bill into his jeans and walks back to the briefcase. He picks it up and swings it hard into the bin. The impact clangs out into the night. After two more blows the briefcase starts cracking and the bin begins to fold inward. The headlights isolate him from the darkness as though he's on a stage.

He stops thrashing the briefcase, swings his arm back, and throws it high in the air. It hits the roof of the supermarket and doesn't come back down. He leans over the bin and starts shaking it, pulling it from side to side, wrenching it back and forth until it tears from the bolts, leaving jagged holes in the bottom. He holds it high above his head for a few seconds, then throws it at the supermarket doors. It bounces off with a metallic thud, the dents in it stopping it from rolling away once it hits the ground. He picks it back up and throws it harder. This time the glass cracks. The third throw gets it through the glass doors. The alarms are instant.

He walks back to my car, clutching his stomach, and when he pulls his hand away I can see it's red. He's bleeding. He leans against the car and watches the supermarket.

I turn around and study the service-alley gate. Ten feet tall and made up of chain-link wire. I'm sure I can scale it without being heard over the alarm. I do just that, climbing it like a large spider. I follow the alley until it circles toward the back entrances of the shops in the mall. I scale another fence and hit the ground in some industrial section, perhaps an auto body shop—it's too dark to tell exactly. Then over another fence and into somebody's backyard. I climb into a park, and start to circle my way back toward my car. By the time I get there two police cars are in the parking lot, but probably no Cyris. With thousands of dollars in the car I'm lucky not to be walking home right now. I guess it's a school night for all those joyriders out there. I do a U-turn, pissed off that I let Cyris get ahead of me, but what could I do? Wait for him to stop breaking glass doors then run after his car?

I keep my foot on the accelerator, hovering between thirty and forty miles per hour. I can't afford to be too late. Cyris already has ten minutes on me and I doubt he took his time driving to Frank's. I also doubt there's anywhere else in the world he'd be going right now.

I wonder if I'm already too late.

# CHAPTER FORTY-TWO

There's no other traffic, no reason to stop at any red lights. Cyris sure wouldn't have. He's fueled with rage just as I was fueled with despair the other night. I've raced these lonely streets before, but the fuel that has me speeding is different from the mix that burned through my veins on Monday. I don't get lost on my way to Frank's house, not like Monday morning, and when I turn into the street the first thing I see is the silver Mercedes still parked on the side of the road. Maybe it's purely for show.

I drive past Frank's house and glance in. Lights are burning inside, but I can't see his Mercedes. It's probably in the garage. I pull up two houses further down. My Honda isn't here, at least not that I can see. Either Cyris has been and gone or he isn't coming. I kill the engine, kill the lights, and wait. I look around the street for any signs of life, but it seems like life on this expensive street has died since I was here earlier. I look at my watch. It's nearly one o'clock.

I stroll over to the house, knowing that slow movement attracts less attention. I don't pause at the cobblestone walkway, I stroll up it as if I live there. The front door is open. That's not good. No signs of forced entry. Coming here is tearing open a recent memory.

I step forward and stand on the threshold of the hallway. On the threshold of Monday's memory. On the threshold of a new horror to come. I stand still and listen, but there's nothing, so I take a few more steps and repeat the same procedure and get the same result. I put my hands in my pockets where they'll be safe from touching anything. I could just turn away and read about it in tomorrow's paper, but I need to see this. I want to see this—to see what has been done to the man who orchestrated the deaths of two beautiful women.

The lights are glowing in the lounge and it's here that I find him, lying on his stomach with his head twisted, his arms spread in front of him, the carpet beneath soaked in blood. My breath catches at this sight and I suddenly realize why. I have killed this man and the feeling doesn't make me feel sick or guilty. I have killed him, not directly, but as surely as if the metal stake protruding from his chest was placed there by my hand. I step closer and kneel down. The anger I feel toward him hasn't diminished at all just because he's dead. If anything I actually feel like kicking him. I'm not sure what that says about me, and I'm not sure I really want to know.

Frank has that distinguished look you see in middle-aged doctors on TV. His wire-rimmed glasses have been knocked askew, his eyes are open and reveal irises that are more yellowish then green. He wears a grim look on his face that death is managing to hold in place, a look that tells me the end didn't come easy. There is a thin line of blood and drool slipping from the corner of his slightly open mouth. The edge of a piece of paper is sticking from between his lips. I reach forward and grab hold of it, and when I pull, his mouth doesn't even move, but his lower lip is dragged forward, his suddenly revealed teeth giving him the smile of a skull. The hundred-dollar note is damp. I unscrew it, my fingers getting wet. I read the message I wrote across it earlier. *Come near me and I'll have you killed.*

I hide it in one of my many pockets, then jam my hands into two of the others. I turn around, studying the room. Expensive furniture and expensive gadgetry and nice paintings . . . I guess it's true when they say you can't take it with you, even though with his arms spread it sure looks like Frank's giving it a go. I call out for Kathy, but she doesn't answer.

"You deserved worse," I say to Frank, and Frank doesn't answer. He doesn't concede the point, or argue it. He just lies there looking pissed off, and I guess I can't blame him. "You probably think I ought to be feeling sorry for you," I tell him, "but I don't have it in me. You got off easy. Way too easy."

I turn my back on Frank. Tomorrow he'll be all over the papers in the same way his wife was. The cops won't know what to make of it. First Kathy, then Frank, both of them stabbed in the chest with a metal stake. They'll track Frank's movements, and I wonder where that will lead, and can't imagine them coming to the conclusion that Frank paid off a hit man who turned around and killed him. They'll be looking for Landry too, and perhaps they've already found him—though I don't see how. Unless the current has swept him free of that fallen tree and he's on his way to where people go swimming or fishing or hiking.

I drive home. I stay under the speed limit. I'm in no hurry to be anywhere. I pray Cyris isn't taking his disappointment out on Jo and figure he can't afford to. In fact figuring he can't

afford to is the only thing keeping me sane. He's lost his payment from tonight and won't risk losing the fifty grand he
thinks he's getting from me tomorrow. I knew the risk when I
wrote out that note; of course I thought I'd be able to follow
Cyris first to Frank's and then to Jo. I wasn't expecting him to
take out his rage on a supermarket. I was expecting to be sitting in my car waiting for him. When I decided to leave that
note for him, well, I didn't know at the time if that was a good
idea or a bad one—it just seemed like the thing to do. Right
and wrong can only be decided by how Jo is being treated.

There is little in the way of traffic. None on my street.
There's a big black cat sitting in the middle of my driveway,
which plays chicken with my car before deciding there can
only be one winner and scampers off over the fence. I load
the money into one of the plastic bags from the supermarket
where I shopped earlier today. I head inside and brace a chair
beneath the handle of the back door in an attempt to lock it.
It's getting close to two o'clock, which, for me these days, is
actually somewhat of an early night. I stand in the kitchen
drinking a glass of water and I stare out the window at the
dark sky, and for once I will be asleep before seeing the purple
light of the killing hour. Dawn will arrive and I won't see it.
Evil will be here and I have a really bad feeling that I'm yet
to see its best work.

# CHAPTER FORTY-THREE

My cell phone pulls me from a world of dreams into a world of nightmares. I reach from beneath my blankets and walk my fingers over the nightstand until I find it. When I pick it up I don't bother wasting any hellos. I know who it's going to be.

"Hey, asshole," Cyris says.

Cyris isn't a morning person. I think back to Frank's body and decide that Cyris isn't much of a night person either. "Yeah?"

"You got the money?"

"I got it."

"You better show up, otherwise I'll . . ."

"Yeah, I get the point," I tell him. "I'll be there."

"It's a hundred grand."

"What?" I ask, sitting up. "What in the hell are you talking about?"

"You heard me."

"No, because it sounded like you said one hundred grand. That wasn't the deal."

"It's the deal now, partner."

"I can't get that sort of money."

"Get it."

"I'm not a bloody bank. We had a deal."

"So did I, with somebody else. Deals get broken, partner. Get used to it."

"That's not my fault."

"No, but it's your problem. Listen, I'm not an unreasonable man. You come with fifty grand tonight, and I give you an extra couple of days. I'll keep the goods while you keep on paying."

The insane-sounding Cyris from the last few nights has been replaced by somebody who seems to be putting more thought into this. I try to think how I could get that sort of money. If I actually had to. I try to sound as if I'm really struggling to come up with an idea, but of course it isn't a problem. Frank helped me out there. "I'll take out another mortgage on the house," I lie. "I'll get the hundred."

"See? This is why I have faith in you, Feldman." He hangs up and my cue to start the day has arrived.

I pull back the curtains to a typical summer morning. I have a fast breakfast containing nothing healthy before dumping the plastic bag of money onto the dining room table and counting it out. It takes me over thirty minutes and the final result is one hundred dollars short of one hundred grand. One hundred grand divided by two. That's how much Kathy was worth. How much Luciana was worth.

I put the money back into the bag, walk to my bedroom and add another hundred dollars from my top drawer before hiding the bag in the ceiling. The rest of the money from my top drawer I stuff into my pockets along with the note I found in Frank's mouth. Then I spend fifteen minutes on the phone to various builders, trying to find somebody who can come around and fix my back door. Most of the guys think the job is too small, but can come take a look in another few weeks. In the end I get hold of a young-sounding guy who says he can take a look at it later on today. I tell him if he can come and fix it today, I'll pay him twice his usual rate. He tells me that's a deal, and we fix a time.

It's nearly midday, the sun already well on its way into a cloudless sky. A warm nor'wester blows across my face, suggesting the day will only get hotter. I have so much summer cheer it's bleeding from my pores.

I climb into the rented Holden and push my thumb in on the cigarette lighter. I back out of my driveway and pause outside my house. I realize I haven't even checked my mail for the last few days so I still don't know what that kid jammed into my letterbox on Monday. There's a whole bunch of other stuff in there now. Bills, probably. Perhaps some junk mail, crap like pizza vouchers and shop brochures. The cigarette lighter pops back out. I hold it against the one-hundred-dollar bill I wrote on. It starts to melt and I hold it out the side of the car as it shrivels away, surrounded by black smoke. Then it crumbles into small pieces and I set them free into the warm breeze.

For the entire drive into town I contemplate the value of life. Jo is going to cost me a hundred grand, exactly what Kathy and Luciana cost Frank. Saving a life is twice as expensive as ending one. It's all about supply and demand. Economics. You get what you pay for.

I park directly outside the gun store recommended by the army surplus guy with the flabby upper arms. When I approach the shop I keep glancing around the street to see if anybody is watching me. I don't know who I'm looking for. Cyris, maybe. Or a cop. Another Landry. Or the way this week is turning out, perhaps even Landry himself. I swing open the door and step inside. A buzzer goes off somewhere letting staff know I've entered the premises. There are rows and rows of guns that look impressive, as if guns solve a lot of problems in this world rather than creating them. The air-conditioning is turned on full, the motor humming in the background. There are no customers, just one man behind the counter reading a newspaper with news in it that I helped make.

I approach him, but he doesn't look up from his paper until I reach the counter. He looks around forty years old, a tall man with a joined eyebrow that makes the bridge of his thick glasses look like they're growing a beard. His smile disappears when he sees the working over I've been given. There's a moment where I can see him taking it all in, and he knows why I'm here.

"Morning, sir. What can I do for you today?" He manages to sound both polite and unhelpful. His finger is holding the place where he'd been reading. He obviously wants to get straight back to it. He doesn't want to deal with the likes of me.

I ask for the name the thousand dollars bought me.

He nods slowly and stands up straight, losing his place in the paper. "I'm Arthur," he tells me, but he doesn't sound excited about it, and looking at his eyebrow I don't blame him. "You're the guy Floyd was telling me about, aren't you."

"Yes."

"You're the guy who's hunting deer."

"That's me."

He takes a few seconds to adjust his glasses. "I don't think I can help you," he says.

"Please."

"What is it you want, mister?"

I point to a picture of a pistol on the wall. In the picture it is stripped down. The parts are labeled. I can make out a few of the words. *Firing pin. Slide. Breech block. Safety mechanism.* If he gave me that exact pistol in that condition I'd be screwed.

The salesman turns and looks at the picture.

I tell him that's what I want.

"That might be what you want, but you can't have one," he says.

"If it's a matter of money . . ."

He shakes his head. "It's a matter of many things," he says. "That up there, that's a Colt Combat Elite," he says, not quoting from the poster. "Fine pistol. Not available here. Never available to anyone without a license."

"Then what do you have that is available?"

He gives me a funny look. Scrolls his eyes over me. Up and down, slowly, taking in the beatings I've had this week. "What kind of trouble are you in, mister?"

I shrug. "No trouble. I just want a pistol for home. For self-defense."

"They're illegal to use anywhere but a firing range."

Again I shrug. "I'm prepared to pay for quality."

I leave it at that. Let him make up his own mind. He's either going to sell me the gun or he isn't.

"I can get into a lot of trouble selling you a gun."

"And five thousand dollars should compensate you for that."

He shakes his head. "Five thousand, no. Ten thousand . . . now that's a different story."

I pull some money out and slowly flick through the notes like a card dealer showing off. His eyes never leave it. I put the entire amount on the counter. Arthur looks from left to right.

His eyes hold on the door for a few seconds as if he's mentally trying to lock it, then he looks out the windows with the iron bars running down them. Nobody around.

"Are you a cop?" he asks.

"Do I look like a cop?"

"I'm not asking if you look like a cop," he says. "I'm asking if you are a cop."

I shake my head. "No."

"Are you sure?"

"I'm sure. I promise you, I'm not a cop."

"If you are," he says, "this is entrapment."

I don't know if it's entrapment or not. I only have a vague Hollywood understanding of what that even means. "Exactly," I tell him. "I'm not a cop and I'm not working with any cops. I'm just a guy who wants a gun for target shooting at a range. Nothing more."

He takes another long, hard look at me. I say nothing as he fights with his temptation. Greed wins out. It always will with a guy like this. Without breaking eye contact, he makes the money disappear much in the same way Floyd did yesterday. He's decided I'm no cop. Cops don't have this sort of money to play with.

From beneath the counter he pulls out a sign that says *Back in 15 mins* and hangs it on the door, checking that it's locked. He comes back to the counter, makes his way around it, and disappears though a doorway. Ten grand is a lot of money for a gun. But it guarantees the fact I'm going to get one. If I showed up with forty dollars and a free hamburger voucher I wouldn't get the same quality of service.

I spin around the newspaper he was reading and study the headline. It's dedicated to Frank McClory. He was found early this morning by an unnamed woman. It doesn't mention how he died or whether it's related to his dead wife, but he must have been found early enough for it to make the paper, but not early enough for there to be any detail. The article is small, proof the reporter had little information and even less time to come up with something dramatic. There's little speculation—that'll come later with news bulletins and tomorrow's paper.

"Shame about that lawyer," the salesman says, stepping back through the door. He puts a wooden box on the counter. He's wearing a pair of thin gloves. That means he doesn't want the gun traced back to him.

"It's not often they get put to such good use," I say.

Arthur starts laughing, then stops when he sees I'm being serious. I can see him considering if I'm the type of person who should have a gun. He pats his pocket. Reminds himself of why he's doing this.

"You're not going to be shooting somebody, are you, mister?"

"It's for self-defense. Home invasions have been in the papers all week."

"I thought you said it was for shooting deer."

"It's home defense, mainly."

"Then you said it was shooting at the range."

"It's that too."

He nods. He gives me another hard look. "Got a driver's license?" he asks.

"What? Why?"

"For ID," he says.

"Why do you need ID?"

"Do you want the gun or not?"

I reach into my pocket. I get out my wallet and pause. This doesn't feel right. He reaches out and I hand him my license and the feeling doesn't get any better.

"Charlie Feldman," he says.

I don't answer him.

"You married, Charlie?"

"Why? You interested?"

He doesn't laugh. "People don't tend to wear wedding rings unless they're married."

I look down at my hand. It reminds me of the conversation with Kathy.

"Okay, Charlie. Before this goes any further, you need to understand a few things, okay?"

"Okay," I say, and I've been in the Real World long enough now to know what's coming up. He's going to threaten me. He's going to tell me that if anybody ever finds out the gun came from him, he's going to be pissed off. He's going to send people after me. After my wife. People that may or may not consist of Floyd.

"I'm a struggling businessman," he says. "This economy— it's a killer. You walk through town this time next year and you'll see a quarter of the businesses that are here now won't be then, just like this year compared to last year. People keep saying things are going to get better, but they don't. This shop—well, I'm hanging on. This time next year, hell, I'm doing what I can to not be one of those businesses you drive past and wonder what happened. You think I want to sell guns to people who shouldn't have them? Of course not. But I have a wife. I have kids. And kids cost a lot of money. I've been in this business for over twenty years, and times have never been so tough. Taking money from guys like you is the only way I can survive. You see what I'm saying?"

"Yeah, I get it. This is where you tell me that no matter what happens, nobody can ever know the gun came from you."

"Exactly," he says. "Before you think I'm some kind of bastard, let me tell you this—I'm selling you the gun because you look like the kind of guy who needs one. You don't look like the kind of guy who's going to rob a bank. So I'm selective. I'm not trying to supply guns to the assholes of the world. You don't look like an asshole. But if the police ever find out this is where this gun came from, then I'm going to be the asshole. I'm going to send somebody to your house, and they're going to fuck you up. You and your wife. And if you're in jail at the time, then I'll have you fucked up in jail. Like I say, I've been doing this twenty years, and I know people. People who make Floyd look like an angel. Now, tell me again that you get it."

"I get it," I tell him.

He looks back at my license. Then he hands it over.

"Come on back through here. It's more private."

I follow him through the doorway. There are posters of guns and girls, sometimes of both. A calendar from four years back with a naked smiling woman stops me from looking around at the shelves full of stock and the cluttered workbench. Part of me just wants to walk away, knows that getting involved with a guy like Arthur is only going to end in a lot of trouble. Only that's long-term trouble—and that's only a possibility. Short-term trouble is certain. I need that gun.

"This is a Glock Eighteen C," he says, putting the package down on the workbench. "It takes a nine-millimeter Parabellum bullet. Nine millimeter is the most famous and frequently used handgun cartridge in the world. It's used in semiautomatic pistols and in submachine guns. This Glock here," he hands it to me by the handle, "has a magazine capacity of seventeen rounds. Of course it's currently unloaded."

"Of course."

"Naturally it isn't designed for target shooting. It's purely a defense weapon. Used in the service industry overseas."

"What, like restaurants?"

"Yeah, good one," he says, his face tightening as he frowns at me. "Police. Military. Armed security."

"Right." I'm holding the gun by the handle, bouncing my arm slowly up and down like gun guys do, getting a feel for the weight. Shame there aren't any tires to kick.

"It's a little over six hundred grams," Arthur says. "A hundred and eighty-six millimeters long, small enough to slip in your pocket. It has an internal safety . . ."

"Meaning?"

He carries on for a few more minutes telling me about the gun. I'm already sold, was from the moment I saw it had a trigger and a handle and a barrel and didn't need any kind of assembly.

"The Glock Eighteen C is fully automatic," he continues, and it seems he could talk forever about the pistol. "There's a switch here," he touches it with his gloved finger, "that selects between semi- or fully automatic. Highly illegal if owned by a civilian in any country."

"Fully automatic?"

"It's crazy," he says. "But you can fire off a whole magazine in under a second."

I imagine doing that. It would be like turning the front of somebody into a zipper.

"So if it can only be sold to the service industry," I say, "how come you have this one?"

"Are you seriously going to start asking me these kinds of questions?"

"No. Sorry."

"Let's get this done," he says. He shows me how to use the

gun, how to load the magazine, how to slip the magazine into the handle, and tells me a few more facts. Then he takes it off me and puts it into the box. Puts the box into a bag. He hands it over to me and we step back into the shop.

"I need some ammunition."

He slowly nods. I don't know if the ammunition is illegal, but he has to go out the back to get some. He includes it in the price. I figure he's a generous guy. Ten thousand dollars. The world's most expensive handgun. I reach out and grab the box of ammo, but he doesn't let it go.

"Remember what I told you," he says. "You don't know me. You've never seen me."

I look at the thin gloves that weren't on his hands when I arrived but were when he first came back out with the box in his hand. "I know."

"And I want your word you're not using it to go on a rampage."

I promise him. Just like any homicidal maniac would.

"I know where you live," Feldman. "Remember no matter where you go, if you screw me on this, I'll find you."

"Nobody will ever know I was here." I tuck the package under my arm, turn to leave, then turn back. "For ten grand I want this too." I grab the newspaper. He says nothing. Doesn't think about his fingerprints all over it. I tuck it under my arm and walk back out into the Christchurch heat.

# CHAPTER FORTY-FOUR

Lying in bed, in bed, and it's comfortable and warm, but his stomach hurts and his head hurts, and it's light outside, but he doesn't want to go into the light because it'll hurt too. He stays in bed because he's tired, because he's been up all night, and his wife has fallen asleep in front of the TV in her bedroom and it's been a long time since they shared a bed together.

When he got home last night, he broke into the morphine stash that he has for his wife, the stash he always promised himself he would never touch, only to find he'd already been at it. Sometimes she's in so much pain that he has to give her some. She can't describe the pain to him, but he knows it's bad, she screams and cries and the muscles in her neck become so tight he's always afraid they'll snap. She hasn't had one of those attacks in over two years now, but he keeps the morphine for her just the same.

Just the same.

Only now it's his.

The duct tape around his stomach is only going to help him for so long. He wishes he could put more tape around his head to keep his thoughts together too. The drugs are getting to him. Last night he was clearheaded. It's as though the crazy, fucked-up personality he was using on Sunday night got stabbed into him, and drugs are making it stay. He hates thinking this way. He hates the pain more. He can't get the balance right.

When this is done, he's sure his brother-in-law can help him out. He must know a doctor who can stitch stuff together. Soon he'll be as good as new. And richer. So far the money angle hasn't worked out. That lawyer bastard screwed him.

That gets him thinking about the revenge, and how sweet it tasted, and how killing Charlie Feldman will taste even sweeter. He's sure of it. It's a horrible world when you can't trust anybody, a horrible world when people don't pay you for the job you have done. He can't for the life of him figure out why McClory would have done that to him. What was he thinking? And then to deny it when he got there to confront him? What the hell was up with that? Did McClory think he was an idiot? Tearing McClory out of the world might have tasted sweet, but he'd rather have had the money. There are still medical bills that he's struggling to cover, and he's hoping to save up enough money to take Macy away—there are other treatments in other countries more advanced than New Zealand, and he'd pay or do anything to give those treatments a shot.

He shakes his head, not just out of his disbelief over last night's affairs, but also to check to see how light-headed the morphine has made him. He can hear the cartoons playing from his wife's bedroom. If she were awake, she would be laughing at them. Sometimes he watches them with her. Sometimes he thinks he's only one thirty-minute episode away from blowing out his brains.

He closes his eyes. He can feel the morphine rushing through his system. He thinks of the hundred-dollar note he stuffed into Frank's mouth and he can't remember if Mc-Clory was alive at that point. He has no idea what Frank was thinking when he wrote that note, no idea where a guy like McClory got the balls to try and end their relationship with a threat, then realizes he was having these same thoughts only a minute ago. How many times has he gone over this? He didn't bother searching the house for the money because there never had been any money. He had just let himself in, done what he went there to do, and then let himself back out. The problem was all that exertion last night opened up the wound in his stomach.

He drifts in and out of sleep and the green numbers on the clock radio tick over quicker than they should. He's sweating, and the room spins, and he wonders if this is the most relaxed he will ever feel. His wife laughs a little, and he thinks she calls out to him, but he can't be sure. He drifts a little more. His wife doesn't laugh anymore. The cartoons are still playing, the DVD player looping one into the other and the other. He needs to do something about his wound before it becomes infected, though of course it probably already is. He can feel the badness from the cut slowly seeping through him. Infecting him. Changing the way he acts and feels and thinks.

He throws back the sheets. They're damp and he contemplates whether he should write a note to remind himself to wash them, but he forgets about the note even as he forgets about the sheets. He gets to his feet, but he's still drifting. He thinks he took something earlier. He seems to think it was morphine, but it couldn't have been, because the only morphine here is for his wife and he wouldn't use that. Maybe he got some more of the good shit from his brother-in-law. He should give him a call when this is over. Maybe he can help with the stomach wound.

He heads into the bathroom and draws himself a bath. He doesn't know if lying in hot water is going to be a good thing because it would soon become hot water full of the dirt and bacteria from his body, so he pulls out the plug and decides to have a shower instead. He stands beneath it for twenty minutes, letting the water soak into the tape. He gently teases the edges as it does so. It's a battle, but one he's determined to win. Sometimes he laughs. Sometimes he cries. Sometimes he feels like putting his fist through the wall. In the end the tape comes away, and blood, about a quarter of a glass of dark blood, falls onto the floor in one large splash, hitting the tub like a wet bloody-nose blow. The bleeding slows to a trickle, but doesn't stop. He uses a flannel to wipe away the flakes of dirt and a few tiny leaves along with the gunk left by the tape.

For a few seconds the world sways. He grabs hold of the showerhead and then the wall until things settle. He looks down and can't see how dark blood can be good. The water makes it disappear. It makes him think that something inside his stomach has been damaged. Isn't there a kidney there somewhere? Or a liver? What about his actual stomach? He realizes he's eaten very little over the last few days, and when he does his stomach burns. Why is that? He studies the skin with his fingers, pulling and poking. It is black in areas, white in others, hard all over, and he isn't sure which color represents the infection. He lets the hot water wash over it.

He gets out of the shower and sits on the bathroom floor

with his back against the bathtub and his towel beneath him. He swabs the wound with disinfectant and it stings like a bitch. He places some medical gauze over the wound, some padding over the gauze, and wraps bandaging around his torso to hold everything in place. He's going to be moving around some more later, so he wraps some duct tape around it all too, just to be sure. When he gets up he doesn't feel like the new man he was hoping for, but it's sure as shit better than seeing dark blood fall out of him.

He wraps the towel around him and goes and checks on his wife. She's awake. She's staring at the TV, but not really looking at it. He's seen her do this before.

"Hey, babe," he says, and the words feel numb, they sound like they're not coming from him.

"Where's Ba-e?" she asks.

She's referring to Billy. Billy was her cat when she was a child. She told him about Billy years ago. Billy has been dead for thirty years. "He's sitting out in the sun," he says.

"Ba-e," she says, and she smiles.

"Are you . . ." he says, then another trip on the morphine wave, and he has to grab hold of the wall to stay balanced. Shit.

"Side-Russ and Ba-e sitting in a tree," she says. "K-I . . . I . . . I forget."

"It's okay," he tells her.

"I'm sorry," she tells him. "I dot mean to forget."

"It's okay," he tells her, and he sits down on the side of the bed and strokes her hair. Something on the TV makes her smile. She forgets all about being sad that she forgets things.

He moves to his bedroom. He runs his hands over the dressing on his stomach. The wound is clean and patched and the pain seems to be just a shadow of what it was earlier. A packet of aspirin sits on the nightstand along with a packet of sleeping pills. Both are nearly empty. He doesn't think he'll need them. He sets the alarm clock. He has a meeting tonight, but right now he can't think exactly what for. He climbs onto the bed. The sheets are damp and he thinks about making a note to wash them, but before he can make one and after he forgets what the note would be for anyway, he falls asleep.

# CHAPTER FORTY-FIVE

The temperature is rising and I have the air-conditioning turned to high. In this heat it's easy to forget I nearly froze to death two nights ago, but easy to remember that Hell is waiting around the corner.

I stop at a coffee shop and insert myself inside another slice of normal life, the type of slice where normal people are doing normal things on a day-to-day basis that doesn't include blood. It's a more upscale café than the one I sat at two mornings ago. All the furniture is made from shiny metal and shiny wood, and several mirrors and paintings have been jammed up on the wall, each an identical distance from the last. I sit at a window where I can keep an eye on the car because the gun is beneath the front seat. I order some lunch from a waitress who's obviously psychic because she says things like *See you're reading the paper* and *Nice day outside*. I especially like it when she tells me I look as though I've been through the wars. I want to ask what her thoughts are on tonight, but decide I might not like her predictions.

I drink coffee and, in a rare moment of healthy consumption, I have a glass of orange juice. I read my ten-thousand-dollar newspaper. It offers up stories about politics and about companies going broke, and it makes me think of Arthur and the economic downturn that is forcing him to sell guns to guys like me, and I wonder how much of what he said is true. I stare at the crossword I would probably half complete if I had a pen. When my bacon and eggs arrive I nearly inhale them off the plate before the waitress can put them down. When I finish I trap a twenty-dollar note beneath the plate as a tip because I'm awestruck by her psychic abilities, and I think how cool it would be to improve at least one person's day, the same way the traffic cop improved mine yesterday. It's a small step, but perhaps I can change the world.

I drive home at a casual speed. I'm in no hurry to be anywhere yet I feel as though I'm running at a hectic pace. When I get home, my next-door neighbor, a man in his late seventies who I see putting golf clubs into his car at least three times every week, catches me in the driveway and starts making conversation. We talk about the weather. He asks how I'm enjoying living in the neighborhood. He tells me if there's anything he or his wife can do for me, just to let him know. I wonder how far his offer would stretch if I told him what I had planned.

When I get inside I start playing with the Glock. It feels more comfortable than it did in the store because I don't have to pretend I know what I'm looking at. Holding it in my hands I feel liberated. I feel like I've beaten the system designed to keep people like myself from owning such a weapon. I also feel like I'm on the right track, that the Glock has evened the playing field. I turn it over in my hand, studying the lines and textures. The cold metal isn't quite metal, according to Arthur, but a high-impact synthetic material that he didn't name. He nicknamed the Glock the *plastic pistol*, but it doesn't feel like plastic. In fact the feeling it gives me is that things might turn out okay.

I pick up the magazine and check to make sure it's empty. I slip it into the gun and slap the butt of it, clicking it into place. Then I play. I point it around the kitchen, the dining room, the lounge. Action Man is having fun. Though *fun* probably isn't quite the right word. I point it at things. I pull the trigger. The slide pulls back. It clicks into place. On each pull my face tightens and my eyes half close as I expect to hear thunder. I feel like a kid playing war. I move around corners, keeping the gun low like they do in movies.

I wonder if I should test it. I could go over to the pasture where I buried the cardboard box and fire off a few shots if nobody is around, but I decide against it. I can't squeeze the drama of being caught into my schedule. I would be charged, fingerprinted, and my fingerprints would quickly match those found at the two dead girls' homes.

I drop the gun into my pocket when there's knocking at the door. It's the carpenter. He's right on time. He's a young guy, maybe only twenty, who talks like a teenager and thinks I must be one too. He calls me *man* every few minutes or so and talks about surfboards as he fixes my back door. I guess I ought to be flattered he thinks I'm young enough to understand. While he works, I put the gun up into the ceiling with the cash hidden up there. Then I change into shorts and a T-shirt. I wait around for the guy to finish. It takes him two hours to strip out the broken door frame and cut and fit the replacement pieces. The door itself is okay. So are the handle and lock.

"You'll have to get in a painter to do the rest," he says. I pay him in cash. "You don't need an invoice, right?"

"No," I tell him.

He smiles the smile of a man who knows he's gotten away with something the tax department doesn't have to know about. I smile the smile of a man who knows that having his door fixed is the act of somebody who is confident they're going to be around long enough to enjoy it. He packs up his gear and leaves and I lock up the house and head outside.

I drive out to New Brighton, the radio off the whole time because nobody can say or sing or advertise anything that'll make me feel any better. I listen to the traffic and to my thoughts and don't really like the sound of those either. The temperature has peaked in the early seventies, but hasn't started its decline yet.

New Brighton has a nice beach that's often ruined by a really killer wind. Sand is always on the move, the wind using it to assault the swimmers and sunbathers. The houses in the area are mainly bungalows and cottages that are stained with sea salt. Anything made from metal is either rusting or in danger of rusting. The gardens that make Christchurch famous don't extend their roots out here. What little greenery there was has dried up and turned to brown weed that crackles underfoot, each piece a potential matchstick.

I park near the mall. Brighton Mall is the only outdoor mall in the city. It used to be vibrant back when I was a kid. I remember my parents bringing me out here. The shops were different from other malls, you had the smell of fish and chips, the sun on your back, the sound of breaking waves only feet away. Now the mall has more empty shops than sales assistants. It's a sign of bad times. It's just like Arthur was saying.

I walk down the mall, I can't help but feel saddened by all

the *For Sale* and *For Lease* signs that I pass. Just before the
end of the millennium a three-hundred-meter concrete pier
was built out here, as though that would bring people back
to a dying suburb, but so far the only thing it has attracted
is fishermen. They renovated the surrounding blocks, threw
up palm trees and slapped paint on the storefronts and walk-
ways. And it worked. For a few months. Until it stopped
working. The pier is still here and has been built so solidly
that it probably always will be. It's opposite the mall, heading
out from above the sand dunes into the ocean. It stands two
storeys high with flights of concrete stairs leading up from
the walkway. A library and cafés are built into the base of
it. I climb the stairs and the warm breeze from below disappears, replaced by air currents that are several degrees cooler.
With the library behind me, its thousands of books perhaps
offering plenty of solutions as to what I could try tonight, I
head out over the incoming tide, passing people who have
their lines over the side to catch whatever fish are dumb
enough to still be hanging around. There are lampposts every
twenty yards: their lights will help me out tonight. Up here
the smell of seaweed is gone, replaced by the smell of blood,
fish guts, rotting skin, and cigarette smoke. People gut their
fish directly onto the asphalt. Teenagers throw fish heads at
their friends.

  I walk out to the end, past wooden seats with peeling paint
and rusting trash bins. I walk to a small non-fishing zone where
people are fishing, leaning against the railing and looking out
over the water. I watch the waves crashing into the concrete
foundations below and feel them shake through the pillars.
The shattering rollers spray plumes of water into the air like
dust. The wind, colder out here, is coming from the east, and
it reaches me without picking up the scent of dead fish on the

way. The water near the shore is gray, but blue beyond the breakers. I look for shapes moving beneath the surface, but see nothing. The cool breeze snaps my clothes back and forth.

I savor the moment, though I keep it short. I bet wherever Jo is, she doesn't have a view of the ocean. Unless she's already in it. I turn around and look at the guys fishing behind me. They look exactly like the kind of guys you don't want to make eye contact with. Cigarettes dripping from their mouths, their hands and necks covered in tattoos, the fishing lines they're using are probably stolen. A sign next to them says *No Overhead Casting*. But signs are like rules for these guys: there to be ignored, and they take pleasure in the knowledge they can do something illegal even in the simple act of fishing. A guy wearing a T-shirt that says *Tonight I'm going to party like you're nine* stares at me as if deciding whether or not I'd make good bait. Head down, eyes down, unmolested I reach the library. I head back to the sand and head north.

Swimmers and sunbathers and kids throwing around a ratty old football make this just another trip to the seaside. A guy throwing a red Frisbee high into the breeze and catching it as it flies back gets in the way of people trying to relax. On the weekend this place will be packed. I walk a hundred yards, then turn around and study the pier. I study the foundations below, the angle where the beach hits the base of the pier where a concrete wall climbs between the two. This is where I'm going to be tonight. I want to know my ground. I need to know my escape routes.

I walk back through the mall to the parking lot. I drive around the surrounding warren of streets to become familiar with them. When I've absorbed all I can I head home. It's nice to see neither of the doors have been kicked in. I make sure my house is secure, then attach pieces of string to the doors and windows, tying the other ends to an assortment of pots and pans. It's a cheap alarm system, but effective.

I bring down the gun. I grab a handful of ammunition and load it into the magazine, slap the magazine into the gun, then set it next to my bed. The day isn't as young anymore, but it still has a long way to go. Knowing I'll need all the energy I can get I lie on top of my bed and set my alarm clock for seven. The sun streams through the window directly on top of me. I put on a pair of sunglasses, prop a pillow beneath my head, and close my eyes.

The sun feels great. Relaxing. It seems easy to forget that another killing hour is on the way. The only question is who is going to be around at the end of it.

# CHAPTER FORTY-SIX

The basement is cold, and Jo can't stop shivering. She's tired, but can't fall asleep. Other than two bathroom breaks that Cyris gave her, she's been roped up against the same drum since coming back here the other night. Which was . . . she isn't sure. It's easy to lose track of time when you're locked in a basement with no view.

When she used the bathroom, she had to leave the door open. Cyris stood with his back to her to at least give her some privacy. The first time, she couldn't bring herself to go. She just sat on the toilet too scared for anything to happen. The second time she barely sat down before things started flowing.

Each time she was brought into the hall, she could hear cartoons going and a woman laughing from a bedroom. She thought about calling out for help, but she didn't. She couldn't face meeting Cyris's girlfriend. The woman had to know Jo was here against her will, she would have heard her, which

could only mean one of two things: the wife was okay with
the fact her husband would bring women home and tie them
up, or the wife herself was tied up and couldn't do anything
about it. If the second of those two options were true, then
why the laughter? And now that she was questioning things,
why would his girlfriend be watching children's cartoons? The
answer to that was obvious—she wouldn't be. Which means
the laughter wasn't coming from a woman, but a little girl.

None of it made sense.

Her trips to the bathroom gave her some idea of the time. It
was afternoon. Probably around three or four o'clock, but perhaps later. Down in the basement it's all the same. In this dark
place on this concrete floor where the cold seeps slowly and
forcefully into her body it's easy to imagine that it's permanent
midnight. Her wrists are sore. He replaced the gag she had in
her mouth with duct tape, and at the same time he gave her the
bathroom breaks, he also gave her water to drink. She doesn't
struggle against the ropes anymore. In fact she hardly even
moves her hands or wrists. The skin there is just too raw. There
are moments where she thinks about how easy it would be to
give up. To accept her fate might just mean dying won't be so
difficult. These moments are brief. She would never give up.
Never make it easy for Cyris. Somehow, she's going to get out
of this. She will see her family again. Her friends. And Charlie?

She doesn't know. Things can never be the same between
them, but what exactly does that mean? She can't forgive him
for what he did to her on Monday night. Can she? No. No, of
course not. However, the fact she's questioning just how much
she can forgive tells her something important—she's not over
him. And he's not over her either. He still has photographs of
her on the walls and he's still wearing his wedding ring.

She hears the basement door starting to open before she

sees it. She looks up as light spills into the room, then has to close her eyes and look away as the light hurts her. Cyris has reached her by the time she can see anything without having to squint. The scent of soap and sweat overpowers her as he leans down, and a moment later a knife touches the ropes that bind her. He tells her to stand, but her legs give way and she falls on her side. He hisses the command at her again, this time adding the sight of his knife as an incentive. It works, and when she gets to her feet he tosses something at her that she can't identify until they hit the ground. Handcuffs. Maybe he has a whole drawer full of them.

When he tells her to pick them up she doesn't refuse. The refusal begins when he tells her to put them on. Handcuffed she will be no match for him. He takes a step toward her and she watches his face as anger and insanity blossom behind his eyes, and she realizes that handcuffed or not she's in the same situation, and that if she pushes the point he'll get those cuffs snapped onto her wrists anyway and beat the hell out of her in the process. The cold metal ratchets into place as she cuffs her hands in front of her.

He leads her up the stairs into the hallway. She can hear the cartoons again, and in the distance a neighbor is mowing lawns, and somewhere between those two noises a chorus of barking from several dogs. The curtains are drawn, but around the edges she can see the dull fading of sunlight. It has to be around six thirty, maybe seven o'clock, she thinks.

He leads her through to the adjoining garage, which looks clinical white under the glow of eight fluorescent tubes. Brand-new tools are hanging neatly on a Peg-Board. Some look new, some look well used. There's a wheelchair lying on its side jammed under the workbench. Did he kill somebody who couldn't walk? Is the wheelchair a souvenir? On the bench is a pile of metal shavings and an open box of shotgun shells, next to them a hacksaw.

"Take off the tape," he tells her.

She reaches up and pulls it away. It hurts. "Please," she says, "please let me go."

He lifts up his hand and points his palm at her. She stops talking.

"If you say anything, I'll hurt you," he says.

"Who does the wheelchair belong to?"

He steps in and uses the back of his hand to strike her. The impact knocks her onto the ground. She looks up at him.

"Get up," he tells her.

She gets up.

"Talk again and it will be worse. You understand?"

She nods.

"Now get in the car."

There are two cars in the garage. One is Charlie's. The other is a dark blue four-door sedan. He opens the passenger door of the sedan for her. She climbs in. As he moves around to the driver's side she contemplates locking the doors, but with all those tools to choose from, it'd only be a matter of seconds before he forced his way in. He climbs in, immediately telling her to shut up again even though she hasn't said a word. He tells her to be still while they wait for the darkness to arrive. She slowly nods. They wait silently in the car as it gets darker outside.

She's more scared now than she's ever been.

Scared of the dark.

Scared of Cyris.

Scared of Charlie.

She says nothing as she waits beneath the glare of the fluorescent lights.

# CHAPTER FORTY-SEVEN

The problem with sleep is you never quite know whether the nightmares are real. Bad things are happening. People are dying and I'm the reason, and I can't seem to wake myself. The sad part is that this is no dream.

I sit up and stare at my bedroom wall where a few slivers of sun rise slowly toward the ceiling. I try to shake the tiredness off, but it begs me to stay. My sunglasses have fallen off and are resting on the floor. I use my T-shirt to wipe away sweat that's layered across my body. I glance at my buzzing alarm clock and the red numbers say it's time to go to work.

The tiredness fades as I dress in my fatigue gear, but the nightmare remains. I put on my vest and load up the pockets. A quick scan in the mirror to make sure everything looks okay tells me nothing is okay. If I show up dressed as G.I. Joe he's going to know something's up. Getting the fatigues is turning out to have been a dumb idea. I strip back down and

dress more casually. The night is warm, but I put on a jacket
to conceal my gun, and anyway, it'll be cold up on the pier. I
tuck the Swiss Army knife into my jacket pocket. I drag the
money from the ceiling and rest it on the living room table.

Our meeting is over two hours away so I get something to
eat. I grab a packet of instant pasta from the cupboard. Just
add water and a microwave and eight minutes of my time,
which I use up unloading and then reloading the gun over and
over just to make sure the bullets are still in there. I dish out
the pasta and sit down at the table in the silence of my house
and slowly eat it, thinking of dead men walking toward gas
chambers after their last meal. Maybe I should have cooked
something better. A roast dinner, or I could have ordered pizza
or Chinese. The pasta tastes okay, but I think with my current
appetite even a gourmet meal would taste bland. I dump the
dishes in the sink and I'm about to wash them when I realize
it's pointless. I could be dead by tomorrow. The confidence I
had at the beginning of the day when I arranged to have my
back door fixed has gone the way of the dinosaur.

When there is an hour to go, I grab the gun and slip it
inside my jacket, sliding the magazine in next to it. I take a
handful of extra bullets and drop them into a different pocket.
They click against each other as I walk. I probably won't need
the extras. If I can't kill him with the first seventeen shots
there won't be much hope of killing him with the following seventeen. I grab the rest of my gear, which consists of
the binoculars I bought yesterday and now also a flashlight,
some rope, and Landry's handcuffs. I hold the handcuffs and
stare at them for a few seconds, putting them into context,
the context being I was wearing these when I thought I was
going to die. I picture Detective Inspector Bill Landry's corpse
turning gray in the river. He's probably turning a color I don't

ever want to see. Something between white and purple. His eyes are open and milky white as the sun beats down on him. His skin will be slipping off, his body bloating, the insects will be . . .

I can feel my pasta starting to move in my stomach.

Time to move.

I load the money into a dark blue canvas bag, which I put into the back of the car. I leave for New Brighton a little earlier than I needed to, so I drive a little slower. The sky is clouding over and I can't see any stars, can't see the moon. I park right opposite the pier. I watch my watch for a while. Then I grab the canvas bag and the rest of my gear, and head back up the sandy steps. The day has gotten colder than I thought it would. The wind is stronger. It feels like there's a storm coming.

The library is closed, the lights off. There are a few fishermen still on the pier, the same kind of guys I saw earlier today, some of them drinking beer, some of them drinking out of bottles with paper bags around them, all of them smelling like cigarettes and fish guts. I walk among them, making eye contact, strolling boldly. They look at me and look away. They can feel, as I do, the change within me, and they sense this the same way a dog senses fear. I stand at the end of the pier and gaze out at the water. It's rougher than it was this afternoon and the vibrations through the concrete are stronger. The air tastes of salt. I turn my back to the water and lean against the rail. Beware: Action Man is here.

The guys with the fishing poles are in the process of packing up. The way the weather is changing, they're probably thinking the same thing I'm thinking, that within the hour the skies are going to open. There are others on the beach still walking, most of them with dogs, but they're moving quickly now, some of them even breaking into slow jogs. Across the road cars are starting to pull away. The day is over for all these people.

I rest against the railing and stare out at the lights of the city. They represent life and activity—and so much ignorance. The pier is empty now and this suits me fine. It will also suit Cyris.

I push off from the railing and walk back halfway to the start of the pier. I stop at a garbage bin a hundred yards away from the library. I stuff the rope and flashlight into it, loading them onto half a dead fish. I keep the gun in my pocket. The wind is making my eyes water. I stay by the bin and I wait and I watch the road.

The killing hour is coming early tonight.

# CHAPTER FORTY-EIGHT

He likes to drive in silence because silence is golden. His mind is busy with thoughts, and when he spells them out, when he follows them, they all have the background music of one of his wife's cartoons. When he thinks that he wants to kill Charlie Feldman, he's thinking it lyrically. It's annoying. In the past he's tried getting headphones for his wife, so she can just listen to her cartoons without the need for him to hear them, but the headphones make her scream and cry and thrash about like a fish out of water. So right now his thoughts of cutting Charlie open and getting paid his dues are coming in a sing-song voice.

The headache came back not long after he woke up. And his stomach isn't any better. The bravest thing he's done all day is resist the urge to take another shot of morphine, but what he did do was take more anti-inflammatories and over-the-counter painkillers. Okay, that's not all he did—he brought some morphine along with him. He doubts he'll need it, but one thing he learned in the army is it's best to take a gun and not need it than don't take one and find yourself getting shot at. Same logic applies to pain medication. The result of what he has taken since waking is he still has the headache, but at least his thoughts are his own. Mostly. But there are still random thoughts slipping in there. When he looks at the woman he wonders how she would taste if he bit into her. The hate between them would surely make her taste sour. He knows that's not normal. She's looking at him, looking at him, looking at him as if he's crazy, and he hates that look, and he hates the crazy thoughts even more. He can't wait for all this to be over.

When they get to the pier he kills the motor. He has very little to say. So does she, apparently, but that's because he hit her earlier and told her to shut up. He knows he's going to have to kill her at the end of all this because she knows who he is and where he lives. She is what the army would have called *collateral damage*. Feldman is too. So was the cop. And the lawyer. It's been a collateral damage kind of week. All that matters is getting paid. Years ago he might have thought different. But after his wife was hurt, he learned people don't give a shit about you when you need help. It was only a matter of days after Macy tried to kill herself that he figured out the whole world could go and fuck itself.

He leans to his side. He takes out his cell phone and his wallet and puts them into the glove compartment. He never takes them on a job. He would never take the risk of leaving one of them behind by accident. The next day's headline would be *Killer Leaves Driver's License at Scene*.

"Let's go," he tells the woman.

He wraps a towel over her wrists to hide the handcuffs. He

pulls her across the driver's seat and outside. It's gotten pretty windy over the last fifteen minutes. Feels like rain is on its way. He looks at the pier, but it's too dark to see if anybody is on it. Feldman is out there somewhere, he can feel it. His car isn't here. In fact the only car here is . . . he looks at the Holden. The Holden. It looks familiar, but he has no idea where he saw it last, if indeed he did. Of course there are probably ten thousand identical ones within twenty miles.

They cross the road. He keeps looking back at the Holden. Something about it bugs him.

They walk toward the pier as the wind begins to pick up around them.

# CHAPTER FORTY-NINE

They cross the road, Cyris glancing at the Holden that was parked outside the shopping mall last night, and I'm starting to wonder if he recognizes it. He can't. Too many of them on the roads for that. There's nobody around now. The beach is ours. For all my planning we may as well have been back out in the woods.

They disappear from view as they reach the steps. I take the pistol from my pocket and tuck it into the waistband of my pants around the back. The wind is getting stronger, whipping the sand up much higher now. I'm thankful for the jacket. Cyris and Jo reach the top of the stairs. He lets the wind push the side of his overcoat out so I can see the shotgun beneath. It looks like Landry's Mossberg, except it's shorter. Either it's a different weapon or he's cut off part of the barrel. I hold my ground. Jo has her arms in front of her with a towel over her hands. No doubt they're tied together.

He smiles at me when he's within talking distance. "Glad you could make it, buddy."

I look at Jo. No obvious signs of assault. "You okay?"

She nods, but doesn't say anything.

"She's just peachy, just peachy," Cyris says.

Jo is still wearing Landry's pants and jacket, and she's still wearing her bra beneath it. I try to think of that as a good sign. They stand next to each other, about fifteen feet from me. The wind makes it difficult to hear. Jo lets go of the towel over her wrists and the breeze catches it like a kite and yanks it into the night.

"Unlock the handcuffs," I shout, looking at her hands.

Cyris pulls the keys from his pocket, turns toward her, then turns back to me. The wind has his scraggly black hair standing on end. The grin on his face tells me he's about to do or say something he thinks I haven't expected. He raises the keys in the air and they follow the path of the towel.

"You bastard," I yell, moving to the side of the pier and looking over the edge. All I can see is black sand and water and I can't tell which the keys have hit. "Why the hell did you do that?"

"Stop pissing around, partner, and give me the money."

"The money's here. Let her go."

"Looks like we need to develop some trust." He pulls a knife from his pocket and touches the blade against Jo's face. I've seen how quick he is with that weapon.

I put the bag of money down and step back. "It's all there, I swear."

"On your life." He laughs. I don't get the joke. "Take another step back," he says, and I do, so now I'm three feet or so away from the garbage bin.

He pushes Jo forward until she's level with the bag. He points the gun at her and forces her to crouch down and open it. She follows his instructions, and holds it open so he can see inside. One hundred thousand dollars, stacked neatly, looks back out at him.

He looks up from the money. "Very good," he says.

She does the bag up and stands back up.

"Now let her go."

He shoves her in the back, and I manage to catch her before she falls. I realize I should have let her fall and drawn my pistol instead. I realize he's done this so I would instinctively react to catch Jo rather than whatever else it was I had planned.

"One more thing, asshole," he says.

I look up knowing exactly what it is I'm going to be seeing, and then seeing exactly what I feared it would be. He has the shotgun pointing at us.

"We had a deal," I protest, stalling for time.

"A deal, uh huh, we had a deal, and I upheld it, partner. I gave you the woman, I gave her to you in one piece. Untouched, just like you wanted her. What in the hell is your problem?"

I start maneuvering Jo behind me, away from the blast of the gun. I keep pushing at her, reaching behind myself, knowing Cyris will think I'm doing one thing when I'm actually doing another. He thinks I'm being noble. I'm just reaching for my gun.

"You've got your money. Now leave us alone."

"No."

My fingers curl around the handle. One false move and I could shoot myself in the ass.

"I called the police," I say.

"Bullshit."

"They're watching right now." I slowly pull the gun upward before putting my finger into the trigger guard. At the same time the breeze whips a load of sand off the beach into our faces.

"I'd better put on a good show." He pumps the Mossberg. The shell crunches into place.

"I have more money."

"How much more?"

"Fifty grand."

"Why don't I believe you?"

I can see he wants to. His head is slightly cocked to the side as if the sound of dollar signs crunching inside his mind is heavy. He's contemplating what he can do with a hundred and fifty grand. Then he smiles. He has finished contemplating.

"I can get it for you."

"When?"

"Tomorrow morning."

He lowers his gun. Just slightly, but it's all I need. They say money can't buy happiness, but they're wrong. A make-believe fifty thousand dollars has just brought me all the happiness I need.

I bring my arm around, not wanting to fire a gun in public, but not knowing what other option I have. The gun appears in one smooth, sweeping movement that makes Cyris's eyes open wide. I pull the trigger and the gun must be in full automatic mode, because within a second the clip is empty and the recoil has pulled the gun upward and it's pointing at the sky. Cyris's shotgun sounds like thunder, then metal rain fills the air as pellets from the cartridge spray across the railings, but I don't feel the tug of any impact. The gun falls out of his hands. I must have hit him. I pull the trigger on my gun again, but it's empty.

He has one arm hanging by his side, but he reaches down

to the shotgun with his other one. I run to him before he can get to it, and he realizes that's how it's going to be, and he stands up straight and throws a punch at me that I manage to duck. I crash the gun into the side of his head. It jags off his skull and Cyris cries out as his head snaps sideways. The momentum from his swinging punch tugs him forward and he crumples into a heap next to his shotgun. I kick the Mossberg further away. I kick the knife away too. I step back and study him. He's perfectly still. I kick him. He doesn't move. But I've gone through this before with him.

Jo moves up behind me. "Is he dead?" she asks.

I shake my head. I dig into my pockets for Landry's handcuff keys and pull them out. We try for a few seconds to undo her cuffs, but it's obvious the key won't fit. "You should go and search for the keys."

"Are you serious?"

"Yes."

"There's no chance of finding them," she says.

"There's no chance of finding them if you stay up here," I tell her.

"Charlie . . . what are you going to do?"

"I'll come down in a minute, okay?"

"Charlie?"

"I've got a couple of things to do."

She slowly nods. "You don't have to do this, Charlie. We can take him to the police."

"If he ever gets away he'll come after us. You know that, don't you? Or in ten years when they let him out for good behavior. It's either him or us, Jo. What do you want me to do? Let that happen? He has to pay for what he's done."

She doesn't answer. Instead she raises her cuffed hands over my head and embraces me. We hold each other while I keep my eyes glued to Cyris. He's not moving. We let go and she runs along the pier as the wind helps her along.

Sand flicks my face and I use my hands to shield my eyes. So much of it is in the air I can't even see the beach. I have no idea how we'll find the keys. As I walk toward Cyris I load the magazine of the Glock back up. I find the switch to change it between full auto and single shot. The urge to kill Cyris is with me, and it's the sort of urge I want to give in to. I don't doubt he'll come after us when he's released from prison after spending the appropriate amount of years that balances the scales for killing at least four people. I grab the rope and Landry's handcuffs from the trash bin.

I want to kill him. The plan has always been to kill him.

I just don't think I can.

I guess I knew that all along. It's why I have the handcuffs. And the rope.

I use my foot to roll him onto his back. There's blood on his shoulder, but nowhere else. He's wearing a bulletproof vest. The Glock has stitched a diagonal line from the bottom right up to his top left, then stitched one bullet into him for luck. The same anger that burned through me when I found Frank leaving a briefcase full of money is burning through me now. I snap the handcuffs around his wrists. The moment the second bracelet is in place he seems to snap out of his fugue. He shoots both hands upward, hitting me in the jaw. The gun goes skittering into the darkness. I reach out and the rope wraps around his neck. It pulls him into a sitting position. I move forward and wrap it around his neck once more. He pushes me off him and tries to unwrap himself. I pull hard on the rope and he follows the direction, getting to his feet. He rushes me, crushing me between his body and the lamppost. My head clangs against it, and when I look down I see four of his legs getting tangled in two sets of ropes. He tries to keep balanced, but the rope is wrapped around him and the hand-cuffs make it that much more difficult. I grab hold of the rope and twist my body aside, pulling him into the lamppost. Then I push my body weight into him, lifting him onto the railing. I hold him at the top and we seem to realize at the same time that he's balanced to go either way. All of a sudden he stops fighting me and I stop pushing.

I'm not sure if I meant it to go this way or not.

"We can be partners," he says.

"Go to Hell."

His hands reach out and grab the railing as he falls. He hangs there, and I take the time to tie off the end of the rope around the lamppost. He sees what I'm doing and knows he should have let go and taken his chances with the water.

"I fucked your wife," he tells me. "And I'm going to fuck her again when this is over."

I kick his fingers and then he's gone.

He doesn't make a sound as he falls the fifteen feet. But the rope does. It comes to a sudden snap, then strains against the side of the rail, moving back and forth in small sudden move-ments. It sounds like grinding teeth. When I look over the edge he's swinging from side to side. He's managed to wrap an arm around the rope to take the impact from his neck. Twenty feet below him is the ocean.

I turn and look back at the pier. Our struggle, from the moment he arrived, has brought us two-thirds of the way toward the end. I make my way over to my gun and spot Cyris's black satchel just ahead of it. I pick it up, curious to see what he had planned for us tonight, and find a bottle that holds around a liter of gasoline, a lighter, and a knife. I can only imagine.

Cyris is still swinging, his hands on the rope to keep him

from strangling. He's trying to untangle his neck. I open the bottle of gasoline and pour a quarter of it onto the leather satchel, then I lie down and put my hand through the railing. I'm on automatic now. This path I'm taking is one I don't even want to consider veering from. I dump the contents of the bottle, getting as much fuel onto Cyris as the wind will allow. I stand back up, then look down so I can see his eyes as I take the lighter from my pocket. I can see little because of the sand swirling around us. I tie the handle of the satchel around the rope so it has enough room to slide, then use the lighter to set fire to it. Even in the strong wind it catches immediately. I let it drop and it spirals down the rope quickly toward Cyris. The wind pushes it around, but doesn't blow it out. Cyris swings harder as he struggles to untie the rope around his neck with his handcuffed hands. Short, jerky movements. The satchel reaches his hands and he cries out and pulls them away, but then the noose starts choking him so he has to put his hands back.

His hair catches fire. So does his beard.

For a few seconds I almost feel sorry for him.

Almost.

He struggles as the fire jumps onto his clothes.

He doesn't scream. Always the tough guy to the end.

I lean over the railing and set my sights on my target with the gun.

Action Man: it is time for all this to end.

# CHAPTER FIFTY

Swinging around, swinging around, this is so bad, yeah, yeah, and the pain is intense, and the handcuffs dig into his wrists and he can't fight his way out of them and he can't fight the rope around his neck, can't fight the fire, and if this is what revenge is, it tastes horrible, fucking horrible. His fingers are on fire, his body is on fire, and he swings in the breeze and gravity pulls at his body while there's nothing, nothing, nothing he can do except burn. Burn to death, burn to ash. The fire evaporates his tears before they fall, and there must be a way, must be, yeah, must be a way he can escape this.

Only there isn't.

He can feel the knife wound in his stomach stretching open under the weight of his own body. It hurts, but not as much as the fire. The headache, of course, is taking this moment to remind him that the headache is king and won't be forgotten. His chest and stomach are sore from the gunshots. He doesn't know what the hell Feldman shot him with, but that pistol was fully automatic. Had to be a dozen shots coming out of that thing. He sure as shit didn't get to play with anything like that in the army.

The skin on his fingers and the skin on his face hurts, hurts so much. The sound it makes is horrible, the *sizzle-sizzle* of meat cooking, of skin cooking, and the smell, the smell is almost as bad as the pain. He's going to die here. He's never going to see his wife again, and for what? A hundred grand? Shit.

He looks up and the night around him is shimmering through the flames. He pulls his hands away from the flames and the rope tugs into his throat, cutting away his chance to breathe in the burning oxygen. The night starts to darken and he can feel himself falling now, falling now, falling into another world where death will be a release from this pain. . . .

Yet when he falls he finds only a cold darkness. It surrounds him. A cold darkness that isn't cold enough to soothe the pain, but it comes close. He opens his eyes and can see nothing. The rope is around his neck, but no longer taut. He kicks out, pulls with his arms, and a moment later he breaks the surface of the water. The remainder of the rope is still swinging in the wind above him.

He is free.

He sucks in a deep breath, then dives back beneath the surface. The cold fights the heat, and is now beginning to numb some of the pain. The salt stings the blisters on his face and neck, and his fingers are stinging too, but the pain is good, the pain is bliss, because the pain means he's alive.

The wound in his stomach, the knife wound from Monday morning, doesn't hurt. His shoulder does from the bullet, and his chest and stomach hurt from the impact from the rest of the bullets. The bulletproof vest he put on knowing Charlie had enough time to come up with a plan is weighing him down. It's becoming waterlogged and he realizes he could drown here.

He kicks harder, and when he breaks the surface he's moved further from the pier. The swinging rope is impossible to see. He buries himself beneath the water. He's struggling to breathe because his upper body is sore from the impact of the bullets, and he's struggling to breathe because he keeps getting pulled into the darkness beneath him. He kicks toward the beach, treading the waves. When he reaches the shore he falls onto his stomach, his face pressing into the sand. More sand whistles around him and bites into his wounds. He forces himself to his knees. He reaches into his pocket. He prays the vial of morphine hasn't been broken. It hasn't. Another pocket and there's a syringe. He pulls it out of the wrapper. He uses his teeth to pull the cap off the needle.

The pain is becoming overwhelming.

The needle plunges into the vial, and then plunges into his arm.

He tosses the vial aside, but puts the cap back on the syringe and into his pocket. He doesn't like the idea of some poor kid finding it in the sand tomorrow or stepping on it.

The pain starts to dull. He closes his eyes. There has to be something, there has to be something he can do, somewhere to go, or somebody to help him. But he's alone, just as he's always alone, and he gets to his feet and heads down the beach. It's dark and he has only a vague idea of where he's heading, but already his mind is focusing, focusing, focusing on his next move, but not focusing, yeah yeah, things are becoming not so much his thoughts anymore, he wants to make people hurt.

He wants to make Charlie Feldman suffer. And there's that bag full of cash too that is rightfully his.

He will get to taste revenge after all, he will get to taste it and after this, after all of this, he knows it will taste better than bittersweet.

He reaches back into his pockets and it only takes him a few seconds to hunt out an extra set of handcuff keys. After last night, he's decided to always carry a spare set, and this set consists of four different types of keys. One of them fits.

With a ferocious appetite he drags himself toward the road. And that's when he sees her, the woman who has been living in his basement the last few days. He heads toward her.

# CHAPTER FIFTY-ONE

Water and fire. How can I have been so foolish? I look down at the rope and the black water and no Cyris. The rope has burned through and I'm an idiot for not seeing it would happen. As I watch another piece breaks away.

I turn from the railing and run down the pier. My lungs hurt and my legs ache. The knowledge I carry is heavy. I wouldn't put any money on Cyris having drowned.

I run toward the steps. The air is slightly clearer. It's still windy as hell, but I can see. The wind has pulled maybe five thousand bucks from the canvas bag, which hadn't been closed all the way. The money swirls around, spent on the air by invisible fingers. I close the bag and take it downstairs, along with the shotgun. The KA-BAR is tucked into my back pocket so the handle points upward. Sand blows in from the dunes, rolling along like low, grainy storm clouds. Cyris is still alive. I don't doubt it. I shot him. I hanged him. I doused him in gasoline and set him alight, turning him into a swinging candle. Then I tried to drown him. At the start of the week I stabbed him. Only stands to reason it's going to take witchcraft or a nuclear bomb to finish him off.

I get down the stairs. The bag is awkward to carry until I'm able to hook the straps over my shoulders and wear it like a backpack. I have the pistol tucked into my waistband, and I carry the shotgun so it's pointing down at the ground. If anybody sees me they'll call the police, and who's to say at this point that that isn't such a bad idea.

There's way more sand blowing around at ground level. I hold my hand to my face and peer between my fingers to shield my eyes. Even so sand slips through my fingers and I have to keep blinking it away. I can't see Jo. I reach the waterline. I can't see Cyris.

Can't see a damn thing.

"Jo?"

No answer. I shout out her name louder. The wind is strong, but not strong enough to whip her name away so nobody can hear it.

I head back to the pier. My legs are heavy in the sand. I keep my left hand in front of my face and my gun ahead of me. I reach the back of the pier, which is somewhat sheltered because of the wall of the library and the steps. There's nobody here. No Jo. No Cyris. No ghosts. I'm making a mess out of this.

"Jo!"

I move back toward the water. I point the gun in the direction that Cyris ought to be coming from, only he isn't.

"Jo! Where are you? Jo?"

Nothing. Did she slip and did the water wash her out? No, because she would have screamed. She would have called for help. The problem is I already think I know what's happened. I just don't want it to be true.

I turn from the crashing surf and head back to the road.

The car Cyris arrived in has gone. He's gone, and there's no reason to believe that he hasn't taken Jo with him.

I run my hand through my hair. I crouch down, the weight of the money almost enough to pull me back. This is unbelievable. There's a moment—just a brief flash—where I think everybody would be better off if I just put the shotgun in my mouth and made fractal patterns in the sand.

I run over the road and dump the money in the trunk of my car. I put the shotgun in there too. I keep the pistol on me. I have no choice now but to go to the police. The time for the police was on Monday, not now, not in the dying hours of Thursday, but what else can I do? I'll go and I'll pray they can find Jo, and what can I tell them that will help?

Nothing.

I start the car. The KA-BAR in my back pocket digs into me. I pull it out and sit it on the passenger seat. As I pull away from the side of the road with the engine revving loudly, I'm reminded of Monday morning. My heart was pounding so hard it sounded like I was knocking at Heaven's door. Things weren't as sharp as they ought to have been, I was seeing the world through a haze of beer, adrenaline, and fear. Not seeing the van parked outside the pasture where there was no longer a dead man was bad enough, but finding it outside Luciana's house was far worse. It was a sign that I was too late. I pulled in behind it. If I'd left right then things could have turned out differently for Kathy, for all of us. I was angry at that guy six months ago in the bar—he was the reason I had no cell phone. He was the reason I couldn't call and warn anybody.

It was as if Cyris had come back from the dead. The boundaries of my imagination were limited by the gravity of reality, so all I needed to be scared of was reality. But I was getting way too much reality. That's what the Real World is all about. I climbed from my car, taking the flashlight. It was no gun, but my tire iron hadn't been much of one either. I slowly approached the van and slid open the door, jumping aside in case he was in there. But he wasn't. The van was empty. It wasn't a moving mortuary with handcuffs and leather straps hanging from the roof and rails, no signs of blood and hair pooled into the corners and caked into the floor. Sort of like the *Scooby Doo* mystery van, those meddling kids moonlighted as sexual predators. For a second all of that was there and more, and then it vanished. Just faded away as my imagination slowly let it go.

I moved to the front. There wasn't any blood on the seat. I couldn't understand it then and still can't understand it now. Cyris should have been dead. I felt cheated and I still do.

The keys to the van were hanging in the ignition. I bent them until they snapped. I left the shaft buried and tossed the remainder beneath the van. Cyris wasn't going anywhere.

I headed up the driveway. Every light was on and the door was unlocked. I slipped inside and entered the kitchen. I'd hoped to find a knife block with a selection of serial-killer blades, but there was nothing except empty cups, a spoon, a potato peeler, and a spatula. I didn't want to start rummaging through drawers in case he heard me, so, keeping the flashlight as my weapon, I started moving around the house. The lounge bisected the hallway at its halfway point. A quick glance to my right showed no movement so I went in that direction. I was sure I'd find Luciana in a bedroom, but I was wrong. I didn't even need to check. The bloody footprints coming from the bathroom told me where she was. They were the sort of prints that suggested somebody had sloshed around and stomped through a lot of blood. They were the sort of footprints you never want to see. I'd been hoping for the best, but preparing for the worst, and the worst was what I was about to get. Standing outside that bathroom with bloody prints heading to the adjoining garage, I came to understand that there was no hope at all.

I opened the door and saw things that met my expectations, and others that didn't. Luciana was in there, but not gagged and tied up and whimpering. She was gagged and tied up, but dead. Her open, lifeless eyes locked onto the guilt I deserved for failing her. The gag in her mouth that held in an eternal scream was a torn strip from my T-shirt. Her recently washed hair was wrapped around the taps, stopping her body from sliding further into the bath. Her wrists were tied together. The dark blood looked like patches of oil. It covered her. It had splashed everywhere. The stake had been driven into her chest.

The walls. The side of the bath. The floor. Patches of the ceiling. Everywhere there was blood. I made it two steps from the bathroom before doubling over and throwing up. I vomited right on top of the bloody footprints.

The bloody footprints gave me a map and a few seconds later I followed them. I knew the house was covered in evidence of my existence: my clothes, fingerprints, hair and skin, saliva on the beer bottle, footprints, vomit. I'd have needed to spend days there trying to hide it all, and even then I'd just have left more behind. I trusted that because I had no criminal record, the police had no way of tracing me.

The garage door was open and the handle smeared with blood. Cyris had stolen Luciana's car. Snapping the keys in the van had been pointless. He was out there driving to

Kathy's house, pursued only by the dawn and his enthusiasm for killing. Both would catch him. I fished Kathy's number from my pocket. The search for a phone began and ended what felt like an hour later. Each lost second fell heavily on me. Each breath I sucked in was one less for Kathy.

I dialed while running outside to my car. I nearly lost control because of my sweaty hands, and the result was a beeping that told me I'd called a nonexistent number. I reached the end of the driveway and had to use my teeth to pull the antenna up on the phone. This time I got the number right. The only problem was the number was busy.

I rang the police. I got the phone up to my ear, but it slipped from my wet hand. I juggled the flashlight trying to save it and ended up losing both. Just before the phone cracked into the driveway I heard the shrill voice of a female dispatcher. The flashlight still worked, but the phone didn't.

I didn't hang around. I thought of going to a neighbor's house, but what neighbor would have let me inside? My tires screeched as I pulled away from the house. It was still dark, but the edges of the sky were fading to the color of a dark bruise. Dawn was approaching, and the early morning was beginning to wash away the night with a cold light that made everything look bleak. There were more cars on the road. I ignored the toots and the flipping fingers of the drivers as I swerved around them, driving with all the skill of a man who has no skill but only desperation.

My short ragged breaths tasted of vomit. I had to keep wiping my sleeve across my forehead as sweat itched my skin and tickled my eyes. I slammed the car through the gears. The sky kept on lightening, the purple light filling the killing hour and, as night fell away, life was being injected into the new day around me. The trees and the plants and the lampposts—

they all looked purple, and where there was light there was life, but where I had been there was only death. Somewhere on the other side of the world people were arriving to Sunday night and the early hours of Monday. Light and dark. Good and evil. The purple hour had brought me into Hell. Everything around me looked like it belonged on some foreign planet, a planet where Evil still lurked and He is a god there, and the world is full of only dark because Evil: He is dark. Then I realized I already was on that planet.

It took just under ten minutes to get to Kathy's. There was a dark sedan parked there that hadn't been there before. I ran up the driveway glancing around the garden. Trees and bushes and if there was a hiding Cyris I didn't see him.

All the lights were off. I thought about yelling out, but that would only make Cyris hurry. I started with the ground floor, succeeding only in turning it into an obstacle course that chewed up more time. I reached the second floor just as the car outside started and revved loudly. I got back to the front door in time to see Cyris pulling away from the house.

I found her in the master bedroom. I found her and my fingers unrolled and the flashlight thumped onto the carpet. I didn't bother walking inside because I could see what I needed to from the doorway. I stepped back, crying as I stumbled down the stairs. I fell twice, each time catching hold of the banister. I tripped on the driveway and skinned my knees and hands, but I felt no pain. I paused at the car, my mind empty. It was as if all thought and all fear had fallen through a trapdoor into my heart. In the passenger seat were my shorts. They were covered in blood. Cyris had put them there.

If we'd gone to the police . . .

But we hadn't. And it's a mistake I'm correcting now. Albeit way too late.

The cellphone rings and I'm back in the present. I'd forgotten I had it. I have to pat at my pockets to figure out where it is. When I look at the display I see the number is blocked. I know who it's going to be.

"Where is she?" I ask, opening the phone.

"She's with me," he says.

"I'm going to the police."

"And I'm going to kill her," he says. "I want my money."

"You'll kill us anyway."

"I probably will. But right now she's alive. And in five minutes she won't be. If I see one cop I'm going to gut your wife like a fish. You've got five minutes to get here."

"Get where?"

"Where it all began," he says, and he hangs up.

I look at my phone. Not calling the police in the past hasn't worked. Being arrested by Landry didn't work either. Maybe now is the time to give them a chance.

# CHAPTER FIFTY-TWO

Jo thinks her arm is broken. It happened on the beach. One moment she was looking for the keys, eyes down studying the sand, knowing it was pointless. Then Cyris was with her again. He was angry. Before when he hit her, when he manhandled her, that seemed tame in comparison to the beach. He struck her in the face with a closed fist. She tasted blood. He twisted her arm and she felt and heard something snap, and before she could scream he pushed her face-first into the sand.

That was the moment she was sure she was going to die. She was going to suffocate. Or he was going to drag her into the water. Where the hell was Charlie?

He hit her again. Hard. Right in the side of the head. Things got dark then, and she could feel herself being dragged by her broken arm, but the pain wasn't there, and she wasn't really there either, she had gone somewhere else, her mind leaving her body.

She came to again in the car. She was lying in the trunk. At least that's what she thought. It smelled like a car, and she could hear the engine and the space she was confined in was bouncing around, and every now and then it would light up red as he put on the brake lights. When she went to scream, she couldn't. Her mouth was taped closed. Her hands were still cuffed in front of her, but tape had been run up the length of her forearms, keeping them pinned together.

The car pulls over and goes dark. The door opens and closes, then the trunk is popped open. Cyris stands there looking down over her. He looks bad. Disfigured, almost. Burned. What the hell happened? He has a coil of rope over his shoulder. He has a black satchel in his hand. He reaches in and grabs her by the hair and pulls her out. It hurts more than her broken arm.

"Let's go," he says, and drags her until she can find her feet.

She's at the pasture Charlie pointed out to her. In the distance are what he was calling Dalí's trees. She doesn't see why. There's a wire fence and Cyris climbs over it then pulls her over.

"Don't worry," he tells her. "Your husband is on his way."

They walk through the pasture—well, Cyris doing the walking and Jo is the one being pulled. She imagines this is what the girls went through the other night. She is petrified. So scared there's every chance her heart will stop before they reach the trees. Last time Charlie came here he was trying to save a stranger, and he failed. Last time he had a tire iron and no shotgun. This time it's all opposites. The only thing that hasn't changed is Charlie—he's the wrong person to be coming for her.

They reach the trees. Cyris switches on a flashlight. The trees look like they've been dragged from the set of some

B-grade sci-fi movie, perhaps the same one she seems to be caught in. Everything is eerily silent, as if the sound guy came along earlier and packed the bugs and insects into containers and took them away.

There's a clearing up ahead. He pushes her hard into a tree. "Move and I'll cut your arms off," he tells her. She believes him. She doesn't move.

He wraps a piece of wire so it goes around her neck and around the tree. It's tight. Any tighter and it'd cut off her air supply. Then he stands in front of her. He stares at her. He looks her up and down and she thinks he's determining her worth. He hates her. He's going to kill her. The best she can hope for is that he does it quick.

He steps forward, tugging at a roll of duct tape. He wraps pieces around her waist and arms, so she can't move her hands anywhere. Then he disappears. He moves past the edge of the clearing. He moves into the darkness. He's gone for five minutes. And then he comes back.

"Your husband is here," he says.

She tries to beg him to leave them alone, but her words are muffled against the tape.

He steps behind the tree. The wire around her throat suddenly gets tighter. She can feel her eyes bulging out. She can't breathe.

There is movement ahead. Charlie is sneaking through the trees. Suddenly he appears at the edge of the clearing. He sees her, and she knows that he knows it's a trap, just as he knows if he doesn't run forward to loosen the wire around her throat she's going to die. He freezes. She doesn't know what she would do in his situation, but she knows she wants him to help her.

"Hold on," he says, and he runs forward, pointing the shotgun all around him as he does. There's nothing to shoot at. He reaches her and tries pulling on the wire, but there's no slack, and it only gets tighter when he pulls it outward. "Fuck," he says, and he moves behind the tree. "Fuck," he repeats, and she hears him putting down the shotgun to try and loosen the wire.

She knows how it's going to go from here.

She suspects Charlie knows too.

The wire slackens off. She pulls in a deep breath. Then there's a thud, followed by a bigger thud. She's heard enough people getting hit in the head and falling over this week to know what's just happened. She begins to cry.

Cyris drags Charlie out in front of her. He tosses the black satchel onto the ground. The material has taken on a plastic look and the zip has been gummed open. It's been burned. He uses the rope he brought to secure Charlie's ankles. Then he claps a set of handcuffs onto Charlie's wrists. He throws the rope over one of the branches. He grabs it and pulls down. He goes about his work methodically and without delay.

Charlie's feet are dragged into the air. Cyris keeps pulling on the rope. Charlie's jacket falls over his head and hangs from his arms. The handcuffs stop it from coming off. His T-shirt bunches up around his chest.

Cyris moves to his satchel and a moment later a can of lighter fluid comes into view.

Oh, Jesus.

Jo struggles against the duct tape, against the wire, but it's no good.

Cyris pops open the can and starts spraying it over Charlie.

# CHAPTER FIFTY-THREE

Yeah, he likes it out here, yeah, he likes it out here a lot. That's why he's come back, to the home of his failure, the home of his nightmare. He's come to right the wrongs and, this time, this time, there will be no wrongs. He likes it out here, yet he hates it too, because it represents all that's bad in his life: the wound to his stomach, the money that he lost. His mind isn't operating the way it ought to be; his thoughts aren't balanced—or are they? Hate and like balance each other out, don't they? He isn't sure, and this ought to really scare him, but the night is warm, the wind has died down, the pasture is silent, and revenge is at hand. Life is good.

Life is bad. Because the headache is back and it's raging out of control and it's all Charlie Feldman's fault. Charlie is really going to pay—big time. He's going to wish he was dead and he's going to keep on wishing that. Death lasts a long time, yeah, a real long time, but for Charlie the dying itself will last forever.

His body is fucked up and once he gets home tonight, he'll call his brother-in-law. He'll get help. He can't go on like this any longer. The tin of lighter fluid is half-empty and he wishes he had brought along more. He wishes he had several liters so he could make Charlie cook for hours, but all he had access to was the last tin in the car. Maybe he ought to just burn a limb at a time. Or maybe he ought to burn the bitch first and make him watch. Setting them alight at the same time would be a waste, and anyway, he doesn't have enough fluid for both. His hands shake at the prospect of having so many things he can do, and he has plenty of time to decide. He's experiencing something he hasn't felt in a long time—excitement.

His mind is throbbing and he raises a hand to the side of his head. When all this is over he will go home and take more painkillers. He doesn't know where he'll get them, but he'll find a way. Maybe he should call his brother-in-law. Shit—didn't he just think that?

His mind is wandering. He looks at Charlie. Charlie is starting to come to. Then he looks down at the lighter fluid in his hand. It would be a waste of money if he didn't use the entire tin.

So many options. Life is good.

# CHAPTER FIFTY-FOUR

My world is upside down.

I remember seeing those contraptions on TV where you can hang upside down from a bar, clipped on with special shoes. It's supposed to be relaxing, to do something positive for your body—maybe realign your spine or soul or consolidate your positive energy. It's pretty obvious the person who invented it wasn't soaked in lighter fluid at the time.

Cyris has his eyes fixed on me, but he's not really seeing me. I think he's gone somewhere, he's gone to whatever place his mind sometimes takes him. Could be a happy place, but I hate to think what a happy place for a guy like this could be. He has my KA-BAR knife tucked into the waistband of his pants.

The fluid smells like eroding batteries. It comes at me in sharp little streams, splashing onto my face. My nose begins to burn. It leaks into my sinuses as I cough. The back of my mouth feels like it's been ripped to shreds. My eyes are burning a hole through to the back of my skull.

The pain spreads like ripples in a pool of gasoline. I cry out and clutch my hands to my nose. I start shaking my head, hard enough to become disorientated. I'm desperate to suck in more air, but I can't. Cyris keeps spraying more fluid at me. I wriggle around on the rope like a worm on a hook, knowing the more I scream, the more fluid he'll get into my mouth. Then suddenly he stops. He's either got tired or he's thought of something else to do. He takes a few steps back and holds a hand against the side of his head. Does he have the same headache I have? My breath tastes of fire and feels ragged, as if I'm swallowing a well-used chisel.

I start to choke. He starts to laugh. I wonder how far away the police are. I phoned them just before I got here. I fought with the decision the whole drive. They'll come here, won't they? All I have to do is keep Cyris talking.

"It'll hurt more once I've lit it. You do know that, right?"

"Listen, Cyris—"

"They say the true torture is in the anticipation. I'm interested in your opinion."

I look over to Jo. I blink away the tears, but more keep coming. A sharp pain continues to race back and forth from behind my nose to my brain.

I grit my teeth, then spit out a sentence. "I know why you killed them."

He shrugs. "What are you talking about?"

"Frank McClory paid you to kill his wife." My head is throbbing. Just how long can a person live hanging upside down? Before being set on fire? "Frank knew he'd be the prime suspect so he wanted you to kill Kathy in a unique way. Killing Luciana diverted focus away from Frank because it made the women look like they'd caught the attention of a complete psychopath. He didn't want them killed at home because he didn't want to be the first one on the scene. He wanted them found together, but I ruined your plans."

"The plans," he says, his burnt face contorting so he can fit the words out in one large clump. "You-ruined-more-than-just-my-plan, you-ruined-my-fucking-life." Then, relaxed all of a sudden, he's waving his hands like a conductor, as if his small outburst never happened. "Go on."

"This sadistic lunatic thing is just a facade to hide what you really are."

"And what would that be?"

"A cold-blooded killer. A paid hit man."

He starts clapping. A slow, patronizing round of applause that would make stage actors sick to their stomachs. "Ladies and gentlemen," he says, "the one and only Charlie Feldman."

"I just hope my handwriting wasn't too messy on that hundred-dollar note."

The clapping stops as if some invisible force has just grabbed his arms and frozen them in the air. His lips become a thin scar. They stay that way for a few more seconds before forming into a grin. It becomes the sort of smile I'd expect to see on a demon.

"You took my money?"

I nod and my body begins to swing around in a small arc.

"You took the money." He starts to laugh, but I doubt he finds it that funny.

"You killed Frank for nothing," I point out.

He seems to think about this. "His bad luck, I suppose."

I suppose it was. Just like it was Kathy and Luciana's bad luck. Just like it's Jo's bad luck, and mine. What can you do against it? Carry a four-leaf clover? A gun?

"Do you know what I had to go through to earn that?" he asks.

"I know."

"You think it was easy?"

"I think you enjoyed it."

He shakes his head. "No," he says. "I don't enjoy any of this. It's just a job."

He reaches into his pocket and pulls out a cigarette lighter. He runs his thumb over the metal wheel; it strikes the flint, a few sparks appear, then a flame. He seems pleased with himself. The look on his damaged face suggests he's taking all the credit for inventing fire. He walks over to Jo. Her eyes widen and she tries to push herself further into the tree. The miracle of camouflage is no kinder to Jo than it was to Kathy.

"Leave her alone."

He doesn't answer.

Instead he picks up the lighter fluid and sprays more of it into my face.

My head starts to pound, and seconds later vomit erupts from my mouth, spraying over my nose and eyes, onto my forehead and into my hair. My nose becomes full of it and the taste consumes my mouth, ridding it, at least, from the taste of lighter fluid. I choke as lumps of digested pasta and coffee flow from me, but pieces get lodged in my mouth and throat and stick beneath my tongue. I wipe my hands at my face and spit out what I can. Cyris pulls himself away and stumbles onto his butt to avoid the mess. He sits there, one hand across his wounded stomach, the other wiping at his face.

I swing in a bigger arc and my limbs come close to breaking. Even though I'm upside down, my hanging jacket isn't, and vomit starts to pool into the creases and drip into pockets. I can see it pooling in the inside pocket, on top of the Swiss

Army knife I bought from Floyd. I think of the game-show host. He tells me if I'm good enough I can still get hold of one of the few remaining prizes up for grabs. He asks me if I'm man enough to do any grabbing.

I pull the jacket closer and reach into the pocket.

"Hey," Cyris says, and I look over at him. He's gotten up and walked over to Jo.

He has the KA-BAR knife in his hand. Where in the hell are the police?

"Don't," I tell him.

But he does.

He drives the blade deep into her.

# CHAPTER FIFTY-FIVE

He wants to open Charlie up from sternum to eyeball with the knife, and he'll do it too, he'll do it soon, but he'll open up the bitch first. He can already see how she'll look with her limbs severed and her face all torn open. The thought does nothing to excite him, nothing at all. The entire process of killing her will be mechanical, but at least it'll be over.

She's looking at him, staring at him, her eyes bugging out of her head, and even though she must have known where tonight was going to lead, she looks surprised. He twists the handle in her stomach and he can feel her through it. He can feel her pain as her body moves beneath it. He can feel the blood running down the handle. He can hear Charlie yelling at him and thrashing about on the rope.

He has stabbed her in the same place Charlie stabbed him. It's not fatal, not yet, but it will be. Already he can feel her life slipping away. The satisfaction he feels is meager. Meeting this woman and meeting Charlie and meeting Frank are the worst things that have ever happened to him. As he takes his hand away and touches the side of his burned face, he knows life will never be the same. He looks into her eyes and he can see her dying, he can see her slipping away. He clamps a hand over her mouth to feel her dying breath against his skin. It gives him strength. It makes the back of his neck tingle, it makes the muscles in his arms and legs quiver, but it doesn't make the pain go away.

He stares into her eyes. He keeps his hands on her mouth. Her breath against his skin is weak and warm. He steps away. The knife is sticking out of her the same way it stuck out of him on Monday morning. *Welcome to my world, bitch.*

He turns toward Feldman. Feldman is reaching up toward the rope. He has something in his hand. A pocket knife?

It's something sharp, because a moment later Feldman is hitting the ground. He's landed on his front. He's getting to his feet.

Cyris points the Glock at him.

He has this covered.

He steps forward and uses the zippo to set Charlie on fire.

# CHAPTER FIFTY-SIX

The fire is on me and there isn't a thing I can do about it. There has to be something I can say to stop all of this, to take all of this back, to make it as if it never happened, but it seems . . . seems that isn't going to happen.

The flames chew my jacket, rising hungrily upward, and I reach out to wave them further away from me. Jo is forgotten now, and Kathy and Luciana, and Landry. The fire has taken me to another world, and this world looks a hell of a lot like Hell. I know Hell is other people, but it's not—it's just two people, Cyris and me. I flap my arms and pat at the flames, burning my fingers. The handcuffs keep digging into my wrists.

I drop to the ground and start rolling. I tear at the jacket. I manage to pull it upward, sliding it and the fire over my head. It singes my hair and I force my eyes shut as the tears inside them seem to boil. Then the jacket's off my head and on my arms where I'm able to push it only as far as the handcuffs. I start kicking at it, stomping it into the ground, the flames finding the lighter fluid on my jeans. I push my feet at the jacket. The fire has weakened it enough to tear apart. It leaves me with gloves that have huge tassels on the ends. Tassels of fire. I kick at them, smudging them into the dirt. The technique works and the flames disappear. Red embers flicker from the material.

I get to my feet. Cyris is laughing at me as if I'm the funniest thing in the world. Perhaps I am. But it's hard to concentrate when you're laughing, hard to stay focused. He fires the Glock. It's loud. I don't feel any pain, but I feel something tugging at my chest. I look down at my vest. My binoculars have been shot. I turn and run. There's another gunshot, this time another tug, this one somewhere in my back. All that tugging and I lose balance and strength, and I make it a few yards into the darkness before falling over.

Cyris comes in after me. There's pain in the side of my chest from the impact of my binoculars being shot, and the side of my back hurts from a bullet. Cyris grabs my ankles and starts dragging me.

"I prefer it like this," he grumbles, but I don't think he does. I think he preferred back when he hadn't been stabbed in the stomach or set on fire.

He starts dragging me back the way we came, probably so he can kill me in front of Jo. I dig my fingers into the dirt, looking for something I can use to fight him with. Leaves, twigs, moss, grass—nothing helpful. No branches, no rocks, just a whole lot of nature and . . .

My fingers wrap around a cold, solid item, something L-shaped, something heavy and metal with a socket at one end. As I tighten my grip on it, the Real World shimmers and darkens, then darkens some more, but doesn't disappear.

I'm not going anywhere. Fuck that. Right now, I'm all out of failing.

At the edge of the clearing Cyris lets go and leans down over me.

"I'm going to enjoy this, partner," he says.

I doubt that he will. I swing the tire iron as hard as I can.

# CHAPTER FIFTY-SEVEN

Something hits him hard. An iron bar of some type. It gets him in the jaw. Right in the front of the mouth. It plows through his teeth, turning them sharp and ragged. He feels his burned lips split open. Bits of shattered teeth are stabbed into his gums and tongue. He fires the pistol and knows the bullet goes astray.

Then the same thing hits him again. This time in the side of the head. His head snaps back and his view of the world changes. He can't help himself, but he lets go of the gun and brings his hands to his mouth, his fingers probing and assessing and trying to repair the damage. He can feel blood rolling down the side of his face. Can feel his mouth filling up with the stuff. He spits some out. Teeth come out with it. He doesn't know where he is. He doesn't think he's anywhere. But if he had to guess—he'd guess this was death.

The forest pulses. Its expands, it shrinks, it's there and then it isn't. Same for the sky. The stars get bigger, they get smaller, they get brighter, they disappear. The pain in his head pulses, it gets bigger, it doesn't get smaller, it grows. So that's not pulsing. It's just increasing.

He closes his eyes. He can hear a beach nearby. Seagulls. The waves crashing against the shore. He's lying down. He can't remember how he got here, but he loves the beach. It's his favorite place in the world. Once, when he was a kid, he ran away from home because his dad used to beat the shit out of him, and he stayed at the beach for four days until the police found him and took him back to his dad so he could be beaten some more.

He gets to his feet. He doesn't recognize this part of the beach. There are a few trees nearby. The sun is out. It's incredibly bright, as if it's only a few feet out into the sea rather than a million miles away. Like the forest before it disappeared, the sun is pulsing too. No, not pulsing, but disappearing then reappearing, like somebody is hanging a dark sheet over it and pulling it away every few seconds and then putting it back.

He starts walking. The sun is getting annoying, and he lifts his hand to shield his eyes. There are people here. He's not sure who they are. People from the army, maybe. He walks toward them and they seem happy to see him, but they seem unhappy about the sun. He starts shaking hands. There's some back slapping and a lot of people saying *How have you been*. His wife is here too.

"Babe," he says, and he wraps his arms around her.

"I love you," she tells him.

"Your legs—they're back," he tells her.

"The hedgehog gave them to me," she says.

That makes him happy. He hugs her tighter, then lets her go and holds her hand. She leads him away.

"Where are we going?" he asks.

"We're going on a journey," she tells him.

"A mission?"

"Something like that. Here, I got you something," she says, and she hands him a flashlight.

"What do I need this for?" he asks.

"To light our way."

The flashlight is on. He turns it off. Then he turns it on again. At the same time he does that, the sun fades, it appears, it fades. The flashlight, somehow, is connected to the sun. It makes him smile. Smiling hurts. There's something wrong with his mouth. He cries. Crying makes his head hurt. There's something wrong with his head.

"I have the world's worst headache," he tells her.

"You have the world's worst headache," she tells him.

"That's what I just said."

"That's what you just said," she says.

He doesn't know why she's doing that. It's annoying. The world's worst headache is getting worse.

"I need to sit down for a bit," he tells her.

"Not yet," she says. "Let's just keep walking. There'll be plenty of time for sitting down later."

# CHAPTER FIFTY-EIGHT

I pick up the gun. Cyris is walking in a slow circle. He's holding the flashlight. He has it pointed at his face, and he's flicking it on and off. On and off. I keep the gun pointed at him as I move over to Jo. She's still alive. I pull the tape off her face and blood comes out of her mouth.

"Hang on, Jo, please, you have to hang on."

"I . . . I want you to, to . . ." she says, and she sounds out of breath, and I know what she's going to say. She wants me to shoot him.

I put my hand up to my lips in a shushing gesture.

"Charlie . . ."

I reach into one of my pockets. My cell phone is in there. I pull it out. Then I switch it off.

"Charlie?"

"I called the police earlier," I tell her. "They're on their way. The phone line has been open the entire time. They've heard everything," I say, but I don't want them to hear what's going to happen next.

"Then where are they?"

"They can't be far," I say.

"Shoot him. Please, Charlie. Shoot him."

"He's done," I tell her. "Look at him."

"This isn't like it was six months ago at that bar, Charlie. You need to shoot him. I won't hold it against you."

Cyris starts patting the trees. And talking to them. I can't hear what he's saying. Then he smiles at one tree more than he's smiled at the others. It must be his favorite. Not that it's much of a smile. Dark blood falls from his mouth in hanging clumps. Some teeth are on angles, some run flat against the roof of his mouth. Others are split, most are completely gone. But he keeps smiling. He hugs the tree. He wraps his arms around it and talks to it, and then when he pulls away he keeps one hand on the tree and the other on the flashlight, on off, on off. Over and over.

Then he starts walking. He doesn't go anywhere because he keeps holding on to the tree, but his legs are going up and down, going through the walking motions. He tells the tree something, and I'm guessing he might be talking to his own personal ghost.

"Help will be here soon," I tell her. "Just focus on staying with me. Please."

"I'm not . . ." she says, and she coughs for a few seconds and I think she swallows down some blood. "I'm not going anywhere," she says.

I want to unhook the wire from around Jo's neck, but I also don't want to take my eyes off Cyris.

"Charlie," she says.

"Yeah?"

"He's a bad man," she says. "If anybody deserves to die, it's him."

"I know."

"There's no way the police will send you to jail. He killed one of them," she says. "They're probably going to give you a medal."

I'm not so sure about that. In the distance I can hear sirens.

"Charlie . . ."

"I know," I tell her. "I know."

Action Man, do your thing.

I point the gun at Cyris. My back is hurting. I can feel blood dripping down my side. The wound back there is starting to feel like it's on fire. I adjust my aim. Cyris's head is moving side to side slightly in his mock walk. He looks as happy as a man can whose mouth has been shattered and whose face is burned. He seems . . . well, strangely, he seems at peace.

I pull the trigger.

My arm bucks upward from the recoil. The bullet catches Cyris in the side of the head. His head snaps to the side and blood arcs out from the wound and then he drops like a rock, breaking his grip from the tree. I feel no pity for him. Only revulsion. He lurches upward, his throat gargling as blood bubbles from his mouth. He starts to convulse, one hand flipping from palm up to palm down over and over two or three times a second. I fire another shot into him, this one also into the head. The convulsing stops.

I lower the gun. This is how it feels to kill a man. I've played my part in the deaths of four others this week, mostly through bad decisions and being a fuckup, but not this—this is cold-blooded, calculated, not even self-defense. I've killed Cyris and if the game-show host came and asked me to sum up how I felt in one word, I'd say *fantastic*.

I think Jo is feeling the same way. Or close to it. She remains silent the whole time. The game show is ending. The purple light of the killing hour is here. Evil has gone. He is not dead, but he has forgotten my name.

Remembering all too clearly the mistake I made the other night, I keep the gun pointed at Cyris. I walk up to him. He looks dead. I don't doubt it, just as I don't doubt one more shot into his head isn't going to hurt. So that's what I do. I can sense Kathy and Luciana watching me, but what I can't tell is whether or not they approve. I would hope they do.

Jo looks scarily pale as I walk back over to her. I drop the gun. Cyris won't be coming back from the dead this time. I move behind the tree and loosen the wire, and Jo manages to stay on her feet for a few seconds before slumping down. The sirens are getting closer. They're almost here. The knife is sticking out of Jo and that's where we leave it. It's probably the only thing stopping her from bleeding to death.

"You're going to be okay," I tell her.

"We're going to be okay," she says, and she grabs hold of my hand and tightens her grip on it.

I can see lights flicking through the trees. Help is here. I keep holding my grip on Jo's hand as the voices get closer, and then they are here, guns being pointed at us, somebody is shouting, but I don't let go of Jo, not until I'm pulled away. I'm pushed facedown into the ground and I'm put in handcuffs and the wound in my back brings me close to checking out for a bit, but I hang on. I'm able to turn my head toward Jo and watch as they help her. There are more voices, then paramedics arrive, and they tell us the same thing me and Jo told each other a few minutes earlier—that we're going to be okay.

A guy introduces himself to me. His name is Detective Schroder. "Want to tell me what happened here?" he asks.

A couple of officers get me to my feet. Suddenly they seem to realize I've been shot too.

"Not until I talk to a lawyer," I tell him, and Kathy and Luciana would be proud, and Landry wouldn't be. Still in cuffs, I'm carried to an ambulance on a gurney, and from there it'll be a trip to the hospital. And then to the police station. It'll sure as hell make a nice change from all this nature I've been seeing lately.

We travel through the Real Word, and Jo's words travel with me—*We're going to be okay*, she said. And after all we've gone through, there's no reason to doubt her.